SUCCESSOR'S
PROMISE

BY TRUDI CANAVAN

The Magician's Apprentice

The Black Magician trilogy
The Magicians' Guild
The Novice
The High Lord

Age of the Five
Priestess of the White
Last of the Wilds
Voice of the Gods

The Traitor Spy trilogy
The Ambassador's Mission
The Rogue
The Traitor Queen

Millennium's Rule
Thief's Magic
Angel of Storms
Successor's Promise

TRUDI CANAVAN

SUCCESSOR'S PROMISE

Book Three of Millennium's Rule

www.orbitbooks.net

ORBIT

First published in Great Britain in 2017 by Orbit

Copyright © 2017 by Trudi Canavan

The moral right of the author has been asserted.

A CIP catalogue record for this book is available from the British Library.

Hardback 978-0-356-50116-1
C format 978-0-356-50117-8

Typeset in Garamond by Palimpsest Book Production Limited, Falkirk, Stirlingshire
Printed and bound in Great Britain by Clays Ltd, St Ives plc

Papers used by Orbit are from well-managed
forests and other responsible sources.

Orbit
An imprint of
Little, Brown Book Group
Carmelite House
50 Victoria Embankment
London EC4Y 0DZ

An Hachette UK Company
www.hachette.co.uk

www.orbitbooks.net

PART ONE

TYEN

CHAPTER 1

The sound was more felt than heard, a deep concussion that shivered up through the feet and vibrated in the chest. As one, all of the wheelmakers looked up; then, as the sensation faded, they turned to Tyen.

He glanced from one to the other, a growing, formless dread reflected in their anxious expressions. All were still, so the small movement near the main door to the workshop immediately caught his attention. A human-shaped shadow was taking form, rapidly sharpening and darkening. A woman, her mouth set in a grim line.

"Claymar Fursa," he said, and as the others turned to face the sorcerer their expressions changed to respect and they touched two fingers to their heart to acknowledge their leader. Tyen followed suit.

"Tyen Wheelmaker," the woman said as she emerged into the world. "The Grand Market has been attacked. We need help." She looked around. "From all of you."

Tyen nodded. "The attackers?"

"Gone." She drew a deep breath and let it out, her eyes dark and haunted. "Half of the roof has collapsed. Many are buried."

The wheelmakers exchanged horrified glances. Tyen picked up a rag and wiped at the grease on his hands. "We will go immediately."

She nodded, then faded from sight.

"I'll take you," Tyen offered. The other wheelmakers moved

away from the machines they'd been working on and joined him in the only clear space in the room, the area in front of the main door. Each took hold of another worker; men and women linked by touch.

"Ready?"

A murmur of assent followed, then all sucked in a deep breath. Tyen drew magic from far above them, saving what imbued the city for weaker sorcerers with a shorter reach. While Doum was a world rich in magic, and the gap he left would soon be replaced when what was around it flowed in to fill the void, he would hate to be the reason other sorcerers were unable to help at the disaster site.

As he pushed away from the world, the workshop seemed to be bleached of colour and all sound ceased. He could feel a fresh indentation in the substance of the place between worlds coming from the direction of the Council House, no doubt where Claymar Fursa had pushed through it to reach them. Conscious that he and his employees could only last in between worlds for as long as they could survive without air, he sent them quickly upwards, passing through the ceiling and first floor into a muted blue sky. Looking over Alba, the largest and most famous city of clayworkers in Doum, he sought the familiar arched profile of the Grand Market building.

When he found it, he paused in shock. Fursa had been understating the damage, or more had occurred since. Only a quarter of the remarkable undulating roof, constructed by cementing together layers of flat bricks, remained.

He propelled them towards it.

The Grand Market had been a beautiful building. Inside were stalls selling the best of the city's wares, attended day and night. *Why would anybody try to destroy it?* he wondered. Had the attack come from a rival city, or from somewhere outside the world? An attack on the Grand Market was an attack on Alba's main source of income. It was also an attack on the place he'd invested five cycles in making a new home – a place he loved more than his own home world. Anger stirred within him.

No doubt the Claymars, elected by the workshop masters of Doum's cities, knew more. He could seek information by reading their minds, but they, like many peoples of the worlds, outlawed mind reading without permission. He'd made a habit of obeying that law, at the least because it would only take one slip for him to reveal that he had broken it, and the acceptance he had sought would be lost. He might have their respect as a powerful sorcerer and the inventor of the world's first potting wheels powered by magic, but as an outsider he was still regarded with suspicion.

The city below flashed by in a blur. The broken edifice enlarged, gaining detail along with proximity. As they neared the ragged, broken walls, a great pile of rubble appeared within the shadows between them. The debris glittered with fragments of shattered glass. A few remnants of the stalls within poked out of the mess, but the wares and occupants were well buried. People were lifting and carrying fragments away. Others lay on the floor among the surviving stalls, clothes stained with blood, some moving, some not.

The sight brought unwelcome memories of a collapsing tower and a wave of guilt. Tyen pushed both away. It had been ten cycles since the tragedy of Spirecastle's collapse – cycles being a substitute "year" measurement sorcerers and inter-world traders used, since no worlds had years that exactly matched – but he still recalled it clearly. The determination to assist hardened in him. *This time I can do something to help*, he told himself. *If they'll let me.*

He took his workers downwards, seeking a safe place to arrive. He decided against bringing them back into the world inside the building, in case the remaining section of roof fell. *Fursa did say we were the nearest sorcerers, so there may not be many others there yet. I had better shield everyone in case the walls collapse outward.* The plaza outside the building was crowded with onlookers. Helpers were rushing out of the building, tossing debris onto steadily growing piles, then hurrying back in. With no clear space to arrive in close by, he chose an area twenty paces away and waited for the people standing there to notice and move out of the way.

It did not take long. Seeing the partly transparent group, the onlookers hastily shuffled aside. When the space was clear, Tyen brought his workers back into the world. All sucked in the dry, dusty air and began to cough. Some pressed hands to their faces as the physical manifestation of emotions, absent between worlds, suddenly returned. But as they drew deep breaths to recover from the journey, their shoulders straightened, and the hands that had gripped a neighbour in order to be carried along with Tyen now patted and squeezed in reassurance and support.

"Let's see what we can do," Tyen said, and started towards the building.

As they entered, he looked up at the remaining ceiling. Only one of the five tall central columns remained. He drew magic and stilled the air above his workers to form a shield – perhaps a little too strongly, as a chill immediately set the air misting.

"No need for that, Tyen Wheelmaker," a man said from somewhere to the right. "We're holding the roof up."

Tyen sought out the speaker. A familiar old man appeared, weaving through the workers.

"Master Glazer Rayf." Tyen released the air. "What can we do?"

"Do any of you have healing skills?" Rayf asked.

The workers exchanged glances, most shaking their heads.

"I know a little," one of the younger men said. "No healing magic – just bandages and stitches."

"I spent a little time in Faurio in training," Tyen said. *Until a former rebel recognised me*, he added silently, *and it was either kill him or leave.* "I picked up a few basics."

Rayf's gaze moved to Tyen and an eyebrow rose. "You can heal with magic?"

Tyen shook his head. "Only the ageless can do that."

The old man's gaze sharpened at that piece of information about Tyen. No doubt he'd wondered if the powerful otherworlder would age – or rather, what it would mean for Doum if he didn't. His gaze flickered past Tyen's shoulder and he frowned. Stepping a little closer to Tyen, he spoke in a low voice. "Look into my mind," he invited.

Tyen did, and read alarm and an image of the stalls behind him. Behind a line of rubble-removers, between pots stacked up in a surviving stall, was a deeper shadow. Within that gleamed a pair of eyes, fixed on the great pile of rubble.

Then Rayf's gaze returned to Tyen's face.

"I can't read his mind. Who is he?" he hissed.

Stretching his senses behind, Tyen sought the owner. He scowled as he found the man's mind.

This is going to take hours, the stranger thought. *The longer I stay, the greater the chance someone will find me. Why should I risk being taken prisoner when it wasn't me who commissioned the attack on this place? If a Claymar has died, the Emperor won't negotiate for my return. He'll abandon me.*

"His name is Axavar," Tyen murmured. "He's from Murai. A sorcerer of the School of Sorcery."

"Was he one of those who did this?"

Tyen nodded. "Set to watch and make sure he and the other attackers haven't killed any Claymars. The Emperor will only take action against those who commissioned the attack if one of our leaders has died."

Rayf's eyes narrowed. "Who did?"

"He suspects the Muraian merchants."

A hiss escaped the old man. "Punishing us for setting a minimum price, no doubt. Which merchants?"

"He's not thinking about anyone in particular. He's an underling. Too young to have gained any authority."

And not at all bothered by what he and his people had done

7

here. Tyen shook his head. It was unbelievably callous to kill people for refusing to sell their goods at too low a price to survive on. If Axavar's thoughts were correct, the merchants of Murai had reasoned that their own survival depended on being able to on sell the goods of Doum at a reasonable profit – though Tyen suspected "survival" did not mean they faced starvation, but a reduction in their great wealth.

"What do you want me to do?" Tyen asked.

Rayf hesitated, his face tight with indecision; then as someone called his name, he brightened a little. They both turned to see several red-robed men and women striding into the building, one heading for Rayf while the rest spread out towards the injured.

"Ah, good. The Payr healers are here." The old man turned back to Tyen. "Follow him when he leaves. Find out who else is responsible, and if the Emperor is behind it."

Tyen nodded. He drew a deep breath, then shoved himself out of the world, stopping when he could barely make out his position in relation to the room. He would have appeared to vanish, unless someone looked closely. Moving in a wide curve, he approached the Muraian from behind.

At the last moment, the man turned and saw Tyen. And fled, flashing into the place between and streaking away.

Tyen gave chase.

The ruined Grand Market faded from sight. The substance of the place between roiled on either side of Axavar's fresh path. As Tyen began to gain on him, the man increased his speed. Tyen could have caught up, but he held back and let the man widen the gap between them. Better to let Axavar think he'd lost Tyen so he'd go straight to his destination.

Which was most likely the rest of the sorcerers who had attacked the market. Tyen would have to approach carefully, keeping out of sight. It was unlikely a single Muraian sorcerer was strong enough to be a threat to Tyen, but he could not guess how powerful they might be together. He also needed to avoid giving them the impression he was the beginning of a counter-attack from Doum, or some might return to Alba and attack it again.

Once past the midpoint between worlds, where nothing was visible, shadows slowly emerged from the whiteness. A city spread below them, growing rapidly more distinct. It lay at the bottom of a cliff face over which a great waterfall tumbled, covering the city in a ceaseless mist of spray. The river at its base divided the city, but the two halves were stitched together by a succession of graceful bridges.

This was Glaemar, the capital of the most powerful country in Murai and home of the Emperor, who ruled all but a few distant lands too poor to tempt a conquest. Tyen had visited it around the time he'd settled in Doum, curious to see the wealthy and powerful neighbour and main customer of the potters' wares. While Glaemar's climate was cooler than Alba's, the culture was more refined – and less friendly. Wealth and power resided in hereditary lines and the poor were kept in perpetual bondage. Sorcerous ability offered only limited freedom from rigid class expectations.

It reminded him too much of where he had come from, of the great Leratian empire that had conquered and colonised most of his world – though the city of Beltonia, with its advanced sewage system, was considerably less smelly than Glaemar's sluggish covered ditches.

Axavar plunged towards his home world, only slowing at the last moment to alter his position within it. Tyen continued to follow at a distance, knowing the other's lesser magical ability meant he'd have more trouble seeing others in the place between. Finally Axavar dove towards a large building with a square inner courtyard.

Tyen remained high enough above the city that he would be only a speck to people below. Even so, he created a globe of stilled air around him as he emerged into the world, both to hold him in place and to shield him. He waited, and soon Axavar's mind became readable as he arrived in the world.

He'd arrived in the School of Sorcery. Footsteps sounded from all directions as other sorcerers responded to his call. Faces appeared in his mind as men and women peered down from balconies. More strode out from archways below them. All stared as Axavar babbled an explanation and warning.

A sorcerer had seen him, he told them. Might have followed him. Might arrive here at any moment.

Axavar sensed radiating lines of darkness flare around the sorcerers as they drew in magic in readiness to deal with a possible intruder. But Tyen had no intention of confronting them. Instead, he searched their minds. He learned that Master Rayf had been right. When the Claymars of Doum had set minimum prices, the Muraian merchants had decided to punish them, hiring five graduates from the Glaemar School of Sorcery to travel to Alba and destroy the Grand Market.

They knew the Emperor would punish them if any of Doum's leaders died. Muraians did not consider the deaths of the men, women and children working in the stalls important because in their culture shopkeepers were of low status. Only people of authority mattered. But in Doum, trade was controlled by the families of the potmakers, brickmakers, tilemakers and other producers – including relatives of the Claymars. Family members who didn't have artistic talent but had skill with numbers and negotiation were as valuable as creators, since they freed the artisans to concentrate on their work.

Axavar's colleagues were looking at the head of the School of Sorcery, a woman named Oerith. She doubted a single Doumian sorcerer would dare attack the school. However, they would seek information, and once they knew why the Grand Market had been attacked they might return to take revenge on the merchants, or even attack the Emperor. The school would be blamed for Axavar revealing himself. Unless she acted quickly to warn everyone. The names of the particular merchants behind the attack had never been revealed to the school, having been communicated through an intermediary, but the Emperor probably knew them, or would soon when the news reached him. She gave orders for the school to post a guard and be ready to defend itself, then pushed out of the world, her mind going silent.

What should I do? Tyen wondered. He expected, for a moment, to hear Vella's voice in reply, but he'd left her securely hidden in his house.

Rayf wanted the merchants' names. Tyen could search for their minds in the city below, but it would take too much time. Oerith believed the Emperor would know.

Tyen turned his attention to a great sprawling building at the base of the cliff. It lay beside the waterfall, where its occupants would have access to the cleanest water. He sought minds within. It did not take long to find Oerith. With so many people employed in pleasing the Emperor, it was easy to find him. Oerith was already in the audience chamber. As she finished warning of the sorcerer who had followed Axavar, she turned to look at five men kneeling nearby.

The merchants, she guessed. Tyen moved to their minds, and confirmed it. He had their names. He could go.

But then, through their ears, Tyen heard the Emperor break into laughter.

Shifting to the ruler's mind, Tyen went cold. The man was amused. He had no intention of disciplining the merchants. Instead, he was considering how hard it would be to invade Doum properly.

Heat chased away the chill as Tyen's earlier anger resurfaced, but he held himself still.

If I interfere, I could make things worse.

But if he did nothing, the place he'd worked so hard to make a home in, and that he had come to love more than his own world, could be destroyed.

Yet he did not know how powerful the sorcerers the Emperor

kept close by for his protection were. They were sure to be a substantial force.

Looking into the minds of the men and women closest to the leader, Tyen counted how many were sorcerers. He'd faced this many before and survived. What of their strength? Many were considering Murai's chances against Doum if this led to a conflict, but while they thought themselves a superior force, none had experience of inter-world battle and more than a few appeared to have inflated ideas of their worth.

To confront the Emperor would be a risk, but one Tyen was willing to make for his new homeland. Taking a deep breath, he pushed into the place between worlds and skimmed downwards.

He did not plunge through the roof of the audience chamber, however. That would be too threatening. He wanted to make the Emperor think twice about making Doum an enemy, not jump to the conclusion the neighbouring world was retaliating. So he arrived a distance from the room, then approached a guard.

The man – a captain – jumped, having not noticed Tyen arrive.

"I wish to speak to the Emperor on behalf of the people of Doum."

The captain narrowed his eyes at Tyen, doubtful that anyone important would send such a filthy emissary. "And you are?"

"Tyen the Wheelmaker, of Alba." Tyen snorted. "And I would have taken time to dress for the occasion if it had not been more pressing to prevent a war between our worlds." He pushed out of the world, skimmed past the man, then emerged and stared haughtily over his shoulder. "Would you prefer I find the Emperor myself?"

The captain straightened. "No. I will take you to him." He indicated that Tyen should follow, then set off through the palace.

During Tyen's previous visit to Glaemar, he'd observed the palace exterior, but having no official reason to enter, he'd had no opportunity to see the inside. It was not what he expected. Instead of the usual glut of precious objects and rich decoration crowded together in a show of wealth and grandeur, the interior was open and uncluttered. No solid walls divided the building into rooms, just rows of columns. Archways opened onto atriums which allowed sunlight and moisture in, sustaining artfully arranged plants in enormous pots. Pergolas stood within the larger of these. The effect was a blurring between interior and exterior. It also meant that the mist from the waterfall, carried everywhere on gentle breezes, kept the air moist and cool.

Yet the palace was not empty of artwork. Here and there a graceful sculpture stood among the columns, the plant pots were from one of the best of Domra's potteries and the floors were covered in mosaics equally as impressive as those Tyen recalled lined the approach to the formal palace entrance. If the mosaics covered the entirety of the complex he'd seen from above, they must spread over a space as great as a large village, maybe even a small city.

No doubt many of the wealthier houses in Glaemar, and other Muraian cities, also decorated their homes this way. Anything considered good enough for the rulers of a country or a world was desirable for those with ambition and the need to appear prosperous and powerful. Looking closer, he realised that the tiles were all glazed. Pottery, not stone.

Little wonder the merchants got a bit touchy about the Claymars controlling prices. There must be a thriving market in this single product, on top of the pottery and pipes they buy from Doum.

He passed diplomats and courtiers, bureaucrats and servants. The latter were all young and attractive, he noted, though they wore plain but simple clothing cut of the same cloth. *I guess in a place so open, the servants can't be hidden, so the Emperor makes sure they aren't offensive to the eye.*

A couple of people in a different but more decorative uniform paused in their conversation to stare at him. Some began to follow; others hurried away. Sorcerers, he read from their minds, placed here to inspect all visitors to the Emperor. They did not like what they could see of him – which was an otherworlder in Doumian garb whose mind they could not read.

Yet none intercepted him, and he knew from the minds he read that he was indeed heading towards the audience chamber. At last, they reached internal walls. A pair of enormous doors stood between him and the Emperor. One of six guards standing outside hauled one open. The captain checked his stride, surprised, then shrugged and led Tyen into the room. He stepped aside and indicated that Tyen should advance ahead of him.

Walking past, Tyen was immediately struck by how dark the room was. It was completely enclosed, unlike so much of the palace, and the only illumination came from the flames of lamp bowls set in alcoves.

A middle-aged man stood at the centre of the room. He wore a plain robe of gold fabric over which a vest of glazed beads had been draped. The latter's humble appearance surprised Tyen at first, until he reminded himself that the world of Murai had few clay deposits. *What you don't have you covet*, he mused, *which has been an advantage for Doum . . . until now.*

Two of the sorcerers who had followed stood to either side of Tyen, and from them Tyen learned that the line of men and women along the back wall were also sorcerers. The Emperor had been informed of their inability to read Tyen's mind. He had, against their advice, decided to stay and meet the messenger from Doum.

A movement drew Tyen's attention to five men squatting nearby, their gazes fixed on the floor. They were well-dressed and ranged from an age a little younger than, to twice the age of the king. The merchants. The head of the School of Sorcery stood behind them.

As Tyen turned back to the Emperor, the man's eyebrows and chin rose in affront at the messenger's lack of respect. Reminding himself that he did not want this encounter to result in more violence, Tyen dropped into the same pose the merchants had assumed.

"Who is this?" the Emperor demanded in Muraian, the words echoing in the room.

"Tyen the Wheelmaker," the captain replied from somewhere behind Tyen.

The Emperor's voice filled the room with scepticism. "The Claymars sent a servant to negotiate on their behalf?"

"No, Emperor Izetala-Moraza," Tyen replied. Then, since he'd read from the man's mind that the ruler knew the Traveller tongue, he continued in that language. "The Claymars sent me to discover who attacked the Grand Market in Alba a short while ago, and why. I followed one of the sorcerers, a man they left behind to check whether a Claymar was among the dead—"

"And was one?" the Emperor asked, also changing to the language of the Travellers.

"I do not know, Emperor."

"Well, you have found the culprits. You may ask them their purpose."

"I have already gained that information, Emperor."

"Then why are you here?"

Tyen met the man's gaze. "These merchants have attacked Doum, Emperor," he said, letting an edge of hardness enter his voice. "That could be interpreted as an act of war." Tyen paused, then rose to his feet. "What I want to know now is: what are *you*, Emperor Izetala-Moraza, going to do? Do you object to their actions?"

The ruler's chin rose again, but he did not speak, pausing to consider his reply. As Tyen read the man's mind, his stomach sank.

"I do not approve," the Emperor said. "They took a great risk, and should have sought my permission." The ruler gave the merchants a hard look, and the men cringed and began to wonder if they had misjudged him. "But they have the right to act upon the Claymars' refusal to negotiate."

"So you will not punish them?"

The Emperor's gaze snapped back to Tyen. "Only if Claymars were harmed." *I suppose I'll have to make a show of it*, the man grumbled. *Those Claymars are a pathetic excuse for rulers. They're just artisan-servants, given temporary leadership of the unruly, arrogant mob they called their "citizens".*

"Remind them that they brought this on themselves," the Emperor continued. "Refusing to honour agreements. Selling Muraian commissions to other worlds. It will not be tolerated."

Tyen scowled. "If you will not pay a price worthy of their time and expertise, why should they not seek customers who will?"

"They have always supplied us," the Emperor said. "It is an ancient arrangement, supported by the Raen—"

"The Raen is dead."

The Emperor's expression became stony, his lips pressed together with displeasure. An uncomfortable, angry silence followed. Tyen had broken a taboo by speaking the truth. *A pretty recent taboo, in the scale of history.*

Who is this upstart? the Emperor was thinking. *Someone powerful. Someone strong enough to not fear me or my sorcerers. Yet his accent is unfamiliar, and though he looks similar to the people of Alba there is a strangeness about him. Could he be an otherworlder? Yes, I think he may be.*

"Why do you care?" he asked. "You are not of their world."

Tyen crossed his arms. "Doum is my home and its people my family. I will do what I must to defend it."

"Then defend it. Convince the Claymar to abandon this foolishness over pricing."

"I would never be so arrogant as to tell them how to live their lives and run their businesses," Tyen replied. "But I can see it will not be easy to convince you to do so as well. Except, perhaps, by removing all magic from this world so that you remain isolated for a few hundred cycles. That would be bad for trade, I imagine."

The Emperor stared at Tyen. Oerith took a small step towards the ruler. The Emperor gestured for her to stay where she was.

16

"Only the Raen was that powerful," he said.

"Not only."

"He would have killed you, had he found you."

Tyen shrugged. "As it turned out, he didn't. I'm sure you know this is a small world. I know of at least two people with enough reach to strip all the magic from it, and I would not be surprised if there were more. Even if it was beyond my ability to take all the magic in one go, I could still make sure Glaemar sits within a void so large it will take cycles to fade. Since you may doubt I speak the truth . . ." Tyen stretched out with his mind, expanding his senses until he estimated he'd encompassed the whole city, then drew in half of the magic, taking it in radiating bands. What remained would quickly spread to fill the emptiness, ensuring no sorcerer engaged in something important, such as lifting something heavy, was robbed of all power.

Gasps filled the room as the sorcerers within it sensed what he had done. Then, before any could panic and attack Tyen, he let the magic go again. It flowed out, temporarily making the palace intensely rich in magic. Shock turned to wonder. Fear to relief.

"I will leave you to reconsider your position, and whether these men –" Tyen glanced at the merchants. " – deserve punishment for killing the families of Doum's artisans and Claymars." Tyen was gratified to see that the Emperor was reluctantly doing exactly that, despite his anger at being threatened. "Thank you for hearing me, Emperor. I wish you good health and fortune."

Not waiting for a reply or a dismissal, Tyen took some of the excess of magic in the palace and pushed out of the world.

Once deep into the place between worlds, the glow of satisfaction faded and he began to worry. How would the Claymars react to him approaching and threatening the Muraian Emperor on their behalf, without consulting them first?

Will they be angry or grateful? Have I made things better or worse?

He wished he could discuss it with Vella. Thinking of her

hidden in his house, he realised that by threatening the Emperor of Murai, he might have made himself a target. While he was reasonably confident he could defend himself, the Emperor might seek a petty revenge that the Claymars would not react strongly to by wrecking Tyen's home. After today, he would start carrying her again.

He found his and Axavar's path from Doum to Murai and followed it in reverse. The stall within the remains of the Great Market began to emerge around him.

And then he sensed a shadow. Someone was following him.

Alarmed, he skimmed across the world, drawing them away from the ruins. To his relief, they stayed on his trail. He lured them out of the city, seeking an unpopulated place where he could confront them without risking harm to others. In a dry lake he emerged in the world, gasping as his body, starved of air, suffered the price of travelling for so long where it could not breathe.

A faint human shape began to form a few steps away. A feminine outline, clothed in a long shift dress. Oerith? One of the Emperor's sorcerers come to challenge him? Or had he sent her to relay a message? Perhaps a counter-threat?

Her face was not very Muraian, however. She had darker skin and straight black hair. And then, with a shock like lightning spiking through his body, he recognised her. As she arrived, she took a breath to speak, but didn't gasp for air, a sure sign of an ageless sorcerer.

"Tyen, wasn't it?" said the woman who had refused to resurrect the Raen. "Do you remember me? Or perhaps I never told you my name. I am Rielle."

CHAPTER 2

"I picked up that something was amiss from the palace servants," Rielle explained, "and it didn't take long before I saw you though other eyes."

She looked different, he noted. Older, though that was to be expected. Taller than he recalled, but perhaps only because his first impressions had been of a desperate and vulnerable young woman. She was as beautiful as he remembered, and as she smiled he looked down to stop himself staring at her.

"And you followed me," he pointed out, part observation, part question.

"I thought you might like to know that the Emperor started planning to have you assassinated once you left."

"Ah," Tyen sighed. "Of course he did."

"His sorcerers were trying to talk him out of it. More out of self-preservation than disagreement."

He looked up. "Do you think they will succeed?"

She pursed her lips. "Even odds, in my opinion. The Emperor does not like being threatened, but he could not help noticing how powerful you are. He may attempt to punish you in other ways instead. You should make sure you and anyone you care for is well protected or hidden."

He nodded, his mind immediately going to his workers. While he considered them as much friends as employees and would hate to see any harmed, he would feel bad if *any* citizens of Doum

19

suffered because of him. And then there was Vella. But the Emperor could not possibly know about Vella.

Except Rielle, now. Her mind was hidden to him, which meant she was more powerful and could read his mind if she wanted to. It was disconcerting. The only other person he'd encountered with stronger powers than his had been the Raen, and he'd assumed the Raen was *much* more powerful. While Tyen did not look into the minds of most people in Doum, he always did with anyone else, and it was a very long time since he'd not been able to.

He could not help wondering what Rielle was doing in the Muraian palace. It was just his luck that the one time he'd used his strength to impress someone they happened to have a stronger sorcerer at hand. Though surely, if she worked for the Emperor, she would not be here warning him of the ruler's intention to assassinate him.

People don't warn you of a threat to your life if they wish you harm. The last time we met, I helped her. As far as I know, she has no reason to hate me.

Unlike most people in the worlds. Or they would, if they knew the truth about him.

He turned his mind from that subject before he could reveal too much, and looked at Rielle closely. She smiled, which surely she would not do if she had glimpsed his secret, unless she was adept at pretending. He wished he could be sure.

"I don't think I thanked you for helping me escape Dahli," she said.

"No need." He shrugged. "I only helped you do the right thing. Did the boy recover?"

"Yes and no." She frowned. "He regained his sanity, but has almost no memories of his time before then."

"Is he . . .? I hope he is well hidden." Perhaps it would be better if Tyen did not know the location of the boy that the Raen had intended to inhabit after his resurrection. The silence of

Rielle's mind made the possibility of running into another sorcerer more powerful than him seem greater.

The look she gave him was full of amusement and gratitude. "Yes. He's in a safe place with good people, living far away from me." She sighed. "I feared that if I kept him with me, I'd draw him into more strife, but I've managed to keep out of trouble for five cycles so perhaps I didn't need to worry."

"And in all that time we've been living in worlds right next to each other."

Rielle lifted a hand in a graceful, negative gesture. "Oh, I've only been in Murai for a few months." She looked towards the outskirts of Alba. "I work for a team of mosaic-makers. The Emperor commissioned work from them. They like the climate in Glaemar, so they accepted his invitation to take up residence in the palace while they complete the job."

"So you work for the Emperor." Tyen raised an eyebrow. Did that make them enemies?

She turned back to look at him. "I work for people who work for him. While the mosaic-makers are decent people, I am not truly one of them. I am an outsider with a useful skill."

Tyen nodded. "I know how that feels. Though I've worked hard to make a home for myself in Doum, sometimes they still treat me as an otherworlder."

"Even after five cycles?"

"Even after five cycles."

She looked sad. "I have wondered how long it would take. I can never go home. I don't want to always be the outsider."

"I am also unable to return to my world." He frowned. "Did you learn why I was visiting the palace?"

"The merchants attacked a marketplace here. They are upset about the prices the Claymars have set on their goods." She paused. "And no doubt you read what they are contemplating doing, if they do not get their way."

"I won't let them invade Doum," he warned. Then he grimaced.

"If the Claymars let me prevent them. They are so touchy about me getting involved in anything other than making pottery wheels that I have to wonder if they'd rather Murai conquered them than I did anything on their behalf."

She chewed her lip again. "Being an otherworlder might have advantages, though. I suspect the Emperor would be more likely to compromise if he didn't have to do it to their faces. Would you negotiate on their behalf, if the Claymars let you?"

Tyen considered. "Yes. Yes, I would – though if the Emperor doesn't like being threatened, haven't I just ensured he won't listen to me?"

"No, more the opposite. He may hate you for defying him, but he will respect you for having the strength and boldness to do it."

He grimaced. "I'm not sure I like the idea of negotiating with him directly. Perhaps Murai needs a representative too. Not that I know any Muraians I'd prefer." His heart skipped as he realised who he would most like to work with. "Could you convince the Emperor to let you negotiate on his behalf?"

Her brow furrowed. "I don't know." Her tone was heavy with reluctance. "It's not that I don't want to help you, but I have no experience or training in this kind of work."

"Neither do I," Tyen told her. "But if we do nothing . . ."

". . . these two worlds may declare war with each other," she finished. "Very well. I'll consider suggesting it."

He smiled. "Thank you. I have to get back to Alba to tell them of what I know and help in the Grand Market."

"I should return to the mosaic-makers. I left them in the middle of a design meeting. Shall I look for you in Alba?"

"Yes. Ask for Tyen Wheelmaker. Most people will be able to direct you to my workshop."

She inclined her head. "Until then, Tyen Wheelmaker, I wish you well."

He waited as she faded out of sight, not wanting to push out of the world on her heels, even if he then travelled in a different direction. When she had vanished completely, he moved into the place between and began to skim towards the city. As he emerged in the Grand Market, his heart began beating quickly, but not from fear or apprehension.

Rielle! Of all people to find living in the next world!

Then he sobered. If Dahli knew where she was, he would be even more pleased. But the Raen's former most loyal servant would, at worst, want to punish her for refusing to resurrect Valhan. At best, he'd try to force her to tell him where to find the boy, so he could complete the Raen's resurrection.

Baluka, the leader of the rebels – the Restorers, as they were known now – would like to know his former fiancée was alive and well. He might not want to know her location, however, because he was not a powerful sorcerer and if others read that information from his mind it could eventually reach Dahli.

Her secret was safe with Tyen, and it was one he was happy to keep. He'd always been curious about her. He knew she had lived in the Raen's palace before his death, and that Dahli had taught her how to use magic, and to become ageless. The first time Tyen had seen her, she had been about to resurrect the Raen, but when she'd discovered it involved sacrificing the mind of an innocent boy, she'd rescued him – at no small risk to her own life. He'd followed her, helping her escape Dahli.

Tyen had admired her for that choice. It surely indicated she had strong morals and the courage to stick to them, even if in the process she became a traitor. Perhaps she would understand the choices he'd made in his life. He'd sometimes daydreamed that they met again, and became allies, friends and – when he was being particularly fanciful – possibly more.

The first part just happened.

He began to smile, but as he stepped out of the Grand Market stall, his good cheer evaporated. Little progress had been made since he'd left, but then he had not been gone all that long.

Sorcerers were now removing rubble from the huge pile, carefully lifting it piece by piece by magic lest they disturb and harm anyone trapped below. From them he learned that no minds had been detected beneath the rubble, but all hoped that some of the buried market workers might be alive but unconscious. The injured and dead recovered so far had been removed. He sought Master Rayf, finding the old man standing by the door talking to Claymar Fursa.

Rayf saw Tyen approaching first, and as his lips moved, Fursa turned to frown at Tyen.

"Tyen Wheelmaker," Rayf said. "Were you able to follow the Muraian?"

"Yes." Tyen related all that had happened. Claymar Fursa's frown deepened to a scowl on hearing of Tyen's threat to strip the world of magic. "That is a dangerous bluff."

"It was no bluff," Tyen replied, meeting and holding her gaze. Her eyes narrowed, and he did not have to read her mind to see she didn't believe him.

"Only the Raen could do such a thing," she scoffed.

"That is what he wanted the worlds to believe," Tyen replied.

"I heard that he killed anyone he encountered whose strength approached his while they were too inexperienced and skilled to challenge him," Rayf said. His attention returned to Tyen, suddenly appraising.

"Unless he recruited and trained them to be his servants," Fursa added, her eyes narrowing.

"Plenty of powerful sorcerers were born during the twenty cycles the Raen was missing," Tyen told her. "I'm not the only one he didn't get the chance to eliminate." Then he shrugged. "Besides, Murai is smaller than the average world. A sorcerer doesn't have to be able to take all magic to have a great impact on a world's strength. I could make life very difficult for the Emperor, if I wanted to."

Fursa's gaze slid away, her lips pressing tight. "Even so," she said, her eyes still averted, "you should not have threatened him without our agreement."

Tyen nodded. "I only did so because he was considering doing worse than this." He gestured around them. "But I assure you, I will not act without consulting you again." He told the pair of Rielle's visit, advice and offer, referring to her only as an otherworld sorcerer he had met before, who was working as a mosaic designer. "She is a moral person."

"She has seen to the heart of the matter." Rayf nodded. "It is unlikely the Emperor will compromise if he speaks to us directly, as it will be seen in Murai as a sign of weakness. But if an intermediary negotiates on his and our behalf, he can distance himself from the decision." He smiled at Fursa. "As can the Council."

Fursa crossed her arms. "Yes, but the Council must decide who will represent us. There may be better candidates for the role."

Suppressing a sigh, Tyen glanced back at the sorcerers digging in the rubble. "I can do no more right now than offer my assistance. When you have decided, let me know one way or the other. You know where to find me." He looked at Rayf. "I'm sure there's something more useful I can be doing here."

The old man glanced around the building. "No, we have it well in hand."

It was not the answer Tyen was expecting, but as he looked closer at the activity in the building, he realised that another large group of sorcerers had arrived while they were talking, and the entire surface of the huge pile of rubble was stirring as bricks were carefully removed. Healers hovered nearby, waiting in case a living victim was uncovered, but with the grim certainty that their services would not be needed.

Tyen nodded. "Indeed you have. I had best get out of your way, then."

He faced Fursa and pressed two fingers to his heart, nodded in respect to Rayf, then pushed out of the world and skimmed upwards, through what remained of the Grand Market's roof.

Locating the familiar shape of his home's rooftop from above, he headed towards it. He plunged through the ceiling but stopped on the upper floor, at the top of the stairs, instead of returning to the workshop with its unfinished wheels. Once air surrounded him again, he scanned the minds around him. The workshop was empty, his employees still helping at the Grand Market. His neighbours were fixed on their work, domestic tasks, trade or exchanging reports about the attack. No spies watched him. Nobody was paying him the slightest attention at all.

The only person who could be watching without me detecting it is Rielle.

He dismissed the idea, then hesitated and made himself reconsider the possibility. It would not be hard for her to find this place. He was famous enough for his magic-powered pottery wheels that he could be found easily by simply asking a few questions of people on the streets.

Why watch him, though?

Could she have warned him of the Muraian Emperor's intention to have him assassinated in order to gain his trust? When she advised him to consider the safety of the people he cared for, had it been in order to read from his mind who those people were? His stomach sank as he remembered who he'd thought of when she had.

Vella.

He hadn't thought about Vella's hiding place, however. Still, he hurried to the toilet and pushed inside. The commode was made up of a wooden box with a hole in the top, in which a large funnel was suspended. The funnel emptied into one of the ceramic pipes that, until recently, Muraian merchants had bought and sold on to other worlds. Carefully lifting the box and funnel off the pipe, he reached under the base. The odour of urine and faeces that always lingered despite regular cleaning grew a little stronger, and he took care to avoid the bottom of the funnel. No toilets in the worlds were as well plumbed and ventilated as those of his home world and city.

26

He groped around inside the wooden base. As his fingers met a familiar bundle, he let out a sigh of relief. Unhooking it, he tucked it under his arm and replaced the seat. He then sat upon the commode. A pouch was uncovered as he removed the wrapping, a firm but slightly flexible object inside. Through holes in the fabric he could see the familiar leather of Vella's cover.

When he'd first settled in Doum, he had spoken to Vella at least once a day, torn between keeping her safely hidden and the need to talk to someone familiar. He also did not want to abandon her to the unconsciousness state she remained in when not touched by a human.

But when he'd adopted the local garb to help fit in with the locals, carrying Vella had become a problem. Since the climate was warm, Doumian fabrics were thin and showed the outline of objects lying beneath them. When people began asking what lay beneath his shirt he'd had to find another hiding place for her.

The busier his enterprise had grown, the less time he'd had to talk to her. His daily chat changed to one every second day, then every three or four days, and the intervals had slowly grown larger. Yet if he waited too long, he began lying awake at night worrying if she was still there. So their chats had become irregular, middle-of-the-night affairs.

As always, she was slightly warm as he slipped her from the pouch. Affection and a little guilt rose within him. While he considered his employees friends, none were as close to him as Vella. He wished he had spared more time to talk to her. He considered his promise to find a way to restore her to human – an idea he'd not had much success pursuing since most sources of knowledge were now in the hands of people who considered Tyen a spy and traitor.

Since she would have read his mind at the first touch of his skin, he did not have to explain all that had happened since he'd last talked to her. He opened her covers and looked down at the familiar unmarked pages. Words began to appear.

Hello, Tyen. I see it has been a day of ill news.

Yes, though it was not all bad.

No. Yet you question whether to trust Rielle too.

Nothing in particular gives me cause for suspicion, but I can't help feeling I shouldn't assume anything. I've only met her once before. All I know about her comes from Dahli and Baluka — what they told me and the occasions they thought about her. Also, if I am to negotiate on behalf of Doum and the Emperor sends her to represent him, I must treat her as I would anyone else in that position.

That is wise.

She refused to destroy a young man so that the Raen could be resurrected, so her morals are strong, but she chose to join the Raen before then. I can't see how anyone could do the latter without making some moral compromises.

Dahli could not have read her mind. Perhaps she was only pretending to be a willing subject.

The Raen would have read that from her mind if she was.

Would he have? You read from Dahli that Valhan said he was not always able to read her mind.

Tyen drew in a sharp breath at the reminder. No surprise, then, that she could read his mind. *Yet that means the Raen could read it some of the time. It is hard to believe she could have concealed disloyalty, considering how difficult it is to keep from your thoughts the things you don't want others to see.*

Perhaps she was loyal then changed her mind about him later.

Or he didn't care as long as she did what he wanted. He chewed the inside of his cheek. *I wonder, would she tell me if I asked.* He frowned. *Though it would be impolite to pry. I don't want to anger her, whether we end up negotiating on behalf of our worlds or not.*

If you wish to know more, Baluka may be able to give more insight into her character.

That would mean telling him I've met her recently, which she might not like.

You do not need to tell Baluka you've met her. You only need to prompt him to talk of her.

He nodded. *That won't be hard. He does like to reminisce.* He drummed his fingers on her cover. *A visit to Baluka, then.* He looked up, focusing beyond the toilet door as a plan formed. To arrange a meeting with Baluka, he must leave a message at one of several pre-arranged locations in other worlds. He would need to change into clothing that wasn't so obviously from Doum in case anyone recognised it and guessed he was living here. He looked down at the page again. And he'd better take Vella with him, in case the Muraian Emperor or merchants sent someone to loot, damage or destroy his house.

He closed Vella, slipped her back into the pouch, then draped the strap around his neck. Emerging from the toilet, he entered his bedroom and opened the clothing chest. Under the shirts and trousers he wore regularly lay clothing he wore whenever travelling through the worlds. It was deliberately unremarkable, designed to allow him to fade into a crowd. Of commoners, of course – it was impossible to predict what garb might be fashionable among the rich and powerful.

From the selection he chose a long-sleeved shirt, rugged trousers, warm socks and leather boots and a long woolly jacket. Once dressed, he checked the hidden pockets of the jacket. In one he found some precious stones, still the most reliable currency across worlds – even more so since the alliances and peace the Raen had maintained had crumbled.

He turned towards the door, then hesitated and looked back at his desk.

"Beetle."

A muffled hum came from the topmost drawer. It appeared to open of its own accord, allowing a pair of antennae to escape. The mechanical insectoid crawled partway out.

"Come out. Close the drawer. Come here."

It scurried up onto the desktop, leaned down and nudged the drawer closed. Wing protectors sprang open and the fine wings within blurred and carried the little machine to Tyen's outstretched hand. He picked it up and slipped it into an inner pocket of his coat. Through the layers of fabric, he felt a faint vibration.

"Be quiet," he told it. The sensation stopped.

Beetle's primary role nowadays was to guard Tyen's savings. He hadn't set it to watch over Vella, since too many people knew he'd used it to protect valuables before and would reason that if it was guarding the book, the book must be precious to him. Now that he was resigned to the possibility that someone might invade or destroy his home, he would rather ensure Beetle's safety by taking it with him than sacrifice the insectoid over some jewels and coin.

Heading downstairs, he left a message in case one or all of his employees returned, telling them to take the rest of the day off. He glanced around the workroom once and, seeing nothing that needed immediate attention, pushed out of the world.

Rather than creating a path in the place between that led directly from his workshop, he skimmed across the city a few times before heading across the country to another city. After returning to the world in a busy marketplace to take a few deep breaths, he withdrew again and propelled himself downwards.

A slightly greyed darkness surrounded him. Few sorcerers would willingly skim into the ground. *Few sorcerers who were not ageless, that is*, he corrected. To do so, he must be able to travel fast enough to emerge on the other side of the world before suffocating.

It was not a danger for an ageless sorcerer. The same knowledge they applied to stop ageing could be used to heal, so they could mend the damage from a lack of air when they arrived in a world. But even for the ageless, instincts rebelled against venturing deep underground. It just *felt* perilous.

Tyen propelled himself faster and faster. By the time he reached the other side of the world, he had gained so much speed that he shot up out of the ground and into the night sky before he could react and stop. Reversing his path, he descended most of the way to the ground.

He was above an ocean, and had to create a platform of stilled air under his feet to stand on when he emerged back into the world to breathe. When his head stopped spinning and the need to gasp for air faded, he drew in a few more deep breaths to last him for the next leg of his journey and, gathering his bearings from the stars, returned to the place between.

Land was not far away – a peninsula edged by fishing villages. In a temple on top of a promontory, he found what he was looking for: an official arrival place for world travellers. Most worlds had them as a means to locate safe paths through the place between. All but a few priests were asleep within the temple. He skimmed to the departure point, a simple stone circle, then pushed away from the world, following a familiar, well-established path. The night-shaded scene bleached to pure white, then gained form and shadow as he passed the midway point between worlds and neared the next.

He arrived in another temple, this one ruined and surrounded by snow-coated mountains. Cold air filled his lungs. He pushed onwards to another world and a small grotto with an altar and several worshippers, then skimmed across the surface of that world to a huge, empty cave where a defaced statue emerged from a wall. Marks on the floor indicated routes to four neighbouring worlds. He stepped onto one and launched himself away, travelling on to a world of mist.

From there he hopped from world to world, arrival place to arrival place. Occasionally he passed travellers in the place between. All avoided him. Sorcerers were still skittish about meeting others in the whiteness, despite it being more than five cycles since the Raen had imposed his restrictions on travel between worlds. For some, it was impossible to break a lifetime of dreading a shadow in the whiteness, and possible death as punishment for breaking the ruler of worlds' law. For others, it was the newer fear of encountering people they had wronged, now that they could no longer rely on the Raen for protection, or the threat of sorcerer thieves and gangs who robbed travellers, or worse.

As Baluka had often said, the end of the Raen's laws had freed the unscrupulous as well as the oppressed. In many parts of the worlds, the Raen's allies had been replaced by new tyrants. They kept the Restorers busy administering justice and imposing new laws. Revolution hadn't brought prosperity or freedom to all, and even those who simply hadn't benefited from the Raen's death to the degree they'd hoped for had grown angry or disillusioned. They demanded more of the Restorers than could ever be delivered, and Tyen did not envy Baluka the task of trying to keep everyone calm, if not satisfied.

He paused to catch his breath in a night-veiled garden. *Baluka would be so happy to learn that Rielle was alive and well. It feels unfair to not tell him. I could ask her if she minds whether I do, but perhaps it is better he doesn't know I am in contact with her.* Baluka was a sorcerer of average strength – powerful enough to travel between worlds, but not enough to become ageless. That meant plenty of sorcerers could read his mind.

Tyen knew his hesitation came out of a habit of never revealing more than he had to. It was a habit borne out of spying. Though sometimes he wasn't sure if he truly earned the title "the Spy", given to him when the Raen's allies had spread rumours about him to weaken the rebels. He did not actively seek information for anyone; Dahli and Baluka simply expected him to tell them whatever information he gained that they ought to know. He'd done so, for both of them, over the last five cycles. About each of them to the other too, in order to keep them both believing he was on their side.

Whose side am I on? He wasn't sure any more. Perhaps neither. Perhaps his own. *No, if I'm so selfish, why do I care about the people of Doum? Or whether there is violence and injustice in the worlds? Or that Vella had been trapped inside a book against her will?*

If anyone had asked, he'd have told them that he was keeping in contact with Dahli in order to keep track of what the man was up to, and staying in touch with Baluka in order to have a reason to stay in contact with Dahli. But it went deeper than that.

If Dahli found a way to resurrect Valhan, all sorcerers would have to choose between an alliance with him or fleeing and hiding – if there was anywhere the Raen's influence did not reach. Tyen would be one of the first to know. He could warn others.

Whatever method Dahli found to resurrect Valhan might work to give Vella a body. Though Tyen would not destroy another person in order to do so, Dahli might find a way that did not. Dahli knew Tyen wanted to restore Vella, but Tyen had made it clear he would have no part in killing someone in order to achieve it. So in order to have another reason to meet up with Dahli, he had admitted that he was keeping in contact with Baluka, and was willing to pass on information.

Baluka believed that Tyen was spying on Dahli for the Restorers. While Tyen had no qualms about spying on Dahli, working against Baluka made him uncomfortable. Baluka was the closest thing he had to a friend, after Vella. He looked forward to their meetings and reminiscing about the past. He took great care to ensure that the information he passed on could not harm his friend.

When Rielle reads all this from my mind, she'll understand, he told himself.

Tyen passed three more worlds before stopping in a darkened room. Using a little magic, he vibrated a speck of air until it glowed. A familiar basement surrounded him. The rotting wooden shelving leaned even more precariously than it had the last time he'd visited. He ducked under and past, climbed a creaking set of stairs and opened the door at the top. Noise battered him as he joined the traffic of a narrow, crowded street. The pungent smells of a bustling city filled his nose. It was impossible to tell what time of day it was, but some instinct told him it was early morning. Not that it mattered. He'd been in this place at many times of day and never seen a change in the number of people out and about.

He let the flow of them take him far from his arrival place, then as he neared his destination, he pushed and dodged his way into side streets, across a small marketplace and into an alley so narrow all had to walk sideways to pass the people coming from the opposite direction. The flow was so persistent that it was easier to walk to the end of the alley, then join the line walking back the other way so he could simply step into his destination, a drinking establishment, when he reached it, rather than push through the oncoming people.

Within, it was quiet, only a few customers standing at the tables. He scanned their minds as he moved to the counter . . . and froze with his hand hovering above the bell.

It's him! one was thinking, his heart jolting with fear and triumph. *It's the Spy. Our source was right!*

As the man turned to signal to his friend, who was watching from across the other side of the room, Tyen pushed out of the world.

Immediately three shadows darkened the place between. Tyen skimmed to the nearest well-used path leading out of the world, his pursuers close behind. Once on the path, he threw the full force of his strength into travelling, propelling himself to the next world and the next, and onwards.

The shadows were gone by the second world. Still, he kept up the pace. Though he kept to established paths, they might be able to track him by guessing which direction he'd taken, and searching the minds of people near to arrival places to see if he'd been observed. Ten worlds away, he stopped and stepped off a stone-paved arrival place into thick forest. He fought his way through the vegetation for a hundred paces or so. His time avoiding allies had taught him that the best way to throw off trackers was to use non-magical means to travel. But he wasn't going to get very far here. He needed to use a different ploy.

He pushed a little way out of the world, then stopped and spread his awareness out around him. Drawing in some of the substance of the place between, he smoothed it over the furrow his passage had created. Moving further into the place between, he covered his trail again. The result was texture like recently raked sand, but it would soon even out. Only a sorcerer who knew this was possible would look closer and notice the signs of a hidden path.

The only sorcerer he'd known who could do this had been the Raen. Vella had no knowledge of the trick. It had taken him a cycle of experimenting before he was able to master it, and he did a poor job compared to the dead ruler.

He'd had a lot more time to practise, Tyen reminded himself. *I'd be pretty good at it after a thousand cycles.*

After stopping to hide his path two more times, he continued on to the next world, arriving gasping for breath. As he recovered, he considered the reaction of the sorcerer who'd recognised him. The man had been surprised, but only that Tyen had actually appeared as they'd been told to expect. Then he'd felt a mix of fear, hate and opportunism. The latter intrigued Tyen. Their reason for waiting for him had less to do with revenge for Tyen spying on the rebels than with some idea they could profit from him. Perhaps by taking him captive. Perhaps only as a trophy corpse. Perhaps they'd heard that he possessed a book containing the secret of agelessness, and hoped to take it from him.

Perhaps, together, the ambushers would have been strong enough to succeed.

Tyen doubted it though. He'd not have lost them so easily if they'd been that powerful. He should worry more that someone had told them where he might turn up. That person could only have learned the location from Baluka. Either they'd read the rebel leader's mind or Baluka had told them.

If they knew of one location Tyen left messages at, they might know of the others. He could check these places to see if anyone was lying in wait, but even approaching the sites might be dangerous. Finding out more about Rielle would have been useful, but not vital to his efforts to help Doum. It wasn't worth the risk.

But he would have to get to the bottom of it eventually. In future, he might have something important to tell Baluka. He would have to find another way to contact his friend. Frustrated and worried, Tyen pushed away from the world and began a long and convoluted journey back to Doum.

CHAPTER 3

T he clay was cool and sticky. It smelled oddly clean for something that had been dug out of the ground, but then, it had been expertly refined before arriving at Tyen's workshop. Stones and organic matter had been removed, as well as air bubbles. All that remained to be done before it could be worked was a light kneading. He carried it over to the sturdy table he used for the purpose, and began rolling and pressing it under the heels of his hand.

As he kneaded, his mind worried over recent events and future possibilities. It was three days since the attack on the Grand Market and he'd not heard anything from the Council. Three days. Were they taking the threat from Murai seriously? In his imagination the Muraian merchants' thoughts still steamed with avarice and a desire to teach the makers of Doum a lesson, and the Emperor's burned with the prospect of conquest.

If the Council *was* taking the threat seriously, had Tyen not heard anything because they did not trust him, as an outsider, to negotiate on their behalf? If they chose a Doumian representative, would the Emperor refuse to cooperate, as Rielle had warned?

He looked down. The clay was supple and consistent now. He peeled it up off the table and began to press and roll it between his palms.

Why hasn't Rielle come to see me?

Perhaps the Emperor was as reluctant for an outsider to speak on his behalf as the Council was for one to act on theirs. Rielle had hesitated at the prospect, and may have decided against suggesting it to the Emperor. Either way, he had hoped she would tell him in person, whatever the news was. He wanted to see her again, though he had to admit, the prospect filled him with as much anxiety as eagerness.

She is, as far as I know, the most powerful sorcerer in the worlds. More powerful than me. That makes her potentially dangerous, not least because I can't read her mind and she can read mine. I should avoid her. I have too many secrets. She is sure to learn, eventually, that the rumours about me are true. Mostly.

And yet, if she did find out by reading his mind, she would also know why he had done what he'd done. She would understand that he had acted without alternative choices, or with good intentions.

She was the one person he knew of in the worlds who was like him too. Not just because they were both strong sorcerers, able to read the minds of nearly everyone they met. He knew that, like him, she had come from a world so weak that too little magic existed in it to transport a sorcerer out of the world. The Raen had taken the last of it from hers, and he suspected that, between himself and Kilraker, the only strong source of magic in his world had been drained when he'd left and Spirecastle fell.

Like him, she was a fugitive. They were both considered traitors outside their home worlds. They were both young and lacking in experience when compared to most ageless sorcerers of the worlds.

If the leaders of Murai and Doum knew all this, they would never choose us to be their negotiators.

He sighed. What would they do instead? Would the Emperor heed Tyen's warning or ignore it? Would the Council forbid Tyen to carry out his threat of draining Murai of magic if the Emperor invaded, preferring war to accepting the help of an otherworlder?

The clay was now a smooth, perfectly round ball. He considered the weight of it in his hand, then judged the distance to the wheel. Slamming it down onto the turntable was satisfying. Even more so when his aim proved good, as it was now, lodging the clay right in the centre. Drawing some magic, he applied it to the boiler he'd installed under the floor. Pistons and cogs began to turn, the motion transferring through an arm to the wheel. The clay started to revolve.

Wetting his hands and a rag, he squeezed a generous amount of water over the mound of clay, then again, and once again to be sure. He braced his elbows on his knees, leaned down and pressed the spinning clay between his palms.

What right do I have to interfere? he asked himself. *Does five cycles of working towards making a life here justify harming another world to ensure this one stays the way I like it?*

He couldn't go home, so he had no choice but to try and make a new one somewhere, but wherever he went, wherever humans could survive or thrive, people had made a prior claim to the land. That left only two choices: live by their rules or disrespect them. He'd settled for living in a place with rules he could live by, hoping that he would eventually earn the locals' trust and acceptance.

Five cycles was nothing compared to the countless generations the local artisans here had spent developing their skills and styles. Surely those men and women would rather a friendly sorcerer protect them than face an invasion of Muraians who considered them nothing more than unimportant servants.

They may want to try standing up for themselves first. Doumians don't like owing anything, money or favours, to anyone as well. I admire them for that, even if it is a source of annoyance.

Perhaps it would help if he reassured them that all he asked for in return was to live a quiet life in their world. A letter perhaps. Or would it be better said in person?

Continuing to douse the clay with water, he gently and firmly persuaded it into a smooth dome. Once satisfied that it was perfectly centred, he began to squeeze and elongate it, then squash it down into a mound again, over and over. Like the kneading, this worked the clay to a more even consistency, but also introduced more water. Slowly the clay grew supple and pliant.

What if the Council do decide to accept me as their negotiator?

His hands twitched, and he had to re-centre the clay.

What was it that Rielle had said? *"I have no experience or training in this kind of thing."* Neither did he. Though he had led the rebels for a while, there had been little need for negotiation among people who had one goal, with no room for compromise. Rielle, on the other hand, had lived for a time among the Travellers, who were skilled barterers. Did that mean she was more likely to be better than he at negotiations? Perhaps she had been bluffing when she'd claimed to be ignorant of such things. Though her ability to read his mind was her greatest advantage – by far.

What could she learn that she could turn against him? That he had a magical book of immense knowledge? Baluka and Dahli knew of it. Since a sorcerer stronger than Baluka could read his mind and learn about Vella, Tyen hadn't expected her existence to remain a secret. Instead he'd relied on remaining hidden, and his greater strength, to keep her from being taken from him. Rielle was strong enough to steal Vella. He could only hope she wouldn't.

Rielle could tell the Emperor that Tyen had spied for the Raen, but since the ruler had benefited from agreements with Valhan, that would only raise Tyen in his eyes. She could tell Baluka, but Tyen could counter that by revealing to his friend why he'd done it. He was sure Baluka would understand. He hoped so, anyway. He doubted Rielle would risk approaching Baluka, when Dahli might have spies watching the Restorers.

What advantages might Tyen have over her? He could tell Dahli where she was. He could tell the Emperor that she had prevented the resurrection of the Raen.

I can't tell him either. She would never speak to me again. I can't even threaten *to tell him that.* He would not take advantage of her in any way.

But what if doing so was the only way to protect Doum? While she might prefer to steer the two worlds towards peace, the Emperor would expect her to produce an agreement that was as profitable to him as possible. Tyen remaining on good terms with her as well as protecting Doum would not be easy.

He would find a way. He was determined to achieve both. If the Claymars gave him the opportunity.

The clay was ready now. Smooth and malleable. He placed his fingertips on the top of the mound and pressed downwards until he had created a hole that reached almost to the turntable surface. Sprinkling in enough water to keep the newly exposed clay wet, but not so much that it formed a puddle, he began to pull outwards. His hand on the outside guided the shaping of the cavity, telling him how even the walls were. As his fingertips reached the top, he ran them over the edge to round it. Then he wet his hands and returned to the centre of the bowl, checking and adjusting the shape as he worked up to the rim again.

After a third working he stopped. A simple bowl now sat upon the wheel, its base still affixed to the turntable. He reached down to a hook on the side of the wheel and lifted off it a length of wire with two sticks attached to either end. Holding the sticks, he stretched the wire between his hands and pressed it close to the turntable surface with his thumbs, then pulled the wire through the bottom of the bowl, slicing through the clay. As it came through the near side, the vessel caught and slid with it to the turntable edge, but Tyen stopped before it could topple off.

He scooped the bowl up and carried it to drying shelves nearby; then he stepped back to consider his work.

It was an unremarkable bowl by an unremarkable potter. At least, it would be if it survived the firing and glazing process. It might rise above its humble beginnings, if the glazing turned out well, but he knew that it was barely any better than the pieces his teacher sent to her tub of rejected work, destined to be dissolved into a slip for casting moulded pottery.

But I'm not running a famous pottery business, so it will do for me. He sighed, shrugged and began cleaning up.

After he'd left Baluka and the rebels five cycles ago, he'd sought a place to live quietly, away from the chaos created by the death of the Raen. A vague idea about doing good to balance the bad had led him to Faurio, the world of healers, but when he was recognised by a former rebel he'd had to leave.

He'd had no aptitude for healing either. When struggling to focus on studying, he had daydreamed about Doum, where he'd met Baluka and the Raen a few times. A world with an abundance of clay and potters. He needed a way to earn a living other than sorcery and mechanical magic. Pottery appealed. It was a literal connection to land. Down to earth. Humble. So he found a country in Doum where the people had similar stature and colouring to his, and he paid someone to teach him.

Things had not gone quite as he'd hoped.

Even when he'd gained a reasonable skill with and understanding of clay, it was clear he had no talent for it. In a place where the existing potters' skills had been developed to a level unsurpassed in most worlds, nobody wanted to buy the pots of an average, unremarkable potter – and less so when they learned they were made by an outsider. A pot made in Doum by an otherworlder was not a true Doumian pot.

While Tyen had learned and practised, his attention had strayed to the tools the potters used, especially the wheels, and his mind became distracted by ideas for improving them. He questioned every feature, or lack of them. Eventually Porla, his teacher, had grown tired of his complaints and given him an old wheel to modify as he pleased. Thinking he would only try a few ideas, he started to work. Within days, he'd created a potter's wheel that used magic, not water, animals or people, to power it.

He'd hidden it for nearly a whole cycle, afraid that if otherworld merchants saw it they'd talk about it in their worlds, and eventually someone would recognise the work of the "inventor" of mechanical magic and come to Doum to deal with "the Spy". But during his journeys out into the worlds to visit Baluka and Dahli, he'd seen more and more instances where mechanical magic had been applied to ordinary tasks, and soon realised his wheels would be just another example among many. So he demonstrated his prototype to his teacher.

Porla had been impressed but cautious. She had him make one for her, and a boiler, and teach one of the sorcerers who ran her kilns how to heat the water. Soon they'd worked out how to utilise the heat of the kilns to run the wheels. Within a few months, Tyen had his own workshop and was training employees to make the wheels and boilers, and install his system across the world. By the end of his fifth cycle in Doum, he had a comfortable income and a small amount of local fame.

He'd come to Doum expecting to be covered in clay most of the time. Instead it was grease he washed off every night. To avoid losing his hard-won pottery skills, he tested every wheel the workshop produced, even though it meant he had to thoroughly clean it before presenting it to the customer.

With the last traces of clay wiped away, he dumped the cleaning cloths in the sink, dried his hands, hung up his apron and started up the stairs. Usually he spent his evening eating with friends at one of the many inns. If no social gathering was planned, he'd tinker with machine parts, making small, harmless insectoids to give to the children of employees or friends. In the three days since the market attack, most Albans had stayed home, afraid to be in public places, so he'd been eating out alone.

As he reached the top stair, a sudden rapping made him jump. He turned and descended. As the sound came again, he located it and headed to the main door of the workshop. Seeking the mind beyond, he was relieved and intrigued to find a messenger waiting. He opened the door.

The sack hanging over the man's shoulder was slack, so this was probably one of his last deliveries of the day.

"A message for Tyen Wheelmaker." He held out a small parcel in both hands.

"Thank you," Tyen replied, taking it and giving the man a coin.

He closed the door and turned the parcel over in his hands. It was an all too familiar weight and size. He tore open the wax-soaked fabric. A small glazed tile fell out into his palm. On it a small insect had been painted.

Well, he thought, *this is badly timed.*

Venturing out into the worlds was the last thing he wanted to do when news from the Council and Rielle could come at any moment. But then, it was unlikely that the Council would contact him at night. Or Rielle, when he considered it. She could easily find out what time it was in Alba. Since trade was common between the two worlds, calendars showing how the days, seasons and years of both aligned were available in both worlds. The merchants of Murai prided themselves on memorising such details of the worlds they traded.

So really, there was nothing stopping him from answering Dahli's request for a meeting.

The tile was green, which meant the matter wasn't urgent. Yet Dahli rarely sought Tyen out. As long as Tyen met up with him every quarter cycle or so, and promptly reported anything important, he was satisfied. The few times Dahli had initiated a meeting, it had been to warn Tyen of a threat, and now, after the ambush, Tyen could not afford to risk that Dahli's reasons for summoning him weren't related.

Ascending to his bedroom, he changed and moved Vella from an inner pocket he'd sewn into his work trousers to the satchel made to stow her in. As he slipped her under his shirt, the reassuring warmth of her cover touched his skin through the holes in the satchel fabric. Through this contact, she could see through his eyes, and they could converse when between worlds. Checking other pockets, he found Beetle still inside the coat from his earlier trip.

He gathered magic and pushed away from the world. The room faded like old cloth left in the sun. As before, he took a fast and convoluted route around the city and dove through to the other side of the world before leaving Doum. Hopping from world to world, he backtracked, looped in circles and stopped to hide his path – precautions he hadn't made a habit of for a long time, but which the failed ambush made seem necessary again.

Though Baluka had always denied the rumour that Tyen had been a spy for the Raen, it hadn't stopped some rebels from believing it. The fact that Tyen had not submitted himself to tests to prove his innocence damned him in their eyes. For the first few cycles after the Raen's death, a trip through the worlds was as likely to include evading pursuit as not. Gradually these chases had grown less common, then rare, and he'd not had to shake off pursuit for a long time now. Either those previous pursuers had learned that he was always going to be faster than them and had given up trying to find him, or more important matters than revenge had distracted them. Or perhaps they finally believed Baluka.

If only he was right. Tyen felt a familiar guilt, not dulled by time, followed by a dogged certainty that agreeing to spy for the Raen had been the only sensible course of action at the time. If he hadn't agreed to, the man would have killed him. Tyen had used his influence with the rebels to prevent a confrontation between them and the Raen and, when he could no longer hold them back, he'd worked to minimise the deaths.

Yet despite the guilt, he continued spying. All the reasons and excuses circled through his mind. Keeping an eye on Dahli. Staying friends with and protecting Baluka. He had to admit to a little pride. He was good at gaining people's confidence and convincing them to trust him. Aside from making insectoids, it might be the only natural skill he had. He may as well use it for a good purpose.

Does that purpose also include preventing Valhan's return? he asked himself.

He knew from his time scouting for the rebels that as many people in the worlds would welcome the Raen's return as wouldn't. The man had been both loved and hated, monster and saviour, master and servant. The worlds had benefited and suffered from his death, and would again if he returned.

If he considered only how it would affect him, Tyen had to acknowledge that the Raen had been, and would be again, both a potential threat and benefactor. Valhan had not killed Tyen when they'd met, when he was known to kill new powerful sorcerers. He'd struck a bargain: Tyen would spy for him in exchange for Valhan seeking a way to restore Vella. The Raen might have died before he had a chance to fulfil his side of that deal, but Tyen knew from Dahli that the ruler had made progress and intended to finish the task after he was resurrected.

Dahli, too, was proof that the Raen did sometimes spare powerful sorcerers who were useful and loyal.

If Valhan returned, Vella had a better chance of regaining her body. But was the cost too high? Did the Raen's bad deeds outweigh his good? Surely it was better to do less harm than good – and Tyen could not say that Valhan had achieved, or even aimed for, that. The worlds might be in upheaval now the Raen no longer controlled them, but they might be better off without him in the long run.

Or they might continue to descend into chaos and more would die as a result, and Tyen, by refusing to help Dahli resurrect Valhan, would be to blame.

What do you think, Vella? Am I doing the right thing?

"*I think you are doing your best to not take a side,*" she replied, her words sounding clear in his mind since they were between worlds. "*Positioning yourself so that you can minimise the harm done if Dahli succeeds while maximising the chance to benefit from it.*"

You make it sound so calculated.

"Think of it as 'carefully considered'."

He was nearly at his first destination – a crowded temple where people left requests to their gods painted on tablets and hanging on the branches of ancient trees. Arriving in a secluded corner, he paused to catch his breath before joining the crowds. On a younger and therefore less popular tree, he found coded instructions from Dahli on where to go next. Another journey through the worlds took him to a ruined ancient city emerging from the sands of a great dune, where a tiny change to a depiction of a feast carved into a wall told him his next step. Several more of these instructions followed. Unlike Tyen, Dahli had powerful sorcerer friends able to set up these complicated paths for him, and guards to watch for and warn against anyone seeking him out.

Each time Tyen returned to the place between, he stopped to hide his path. It slowed his journey considerably, but then some of Dahli's instructions required Tyen to travel by non-magical means, which was also time-consuming. The number of worlds he must visit to find Dahli always varied. Sometimes he travelled through a handful of worlds, sometimes several dozen.

Directions given by a butcher in a small rural town had him walk to the next village to a small cottage. He'd have taken it for abandoned if smoke had not been filtering out of the reed-covered roof. So when Dahli answered the door, Tyen paused in surprise. He'd expected to have to travel much further than this.

Though Dahli had altered his appearance, grown a beard and turned his hair white, Tyen knew him even before he looked into the man's mind. Dahli's way of standing and moving always remained unchanged, as did the way his gaze never wavered where most people would look away out of politeness or respect.

"Yes, it's me," Dahli said, then stepped aside and held the door open.

Tyen moved inside. The cottage interior was a single room with a dirt floor strewn with bundles of the same reeds that

47

formed the roof. A bed hung from a sturdy beam at one end, a table and two stools occupied the other. In the centre, a fire burned within a simple ring of stones, the smoke lingering beneath the rafters before it found its way outside.

It was not Dahli's home, of course. He was only borrowing it from the owner for a few hours. The man waved to one of the stools, then sat on the other. For a long moment after Tyen had settled, Dahli sat rubbing his hands together lightly, his expression thoughtful as he considered how to begin. All of which made Tyen tense and impatient, despite being able to watch the man's deliberations.

"Do you have anything to tell me?" Dahli eventually asked, raising his eyebrows.

Tyen shook his head, then stilled as he remembered that he did. "Actually, yes. A few days ago I tried to leave a message for Baluka at one of my usual places and found three sorcerers lying in wait for me."

Dahli's frown was the only outward sign of his surprise. "Do you know how they discovered the location?"

"No. I didn't stay long enough for them to think about it."

"Would Baluka betray you?"

"Perhaps, if he had been given proof of my true role among the rebels."

Dahli nodded, and Tyen was relieved to see the man had not, as far as he recalled, arranged for that to happen – though it was possible he had, then blocked his memory of it, as he had done to his memories of where the records of the Raen's experiments with resurrection had been hidden.

"So why have you arranged this meeting?" Tyen prompted.

Dahli's jaw tightened. "It has been five cycles."

Tyen nodded. He could see Dahli's frustration. *Valhan said . . . no, he hinted, that if Rielle would not bring him back to life, Tyen might*, Dahli was reminding himself. *Tyen is the only sorcerer I've encountered as strong as her.*

"The boy is now an adult, physically," Dahli continued. "I have come to agree with you that we must find Valhan another vessel."

Tyen had never felt comfortable speaking the Raen's name aloud. It seemed too informal. Yet it sounded right coming from Dahli, who had been closest to the ruler of worlds – known as the Raen's "most loyal". Though not as close as he wished to be. Dahli's genuine love for the Raen, though unrequited – perhaps only because it *was* unrequited – somehow made it much easier for Tyen to sympathise with him. That, and the tearing grief he could see the man still suffered. *Is that partly why I don't find it too arduous spying for him? It would be easier to refuse him if he was a man with no conscience or emotion. I see his regrets for what he has done for the Raen. I think he would be a good person, if it weren't for Valhan, and yet I respect his dedication to the man.*

"I never said that exactly," Tyen corrected gently but firmly. "I said we must find another way. I will not destroy someone in order to give the Raen a new body."

"Yet you would for Vella."

Tyen shook his head. "No. The Raen and I discussed other options for her. I suspect he chose the boy because he was short of time. If faking his death hadn't been part of his plan, he would have explored alternatives."

Dahli did not agree, but he did not voice his doubts.

"He would have," Tyen insisted. "It was a part of our deal."

If Tyen was honest, he could not remember the exact terms of the deal now. Perhaps he hadn't been that specific. Yet he did recall the Raen warning Tyen that there might be no way to restore Vella without harming anyone, and then it would be up to Tyen to decide whether to proceed.

Dahli let out a long, heavy sigh. "Well, he is not here to attempt it. If you wish to continue his experiments and apply them to Vella, then you may have your chance to. I will restore my memory and give you all the information he recorded in exchange for your help in resurrecting the Raen. But you must work on her restoration only *after* he is alive and intact."

The flush of hope that had surged through Tyen immediately ebbed away. "I won't kill someone in order to learn how to not kill someone."

Dahli spread his hands. "You need only do it the once."

"No." Tyen held back a growing anger. He kept his voice firm and steady. "I will help you resurrect the Raen when I have a method that will not destroy a person. I know I am asking you to trust me more than you are asking me to trust you, but that is how it must be. I will not murder anyone to bring him back."

"Many more will die the longer we wait to restore him," Dahli warned. "The worlds grow ever more dangerous and destructive. Wars are already raging. How long before they combine to bring strife to all worlds? And I do not . . ." He paused, then shook his head and continued on though he worried that it was unwise to share the next piece of information. "I do not know how long Valhan's hand will survive. It appears to have shrunk a little. To have withered more."

Tyen regarded Dahli with doubt and sympathy. He read from the man's mind that he had woken the memory of the hand's location recently so that he could check that it was safe, but it had taken a few days for the recollection to form. Dahli also feared that he might permanently block his memories of its hiding place, as well as all the other information needed to resurrect the Raen. Suppressing memories was an inexact, dangerous process.

Dahli hoped that the danger of losing the knowledge to restore Vella would persuade Tyen to accept his terms, but he acknowledged that if the only method to resurrect someone was one Tyen couldn't use, that knowledge was of no value.

Sighing, Dahli leaned back in his chair. "I don't have to read your mind to see you won't accept my offer. And I don't need to tell you I am determined to find a way to persuade you."

Tyen shrugged.

"This ambush you avoided . . . will you be unable to remain in contact with Baluka?"

"I have other places I leave messages, though I will, of course, approach them with caution."

"I will ask my contacts if they've heard of any renewed efforts to find you, or if a reward has been offered." The ageless sorcerer was thinking that Tyen must surely have considered that Dahli might have arranged the ambush. *Though he must have also realised that if I did want him dead, I'd have brought an army of sorcerers with me strong enough to do the job. So it took no small measure of courage for him to meet me today. Or trust.* The possibility that Tyen trusted him was small, he mused, so courage was more likely.

Tyen kept his face immobile. It had occurred to him that Dahli might have arranged the ambush, but it seemed unlikely when the man needed so much of him.

"Do you still wish me to keep an eye on Baluka?" Tyen asked.

"Only if it is safe to do so. He is a potential link to Rielle and the vessel. Did you have a particular reason to contact him?"

"Yes, but nothing urgent." When he didn't elaborate, Dahli nodded, accepting that Tyen would not tell him everything as long as he passed on important information.

An awkward silence followed. That was the difference between Tyen's meetings with Dahli and those he had with Baluka. Dahli was never chatty. He did not discuss personal matters. Baluka always did. Tyen considered his doubts that he could get Dahli to talk about Rielle. But then . . . perhaps he could.

"I make sure some of our meetings are purely social," he explained. "Sometimes we just chat. I often learn more from his wandering thoughts than by asking direct questions. While he talks about Rielle, for instance, he doesn't always say what is in his mind."

"Oh? In what way?"

"From his words you would think she was faultless, but he knows otherwise."

"She was disloyal to him and the Raen." Dahli frowned. "But I do wonder if, by persuading her to dishonour her promise to him, we made such changes of heart somehow more permissible to her. Even more likely."

"Were her personal ethics incompatible with expectations of loyalty, in the latter case?"

Dahli nodded in agreement. "Perhaps. Ethics with no basis in practicality, and shifting loyalties due to a lack of experience." A faint look of amusement coloured his expression. "All typical of the young."

Tyen smiled wryly. "I, too, am young and inexperienced."

"I do not expect loyalty from you," Dahli replied. "But I expect you to keep to your side of any deal we make." His smile faded, replaced by a thoughtful look. "I've also wondered if that is the mistake we made with Rielle. If we should have struck a deal."

"Why didn't you?"

"Valhan said she was not the type to make deals. Though . . . when it came to leaving the Travellers, I know breaking her promise of marriage to Baluka was not done lightly. She felt bad about it, even as she was relieved to have been freed from her situation." He shrugged. "It is all in the past now." A movement outside the house drew Dahli's attention. A cart full of fresh reeds was trundling past, pulled by a sad-looking squat animal. "Is there anything else you wished to ask or tell me?"

"No."

"Then we are done." Dahli rose and ushered Tyen to the door. "Travel safely. And do not dismiss my offer completely. I do not know how much of the worlds you see nowadays. Perhaps you should take a look around. Things may be tranquil wherever you call home now, but I assure you they are not elsewhere."

It is hardly tranquil now, Tyen mused. "I may do that. Travel well, Dahli."

Stepping outside, he heard the door close behind him. He started to retrace his steps. Dahli's suggestion sent the back of his neck tingling with doubts. In the last few cycles, Tyen had not seen as much of the worlds. Though he'd travelled through many, they'd been stepping stones he'd briefly touched. He'd not stopped to examine the people and civilisations in them. They could be caught up in all kinds of new strife, but as long as the arrival places were safe and intact he wouldn't know.

With Doum and Murai on the verge of conflict, it was easier to believe that other worlds were descending into war and other kinds of savagery too. Dahli certainly believed it. He also firmly believed the only person who could stop it was Valhan.

Tyen shook his head. *I meant what I said. I will not murder anyone in order to bring the Raen back.* Perhaps all that the worlds needed were people determined to find another way to solve their problems than killing. Perhaps all they needed was time.

He was now more sure than ever that Rielle would agree.

CHAPTER 4

As his bedroom receded into whiteness several days later, Tyen wondered how it was that he could not feel physical sensation in the place between worlds and yet he still knew that he was excited.

"*Your mind remembers how it feels,*" Vella told him. "*Just as those who lose a limb can sometimes have the perception of it still being intact.*"

Do you still recall how it felt to have a body?

"*No. When I am conscious, it is only because I can access and use the mind of whoever touches me. I will only feel what they feel, not a memory of my body. When I am not touching a person, I am not conscious, so there is no opportunity for me to recall my body. I also did not recall my physical self when the Raen held me, when you first encountered him – though I was conscious, I had no access to his thoughts or sensation of his body.*"

I've often wondered how he did that. Perhaps he allowed you enough access to his mind in order to be conscious, but managed to keep his thoughts and memories blocked. I would love to know how he achieved it. I guess if Dahli succeeds in resurrecting Valhan, we could ask.

"*Rielle might know. She had access to the Raen's memories before she stopped the resurrection and saved the boy.*"

She might. Tyen frowned. *It depends how much she learned. Perhaps enough to help me restore you. Would she do it, do you think?*

"*Perhaps – if it did not involve killing anyone or replacing their mind.*"

Asking for help will be risky. I must trust that she will not take you from me. I don't think she will . . . and I'm not making any progress on my own. She might be the help we need and . . . and some risks are worth taking.

The moment the words formed in his mind, he began to doubt them. Asking the Raen for help restoring Vella had been like a risk worth taking, since striking a deal gave the Raen reason not to kill Tyen for breaking his law against travelling between worlds. The deal they'd made hadn't benefited either of them ultimately, though if he hadn't proposed it, the Raen would not have known it was possible to store a mind in an object, and therefore fake his death and arrange his resurrection.

If Tyen made a deal with Rielle to restore Vella, what might she want in return?

He did not get a chance to ponder that. The rooftops of Glaemar were emerging from the whiteness now. He arrived high above the city and started to skim towards the sprawling palace.

The instructions left for him at the workshop were to arrive where the building met the river, at the section furthest downstream. A change of colour in the river marked the spot, a sure sign that this was where the palace artisans worked. The shore downstream was stained with bands of oily colour, smaller, more humble buildings clustering along the water's edge.

The riverside edge of the palace was bordered by walkways and small circular jetties. As he drew closer, he searched in vain for a familiar figure, before arriving on one of the unoccupied jetties. While he paused to catch his breath, his attention was drawn to the palace's glittering, mosaic-covered outer wall. A vast mural, it depicted a procession of lithe and elegant men, women and children draped in fine cloth, gold and jewels, some riding animals, some carried on panniers by well-muscled servants. The scene was broken here and there by smooth, wide arches, and as he admired the work, a woman strolled out of one of them. A shiver of recognition and nervous anticipation went through him.

"Tyen Wheelmaker," Rielle said in the Traveller tongue as she walked out to meet him. "Welcome – properly this time – to Glaemar."

"Rielle Lazuli," he replied. "Thank you for the invitation."

She wore a sleeveless dress of a silvery fabric, loosely belted at the waist with a fine chain. Matching chains formed a simple headdress, some draped across her brow and two long tassels of them hanging down in front of each ear, bright against her straight black hair and brown skin. A single chain around her neck supported a small, finely decorated silver cylinder, sealed at both ends and with a seam at the middle suggesting it was hollow and could be opened. Though both garment and jewellery were simple, they gave an impression of wealth and elegance and he was glad he'd chosen to wear his good clothes for the visit – a simple long shirt and matching trousers of a fine black fabric, and a dark brown jacket. Even so, his attire seemed lacking in sophistication compared to hers.

She smiled and turned towards the building. "Come inside."

He fell into step beside her. She walked slowly, signalling each turn with a small gesture.

"How is life in Alba?" she asked.

He considered how to reply tactfully. "Quiet," he said.

"You must have been to many funerals for those who died in the Grand Market."

"Few, actually. Doumians grieve privately, keeping rites to close family and friends. I was surprised that anyone invited me."

She nodded. "You did not know those who died?"

"Not personally, just as relations of some of my workers."

"Has your work slowed as a result?"

"Yes and no. I've been very busy. I have been doing most of the work so my employees can attend the ceremonies. We've had no new orders since the attack, so I've delayed a few so there is something for my workers to do when they return."

"No orders? Your customers don't blame you for the attack, do they?"

"No, it is only that so many were affected, and Doumians don't tend to buy things when they are grieving. Every major workshop runs a stall at the Grand Market. Nearly all lost relatives."

The chain tassels of her headdress rustled softly as she shook her head. "The merchants pretend that they didn't know their victims were important, but nobody believes it. No good merchant should fail to note the customs of the people they buy and sell to."

"No Emperor either. Nor should he allow merchants to get away with picking a fight with a neighbour without his permission."

She glanced to one side, and Tyen saw a servant lingering in the shadow of a column.

"The Emperor is no fool," she replied, then smiled faintly.

Her tone was mild but he could not have missed the warning, and it sent a chill down his spine.

A small gesture indicated she was about to turn again. He followed her around a colonnaded courtyard and into an area divided by shelving, tables, beds, crates, barrels and plainer versions of the giant pots he'd seen on his earlier visit. Looking closer, he saw that many of the tables were covered in drawings, each in some part covered with small pottery tiles. Workers bent over them, selecting pieces from trays and carefully dropping them onto the drawing. Others appeared to be sorting tiles into colours.

"Your employers?" he asked.

She nodded.

"Is this one of your designs?" The nearly completed mosaic they were passing depicted a table viewed from above, laden with food.

"Yes."

He noted a patch of smaller, dark tiles on a leafy vegetable, and pausing to look closer, saw that it depicted a little insect.

"Impressive work."

"Yes, they are very skilled."

"Yet you thought of this. You are essential to the process."

She shrugged. "I am replaceable. Artists are hardly uncommon in the worlds. Good mosaic-makers are rarer. My only advantage is that I can read the minds of their customers, and so more easily and quickly discern what they want."

They were heading towards a walled section now. As they drew closer, he noticed that the walls were free-standing – panels on stands that could be moved to reconfigure the shape and dimension of the rooms they formed. Fabric hung across some sections, and as Tyen saw a young woman push past one, he realised they functioned as doors.

"Only the Emperor's rooms have solid walls," Rielle told him. "I'm afraid this is as close as the rest of us get to privacy here – and it's a concession only we artisans from other worlds enjoy, since we are unused to such open accommodations."

She led him to the hanging the young woman had emerged from. Holding it aside, she invited him to enter with a graceful sweep of her arm. He stepped through and found himself in a long, rectangular room. At the far end was a bed surrounded by translucent hangings. In the centre was a large square table with an opening in the centre, surrounded by eight chairs – though only four places had been laid on it.

In the closest area, in which he was now standing, low benches had been arranged in a circle. A grey-haired man rose from one, smiling broadly, and Tyen stopped, astonished that he knew the man's face.

"Tarran!" he exclaimed.

His former mentor and friend grinned in reply. Tyen hadn't been sure he'd ever see the old man again after Liftre, the school of magic where Tyen had learned and taught at, had closed more than five cycles ago.

"Young Ironsmelter," Tarran said, walking over and grasping Tyen's shoulders. "It *is* you. I hoped our paths would cross again. You are looking well."

"As are you," Tyen noted with genuine surprise. The old man's skin did not sag as much as Tyen recalled, but was taut and flushed with health. He stood straighter too.

Tarran looked fondly at Rielle. "My most recent student has made sure of that."

"I went looking for a teacher after . . . well, once I was free to roam as I pleased," Rielle explained. "I heard of a school of sorcery that had been abandoned when the Raen returned, so I sought it out. There I found a few ex-students who'd returned in the hope it would be re-opened. One suggested I ask Tarran for lessons, and gave me directions to his home."

"I'd been teaching young new sorcerers," Tarran continued. "All self-taught sorcerers have gaps in their knowledge, but Rielle's were especially odd. How could someone who didn't grow up using magic be ageless yet not know how to fight?"

"He has tricked most of the story out of me." Rielle tried to adopt a disapproving expression, but she could not hide her affection. "Not everything, of course."

"A girl has to keep a few secrets or she loses her mystique," Tarran agreed.

Rielle rolled her eyes. "A ridiculous saying, that one. As if mystique was some kind of commodity women trade on." She looked towards the door. "Ah – here's Timane, my servant."

Following her gaze, Tyen saw that the young woman had returned. Timane smiled shyly as she was introduced, and replied haltingly. To Tyen's amusement, it wasn't that she did not understand Traveller tongue – Rielle was giving her lessons in the language to help her improve her status in the palace – but that she was intimidated by and not a little attracted to him.

Her hair was a deep red and hung almost to the floor. Judged by physical appearance, the two women appeared the same age. That should mean Rielle had been barely past childhood when he'd met her five cycles ago. This made it suddenly obvious that Rielle could pattern-shift – the magical technique that enabled sorcerers to halt and reverse ageing. Which was no doubt why Tarran attributed Rielle as the source of his good health.

"What have you been up to since we last spoke?" Tarran asked.

Tyen shrugged. "Surviving. Making pottery wheels."

"I heard you led the rebels at one point."

"Yes, though not by choice." He resisted glancing at Rielle who, having seen him among the Raen's friends at the failed resurrection, must wonder what a former rebel leader had been doing among his enemies. He drew up memories of a younger Baluka, disdainful of Tyen's leadership, thinking that Rielle might be amused by them. "Fortunately a better leader soon replaced me."

Tarran nodded, and Tyen's stomach sank as his former mentor began considering the rumours about Tyen. "I also heard another story about you, but it was not as flattering. Are you aware of it?"

Tyen grimaced. "The one about me being a spy of the Raen's?"

"Yes. I'm sorry to bring it up. I only wish to be sure you know of it, for your safety." Tarran glanced at Rielle, recalling that he had thought of the rumour when she'd first mentioned that Tyen was living in Doum. He'd assumed she'd already read of it from his mind, and since discussing such accusations would cast an awkwardness over the evening, he decided not to pursue the subject. "Let's not speak of it again."

She nodded in agreement.

"So Liftre has re-opened?" Tyen asked.

Tarran smiled. "Yes. People are returning slowly. Some of the books and valuables taken have been returned too."

"Have you taken up a position there?"

"No. I am too old. I don't have the patience for foolish young students." He smiled at Rielle. "Or rather, I only have the patience for one or two at a time." Her eyebrows rose, but he continued on. "And I am not sure if it is wise, being a part of something so . . . so *visible*. With power shifting in the worlds, Liftre could easily become a target."

"Or it might be the only place where reason prevails," Rielle inserted.

Tarran grimaced. "The struggle to prevent people from so many backgrounds from turning on each other was difficult enough before the Raen returned. Those who seek to restore it now are hardened by war. They have neither the spirit of compromise nor tolerance of difference under which we founded the school."

"Perhaps if they had a common enemy they would be more amenable. 'When no adversary unites . . .'"

". . . society divides'," Tarran finished, nodding. He sighed. "Either way, I have no enthusiasm for politics nowadays."

Tyen had not heard the quote before, and wondered if this was Rielle's contribution to Tarran's great store of wise sayings, or a new one the old man had picked up since leaving Liftre. Had she also learned his form of calligraphy?

"I too would rather avoid politics," Rielle said, her attention shifting to Tyen. "But I find myself in a position where it is difficult to avoid." She smiled ruefully. "Let's move to the table where you can eat while I explain. Lead us in, Timane."

The young woman led the way to the large square table, indicating to Tyen and Tarran where they should sit. She ducked under the table and, a moment later, stood up within the opening in the centre. Around her were several platters covered in slices of meat and vegetables, and little balls of coloured dough. Between her and the corner of the table between Rielle and Tyen was a crescent-shaped black plate resting on a wooden base. Timane stared at it, then tipped some oil from a jug onto the surface. Immediately it began to sizzle.

So the servant is a sorcerer, Tyen mused. Timane glanced at him, saw him watching and blushed. Her mind immediately gave away that she was not a strong sorcerer, but Rielle had been teaching her to use the meagre powers she had.

"The Emperor heard that I approached you after your last visit to the palace, Tyen," Rielle said.

He turned to her and frowned. "How?"

She shrugged. "No doubt he has spies in Doum. He knows that afterwards you proposed to negotiate on behalf of the Claymars. I had all but decided that I would not offer to represent Murai, but this morning he ordered me to do so. I must comply or leave this world."

Tyen winced. "I am sorry. This is my fault."

"Not at all." She waved her hand dismissively. "When I followed you, I knew I was taking a risk. I expected you to lead me to Alba, where my appearance would be noted, and the Emperor would eventually learn of it. I feared only that he would conclude I was colluding with you somehow." She glanced around the room. "I enjoy my work for the mosaic-makers, but I don't value my comfortable life here higher than warning someone who saved my life that he is in danger."

She said it lightly, but her expression was serious. Tyen watched Timane pressing balls of dough flat on the grill with a wooden paddle as he considered how to reply.

"Then I have more to thank you for than I realised," he said slowly.

"Perhaps." A crease appeared between her brows. "You may not feel that way when we begin negotiations. The Emperor has high expectations."

Tyen nodded, relieved that she had decided to stay and do as the Emperor ordered. "I don't know yet whether the Claymars have accepted my offer."

"They will," she told him. "He has hinted *very* strongly that I will deal with no other but you. Which may be how you hoped the situation would progress . . ." She held out her plate to receive a disc of fried dough from Timane. As the girl scooped up another on the paddle and offered it to Tyen, he quickly picked up his plate and held it out to receive it. ". . . but there is always more going on than what is apparent when the Emperor is involved. I must speak as he wishes me to, even if I disagree with what I say. I am forbidden to read his mind. And since I will have to refuse to deal with you if I learn that you have read his mind, I ask that you do not."

"Of course."

Having served Tarran, Timane next placed a small dish filled with thick orange sauce in front of them, making a small ticking noise with her tongue as she did.

Rielle chuckled and spoke a few gentle words in Muraian. "We are being rude, according to Muraian custom, by discussing anything but food while we eat." She gestured to his plate. "Enjoy."

The fried dumplings were a little bland, but with a pleasant crunch from a crisp plant in the mix. The sauce was spicy, leaving his tongue tingling. The servant girl cooked up and served several more, then began to stack slices of meat and vegetable on the grill.

Rielle set down her cutlery. "We may speak now, as the next course cooks."

"Have you remained in contact with the rebels?" Tarran asked Tyen.

Tyen looked at Rielle, wondering if it would be inconsiderate to mention her former fiancé. "Yes. I meet up with their leader now and then."

Her lips pressed into a wry, knowing smile. "How is Baluka?"

"He is well," Tyen replied. "Overworked, if not overwhelmed, by the demands made on the Restorers."

Tarran scowled and made a low noise. "Restorers? The trouble with the idea of restoration is that everyone has a different idea as to what must be restored, and to what degree."

Rielle ignored him. "Does he mention his family?"

"The Travellers?" Tyen shook his head, then paused as a memory surfaced. "He said once that many of them have given up trading between worlds because it had become too dangerous."

She nodded. "Some people believed the Travellers were allies of the Raen, since he'd allowed them to travel between worlds when others could not, and either refused to trade with or attacked them. Some Traveller families found that too many of the worlds along their established path were in upheaval after the Raen's death, making trade dangerous or no longer viable."

"What will they do instead?"

"Settle somewhere they are welcome and wait until the worlds are safe again."

"If they ever are," Tarran added.

She smiled at the old man fondly. "Tarran and I disagree in our predictions for the future. I am optimistic. The Raen was one man. Though his allies assisted in enforcing his laws, they were scant few compared to the number of worlds that exist. Many worlds never felt the Raen's rule and yet they did not destroy themselves. Yes, the sorcerers that were controlled by the fear of him are testing their newfound freedom. Those that do evil will be dealt with, either by the Restorers or by other sorcerers tackling threats to peace and prosperity."

"Or by the Successor." Tarran's eyes gleamed as he spoke the title.

Rielle rolled her eyes as she turned to him. "Then where is he? Wasn't he supposed to be the one to kill the Raen?"

"The Raen killed himself," Tyen pointed out.

"Yes. Doesn't that make the Raen the Successor?"

Tarran shrugged as if to say anything was possible. Tyen

looked from Rielle to the old man and back again, then read Tarran's mind. There was no knowledge there of the failed resurrection. She had not told him, so Tyen would not speak of it either.

If the Raen is resurrected, then he is *the Successor, since he killed himself*, Tyen thought. *I wonder if that was his intention all along.*

"You said you did not believe in prophecy," Tyen reminded the old man.

Tarran grinned. "I do not. But I did say it was a prediction of inevitable change. Only a sorcerer more powerful than the Raen could defeat him—"

"Or not as powerful but more skilled. Or luckier," Rielle inserted. "Or someone politically more powerful, leading enough sorcerers to defeat someone much stronger."

". . . it can also be interpreted as a prediction that someone as strong will *replace* him," Tarran finished.

Rielle grimaced. "They'd have to want to," she said with distaste.

Tyen resisted a smile. It was clear that Tarran did not believe prophecy was a supernatural force which ensured the future proceeded in a certain way. He was more intrigued by the idea that Rielle, as a sorcerer nearly as powerful as the Raen, might step into the Raen's place – and concerned that someone less scrupulous would claim the title if she didn't.

"The worlds would have to acknowledge this Successor," Tyen pointed out. "Willingly and not. The Raen ruled as much through fear as with favours. Something the Restorers have had no choice but to emulate, I fear."

Tarran nodded. "But the worlds do not fear the Restorers like they feared the Raen and his allies. Many of those who supported them in the beginning do not respect them now. Any large group is bound to be rent by disagreement and conflicting ideology and aims." He spread his hands. "They could use the idea of a Successor to forge unity and save the worlds from chaos." He looked at Tyen. "I am sure they would accept Rielle. She was trained by the Raen, perhaps in order to replace him, but her friendship with Baluka would ease any mistrust around her association with him – especially if they believed she was taken from the Travellers unwillingly."

"I am not going to rule the worlds," Rielle said firmly. "Or lie about my past. Especially since Baluka knows the last is a lie and most rebels could read the truth from his mind."

The old man subsided. He knew she was not ready for such responsibility, even if she had wanted it, and he liked her too much to wish an existence on her that was likely to make her unhappy. *Was she in love with the Raen?* Tarran wondered, not for the first time. He searched her face as he'd done so many times since learning that she'd broken her agreement of marriage to Baluka in order to live with the Raen – even after she'd learned the ruler was not the angel she'd believed him to be.

Now there's a question I'd also very much like to know the answer to, Tyen thought. Her mind was, as always, tantalisingly out of reach.

Rielle's eyes narrowed. She glanced at Tyen, catching him watching her, then sighed.

"I was not in love with Valhan," she told the old man. "Believe me, I have asked myself this many times, but always I am certain that the closest I came was admiration for a competent, charismatic leader. Ask Tyen, if you doubt my words."

As Tarran's gaze shifted to his, Tyen frowned in confusion. Then his heart skipped a beat. *Rielle believes I can read her mind!* He looked down at his plate, hoping to hide any sign of the realisation. *That would mean . . . she can't read mine!*

"I do not wish to invade the privacy of such a gracious host," Tyen mumbled.

Rielle let out a soft laugh. "Well, then you'll just have to believe me, Tarran. And now it is time to eat again. Tyen?"

Looking up, Tyen found Timane holding out a steaming offering towards him. He lifted his plate and smiled in gratitude as she filled it. She blushed and focused on filling Rielle and Tarran's plates.

When they had finished eating, Rielle turned to Tyen.

"If I could be the Successor, then Tyen also could be. He is stronger than I. Tyen, were you there when the rebels faced Valhan?"

He blinked in surprise, then hesitated to reply, wondering if it was wise to admit it. Unable to decide, he chose truth over lies. He had too many lies to keep track of already.

"Yes."

The flicker of curiosity in her eyes quickly faded. "Could people be persuaded to believe your presence was the reason Valhan failed?"

"No. We had barely arrived when he killed himself." Tyen swallowed. "And nobody would accept me as the Successor, if I wanted to claim that role."

Tarran straightened. "Because they call you "the Spy"? Why, that could be easily overcome if we spread a counter-rumour that it was malicious gossip spread by the allies to prevent anyone accepting you as the Successor!" The old man's eyes were alight with enthusiasm, and Tyen almost felt guilty as he shook his head.

"Leadership did not suit me before; it would even less so if it were of all the worlds rather than a few hundred rebels." He shook his head. "There are men and women far better suited to it than I – which raises the question: why can't Baluka be the Successor?"

Tarran spread his hands. "It could be, I guess. Nobody is saying it now, but in time they may."

Leaning back in her chair, Rielle tapped her fingers on the edge of the table. "I only hope that, if a Successor is necessary for peace and order, then one comes along soon, and that they are wise, kind and clever. Someone who, unlike me, has experience and training in politics." She shook her head. "Valhan admitted he couldn't predict what his interference in a world's affairs would lead to, and he had ruled for over a thousand cycles. I feel out of my depth just at the prospect of trying to prevent a war between Murai and Doum."

She glanced at Tyen, then smiled ruefully. "Though I suppose I should not admit that here and now."

Tyen shrugged. "I have as little experience as you."

"But you led the rebels."

"We were trying to *start* a war," he reminded her. "Not avoid one."

She grimaced. "What are our chances?" She looked at Tarran.

The old man frowned. "Doum has something Murai wants and it has no army of trained sorcerers." He looked at Tyen. "I fear the odds are not in your favour, if you cannot persuade the Claymars to cooperate."

Tyen nodded. "Or persuade the Emperor that war will destroy what he wants to take."

"I find myself wondering what Valhan would have done, not just to settle this, but about the strife in the rest of the worlds." Rielle shook her head. "Then I'm glad that he's not here, because I suspect the solution would be forceful, possibly even violent. He was not one for negotiation, at least from what I saw."

Tarran nodded. "He'd have told everyone to behave, and they'd have been too afraid to disobey."

They fell silent for a short while, then Rielle straightened and looked at Tyen. "Do you have that mechanical insect?"

Surprised by the sudden change of subject, Tyen nodded. He held open one side of his jacket.

"Beetle. Come out."

A vibration came in response to his first word, then the insectoid scurried out to sit on Tyen's shoulder.

They all jumped as a shriek came from Timane. The servant girl was staring at Beetle in horror. Rielle half rose, two hands extended in a gesture of reassurance as she spoke rapidly in Muraian. Tyen spoke to Beetle, sending it scurrying back into his clothing.

The movement made the servant jump again. She looked from Tyen to Rielle, muttered something, then ducked under the table, surfaced on the other side and hurried away.

"She'll come back when you're gone," Rielle told them. "In her homeland there are several species of venomous insects, the larger the more deadly."

"Tell her I apologise for upsetting her," Tyen said.

"I will. She did see that it was mechanical, but that did not ease her discomfort at the sight of it." Rielle looked in the direction the girl had gone. "Poor Timane. When I came here, she was being bullied by the other servants. I chose her to be my personal servant, and taught her how to use magic. Which might have been a mistake, as she now sees herself as my loyal follower rather than an equal."

"What were you hoping she would become?" Tarran asked.

"Perhaps a friend." She shrugged. "It's been a long time since I had a friend." Her eyes shifted to the items the servant had left cooking on the grill. "These look ready to serve." She took up the spatula and began filling their plates with sweet slices of fruit, then dousing them with hot syrup.

"The reason I asked about – was it Beedle?"

"Beetle," Tyen corrected.

She nodded. "Beetle. Valhan gave it to me to look after, the last time we spoke. He said something regarding it that I've often wondered about." She glanced at Tyen. "He said it was the future."

Something within Tyen's belly flinched and recoiled, as if from a punch. He thought of the deadly swarm of insectoids his former classmate at Liftre had made to defend her home, and begun selling to friends in neighbouring worlds. Insectoids that could easily be modified further to become offensive weapons. Was that the kind of future the Raen had seen? Or did he simply see one where the magically powered machines of Tyen's world were everywhere, slowly sucking magic from all worlds?

"Do you know what he meant?" Rielle asked.

Tyen met her eyes. Surely she was seeing all of these scenarios in his thoughts . . . but not if she was unable to read his mind. In truth, he could not know what the Raen had imagined. He'd barely spoken to the man, really. He shook his head. "Not exactly. He never discussed it with me."

"Then we will have to wait and see." She filled her own plate last, adding syrup with a flourish. "Eat, my friends. A world with good desserts can't be all bad, as a friend of mine used to say."

Glad of the change of subject, Tyen turned his thoughts to the simple distraction of eating.

CHAPTER 5

*S*o *Rielle can't read my mind,* Tyen said. *How is that possible, when I can't read hers?*

Either *she was lying, or your strength is the same,* Vella replied. *She spoke of not being able to read your mind when you first met her, when she had less reason to deceive you.*

She did? I don't remember.

It was five cycles ago, and your mind was on more pressing matters.

He shook his head. All this time he hadn't needed to worry that she might discover he was a spy. Now she need never know. He silently cursed Roporien for the small flaw in Vella's construction that meant she did not always supply information unprompted. She responded to questions and engaged in conversations, and could warn him of danger, but didn't offer information that wasn't obviously related – and how she judged that was a mystery only her creator had understood.

So our strength is evenly matched. Have you heard of that happening before?

It is rare, but not unknown. I have no record of it occurring between two sorcerers of great strength. It is more common the weaker the sorcerers are, but possibly only because they are more numerous.

If the Raen had difficulty reading Rielle's mind, does that mean they were equal?

No. He was the stronger, but not by much.

Then I am nearly as strong as he was.

That fact was astonishing, especially when he considered that the Raen hadn't killed him, when he was known for removing potential rivals. Still, how would the ruler of worlds have known how powerful Tyen was? Tyen hadn't, so the Raen couldn't have read that from his mind. Tyen hadn't demonstrated the extent of his power in any way. The only other way the man could have found out was to test Tyen.

But even so, the only proof Tyen had that he was as strong as Rielle was her claim to not be able to read his mind.

I have to consider that she may be pretending, to make me relax and think about things I'm trying to avoid thinking about. Tyen frowned. *To not allow for this will be to risk failing at negotiations.* Rielle's manner hadn't been that of someone worried that her own mind would be read, he noted, as she should be if she couldn't read his mind. Unless she, too, had worked out that their strength was equal.

If you get her to hold me I could discover the truth, Vella suggested. If she refuses, you'll know she has read your mind.

If she didn't refuse, Vella would learn everything Rielle knew about resurrection. A thrill of temptation ran down Tyen's spine, but he ignored it.

No, I won't trick Rielle into it. You'd learn where the boy is, and that could put him in greater danger. I'd rather have her willing assistance in restoring your body. He drummed his fingers against Vella's cover. *We will wait until after the negotiations are over before we ask her for help, and I'll carry you wherever I . . .*

A sound caught his attention. It came from outside the toilet, where he'd retreated to talk to Vella. It was a rapping, but not quite the tone produced when knuckles met the workshop's front door. When it came again, a shiver ran down his spine. It was definitely coming from the floor below, but sounded as if it were coming from *inside* the workshop.

"Tyen Wheelmaker?" a voice called. "Are you at home?"

A long sigh escaped him. Claymar Fursa. Why the woman

couldn't knock on the front door like ordinary people instead of arriving inside his workshop was a mystery to him.

No, not a mystery. It's pure arrogance. She likes to remind people of her position and power.

He quickly returned Vella to her pouch, and stuffed it inside his shirt. Rising, he pulled the lever that released water into the basin, which spared him the indignity of calling out to Fursa from within the toilet to let her know he was home.

Once out of the room, he walked to the top of the stairs before speaking.

"Claymar Fursa." He briefly pressed two fingers to his chest, and started down. "Welcome. For what reason do you honour my humble home with your presence?"

She moved into sight, frowning up at him in consternation, as if not sure whether he was mocking her or not. "The Council has agreed. You will represent us in negotiations with the Muraians."

He nodded. "I am deeply honoured by their trust in me, and will do my best to arrange a fair agreement between Doum and Murai."

Her gaze dropped to his clothing and her eyebrows rose. He was not wearing his usual workshop clothes, but something more like he'd worn among the rebels. Which was badly timed, as it made him more of an otherworlder.

"We are collating a list of our aims and requirements," she told him. "You will meet with three of us at the High Chamber at midday in three days, so we can inform you of them. Then the day after you will meet with Rielle the Mosaic-maker on the Island of Tiles at dawn."

He nodded. "High Chamber, midday, in three days. Island of Tiles, dawn the day after," he repeated.

Fursa stared at him in silence for a little longer – a ploy she used when she wished to intimidate but which had no effect on him. "I must go," she finished. "Do not be late."

He smiled and watched her fade from sight, amused at her parting words. Treating him like a child only revealed how much she needed to belittle him in order to feel superior.

Turning away, he looked around the workshop. It was Thumb Day: the fifth day of the Doumian week when artisans rested and dealt with domestic chores – though it was not rigidly observed. The Grand Market of each city was closed, so workshops that did not have a stall, like his, opened their doors in order to sell their wares. Those with urgent orders to fill paid employees extra to work.

Just two orders remained to be filled, each for a single wheel. Too little work for himself, let alone his workers. He ought to put out a sign indicating customers could come and browse his wares, but he had a more urgent matter to tackle – which was why he'd dressed as he had. A matter he'd been putting off, but ought to deal with before his time was taken up with negotiations.

It was time he found out if the other places he left messages for Baluka had been compromised.

Returning to his bedroom, he donned his jacket, put Beetle in the inside pocket, took a deep breath, then pushed out of the world. After taking his usual precautions, he set out for the world furthest from the one containing the Restorers' base, on the slim chance that those who hunted him – if they still did – would be less likely to venture that far.

For less powerful sorcerers, like Baluka, it was easier to hide in a crowd than in sparsely populated locations. Their mind would blend with the general cacophony of minds. Only if you knew exactly who you were looking for, and they were stationary and in a pre-arranged place, was it easy to find a person.

So this hiding place was as crowded as the city where he'd encountered the ambushers – a sprawling temple that attracted a constant stream of mask-wearing pilgrims. Tyen created a shield of still air close around himself as he arrived. Using local money he'd purchased on earlier visits, he bought a hooded overrobe from one of the hundreds of temple stores, along with a mask laced with scent. He walked out among thousands of worshippers, weaving through them to join a line of people waiting to enter an altarhouse dedicated to a god of metals.

As he waited, he scanned the minds around him. All were pilgrims. He read thoughts both pious and profane, bored and fascinated. A few were searching for other people, but none were powerful sorcerers or had Tyen's or Baluka's name in their minds.

The line shortened, then he was entering the altarhouse. The air writhed with a stink of sweat and smoke too strong for the scented masks to ease. A gaping square mouth of glowing orange spewed heat. Pilgrims hurried forward, tossed discs of metal into the furnace, then fled.

Tyen's turn came. As he approached the furnace, he slipped a small twist of paper between two coins. He threw them in and watched the minds of the priests tending the furnace. As the powder within the paper exploded, making a loud pop, the priests jumped and exchanged a glance. They would report this to the Head Priest, who would send a message to a sect that kept records of such occurrences. One of the record-keepers would contact an ally of Baluka, and on the message would go, until it reached the Restorers' base and their leader.

This was not the only reason the pop intrigued the priests, Tyen saw. Three pops had come from the furnace four days ago, then another single pop yesterday. They wondered what the gods were trying to say.

Tyen's heart began racing. Outside, a priest handed him a small square of thick, wet fabric. He pressed it to his brow. The pilgrims who had entered before him stood fanning themselves, faces above and below their masks still red from the heat.

The three pops means Baluka sent me a message. One I should have received by now. Perhaps it had been delayed. Perhaps it had been waylaid. But that wasn't the most alarming prospect.

The single pop yesterday will have summoned Baluka here.

He hadn't sent it. Whoever had, had wanted to bring Baluka here, and if Baluka had responded quickly he would already be in the temple. Not having found Tyen waiting, what would he have done?

Tingling all over with worry, Tyen send his mind towards the enormous, multi-winged building that accommodated pilgrims wealthy enough to afford a small room. Lightly jumping from mind to mind, he stopped as he found a familiar one engrossed in conversation with another otherworld visitor.

Baluka had decided to stay the night. His protectors waited in rooms nearby – powerful, fiercely loyal sorcerers who would protect their leader or give him time to flee if he was attacked. The men constantly watched the minds of people around the building, and, to Tyen's relief, hadn't seen anything to give them concern.

It was possible, though, that someone more powerful than them was watching. Tyen scanned the surrounding minds carefully, but found nobody suspicious. Too many people were in the temple for Tyen to search them all, however, and a very powerful sorcerer could seek out minds while outside the city, if they knew where that person was likely to be.

I have to warn Baluka, Tyen thought. *Even if it means revealing myself to whoever called him here.* Oddly, he wasn't as alarmed by the possibility as he expected. *If I am as strong as Rielle, and Rielle is nearly as strong as the Raen was, then I should be able to protect both of us – especially with Baluka's protectors helping. I almost want the ambushers to appear. Then I'd find out who is behind this, and why.*

Baluka was engrossed in telling a story from his childhood to a woman pilgrim, so Tyen had not yet been able to discover if Baluka suspected Tyen hadn't summoned him. Now, as Baluka finished, the man's thoughts returned to his situation. *This would be pleasantly relaxing if I wasn't worried that Tyen hasn't appeared*, he thought. *And whether the worlds are descending into even greater chaos while I'm away* He sighed. *Hurry up, Tyen. I can't stay much longer.*

So Baluka wasn't aware he had been tricked. Resisting the urge to check the fit of his mask, Tyen headed towards the building, keeping his pace relaxed and path indirect. He entered the Visitor's House and paid a novice to tell Baluka a friend was here to see him. Watching Baluka's mind, Tyen saw both hope and disappointment at the message. Baluka liked the woman, and since she was not magically gifted he could see from her thoughts that she was attracted to him. But he did not want to delay meeting Tyen one moment, so he excused himself and returned to his room on the other side of the hall.

Giving the surrounding minds one last sweep, Tyen approached Baluka's door and knocked, taking off his mask.

The rebel leader grinned as he opened it. "Ah! At last! Come in." He closed the door behind Tyen. "Is everything all right? When you didn't respond to any of my messages I started to worry."

"I didn't receive them. You sent more than one?"

Baluka frowned. "Yes. I sent three. Then I received your summons."

The room was divided with a curtain, which did not meet neatly, revealing an unmade single bed beyond. Two low-slung chairs and a small table filled the rest of the space. Tyen stilled the air just within the walls of the sitting area to prevent sound escaping.

"I didn't send it," Tyen told his friend. "Though I did just send one, since I didn't discover you were here until a moment ago."

Baluka's eyes widened. "Someone knows our code."

"And our meeting locations. Three men were waiting for me

in Jarteen several days ago," Tyen said. "Ex-rebels. They believed there would be some profit in selling me to someone."

Rubbing his hands together, Baluka began to pace. "Who offered this incentive?"

"I didn't stay long enough to find out."

"It wasn't me," Baluka assured him.

"I know."

Baluka's mouth thinned a little, but more in grim sympathy than offence at Tyen reading his mind. "Is your hiding place compromised?"

Tyen shook his head. "They tried to follow, but I lost them easily." He grimaced in apology. "I'm sorry. I should have told you sooner. I assumed I was their only target and local matters in my world have kept me very busy."

"Are we safe here?"

"I've checked the minds of everyone around us, and nobody has any ill intentions towards us. I suggest we don't stay long, however."

"That would be wise. Why did you want to meet me?"

"I wanted to tell you about the ambush in Jarteen." Tyen smiled. "Since I have already, I guess it's your turn."

Baluka stopped pacing. "There's a new source of trouble in the worlds." He looked both pained and apologetic. "In some of the recent conflicts we've dealt with, one or more sides have used weapons of mechanical magic."

Something within Tyen's stomach twisted. Baluka radiated sympathy: he knew how Tyen felt about the misuse of his "invention". Yet his regret at having to deliver this news was nothing compared to the guilt it roused in Tyen.

"When their makers claimed to have invented them," Baluka continued, "the people who knew you at Liftre have corrected them. They are so touchy about giving credit to the correct inventor. Unfortunately, the truth has been misunderstood. Too few know that you never intended mechanical magic to be used in war. They believe this development is a deliberate move on your part, whether merely for profit or as part of some greater plan."

The tightness in his middle was now a pain – a ceaseless cramp. Tyen breathed slowly, resisting the urge to rub at his belly. *What did Rielle say that Raen told her – that Beetle was the future?* He swallowed as nausea rose. *I should never have taught anyone mechanical magic. I should have found another way to pay for my tuition at Liftre.*

"So I have to ask," Baluka continued, "is there a way to turn them all off without getting control of each machine?"

Looking up, Tyen regarded his friend with surprise. The possibility hadn't occurred to him. He considered the idea, then shook his head. "Not that I know of."

Baluka's shoulders sagged.

"But that doesn't mean it isn't possible," Tyen added. "All designs have a weakness. Something different for each, most likely. There might be a universal flaw, common to all." *They all run on magic. If they had no magic to draw upon, they would cease working. But once magic returned, they would revive. Unless someone has invented a way for machines to store more magic.* All the insectoids he'd designed could store a tiny amount of magic, so they did not stop operating when passing through a patch of Soot – what the people of his world called the void left when magic was taken from a location.

"I think," Baluka said slowly, "that if you joined us, declaring that you never intended mechanical magic to be used in warfare, and found a way to combat them, the Restorers might accept you—"

"No." Tyen had not intended his voice to sound so cold. He softened his tone. "You know there's no way they would unless I opened my mind to them. We both have secrets we'd rather they didn't see."

Baluka winced, guessing correctly that Tyen referred to how, when the allies had attacked them in the Raen's palace, he'd been searching for Rielle instead of leading the rebels. He bowed his head. "I'd be prepared to let them discover everything about me, if it meant you could join us again. I think they'd forgive you everything, both truth and lies, if we . . ." He looked up. "If we convinced them you were the Successor."

Tyen frowned and shook his head. "The Successor?" *First Tarran, now Baluka? What is going on?* "Why in all the worlds would they believe that?"

"You were there when the Raen died."

"As were plenty of others. Who know he killed himself, and I had nothing to do with it."

"You're stronger than any sorcerer I know of, and I now know about most of the sorcerers in the reachable, habitable worlds."

"Most?" Tyen repeated, then snorted. "Forgive me, but there are plenty who give the Restorers a wide berth."

Baluka did not argue, though by the sharpness of his gaze Tyen knew he was storing that piece of information away. "Do you know of any who rival you in strength?"

Tyen hesitated. *Should I tell him about Rielle? She is what I wanted to discuss with him when I sought a meeting with him before.*

"You do, don't you?" Baluka sat up straight. "Who is he? Not one of the Raen's allies or friends, I hope."

Tyen shook his head. *It's amazing how people never consider initially that the Successor could be a woman,* he mused. Which makes it much easier for Rielle to have a quiet, safe life, so he bit back the temptation to say her name.

"I've met two people in my short life whose mind I couldn't read," Tyen said. "One is dead. If the other had any interest in ruling the worlds, they'd be in charge already." He shook his head. Baluka did not believe prophecies were real. He did, however, know that they could be powerful persuaders – and he was worried that someone would claim the title of Successor and challenge all the good the Restorers were doing, if he didn't find a plausible candidate first. "You said, all those cycles ago, that the Successor might not be the strongest sorcerer, but the one willing to take the credit for killing the Predecessor. By that measure, *you* are the Successor."

Baluka nodded. "Except everyone knows I didn't kill the Raen. As you pointed out: he killed himself." He paused, his eyebrows rising. "Perhaps he meant for no Successor to follow him."

That is far too close to the truth, Tyen thought. *But not for the reason he thinks.* As he had many times before, Tyen wished he could tell Baluka of the Raen's plan to be resurrected and resume his rule when the allies and rebels had destroyed each other. Baluka ought to know there was a chance the Raen would return. But if he did, stronger sorcerers might find out by reading his mind. Perhaps a sorcerer who would like to see the Raen resurrected, who would seek out Dahli and assist him.

"Perhaps people should stop hoping someone will come to rescue them," Tyen muttered. "And fix their own problems."

Baluka gave him an odd look, his head tilted slightly to one side. "You haven't really seen what's been going on in the worlds, have you? You've been hidden away too long. People *are* trying to fix their problems. Preventing and stopping wars is not as easy as you think."

Tyen nearly winced. "I know, and you are doing your best to help." He sighed. This discussion was pointless and he had stayed too long already. "I had better go. I will see if I can deal with these mechanical weapons. If I can examine some, I may be able to find a way to disable them. Do you have any?"

"No, but I will arrange for the capture of a few. I will have someone investigate who tried to capture you, and why, and how they knew our code and where to wait for you – us." He frowned. "We need to arrange some new ways to get messages to each other too."

Tyen nodded. Thinking quickly, he came up with a location where Baluka could leave a message for him. He'd have to set up a chain of couriers to take it to Doum next. Baluka chose another.

"Is there anything else?" his friend asked.

Tyen paused. Mentioning Rielle now might seem odd and even suspicious. Unless he could—

"Wait . . . did you see that?"

Baluka was staring at the curtain. Looking over at the room divider, Tyen saw nothing untoward. He shook his head.

"What was it?"

"I saw an eye, just briefly, in the gap."

Pushing out of the world a little, Tyen skimmed to the other side of the curtain. At once he sensed the indentation of a fresh path. He returned to the world and pushed aside the fabric.

"Someone was here," he told Baluka. "I'll find out who and why."

First taking a generous amount of magic from the edges of the world, Tyen propelled himself out of it and along the path. Soon he sensed a shadow ahead, travelling quickly away from him. He followed, steadily gaining on the spy. Past the midway point between worlds, a room began to emerge from the whiteness. Four figures sat in tall-backed chairs arranged around the centre of the room. One on each side. They watched the spy approach. Then one suddenly rose to his feet, and Tyen guessed that he had been seen. The other three rose hurriedly and all pushed their chairs away with magic, sending them tumbling into the room's corners.

They didn't flee. Tyen hesitated for a moment. If he arrived, they would attack. That he was sure of. They'd have gathered plenty of magic beforehand, ready for a fight. Was he willing to risk a confrontation? He might be wrong about Rielle not being able to read his mind. He might not be as strong as he suspected.

Then I should grab their spy. They might not care about the man, but a bargaining piece of uncertain value is better than none.

He pushed forward and, in a burst of speed, caught up with the spy. The man gaped in surprise as he jerked to a halt, then turned to stare at Tyen in horror. Tyen could feel the spy's feeble attempts to break free, and guessed that the man was not a powerful sorcerer. Probably not ageless either, which meant he'd suffocate if Tyen held him here.

But then so would Tyen. He had two choices: go back to Baluka or continue to the room.

The decision was easy. Returning might lead the four sorcerers to Baluka, and he wouldn't endanger his friend. Better to deal with these men in the world they had been waiting in.

Tyen looked from one sorcerer to the other as he continued towards the world. He recognised none of them. As he arrived, he stilled the air around himself and the spy to create a shield – and another between the two of them in case his prisoner attacked. He breathed deeply and slowly, trying to hide the fact that he was breathless. No point letting his enemies know he wasn't ageless. *Maybe it's time I learned how to be*, he mused.

His captive was gasping for breath, but that had as much to do with fear as lack of air. He began to attack the shield between him and Tyen. The man didn't believe the sorcerers would hold back to save him.

He was right. Tyen's shield began to vibrate as they attacked. He retaliated by sending stilled and heated air towards them, hammering their own protective barriers. A glow to his left warned him that the sorcerer there was trying to heat the air nearby enough to weaken Tyen's shield. He simply compensated by stilling that part of his shield so much it became colder.

That was as subtle as the fight would get until one side or the other proved the weaker, or a human aspect changed the situation. The four men used no projectiles and he did not try to save magic by leaving gaps in his shield – strategies rare outside of weaker worlds like Tyen's own. As time stretched, Tyen began to move the stilled air of his shield slowly inwards, letting go of a layer inside to provide fresh air to breathe while stiffening a new layer outside.

At the same time Tyen looked from one sorcerer's mind to the next, watching their thoughts. They were focused on striking and defending, frightened that if they lost concentration they would die. They would not reveal much of their intentions while so focused. So he pretended to fail a little, letting his shield waver under their assault. At once all four grew hopeful, and he could see what had driven them to risk luring him here.

Either I die or I become ageless, one thought, repeating words he had said many times to the others.

The four of us can do this! another thought. *I knew together we'd be stronger than him. He's not the Raen, just another relic of the past.*

It'll soon be ours! the one directly before Tyen crowed silently, his lips spreading into a greedy smile. *Agelessness! Healing! And who know what other secrets the book contains.*

Tyen's stomach sank. They were after Vella, having heard the rumour – he had no idea where it had begun but suspected Baluka's mind had been read – that the Spy carried a book that contained the secret of agelessness. She was the prize they would gain by killing him, though they also intended to collect the bounties placed on his head.

Tyen considered what to do now. He could keep them engaged until they ran out of magic, or he could release the spy and leave. But he hadn't learned yet how they had known about the code he and Baluka had used, or their meeting places, so he waited and watched, pretending to rally his strength then letting his shield waver again to give them time to think.

They grew even more jubilant, but then suddenly all four minds blurred with fear. They exchanged looks, Tyen seeing images in his mind of figures in the shadows behind the four. Their attack ceased abruptly, and they vanished.

Surprised, Tyen searched the shadows of the room. Sure enough, figures were appearing. Six, seven – eight of them. Tyen's heart began pounding. He had held off the four, but could he fight eight, having used up a great deal of magic fighting already?

Tyen reached for more magic from the extents of the world, but as the first of the sorcerers arrived, the man's mind became readable, and Tyen relaxed. He was the leader of Baluka's protectors.

"Need some help?" the sorcerer asked.

"Not now. You scared them off," Tyen replied. "Is Baluka safe?"

The leader nodded.

The other were arriving, minds blossoming within Tyen's senses. None recognised Tyen. Baluka only brought sorcerers who'd never seen Tyen to their meetings.

"Did you learn the reason for the intrusion?" the sorcerer asked, looking at the spy.

"Yes. They wanted to steal something they believe I possess. So . . ." Tyen looked at his captive. "How did they know we'd be here? How did they know our code?"

"I don't know!" the man exclaimed. "They hired me to check the room, to see if you'd arrived yet."

It was the truth. Tyen sighed and let the man go. At once, the spy faded from sight.

Turning to his colleagues, the leader of the protectors swept his gaze over all of them. "Follow him. See if he leads you to the others."

The men and women exchanged glances, then vanished. The leader looked at Tyen. "A lesser man would have killed him."

Tyen nodded. "A smarter man, perhaps."

I'd wager he's never killed anyone, the man thought, but instead of contempt he only felt envy as he pushed aside unpleasant memories and guilt.

"Baluka is gone?" Tyen asked.

The man nodded. "He gets twitchy when he's away from the

base too long, worried about what the Restorers might be doing in his absence."

"Then I will go too. Thanks for your help."

The man nodded. Gathering magic, Tyen pushed out of the world and headed home.

CHAPTER 6

As Tyen smoothed down the shirt of his most formal set of clothing, the small rectangular shape of Vella pressed against his chest. He checked his reflection in the small mirror of his bedroom, drew a deep breath and picked up the list of terms the Claymars had given him.

Then he gathered his wavering determination, inhaled again and pushed out of the world.

I hope Rielle won't take offence at the tone of these terms, Tyen thought. *I don't think she will, but then she has to give them to the Emperor. Poor Rielle. She'll wish she had never suggested I negotiate on behalf of Doum, or agreed to do so for Murai.*

He almost began his usual skim around the city out of habit, but this time he didn't need to hide his path. Moving through the ceiling and roof of his house, he rose high enough that all of the city was visible below him, then propelled himself to the west.

Do you think there's any chance the Emperor will agree to the Claymars' terms, Vella?

"Unless he is motivated by factors we do not know of, there is almost no chance of it."

As her voice spoke clearly in his mind, he felt his heart lift a little. It was always good to hear her speak. It was the closest she came to seeming physically human. If it weren't for the fact he'd suffocate if he stayed between worlds, he'd slip into the place between whenever he wanted to talk to her.

Do you think the Claymars don't understand what is at stake? Can they not see they are risking an invasion of their world?

"I cannot say for certain without reading all of their minds, but it would be strange if they did. You have not observed any reason they might avoid seeking information about their neighbouring worlds. There is no charismatic leader or restrictive religion with an agenda that works counter to self-preservation. They ought to know where they stand."

So why risk enraging the Emperor?

"Most likely they have adopted a bargaining strategy. They expect to compromise, so they begin with terms most favourable to them."

An approach not unexpected from a society used to bartering a price for what they create. The Emperor should be used to dealing with Doumians too.

"He may not be, if trade has always been handled by the merchants. He may be more used to being obeyed without question."

That doesn't sound at all promising.

Following the roads below him, Tyen traced a path to Fabre, a city a quarter of the way around Doum. Smaller than Alba, it nestled within an arc of tiered quarries cut into a low cliff wall. From these came the glistening clay that formed the whiteware Fabre was famous for. He did not descend into the metropolis, however, but instead headed for a building a little way past the top of the cliff. From above, it was an interlocking complex of rings, the internal spaces filled with greenery. White rendered walls gleamed in the morning sunlight.

The largest of these rings was his destination. At the centre was a pond and in the middle of this rose a circular shelter reached by a small bridge: the Island of Tiles. Drawing close to the world, he began to make out the trickle of water from fountains set around the pond. As he arrived, the sound sharpened and his surroundings regained their full saturation of colour. The shimmering reflection of tiny tiles set into the bridge and its railing caught his eye. A multitude of them formed a mosaic of bright colours that depicted entwined flowering vines. He ran a hand over it. The white grout was rough compared to the smooth glaze.

Will Rielle be impressed by this? he wondered. *She has been among mosaic-makers so long the chances are she has seen the best the craft can produce*

"Tyen Wheelmaker," a voice said.

Tyen turned. A middle-aged man was approaching the bridge, wearing the simply cut clothes most potters preferred, but of finer cloth and with a symbol stitched onto the chest. The sort of uniform an official might wear.

"I am Abler Tithen," the man said. "I will convey the result of your meeting to the Claymars and see that you are provided with anything you require."

"I am honoured to meet you, Abler Tithen," Tyen replied.

The man's lips pressed together into a near-smile, as if he found the formal reply amusing. "And I you," he replied. "The Emperor of Murai's representative will arrive shortly. You will speak to her here." He indicated the island shelter behind Tyen. "There are refreshments waiting."

"Thank you," Tyen replied. "Where will I find you when we are done?"

"When you emerge, I will come out to meet you."

The man took a step back, then turned and walked away. Tyen crossed the bridge and entered the shelter. At once, the sound of the fountains changed, softened yet not amplified in the small space. Two plain reed chairs waited on either side of a round table of the same material, the top woven of finer strips to make the surface as smooth as possible. A pair of glasses stood beside a jug of water and bowls of fruit, little baked savouries and the small salted fish and pickled seaweed that Doumians served to guests.

He put down the documents and sat. He waited, watching the bridge.

After a while, he began to wonder if the Emperor had changed his mind. He considered emerging to ask Abler how long he should linger before concluding the meeting wasn't happening. He decided to wait a little longer; then when he had made up his mind to leave, a faint shadow of a figure began to appear at the centre of the bridge.

His heart leapt, then began to beat quickly. Though it was an indistinct shape, he was certain it was Rielle, but he could not say why. Sure enough, as the figure grew more distinct he was proven right. She was slowly turning in a circle, her gaze combing the shadows of the building and then the island. As she saw him, she smiled, and grew more opaque.

He stood and walked out to greet her. She did not drag in a breath as she arrived, and this reminder of her agelessness sent a shiver down his spine.

"Rielle Lazuli," he said. "Welcome to Doum."

"Thank you," she replied. "I am sorry to be late. The Emperor arranged something to delay me out of some silly idea about looking like he was in control if he dictated the time we met."

"More annoying for you than me, I'm guessing," Tyen replied. "I've been sitting in comfort, not having to pander to a ruler's whims. Come inside. There are refreshments waiting."

"The inside that is still outside," she observed as she entered the shelter. "A concept common to Murai and Doum."

"Not common to any other place within Doum that I have seen. Perhaps it is inspired by Muraian architecture. Did you see the mosaics?"

"Yes." She nodded as she looked around. "Did the Claymars select it for that reason, so I might feel at home?"

"I don't know."

She shrugged. "If they did, then thank them."

"I will."

At his gesture towards a chair, she smiled and sat down. Her dress was as uncomplicated as the one she had worn when he'd visited her in the palace, this time a grey-blue, though she wore no jewellery but the lozenge-shaped pendant. She did not carry anything. Either she had memorised the Emperor's terms, or they were so straightforward she did not need to. The latter was unlikely to be good news.

"How is life in the palace?"

Her mouth twitched with wry amusement. "Busy. The Emperor has commissioned enough mosaics to keep me busy for many cycles. Deliberately so, I suspect, to give me incentive to gain the result here that he wants."

"That is good for the mosaic-makers?"

"Yes, as long as he gets his way. If he doesn't . . ." Her lips pressed into an unhappy line. "I can only hope he will not punish them for my failure."

"You do not know whether he would?"

The wry smile again. "He has made sure I cannot easily find his mind, by leaving Glaemar and taking with him the few people who know where he has gone." She shrugged. "It's not that he doesn't trust me. He doesn't trust anyone."

"So you are communicating via emissaries as well." Tyen chuckled. "The Claymars don't trust me either."

They were silent for a short time, unified in their exasperation and acceptance of the situation. Then her smile vanished and she straightened.

"So, what do the Claymars want?"

He lifted the small stack of paper outlining Doum's terms, and began reading.

"Well," she said when he'd finished. "At least they thought about it. The Emperor simply told me to say, 'Give the merchants what they want or I'll come and take it.'"

Tyen's stomach sank – the same sensation he'd felt on receiving the Claymars' demands. He looked at Rielle and found himself unable to speak. Her gaze moved over his face, searching, and he recalled how Baluka had once said that he wished he could keep his thoughts from showing as well as Tyen did.

Tyen drew in a breath and let it out slowly. He recalled what Vella had said about bargaining. Was the Emperor asking for all that he wanted, knowing he'd have to compromise?

"And yet, he sent you here anyway," he pointed out.

"Yes." She spread her hands. "This may be the position from which he must be seen to begin."

"I interpreted the Claymars' list of terms in a similar way."

"It may also be an ultimatum."

"Or a bluff, to see if the Claymars scare easily."

"It may be directed at you. Would you defend this world if the Emperor attacked?"

"Yes."

"Even if the Claymars did not want you to? Even if they told you not to interfere?"

He frowned. "It is unlikely they would refuse my help."

Her eyebrows rose, demanding an answer.

"Then . . . I don't know. I'd have to make sure it was truly what all the Claymars wanted. And if they did, then perhaps I'd stay and be ready to help if they changed their minds."

She nodded. "That they accepted your help as negotiator is a good sign, at least."

"What about you?" he asked. "Would you help the Emperor invade, if he asked?"

"No."

"What if he made it clear you would not be welcome in Murai if you didn't?"

"I'd move on." She shrugged. "I'm here only for the work, which is not so hard to find that I have to participate in a war to stay employed."

"What if Murai was invaded?"

She grimaced and shook her head. "I do not get involved in local conflicts. You never know whether you'll make it better or worse."

He nodded. "As Valhan told you."

"Close enough." She grimaced. "And here I am, getting involved." She looked down at the Claymars' demands. "What are we to tell those we represent?"

Tyen looked at the papers on the table, then at Rielle's hands, resting where he'd expected the Emperor's terms would lie.

"I don't fancy the prospect of conveying unreasonable demands back and forth to endless meetings like this – despite the opportunity to enjoy your company. I say we behave as reasonable people do, and discuss what a mutually beneficial agreement might look like."

Her smile was not wry or grim this time, but open and full of admiration and eagerness.

"Yes! And present it to both sides, as a suggestion. They may not like two otherworlders inventing terms for them, but if we behave more sensibly than they do, we may shame them into negotiating properly."

"It's worth a try."

Tyen rose and moved to the entrance of the shelter. At once, Abler emerged from a doorway.

"We need paper and something to write with," Tyen told the man. He paused, thinking of the uneven surface of the reed-woven table. "And boards to support the paper."

Abler nodded and withdrew into the building. Returning to his seat, Tyen poured water into the glasses. Soon the emissary entered the shelter with the items Tyen had asked for. As the man left, Tyen pushed a board, writing stick and half of the paper towards Rielle.

"So, where should we begin?"

They started with the original source of contention between the worlds, then worked over the other issues the Claymars had raised in their long list of terms. Hours passed, the time barely noticed. The work was not easy, but they had both seen many different systems of government and trade in their travels, and knew enough of Murai and Doum to guess what ideas they could suggest that would not be dismissed as too strange or unworkable by the Claymars and Emperor.

They stopped when Abler and two women interrupted to serve a meal. The garden was now bright under a midday sun. Tyen realised they had barely touched the food on offer. For a while they ate in silence, then Rielle looked at him thoughtfully.

"Tarran told me much about you," she said. "At least, what he knew of you from before Liftre closed."

Tyen nodded, then frowned as he realised what that meant. Tarran was one of the few people he'd trusted to know about Vella. Tarran might not have told Rielle about Vella, but she would have learned of the book by reading his mind. It was unlikely she hadn't, in the five cycles she'd known the old man. *Then there's no reason to hesitate to ask her for help in restoring Vella.*

He opened his mouth, then closed it again. It was possible she had never read Tarran's mind out of good manners, or Tarran had never thought of Vella when she had. Though the possibility was remote . . . *I had best not mention Vella until I'm sure Rielle already knows about her.*

"Your world sounds fascinating," she continued. "Everything done by machines driven by magic."

"Not everything," he corrected. "Or there'd be no jobs for anyone. The price was great: my world is weak because the machines were consuming the magic faster than it could be produced."

"Tarran said people in your world don't believe creativity is the source of magic."

"It is considered a primitive belief. At least, it is in the Empire. In the colonies and uncolonised south, they know the truth."

"In my home world, using magic is forbidden unless you are a priest."

He nodded. "Because there is so little magic. We both grew up in worlds weak in magic."

"Are you reading my mind?"

He hesitated a moment. "No."

Her eyes narrowed. "So how did you—? Ah! Dahli told you. Or you read it from his mind."

He nodded.

She looked pained. "You must know far more about me than I do about you, since he knows everything about me before I became ageless. I had to open my mind to him while he taught me pattern shifting."

"Is that unavoidable – opening your mind to the one who teaches you?"

"I don't know." She shook her head. "It's probably faster that way, but I think if you knew what you were aiming for, you could teach yourself. The first person to become ageless must have achieved it alone, so it has to be possible. Have you tried to teach yourself?"

"No."

"Why not? You are powerful enough to achieve it. Tarran said you have the knowledge."

"I guess I haven't had a good enough reason yet."

"What reason do you need?" She tilted her head to the side. "Do you believe it should be a selfless act?"

"No." He chuckled. "I'm not so noble that I'd pass up the chance to become ageless unless it had a noble purpose." He paused. "Has anyone done that?"

"Apparently."

"Well, I'm as eager to live as long as I can as most people are. But I know it takes a long time and can strip a world of power. I've read that there are drawbacks." He paused. "Do you mind if I ask what the drawbacks are?"

She smiled. "Of course not." She looked thoughtful, then her shoulders rose and fell. "Dahli said that I would unconsciously change myself to please those who regard me, and if I wasn't careful I would eventually forget what I originally looked like." She frowned. "I've often wondered if my personality would change too. Valhan had a statue of himself in his palace so he knew what he should look like. I've painted portraits of myself and left them in safe places."

"Does it matter, really, if you end up looking different to how you started?" Tyen asked. "It might be appealing, if you didn't like your appearance."

"I would not have thought it mattered much, but maybe after living a few hundred years you feel like you've lost something. I sometimes long to return to who I was, when I didn't know about magic and that there were other worlds – but then I think everyone is nostalgic for a time in their lives when things were innocent and uncomplicated."

Tyen nodded, thinking back to his early years in the Academy. "I read that being ageless can make you feel less human."

Rielle shook her head. "I feel very human. Too human, sometimes. It as though having strong powers makes my human needs and flaws more obvious."

"Yes, I know how that feels. It sounds as though these drawbacks are those that anyone who lives an interesting and long life would have anyway."

She frowned. "All but one, for me – losing my Maker ability. But that isn't something you would need to worry about."

He raised his eyebrows at this piece of information. She had been a Maker, but becoming ageless had removed the ability. Something about this piece of information seemed familiar. Perhaps he had read it from Dahli's mind. Or Baluka's. "Do you regret losing it?"

Her mouth pulled down at the corners. "Yes and no. It did not matter to me. Being ageless has far more benefits." She smiled faintly. "And I am not the only one enjoying them."

He nodded. "Tarran. You've healed him – perhaps even made him younger."

"Both. What I do for him won't last for ever. He didn't want me to transform him into a young man again. He just wanted a little more time and no aches and pains." She met his gaze and lowered her voice. "Though I would rather it wasn't well known that I have that ability, or a certain person I represent here will try to find ways to make me his healer."

"I respect that." Tyen shuddered as he imagined how the Emperor might persuade her to give him a long, healthy life. *He might not be able to harm her, but he might hurt people she cared about, like the mosaic-workers, or the servant girl.*

Rielle pushed her empty plate aside and picked up her writing stick. "That was delicious. Now, we should get back to work before they come to see what we're up to."

So they continued on. During further rest breaks they swapped stories of their homes, of mistakes made while learning magic, and of people they had encountered since learning to travel the worlds. When they finally finished they had only the skeleton of a proposed agreement between the worlds – the best they could do without spending many days on it. Darkness curtained the shelter. Tyen had created a spark of light and set it floating above the table. Rielle took her copy, folded it in three, then stood.

"I must go. I've been gone far longer than expected."

"The Emperor probably intended you to come straight back."

"It will do him good to have to wait for an answer, for once." She looked up and smiled. "You should know, Tarran lives in the world of Roh, in the southern mountains of Puttila, beside Lake Boaleu. I'm sure he would appreciate a visit."

Tyen nodded. "I'd like to see him again."

Her smile widened. The odd angle of light cast her eyes in shadow, giving her expression a sultry mystery. Her lips seemed to curl in an invitation. His heartbeat quickened. Was that a deliberate look she'd given him, or only his hopes altering his perception of it?

"Thank you," she said quietly. "Good luck presenting this to the Claymars. I look forward to our next meeting."

"I, too." He bowed in the manner of the gentlemen of his world. "Best of luck with the Emperor."

She nodded in reply, then pushed out of the world.

He stood in silence after she had faded from sight. Her absence was like the extinguishing of a fire, allowing cool air to seep into the shelter. He realised he was tired, and wanted nothing more than to return home and think over their encounter. Leaving the Claymars' list of terms, half-emptied plates of food and worn-down writing sticks on the table, Tyen stepped out onto the bridge. At once a rectangle of light in the building wall appeared and widened, the silhouette of a middle-aged Doumian man in the centre. Tyen brought out the spark of light, illuminating the way as Abler approached.

He handed the second copy of the suggested agreement to the man.

"Thank you for your assistance. Please deliver this to the Council," Tyen said.

"I will do so immediately," Abler replied. "You may return to your workshop."

Tyen nodded, then drew magic and a deep breath and pushed a little way into the place between worlds so he could skim back to his home.

CHAPTER 7

R oh was a small, warm world. It contained no oceans, just a multitude of lakes. The vegetation was predominately grass – from towering fan-like species as tall as the largest trees of Tyen's world, to tiny plants that sprouted from the smallest accumulation of dust and dirt.

Tyen had explored it briefly, back when he had been searching for a world in which to settle. Doum had already been in his mind as an attractive new home, and he'd found Roh a little boring in comparison. The lack of metalworking technology had put him off, despite his determination to leave mechanical magic in his past.

The southern mountains of the area known as Puttila would be better described as ripples in the blanket of green vegetation that covered most of the world. A maze of lakes lay between them. It took some time, following the convoluted coastlines of several lakes, before he found the first inhabitants. Aquatic grass blurred the line between lake and land, most of it several times the height of a man. The houses were suspended platforms tied to the mature plants, a wider roof hanging above.

He emerged in one, startling a man making rope, and asked where Lake Boaleu was. The man's language was a liquid flow of sounds that Tyen found difficult to speak. His own pronunciation of Boaleu was so far from correct that it took some time to make himself understood. Being able to read minds did not always make communication easier. The instructions he was eventually given were too complicated to memorise, being the steps someone would take if they were travelling in a small boat. He had to stop and question locals several more times before he finally arrived at what he hoped was the lake Tarran lived beside.

When he got there, however, finding Tarran wasn't hard at all. In the middle of the lake stood a spire of rock – the remnants of an ancient volcano's throat. On top of this, among more grass-like vegetation, sprawled a cluster of buildings. From the verandas and pergola posts fluttered colourful banners covered in black marks. If Tyen hadn't been skimming just outside the world, he'd have laughed aloud. The old sorcerer was clearly still keeping up his calligraphy practice – and no doubt making all his students learn it too.

Though it was obvious to Tyen that this was Tarran's home, he could not shake his long-held habits of caution. He continued past the spire and followed the lake to the furthest edge, stopped for a breath, then quickly retraced his steps, creating a dead-end path in the place between worlds. As he set off in a new direction towards the spire, he began concealing his path.

He skimmed towards the building slowly, looking for signs of life. A man scrubbed clothing in a trough; a woman worked in a small vegetable garden; and through a window Tyen spotted a young man bent over a table, wielding a large brush. Then as he passed over the building, he saw an old man leaning on a railing, looking out over the lake.

Descending to the pavement behind the man, Tyen moved the rest of the way into the world, feeling the pull of gravity as he arrived. At Tyen's deep intake of breath, Tarran started and turned. Then he smiled.

"Ah," he said. "Tyen. She kept her promise."

"Promise?"

"To send you here."

"Why wouldn't she, if you wanted her to?"

Tarran grinned. "Jealousy. She wants me all to herself."

Tyen pretended to be impressed. "Your teaching must have improved greatly since you were at Liftre."

The old man chuckled. "Ha ha. Actually, it can only be better when I have fewer students. More time for each." He beckoned and turned back to the rail. "I was just admiring the view. It's a particularly fine one today. No mist obscuring the distance. No wind to ruffle the water."

Walking over to join Tarran, Tyen had to agree: it was spectacular. The lake spread before them, encompassed by green-blue hills. The shore closest to them shimmered as a flock of winged creatures took to the air, their energetic flapping becoming a graceful, unified wave. The lake was partially transparent, revealing shoals of many small aquatic creatures, and one impressively large one steadily making its way past the volcanic plug.

"How long have you lived here?" Tyen asked.

"Three cycles."

"Why here?"

Tarran shrugged. "There's little danger anyone would invade this world. While there's plenty of water and good soil, otherworld crops can't compete with the local plants. There are no great stores of mineral resources to exploit. There's enough to live on, evenly distributed around the world, but only if you live simply. Of course, the Rohins still manage to find things to fight over. They're as human as the rest of the people of the worlds. But they tend to fight about politics or law. Or matters of the heart."

Tyen looked over his shoulder at the building. "Did you make this place?"

"No, I bought it from another otherworlder. One of the Raen's former allies, who needed a more secretive hiding place than this."

Tyen looked into his former mentor's mind, but didn't recognise the ally. Tarran doubted the name he'd been given was the true one anyway.

"What about you? Did you finally get around to becoming ageless?"

"No."

The old man frowned at Tyen. "Why not?"

"The right time hasn't come along." Tyen shrugged. "And it means destroying a world, with the added risk of being stranded in it."

"It doesn't destroy a world to take the magic out of it," Tarran reminded him. "They do recover. And while worlds with magic and no people are rare, they do exist. Though they may be growing more scarce, now that the Raen no longer controls who is becoming ageless." Tarran put a hand on Tyen's shoulder. "You know I'll come and get you if you became stranded."

"And the drawback to being ageless – the risk of irreversible change?"

The old man paused, then drew his hand away. "By the time you're my age, it won't seem that relevant. We all change as we grow older. We constantly evolve into new people. Believe me, I am nothing like the person I was at your age, and I don't mind that as much as you'd expect. While you may end up changing into someone completely different, that doesn't mean it'll be something worse. You have less to lose than Rielle did. She was once a Maker. Now when she creates, the magic she generates is no greater than any other artist's."

Tyen nodded. "Baluka told me she was a Maker. He thought that was why the Raen took her to his palace."

Tarran frowned. "If that were true, why did he have her become ageless?"

Tyen shook his head. He could not tell Tarran the real reason the Raen had recruited Rielle: to resurrect him after he died. The old man turned to face the building. "Come inside. I have some new students, and I should introduce you."

Following Tarran inside, Tyen caught a thought from the man that made his heart skip a beat.

Rielle will probably get here soon, Tarran thought. *If she's taken* all *of my advice and not simply suggested Tyen visit me.* In the next moment a spark ran along Tyen's nerves, as he learned that Rielle had admitted to Tarran that she was attracted to Tyen. That she would like to form more than a friendship. Tarran had suggested she arrange for Tyen to meet her here. Or at least send Tyen to him so he could attempt to find out if his former protégé was at all attracted to her. *If he was interested in meeting for more than just negotiations.*

"More than negotiations"? Tyen mused. *Even in his thoughts, Tarran is endearingly coy.*

The old man glanced back. Tyen quickly smoothed his expression but, judging by the knowing smile that curled Tarran's lips, not quickly enough.

Cunning old romantic, Tyen thought. *I'm tempted to pretend disinterest, just to tease him a little. But that might put Rielle off, and I really don't want to do that.*

Tarran said nothing, however. He led Tyen through the rooms of the house, introducing his students when they reached the workroom. The walls were decorated with calligraphic banners, and Tyen was astonished to find one of his own hanging among them. But despite all the observations and explanations, introductions and chatter, a part of Tyen's mind could not leave alone the question of what to do when Rielle arrived – if she arrived – while he was there. Was what he had daydreamed of coming to be? She was attracted to him. She liked him. She wanted them to become more than friends. Perhaps just lovers. He dared not hope for more. He couldn't say yet if he wanted more than that. Sex was one thing; living with and promising oneself to another was entirely another. They couldn't read each other's minds, which was a challenge they were both unused to now. Even if they could, they might not get along.

Rielle would know, the moment she read Tarran's mind, that Tyen had betrayed a hint of interest. But she would only know that *Tarran* thought so. Tyen had an unfair advantage over her.

Unless I tell Tarran I am. Then she'll know it's not just Tarran's guess.

Yet he couldn't bring himself to say anything. Besides, surely it was better that Tyen told Rielle herself?

As he tried to imagine what he'd say, he floundered. He was no expert on these first steps of intimacy with a woman. He'd not realised Sezee was romantically interested in him until it was too late. Yira had made her intentions clear from the outset, so there had been no guessing and interpretation of hints. Since the Raen's death, he'd discouraged women whose interest went beyond the physical, not wanting to draw anyone into his life until he knew it would not put them in danger. Being able to read their minds meant he knew their expectations matched his, and how best to pursue or encourage them.

That was the key to his disquiet, he realised. While Rielle had made it easier by communicating through Tarran, once they were together he would be reduced, thanks to her hidden mind, to the awkward, clueless man he'd been in his world.

Before his thoughts had a chance to move beyond this point, Tarran led him into a circular atrium and there she was, her back to them as she examined the flowers of a creeper covering half of a wall. Once again, she wore a simple shift dress, this time in a red as bright as blood. Her hair had been put up in a fancy arrangement, jewels glittering in the coils.

Hearing their footsteps, she turned and blinked at Tyen in surprise, then smiled. Her gaze moved to Tarran. When it slid directly back to Tyen again her smile had altered. It became the same mischievous curl it had been before she'd left the Island of Tiles. A thrill shot though Tyen's body, culminating in his groin. Fortunately, she didn't look down, but turned back to Tarran, crossed her arms and lifted her eyebrows in open disapproval.

The old man looked insufferably smug.

Don't let your annoyance spoil everything, Tyen told himself as he stepped forward to greet her with a gentlemanly bow.

"Rielle Lazuli," he said. "What an unexpected pleasure."

She laughed softly. "Not entirely unexpected, I think. I did tell you where to find Tarran, though I could only guess when you'd visit."

"I am fortunate, then, that our timing matched."

"As am I," she replied, then hesitated. "I am glad we have the opportunity to meet outside the formality of the negotiations, and can discuss matters with no danger of eavesdroppers."

He paused. Had Tarran misread her reasons for urging Tyen to visit him? "Is there anything regarding the negotiation you can only tell me here and now?"

"No, nothing," she assured him. She lowered her eyes. A short silence followed. Tyen cursed silently. How had they slipped into this formal manner? He must steer them towards a more relaxed conversation. Tarran was silent, rocking back and forth from his heels to the balls of his feet and wishing he could knock their heads together. Tyen grabbed the first question that came to mind.

"How did the Emperor respond to our suggested terms?"

So much for steering them to a relaxed conversation.

She glanced up. "He sent a rather terse letter. It implied I let you bully me into writing terms favourable to Doum. I am to wait for his official response. What about the Claymars?"

He shrugged. "Much the same."

Her gaze was now on Tarran, who was studying them with no intention of interrupting. "Well, my old mentor, are you going to stand there gawping or take us somewhere we can sit and chat?" she asked, not hiding her irritability, though there was equal affection in her voice.

Tyen covered his smile with his hand.

"Of course," Tarran replied. "I have the perfect location. Very comfortable. Private. I'll make sure you are not interrupted."

The old man set off down a passageway. Rielle looked back at Tyen once, her eyes bright with amusement, then followed.

"I found no path in the place between," she observed. "How did you get here?"

"It didn't seem polite to leave a trail leading directly to Tarran's home."

"So . . . you levitated?"

He shook his head. "No."

When he did not offer an explanation, she glanced back again with narrowed eyes, but didn't press him further.

Leaving the house, Tarran led them down a staircase carved into the side of the spire. It ended at a cave. The opening had been filled in with glassed panels, and a door. The interior was circular, and statues of men and women posed within alcoves in the walls. Large cushions had been fashioned to fit a deep wooden bench built to fit snugly against the walls. It was large enough to seat several people. A crescent-shaped table stood in the centre of the room, the outer curve matching the bench. On it was a flagon of water, bottles of wine, bowls of fruit and other foods that would not spoil quickly.

"I'll tell the cook to start making a meal for later," Tarran said, once they had settled on the benches. *Much later*, he thought as he slipped back out of the door. *If all they become is friends, I will be happy*, the old man thought as he started back up the staircase. He paused on the stairs and looked back at the door. *Anyone else might think I was mad, bringing two of the worlds' most powerful sorcerers together in my home. But I've known them, separately, for five cycles each. They'll be fine.*

Rielle chuckled, and as Tyen turned to her she smiled. "I am sorry, if I have made you uncomfortable. I confess this wasn't all Tarran's idea. I do wish to know you better. I thought it would be impossible, what with the negotiations placing us on opposite sides, but after our first meeting I realised we were in the same position, stuck between the Emperor and Claymars but with our own similar objectives."

He nodded. "Yes, I suppose there are three sides to it, if you include us." He sighed. "These negotiations have shown me that, despite all I've done to make a home in Doum, I will always be an outsider with the motives of an otherworlder."

"Though your motives align with the Claymars, of course."

"Not all." He shook his head. "Obviously I'd rather they didn't make stupid decisions out of pride."

"Are you tempted to search for their minds and make sure they aren't planning anything foolish?"

"Constantly. You?"

"I've tried," she admitted. "No luck. The Emperor has hidden himself too well. Perhaps he isn't even in Murai, and has settled in some neighbouring world, leaving sorcerers to make reports and deliver orders. I'd do that, if I was him."

"Will you leave Murai if he invades Doum?"

Rielle's forehead creased as she nodded. "I'll try to convince the mosaic-makers to leave too. It could be dangerous for them to remain in the palace."

"Where will you go?"

Her expression became wary, then softened. "I don't know. I will try to keep in touch, if you like."

"I would like that," he told her, smiling.

She turned in her seat, to face him. "Are you . . . ?" She paused, searching his face, then bit her lip. His heartbeat quickened as he waited for her to finish. What could she be hesitating to ask?

"Yes?" The word sprang from him, before he could stop it.

She made another little grimace of apology. "Are you still in contact with Dahli?"

His stomach sank a little. "Yes. Not that I have seen him much since . . . We have a way of contacting each other if the need arises."

"So . . . do you know if he's still trying to resurrect Valhan?"

A chill ran over Tyen's skin. He nodded. "Of course."

"With no success?"

"Not as far as I know."

"I gathered as much, or we'd have heard." She sighed. "Sorry. I had to ask. To get beyond that subject." She paused. "There are things I must know about you before . . . well, before I can trust you."

The tension that had been growing in him eased. It was possible that asking about Dahli was the true and only reason she'd arranged this meeting. *It makes sense, though. Five cycles ago, I was clearly one of the Raen's people. But then again, so was she.*

What could he tell her that would show she could trust him? He considered and rejected a few pieces of information. Then the answer sprang into his mind. It was obvious – and she would work it out eventually anyway.

"I can't read your mind," he told her.

She smiled. "I know."

He blinked in surprise, then his heart sank a little in disappointment. "How?"

"Your surprise to see Tarran was the first clue. If you'd been able to read my mind, you'd have seen me anticipating the moment you two were reunited. There have been other moments when it became clear as well."

"I could have been politely not reading your mind."

"Really?" Her eyebrows rose. "You're in the palace of the ruler who wants to invade your new home world, and negotiating a peace on behalf of a world and people you love, and you wouldn't read my mind?"

He chuckled. "Yes, I suppose I would have. I could have been faking my surprise."

"It seemed genuine to both of us – and Tarran knows you much better than he knows me. There were . . . other clues." She shrugged. "In a way, it would be easier to trust you if you *could* read my mind. Then, if you had revealed the boy's location to Dahli, I'd know you were untrustworthy."

"And then it would have been too late."

"No, I made sure it wasn't."

"Of course." He pondered what she had said. "So what else do you need to know to judge me trustworthy?" he asked.

She drew a breath, let it out, then took another. "Why were you there?"

He wondered for a moment where she meant, but it did not take long to guess. "At the resurrection."

She nodded.

He considered how much he could tell her. Not the complete truth, he decided. "After the Raen died, Baluka wanted me to look for you. I noticed a path leading out of the palace and followed it. It was Dahli's. When I caught up with him, I read everything from his mind." That much was true. "I let him believe I had made a deal with the Raen – that I was a spy. He took me to the resurrection as an extra source of power, for defence and to get everyone out of the world if it ran out of magic."

"He trusted you though he'd never met you before?"

Tyen shrugged. "My role among the rebels was to scout and gather information. I'd learned a lot about the Raen. Enough to convince him I was one of the Raen's spies – of which there were plenty Dahli had never known about."

Her eyebrows rose. "He didn't ask you to open your mind?"

"No."

She looked away. "I suppose he was in a hurry." Her eyes snapped back to him. "And he doesn't suspect you now?"

"No more than anyone else." Tyen shrugged.

"Why do you stay in contact with him?"

"So I will know if he finds another way to bring the Raen back." Tyen paused, then decided it was time he tested her in return. "He knows that, with the worlds falling into chaos, many would welcome the Raen's return."

She scowled. "Then they are fools."

"Yet you chose to live in his palace."

She glanced at him, then down at her hands. "Yes. At the time it seemed like the right decision." She winced. "It *was* the right decision, when the other options would have led to my death. He would have killed me if I hadn't joined him. I learned that during the resurrection. I was able to see into his mind, to search out the truth. He was planning to kill me eventually, after I resurrected him."

"That seems . . . strange. He believed you would still resurrect him even after you learned that? Or did he not realise you would be able to read his intentions?"

"I think he knew it was possible, but he believed I would still do it, to save the worlds from the chaos that would follow his death. He'd shown me many places that benefited from his intervention to convince me he was the source of stability in the worlds."

"And you were convinced."

She shuddered. "I was, then."

"So what changed your mind?" Tyen pressed. "It wasn't the threat to your life, was it? It was the boy?"

She straightened. "Yes."

"Despite believing that the worlds would fall into conflict without the Raen."

Her eyes narrowed and she sent him a reproachful look, but she didn't move away. "I wasn't stupid. I knew there would be consequences. But I could not say whether there would be more or less death and suffering than what was happening under Valhan's rule already, or would occur when he returned. He maintained order, not a lack of violence and cruelty. When he showed me worlds, he never kept that from me. And he admitted he could never predict the outcome of his interference."

Tyen nodded. "So you have said before. What I saw of the worlds during my scouting . . . He'd succeeded in some but failed in others. His methods were flawed, even after a thousand cycles."

She exhaled. "What I fear most, right now, is that I know too little to keep Murai and Doum from war. That I might make things worse."

Her eyes were wide with worry. He moved a little closer so he could place a hand on her back. Lightly. Reassuring. Nothing that could be taken as too intimate too soon, he hoped.

"I do too."

She looked up at him. Suddenly her eyes were very large and close. "We can't force worlds to be peaceful. Not without becoming *him*."

"No," he agreed. "All we can do is offer our help."

"And it is only two worlds we are trying to help. We're not trying to rule them all."

"Two is more than enough."

She let out a quiet laugh. "They certainly are." She was not moving away. Her lips quirked into a smile – not quite the mischievous one she had made earlier, but close. His heart beat faster, sending a pulse of excitement through his body.

"You have to stick around to help people," he told her. "Perhaps that was the Raen's mistake: he could have been a benevolent ruler if he hadn't tried to rule all of the worlds. He should have chosen one and dedicated himself to . . ."

She stopped his words with a kiss. Though he had made the kind of gestures he'd hoped would be welcome – drawing closer, a reassuring touch – he was still startled by it. As if he truly hadn't believed she would respond in this way. That she would ever trust him. That such a beautiful, smart, powerful woman could ever possibly want him.

But the firm press of her lips on his made him forget his surprise. They told him otherwise. They told him that she wanted much more. As her arms slid around him, she pressed her body to his. Her breasts pushed into his chest, harder then softer with each of her quickening breaths. One of her legs slid across his, so that more of their bodies touched. There was no place for his hands to be except on her body, and her lips tightened into a smile as he pulled her closer with one, then tentatively slid the other around to where the side of one breast swelled where it was pressed between them.

111

She pulled away a little, and gave him a searching look. He raised his eyebrows, trying to both invite and question at the same time.

Her lips curled into a small grin, this time unmistakably sensuous. He felt her fingers plucking at the buttons of his shirt, then pulling the cloth away. She drew him down onto the cushions and the only thought he had about anyone else from that point on was that Tarran had better not come to check on them for a very long time.

CHAPTER 8

S ounds filtered up from the workshop below. Though yet another sign that the time of grieving had passed, they did nothing to chase away the oppressive quiet of Tyen's room. He picked up an unfinished insectoid, then put it down again, then rifled through drawers of parts and tools. His mind would not fix for long on anything, and the closer he came to the time of his next meeting with Rielle, the harder it was to concentrate.

It was a mistake for us to meet privately, he thought. *If the Claymars find out, they might decide my position has been compromised.*

But they wouldn't, if neither he nor Rielle told them. Why would she reveal their tryst to anyone? The Muraian Emperor would also suspect that Rielle's ability to negotiate on his behalf was weakened. She wanted peace between Murai and Doum too.

Or did she? Rielle was only a temporary resident in Murai. She had not taken on the position of negotiator willingly. If she revealed they had been lovers, it would free her from that obligation, and at the same time strike a blow against Doum, thereby keeping her in the Emperor's good graces and the mosaic-makers in continuing work.

Or perhaps the Emperor had threatened her, or offered a reward, which made pressing for a result that benefited Murai worth her seducing Tyen. That would only make sense if he believed that the Claymars thought having sex with someone put you under their influence. But then who was influencing the other? Who was the seducer, and who the seducee?

The people of Doum were refreshingly disinclined to assign a behaviour as being atypical to either males or females. Women weren't considered more or less sexual than men. It was possible they would not be at all bothered by Tyen and Rielle being lovers. They might even see it as beneficial – greater motivation to find a peaceful solution.

He had less familiarity with Muraian customs or, more importantly, with what the Emperor's possible reaction would be. The man might be angered by the assumption that Rielle had been charmed by Tyen, or pleased that she was willing to use her feminine attractions to manipulate Tyen on his behalf. Tyen didn't know him enough to judge.

I can't shake the feeling his reaction would be bad either way. Which makes me even more certain that Rielle would never tell the Emperor – but I have to consider whether this was all some plan to manipulate me in a way I haven't thought of . . .

He paused to recollect, seeking signs of deceit, but that only led to reliving some very pleasant and distracting memories. Dragging his attention back to the questions that plagued him, he chuckled quietly. *If she only meant to make it hard to concentrate on serious matters, then she has succeeded.*

Whatever the intentions of all parties, Tyen was determined to be as persuasive and flexible at this coming meeting with Rielle as he had been at the first. If his stomach buzzed and his heart raced in her presence . . . well, he would have to rely on his skill in hiding his true thoughts and keeping a calm exterior.

Though Tarran had managed to read him easily enough.

Tarran. That old meddler! Tyen smiled. *I barely spoke to him, and mostly about Rielle.*

He recalled then what the old sorcerer had said about Rielle being a Maker before she became ageless. That reminded him of his plan to discuss it with Vella. He'd put off doing so. When he'd undressed in the cave room, he'd slipped the pouch over his neck with his shirt, keeping her hidden. Later he'd slipped her into his jacket, avoiding touching her cover through the holes in the fabric.

Vella must have seen enough to know what I was about to do, he reminded himself. But she wouldn't know for sure what had happened until he touched her again and read the truth from his mind. Though she could not feel jealousy, and no disapproval had ever been in her comments when he'd had lovers in the past, guilt always plucked at his conscience. It was more intense this time. It hadn't faded.

Because I want more than a passing, physical encounter with Rielle, and that feels like disloyalty.

He straightened in his seat as he felt the truth of that.

I promised Vella that I would protect her and find a way to restore her to a living human being. So what do *I want from Rielle that could threaten that?* He wasn't sure. *To talk to her. To get to know her. To make love with her.* Just the thought of it set his pulse racing. *Does this mean I'm in love?* Ironically, he wanted to ask Vella. She was the only person he could talk to. The only friend he discussed such personal matters with. *And it helps that her answer can only be truthful and free of emotional complications.*

That thought made him wince. Being trapped in a book was so unfair to her. She ought to be able to lie and feel emotions. He should be doing more to help her. He owed her that much. And that was, he realised, the true source of his guilt.

Vella's welfare is still my responsibility, and here I am dreaming about another woman – to whom I cannot make promises of unwavering loyalty. Not when my promise to Vella comes first.

Rielle might not want anything more from him anyway. She might not even intend to sleep with him again. He might be, to her, no more important than the women he'd lain with once or twice. She might not want to become attached to anyone, when Dahli could threaten that person in order to persuade her to reveal the location of the boy who was supposed to have become the Raen.

And then he realised that Rielle too had made a promise that must come first: the promise to protect the boy.

He wanted to talk to Vella even more now. He needed the clarity that came from discussing matters with her. *I can't help her or Rielle or Doum if my mind is distracted by all these questions.* He rose and slipped out of his room, heading for the toilet. Though he wasn't hiding Vella there any more, it was still the best place to talk to her. Claymar Fursa was unlikely to materialise inside the room, at the least.

Once perched on the lid, he dug Vella out of a pocket and removed her from her pouch. When he opened the pages, her elegant script appeared.

Well, well. Haven't you been having fun?

He felt his face grow hot. *I'm sorry. Are you bothered at all?*

No. There's nothing to apologise for, Tyen. On the contrary, it's about time you stopped keeping to yourself. You've been practically celibate since you settled in Doum.

Tyen didn't know what to say, so he changed the subject. *What do you think? Can I trust Rielle?*

I do not have enough information to be certain. The only duplicity she has demonstrated was to disobey Dahli and the Raen's instruction to resurrect him, and secretly meeting with you if she knew the Emperor would disapprove — which would be a move against the Emperor, not you.

Tyen nodded. *Tarran said that Rielle lost her Maker ability when she became ageless. Does this always happen to Makers who learn how to stop ageing?*

I cannot answer that question. That she became ageless at all is unusual. It has been written and believed for thousands of cycles that Makers cannot become ageless.

Perhaps that is only because there are no ageless Makers, because becoming ageless removes the Making ability. Or that Makers who were strong enough sorcerers to become ageless decided not to. Or that Makers are almost never strong enough to become ageless.

Those are all plausible explanations. However, there is an old belief that the worlds will be torn asunder if a Maker becomes a Successor.

A prophecy?

Perhaps. Or a prediction based on information or insight I do not have.

Could it be interpreted the same way Tarran did Millennium's Rule: "a vague prediction of inevitable change"?

It is most certainly vague. Whether it is predictable or inevitable relies on knowledge I do not contain. It would be difficult to prove. Successors have been defeating Predecessors for many thousands of cycles, so a prediction of inevitability is not implausible. The worlds being torn asunder is most likely not a repeatable scenario.

Do you know who thought of it?

No.

How do you know about it?

The source is a notation on a scroll translating a tablet describing Millennium's Rule, written over eight thousand cycles ago. It was described most recently two and a half thousand cycles ago by a pair of ageless scholars who had gathered a great library, destroyed in the wars following Roporien's Succession. One wrote about the scroll in his diary, which was found in the ruins by a scavenger and sold to a king, who held me at Roporien's bidding.

This sounds more like speculation on what would happen if a very rare circumstance occurred than a prophecy.

Or an impossible circumstance, if becoming ageless removes a Maker's ability.

Tyen recalled the sadness in Rielle's voice as she'd told him of her loss.

Being a Maker is a rare ability. She says she didn't care much for it, but I suspect she does feel the loss.

Most well-populated worlds will produce a Maker every few generations. That means thousands of Makers are alive across the known worlds at all times.

I suppose when you put it that way, it's not that rare. How many of those thousands are powerful enough to become ageless?

I don't know exactly, only that sorcerers of Rielle's strength are very rare, so the probability that one would also be a Maker is extremely low.

When was the last time you—?

A sound interrupted Tyen's question: his name, shouted from

somewhere below the stairs. He looked up from Vella's pages and reached out to open the door a crack.

"What is it?" he called back.

"Messenger," one of the workers shouted.

Closing Vella, he stowed her in her pouch and slung it around his neck under his shirt. He flushed the toilet, left the room and moved across the hall to the stairs. A man in the uniform of the Claymars' messengers waited below. As he saw Tyen, he straightened.

"Greetings, Tyen Wheelmaker," he said. "I am here to tell you that Rielle of Murai has arrived early at the Island of Tiles, at the bidding of Emperor Izetala-Moraza. Are you able to meet her?"

Tyen's heart skipped a beat, but he kept his expression and bearing relaxed.

"I guess I can leave now, if the Claymars wish me to."

"They do," the messenger replied. "The meeting is at the same location as before."

"Thank you." Tyen looked at the worker who had announced the messenger. "Could you see our visitor out?"

The young man nodded, and ushered the messenger towards the door. Tyen hurried to his bedroom and changed into his formal clothing. Drawing magic and a deep breath, he pushed out of the world and began the journey to the meeting place. Though he paused to breathe less frequently than last time and travelled faster, it seemed to take twice as long as he remembered. When he finally arrived at the shelter, it was midday. The interior was cast in shadow, but he could see someone moving about inside. The fountain's splash concealed all noise. Smoothing his clothing and his expression, and ignoring the racing of his heart, he walked across the bridge.

The occupant stepped into the entrance, the sunlight revealing the same official that had greeted him last time. Tyen nodded respectfully, keeping his disappointment hidden.

"Thank you for coming here early, Tyen Wheelmaker," Abler

said. "The Claymars have left a new document. Rielle of Murai is being entertained elsewhere to allow you time to examine it."

Tyen frowned and peered into the shadows. He could see a rectangle of white pages, but could not judge its depth. "How long do I have?"

"As long as you need. Ring the bell when you are ready."

Abler stepped past Tyen, crossed the bridge and entered the building. Sighing with impatience, Tyen entered the pavilion and was relieved to find the stack of paper wasn't too thick. It would take some time to read it, but not the rest of the day. He'd have rather had a full day to consider the contents, however. That was a luxury the Claymars weren't intending to give him, so he sat down and picked up the first page.

It was slower work than he'd expected, not due to the complexity of the contents or occasional confusion caused by a writer inexperienced in using the Traveller tongue, but because he had to pause to let his temper cool several times. When he was finished, he rang the bell and concentrated on regaining a calm composure.

Rielle stepped out of the building. She smiled as she headed for the pavilion, and all his annoyance melted away. Her pace was serene, her walk graceful and yet he could not help noting the sensual curves of her body and the quirk in the corner of her smile that suggested she too was thinking of their last meeting.

"Tyen Wheelmaker," she said as she stepped into the shelter. Her tone was warm, but her stance was formal. A roll of paper was coiled within her fingers. "There's no reason to get up to greet me."

He glanced down, realising he was on his feet. He couldn't remember standing.

"Rielle Lazuli," he replied evenly. "Welcome back to Doum."

"Thank you." As she walked over to the table he tried not to stare. Every detail about her was fascinating. How her hips swayed as she walked. How the simple dress she wore, shaped by the body beneath, tightened when she sat down. How the pendant's chain was exactly the right length, so it rested just above the gap in the neckline of her dress, in the dip between her breasts.

"I apologise for my unplanned visit. The Emperor demanded it and expects me back at an unreasonable hour. Though *I* expect to return at a reasonable hour, I would rather not give him any more cause to be annoyed with me than necessary. Let's make a start."

Tyen returned to his seat and looked down at the Claymars' document. "I am afraid I cannot offer good news."

"Me neither." She uncoiled the roll of paper and held it open. "Shall I start? I'd like to get this unpleasantness over with."

"Go ahead."

When she had finished reading, Tyen said nothing in response. Instead he read aloud the Claymars' new demands. Rielle asked a few questions, nodded at the answers and then they both fell silent.

"I see our error," she said eventually. "Instead of giving them a shortcut to the middle of their respective positions, we have provided them with a third position, and two new middle grounds on either side."

Tyen nodded. She was right. "They've started negotiating with us, not each other."

"I guess it's our fault for thinking they'd welcome us speeding the process."

"We denied them the chance to bicker with each other, so now they're bickering with us."

"We've gone backwards."

She set her elbows on the table and pressed her hands to her face. "I knew I wasn't up to this task. What do I know of negotiation?"

Tyen shrugged, resisting the temptation to reach out and place a reassuring hand on her arm. "No more than me," he assured her.

She crossed her arms and moved her hands to her shoulders. "So what do we do now?"

He considered. "Remind them that we are not the enemy."

"How?"

"I don't know . . . just tell them?"

"Tell them they're acting like children?" She let out a bitter laugh. "I'm sure that will be welcome."

"Nothing we do will be welcome," he pointed out. "We're not here to tell them what they want to hear."

"So . . . if our job isn't to make them comfortable, do we aim to make them feel uncomfortable? *More* uncomfortable? That will make them even more likely to consider us the enemy."

"Perhaps . . ." Tyen paused as he considered this. "Perhaps we should say, 'If you make us your enemy, we will be your enemy.'"

A small crease appeared between her brows. "What do you mean?"

"Maybe it's time we gave them an ultimatum."

"You've already threatened the Emperor."

"No, I mean threaten the leaders of the worlds we represent."

Her eyebrows rose. "With what?"

"For the Claymars, my absence. Judging by their unreasonable demands, either they believe Doum is stronger than it is, or they think I will – and can – defend it for them."

She frowned as she considered this. "I couldn't make the same threat to the Emperor, so what do I do instead?" She tapped her fingers on her shoulders. "I suppose it would truly foil the Emperor's ambitions if I swapped sides." Her eyes widened. "I could set up here, actually. Mosaic-makers come here for tiles, so there's a good chance they'd buy designs at the same time."

Tyen's heart leapt. If she swapped sides she would be living in Doum. "Would you do that?"

She pursed her lips. "I've not considered a more permanent home before, but I guess it only has to appear to be one long enough to dissuade the Emperor. Would you leave Doum, if the Claymars didn't cooperate?"

The fresh little flame of hope within him died. "Probably not."

Her smile faded. "Well, then we had better hope they don't call your bluff. Though . . . if they do, you could leave for a short time and return later."

"I doubt they'd welcome me back."

"They might, if you were their only hope of defence."

"It would be harder to monitor the situation from elsewhere."

"Yes, but I can tell Tarran what is going on and you could check with him." She shrugged, unfolded her arms and leaned back in her chair. "This might work. Or it might backfire on us. What is more likely?" Her question was not posed to him, but to herself.

"Do you want more time to consider it?"

She shook her head, slowly at first, then with more determination. "No. The people we represent aren't taking us seriously. I think we have to force them to decide whether they trust us or not, or we'll never get anywhere. If we're never going to get anywhere, then I'd rather they stopped wasting our time."

"Very well," he said. He had more to lose than her since she had no desire to live in Murai permanently, but her point that the Claymars wouldn't take the negotiations seriously until they decided whether they could trust him rang true. "Let's do it."

As she rose, he got to his feet. "I had best return. I will let you know what happens."

"And I you."

She smiled. "Good luck," she told him, and then she vanished.

For a moment, he stood staring at the place she had occupied, holding back his disappointment that she had made no suggestion they meet at Tarran's house again.

But then, maybe I'm supposed to make the second invitation.

Sitting down again, he drafted a short letter to the Claymars, then wrote out a final copy on a fresh piece of paper. Leaving it weighed down with a stone from the garden, he moved into the doorway of the shelter. Once Abler had emerged, Tyen told him of the letter, then pushed out of the world and retraced his path to his house.

The workers were gone, returning to their homes for the evening. He descended the stairs and considered the workroom and the unfinished wheels. If the Claymars did call his bluff and he left for a short time, would he lose all this?

If the Muraians invaded, it was likely he'd lose it anyway.

Sighing, he turned away, but as his gaze moved past the doorway he noticed a small object on the table beside the door where his workers left messages when he wasn't home.

A small parcel of a familiar size and shape. He walked over, tore away the wrapping and stared at the tile inside. His heart lifted and sank, over and over, as hope and dread struggled for dominance.

Dahli wanted to meet again.

CHAPTER 9

As always, Dahli left a trail of directions, each leading to the next, with no clue as to when Tyen would encounter him. The trail was not old, since a few of the directions had been left with people earlier in the morning or afternoon, or the night before. Yet some of the places Dahli had left them were oddly unreliable.

In particular, in worlds at war.

Such worlds had a stink about them, both physical and mental. It was the mingled stench of death, sickness, misery and terror. The smell was a warning not just of the risk of violence and horror, but of becoming trapped in a world stripped of magic.

Whenever Tyen had stumbled upon such signs before, he'd beaten a hasty retreat. Now he had to trust that Dahli wouldn't lead him somewhere dangerous. The trouble was, if Dahli had decided to eliminate Tyen for some reason, leading him into a dangerous or dead world was likely to be part of that plan. The next step would be to ambush Tyen with the help of several well-strengthened sorcerers. So when Tyen found himself in a weak, war-torn world, he quickly backtracked. Moving through three relatively peaceful, magically rich worlds, he gathered a good measure of magic from each. Fortified, he returned to the weaker world to continue along Dahli's path.

The scorched, silent landscape was threaded with lines of men, women and children of all ages, laden down with all manner of objects. From their minds he learned that they were fleeing a battle in the nearby city. The closest of these locals saw Tyen arrive, and though they gave him frightened stares they did not quicken or slow their pace.

Dahli's directions instructed Tyen to skim to the north to a city called Iuhin, so Tyen stopped only long enough to catch his breath, then skimmed away. Iuhin, the directions had explained, was surrounded by a park of ancient trees. On windy days the citizens, when considering a love match, would let loose scraps of cloth with their names stitched on, attached to paper sails. If their "wishes" became tangled in the trees, it was considered a good sign and confirmation of a good match.

He stopped to breathe on the outskirts of another city. People were fleeing this one too. From them he was surprised to learn that he was actually standing outside Iuhin. No green area surrounded a city wall. Instead, all was ash. Hundreds of columns of smoke billowed up from within a great circle of rubble. As he looked closer, he made out what was left of the trees – blackened skeletons clawing upwards from scorched ground.

He skimmed closer, arriving a hundred paces away to catch his breath again, creating a shield in case sorcerer warriors still lingered nearby. The air tasted of ash. People bent with age or sickness, or merely dazed with shock, straggled past him along a nearby road. Among them rolled carts pulled by teams of small, shaggy-pelted animals, piled high with fine furniture. Well-dressed men and women huddled on board. Drivers shouted and lashed out with whips when those on foot did not move out of the way fast enough.

So when shouting came from the direction of the city, Tyen did not pay attention. Neither did the people near him at first. But as it grew louder he detected a note of warning and soon all began to turn and search for the source. A man hurried in their direction, riding two of the small animals that hauled the carts, on a saddle designed to link the pair together. They were galloping as fast as they could bear him, ash erupting at each strike of their hooves.

As he bore down on them, the crowd fell silent. A soft distant tinkling, like thousands of clocks ticking, became audible. Shouts of alarm rang out, followed by screams. Suddenly everyone was running or shuffling as fast as they could away from the city.

Tyen looked past the approaching man and a movement drew his attention. Water was flowing over the ground, but with uncanny speed and defying gravity by flowing up the slope towards him. As it neared it grew sharp-edged and metallic. It steered towards the man as his steeds slowed to pick out a path across rough ground. Before Tyen could make out what it was, the stuff caught up with them. Fire blasted up and surrounded both man and beasts, so sudden and shocking that Tyen let out a shout of surprise.

A shrill sound escaped the beasts and man as they fell and began to writhe on the ground. More flares burst around them, and in moments they were still.

Stunned, Tyen could only watch as more of the deadly stuff flowed towards him. He resisted the terror urging him to run. Instead he widened his shield of stilled air to form a wall protecting the fleeing people, and strengthened it until it began to frost. Small, mechanical bodies surrounded him. Each had a spherical body, with six legs to carry it forward.

Insectoids!

No attempt had been made to make these look like insects or any living form, however. They were moving, self-targeting bombs, and no more. As each encountered his shield, it vanished in a great gust of flame. From beyond him came screams. He spun around. Another wave of insectoids coming from a different direction had reached the stragglers, the mechanical bodies crashing through them like a wave. Burning bodies thrashed. Tyen began smashing at the insectoids, but they moved too quickly and wove among the people so he was in danger of hitting them instead.

Those he struck still burst into flame. He smashed one just before it reached its intended victim, but the fire scorched the man's back anyway. Then another, hidden by the uneven ground, reached the injured man and finished him. Though Tyen tried again and again to stop the insidious little machines, there were too many of them, they were too fast, and they were too often hidden by the uneven ground, sneaking up on people before Tyen saw them.

Then suddenly there were none. Tyen looked around and his stomach dropped. All of the stragglers were dead. The screams he was hearing now were distant – another group running away. He sought the source of their fear and found another wave of death flowing towards them. With no people in the way, Tyen was able to smash at it until all of the insectoids had exploded.

Relieved that he had been able to help some of the people, Tyen turned to stare at the city, searching for other deadly floods of machines. He found none. Whoever had sent them must be there, however. Perhaps through that person he'd find out who had made such terrible weapons. He clenched his fists. When he did find whoever had distorted and perverted the gift of knowledge he had passed on to the worlds he would . . . his rising anger faltered.

Do what? Kill them?

Tyen sighed as his rage shrivelled and died. If not kill them, then what? Threaten them? Beg them to stop? Make them promise not to misuse his invention? He doubted anyone who'd made these flame machines would hold to such a vow once Tyen was gone.

Still, if I head for the city I might be able to get hold of one of the insectoids to study, and perhaps find another way to stop them. He'd have to find a way to stop them exploding when he touched them though.

He doubted anything was left of Dahli's message, but decided to check anyway. As he skimmed past the city fringe, he paused to examine one of the fallen and burned trees. And silently cursed.

127

Tyen follow, was slashed into the charred trunk, written in the Travellers' language.

He stopped to breathe and deliberate. Dahli would not lead him past dangerous worlds if he could avoid it. Perhaps he did not have the time to find a way around them. Perhaps the reason for summoning Tyen was too serious to waste time skirting this world. Baluka was already hunting for insectoids for Tyen to study.

I have to follow Dahli.

Taking a deep, smoky breath he pushed out of the world. Sure enough, a fresh path led away. He pushed himself along it. The scorched city faded to white.

The new world that materialised looked peaceful, much to his relief. He emerged on a flat plain divided into many fields of crops. The air was fresh. The sky was a clear greenish-blue. In a nearby field, several people were bent double, harvesting stalks of rust-orange grain and stuffing them into two huge baskets, which they hauled along as they worked.

It was a relief to be greeted by such a peaceful scene. But something about them set the back of his neck tingling. He withdrew from the world and skimmed closer. The workers' movements were sharp and hurried. As he arrived at the edge of the field, the closest of them saw him and jumped. They glanced over their shoulders then quickly turned back to their task.

Following their gaze, Tyen saw a woman walking along the centre of the field over the stubble of harvested crop, keeping pace with a large cart. Workers with full baskets had hauled them onto their shoulders, and were running to a cart to empty them.

The woman was staring at Tyen. As Tyen met her gaze, she made a half bow. Looking into her mind, Tyen saw that she was a weak sorcerer, but had until recently been employed by the city of her birth to take care of small tasks required of a sorcerer for the benefit of the citizens. It had been an easy, peaceful life.

Then emissaries had come from the Wexel, a warlike people

of a nearby world. Faced with certain defeat by a stronger force of sorcerers and their dreadful machines, the people of this world had joined forces with the invaders instead. That meant adopting the Wexel's enslavement of farmers and the poor to perform menial tasks. Attaching "latches" to the slaves ensured none could rise against their masters, new and old. The mechanism required a sorcerer to be present, so the woman's quiet life had been replaced by one far from home, stuck in fields like this or trying to keep order in the nearby slave quarters.

Seeing the device in the woman's mind, Tyen felt his heart sink. He looked at the nearest worker. Sure enough, something was nestled at the back of his neck, thin legs encircling the throat. The worker's discomfort radiated from his mind, and fear of the pain the machine would inflict at the instruction of the sorceress, or the instant death that came if anyone but her or her kind tried to remove it. Yet it could not see the hatred fermenting there. The woman no longer noticed, used to the resentment she saw in all of them. *Not my fault*, she thought as she yelled at them to hurry up. *Maybe it would have been better if we'd all died, fighting an unwinnable battle, than enslaving most of our people.*

Appalled, Tyen stood paralysed. He could not do anything to help them here and now, but he did not want to accept that. Even if he persuaded the woman to release these people, someone higher in this world's hierarchy would soon come to deal with them. Liberating them would require dealing with the masters, and the Wexel, and that would take time and careful planning. He had enough responsibility trying to stop Murai invading Doum.

A shout drew his attention back to the field. Seeing the woman striding forward, Tyen sought the source of her interest. Through her eyes he saw scorched and flattened crops. *More of this*, she thought. *It's as if someone has been writing on the ground with fire.*

Writing on the ground . . .? Tyen withdrew from the world a little and skimmed higher. Sure enough, characters had been burned into the field. First was an arrow, then the characters for "ruins", "pool", "gather magic" and "follow".

Keeping a hundred strides or so above the ground, he skimmed in the direction indicated by the arrow. The plain stretched endlessly, and he had to stop twice to breathe. At last he noticed variation within the crops, paler areas forming circles and rectangles. From above it looked much like the streets and buildings of a city. Then the first non-flat feature he'd seen in the world so far appeared. A small hillock rose above the plain, upon it fragments of walls, and at the summit was a small, smooth pond.

He paused beside the pool to refresh his lungs and gather more magic, then pushed into the place between. No path led out of the world, but as he moved to hover over the pool, he found a fresh one leading down under the surface. He followed, and once his head was under the level of the water, the trail led away from the world.

The watery light bleached to white, then new shapes began to gain colour around him. It was all rock, with only the occasional grey, wiry plant surviving in cracks here and there. He arrived with a jolt, his senses deceived by the paleness and dustiness of his surroundings into thinking he was further from arriving than he had been.

The air was dry and cold, and a constant breeze whistled in his ears. The ground was hard and covered in dust. Looking down, he saw another arrow, and characters carved into the stone. "Be frugal with magic, as you'll find little here."

A shiver ran down Tyen's spine. He looked around with his mind, and reeled. He hadn't noticed the void because no magic remained to contrast with it. Though . . . he noticed something like mist at the edge of his senses. Concentrating, he saw that it was magic, weak and thinly spread. It flowed from the direction Dahli's arrow pointed.

Pushing out of the world a little, he skimmed in that direction. The source was not far away. It might have taken a day to walk there. A darker smudge appeared in the pale landscape and at first he thought he was approaching a low forest of the twisted trees. But soon it fragmented, and he recognised tents, carts and piles of objects of all shapes and sizes from barrels to boxes to sacks.

Rising a little higher, he made out a huge encampment the size of a city. Most of the occupants lay sleeping, but a few were huddled together at the edges, within walls made up of objects piled on top of each other. Apart from a few individuals bearing armour and weapons, most of the encampment was made up of ordinary people.

Judging that he needed to breathe, Tyen dropped down to an area of sleepers, not wanting to frighten those still awake, but as he reached the ground he held back from arriving. The closest of the sleepers lay with eyes open. Eyes filmed with white and rimed with dust. He looked at the next, and next.

Dead. They were all dead. Suddenly the groups huddling within makeshift walls made sense. They were fortifications, protecting the few survivors of whatever disaster had occurred here.

He had no choice but to emerge in the world. Expecting a stench from so many bodies, he was surprised when the smell of decay was not that strong. No creatures, large or small, appeared to have been feasting on the corpses, and it was as dry and cold as where he had first arrived in this world.

What happened here? he wondered. *And why did Dahli want me to see this?* Because it seemed obvious that the sorcerer did – and perhaps the last two worlds too. Did Dahli want him to see the effect of weaponised insectoids? Looking around Tyen saw no sign of mechanical magic here. But the dead were of all ages, men and women, of varying wealth, much like those who had been fleeing the flame machines. He had not seen a city nearby, or even the tracks of such a large body of people. They must have arrived from another world. But why come here, where there was no magic, or water, or life? Tyen sought the minds of those sheltering within their fortifications, and found the answer.

These people had fled a great enemy in their world only to become trapped in here. Their sorcerers had united to find and transport their people to a new world. They'd mapped a path, making sure each world they passed through was safe and full of magic.

The sorcerers had claimed that this world was full of magic mere hours before they'd arrived. They said that someone must have stripped it all away since their visit. Their sorcerers had then gone in search of water, walking because there was no magic. Some suspected the sorcerers had left because they would be blamed for stranding their people in a dead world, doomed to die of thirst or starve.

Tyen had heard that worlds were being stripped of magic. Had these people been stranded deliberately, or had some unknown sorcerer greedily taken all the magic, not knowing that they were about to pass through this world?

It doesn't matter who is to blame, one of the survivors was thinking. *We'll all be dead soon.* His group's supplies would not last much longer, and they didn't have the strength to raid another's. *Look what we've descended to*, he thought, listing the crimes of his fellow survivors, who'd turned to murder, torture and even cannibalism. He knew he would not accept rescue now, if it came. It would mean living with the knowledge of what he had done. *I only wish I am dead before my brother returns – if he does – and can read the truth from my mind.* He stared off at a distant rocky formation, where he'd last seen his sibling walking away among the sorcerers, and wondered if he was already the last of his family alive.

Pushing out of the world, Tyen rose above the encampment and located the formation. He skimmed towards it, then stopped to search for minds. Nothing. He travelled on, hoping he had enough magic to do this and still get out of the world again.

Soon he'd travelled further than anybody could have walked in the time since the people had arrived, but found no minds. The sorcerers were probably dead.

Returning to the encampment, Tyen discovered that a battle had taken place in this absence. The last of the survivors lay dead of their wounds or exhaustion. Roaming through the camp, he searched for a clue for where Dahli had meant him to go next. Had the man known these people were here, but done nothing to help them? The possibility angered him. *But I didn't either. I could have taken the survivors out of this world straightaway, then returned to look for the sorcerers, if only I'd thought of it sooner.*

He reached the centre of the camp. A space had been cleared, bodies and tents pushed aside. On the ground a single character had been carved. "Follow." Dahli's instruction. Tyen pushed out of the world. The path was very fresh, as if Dahli had been there not very long before Tyen had arrived.

The pale world faded. A wide, oval grassy area replaced it. An arc of tiers or steps rose up it on three sides, suggesting basic seating for an audience. Objects were scattered over both. Looking closer, Tyen saw that they were the same sorts of sacks and boxes from the encampment. This was the world from which the people had fled.

Some sort of enemy had driven them away. He maintained a strong shield and climbed the stairs. A city came into view. Large public buildings and residences lined streets bordered by carefully maintained gardens. Colourful decorations, perhaps for a festival, still hung from lamp posts. Yet everything was quiet. Not one human roamed the thoroughfares.

Extending his mind, he found he was wrong. The city was not completely abandoned. Some had refused to leave, preferring to die at home than leave their world, or believing that the stories of the Raen's death were lies. A few were doubting their decision, wondering if they had time to reach one of the other groups in the world, waiting for their turn to be transported to their new home. But they doubted they'd get to one in time. They could only hope they'd survive, when the enemy returned.

Which, Tyen was finally able to discern, was not the conquering army of a neighbouring world. Once every fifty-two years of this world, lights streaked across the sky. Meteors, Tyen realised. The local people did not understand what they were, only that – before the Raen had struck a deal with the leaders of their world – the celestial attack had brought devastation. Only the Raen had been strong enough to protect the world, and in return their artisans competed to make the most beautiful of objects, the best of which he would choose for his palace.

But the Raen had not returned, and the sky fires had begun to fall. For the first time, the entire world had united, so that they could plan an evacuation to a new world.

So who stripped the first world on their journey, and why? Tyen wondered. Had someone in the destination world done it to stop the mass migration? Had an enemy of this world seen the opportunity to strike at them? Or had an enemy of the destination world sought to prevent an alliance between it and this world's people? It could even be a former rebel or rebels, exacting revenge on these people for their reliance on the Raen in the past.

"It's not often you see a newly abandoned city," a voice said.

Tyen spun around. Dahli was twenty paces away, sitting halfway down the stairs. He looked younger. Though his hair was still white, it and the beard had been cropped short.

"Why?" Tyen asked.

Dahli's eyebrows rose. "Why is it abandoned? Haven't you yet read the minds of those left behind? Or of the stranded escapees in the previous world?"

"Why are you showing me this?" Tyen clarified.

Dahli's lips pressed into a humourless smile. "Because I don't think you'd look at the proof if I told you where it was."

"Proof of what?"

"The destruction the Raen's absence has created. The chaos."

Tyen scowled. "You've only shown me what supports your claims."

"I'm sure Baluka would show you only examples of worlds that have benefited from the Raen's absence, too. What *you* need to do is to seek the whole picture. Or look into my mind. I cannot lie to you, after all."

Tyen was already reading Dahli's mind. He knew that Dahli believed everything he had said. But Dahli could be wrong. He could be seeing what he wanted to see.

"Can you ignore all this suffering?" Dahli asked. "Can you allow it to continue?"

"You have caused enough of it yourself over the centuries," Tyen retorted.

He instantly regretted it. If Dahli thought Tyen disapproved of him, he might no longer seek Tyen's help – and then Tyen would have no excuse to keep an eye on the man.

Thankfully, Dahli only nodded. "I have. I have done terrible things in the belief that the worlds would benefit, in the long term. That Valhan's orders were just. I'll admit, sometimes they weren't. Valhan was by no means infallible, but he was very rarely wrong."

Dahli's unwavering belief made it hard to deny what he claimed. *But Baluka is just as certain the worlds will flourish without the Raen.*

"Look at what's happening, Tyen," Dahli continued. "Then you'll know that sacrificing one life in exchange for the safety of thousands of worlds is not such an unreasonable act."

Tyen crossed his arms. "Is this why you wanted to see me?"

Dahli looked away. "No." His shoulders rose and fell, then his back straightened. "If I give you Valhan's notes on his experiments in resurrection – and let you use a method and body you approve of – will you do it?"

Tyen stared at the man. *He's offering me everything the Raen knew about resurrection.* He was suddenly conscious of Vella's pouch resting lightly against his chest, under his shirt. *Everything she needs to regain the life stolen from her. But the price is bringing the Raen back.*

He looked into Dahli's mind. The man intended to keep his side of the bargain. Even if it risked giving up the secrets he guarded, only to find Tyen could not resurrect the Raen because he would not kill anyone to do it.

It was also his last attempt to persuade Tyen to help him. If Tyen refused, Dahli would begin to search the worlds for someone else strong and clever enough to bring Valhan back – or attempt it by using several strong sorcerers instead of one powerful one. It might take a long time – maybe many cycles – but he'd find a way eventually.

Tyen realised he was breathing quickly. *If I don't agree to this, Dahli will stop meeting me. I won't be able to keep an eye on him. I won't know if the Raen is about to return.*

If he did agree, he would be the most hated man in the worlds. Yet he would become a hero to as many. *Well, I'm already hated by most of the former. At least the latter would stop trying to kill me.*

Tyen realised, then, that he didn't care how either side regarded him. He'd only ever tried to reduce the harm of whatever action he took. So if Dahli was going to find a way to resurrect the man eventually, would it lead to more or less harm if Tyen was involved?

Yes, he realised. *If the Raen returns and learns I refused to help Dahli, he'll kill me. He'll kill Rielle whether I bring him back or not. Unless . . . unless I can make a deal with him. Bringing him is no small favour, so perhaps I can ask for one in return. Perhaps I can ask for her life in exchange.* The chance of the Raen agreeing to such a deal seemed slim, but that was better than no chance at all. *If I help Dahli, I will know if and when he is going to succeed. I can warn Rielle. She might be able to find a place to hide before the Raen returns.*

She wouldn't like that he was helping Dahli, but when he explained why, she would understand. Though it would be better that he didn't tell her straightaway. If it turned out that he couldn't resurrect the Raen, then she need never know that he had even attempted it.

But if I can . . . I'll make sure it takes a long time, Tyen thought. *If I draw out the experiments and do multiple tests every stage, she'll have plenty of time to find a safe place to hide.*

He would warn Baluka too. Perhaps his friend could help Rielle, and she him. Perhaps Baluka would be able to raise another army, and this time defeat the Raen.

Footsteps sounded behind Tyen. He turned to find Dahli climbing the stairs.

"You're hesitating," the man noted. "Yet I have offered you the terms you've demanded all along." His expression was unreadable, but Tyen could see his mistrust growing.

"I am considering it," Tyen admitted. "Weighing up the consequences."

"Like?"

"I will be taking a side."

Dahli nodded. "Obviously."

"I'll need to learn pattern shifting."

"I will teach you."

Tyen considered the sorcerer. He knew that Dahli had taught this to only one person before: Rielle. Dahli was thinking that he'd needed to see into Rielle's mind in order to train her quickly. It was doubtful Tyen would agree to that.

"Thank you for the offer," Tyen replied, "but I have another way to learn it."

Dahli frowned. "Someone else?"

"In a manner of speaking."

"The book?" Dahli's brows lowered even further. "That may take a very long time."

"It might; it might not." Tyen spread his hands. "I will not let you into my mind unless there is no other choice."

"But we . . ." Dahli grimaced. "I don't know how long the hand will hold its information. Valhan was unsure of its permanence."

"Will another cycle make a difference?"

Dahli sighed. "I don't know."

"Before I begin learning pattern shifting I will need to . . . make arrangements. And afterwards . . . where will we work?"

"I have a house in a world sympathetic to our cause, where we should find all the supplies you need."

Tyen nodded. He'd have to leave Doum for a while. If he wasn't going to tell Rielle what he was doing yet, he'd have to come up with another plausible reason. He wanted to spend more time with her before he left. Visiting her when he was working for Dahli would put her at risk. He might lead Dahli straight to her, or to Tarran.

He also needed to settle this conflict between Doum and Murai.

"I can't say how long I'll need," Tyen told the man. "Perhaps a quarter cycle. Perhaps more."

The sorcerer's mouth pressed into a thin line. Impatience and scepticism warred with hope, but both fell before resignation. He needed Tyen's willing cooperation. And that reminded him of another matter he'd intended to raise.

"Very well. Before you go, I can tell you that my people have learned that a group of rebels who have split from the Restorers, claiming they are too soft on the former allies, have decided to track you down. They know you carry a treasure that contains the secret of agelessness." His mouth thinned in a grim smile. "I can deal with them, if you wish."

Tyen paused. It was tempting. He could do without the constant worry that sorcerers might be hunting for him. If they succeeded in finding him, it could make saving Doum and restoring Vella more complicated and dangerous. But . . .

"No," he replied. "If you do, there will always be a risk – even a small one – that Baluka will discover you did so for me. He'd have to wonder why you'd do me such a favour."

"I won't require you to spy on Baluka any more if you do this work for me."

Tyen shook his head. "I suspect the connections I have will prove useful in future, if not for you then for me. It might even help us with our work."

Dahli nodded. "Then I take it you are agreeing to my terms."

"Yes." It came out as a sigh.

"Then let me know when you are free to begin."

Tyen nodded. "I will."

"Do you know where you will go to learn pattern shifting?"

"Not yet."

"I can tell you of a few magically rich worlds that might be suitable."

"I'd rather nobody knew where I was."

Dahli's mouth twitched. Almost a smile. "Very well. Keep me informed. If there are any materials or tools you know you will need, send me a list. I will acquire them in anticipation."

He stook a step back, then began to fade. In a few moments, he had disappeared.

Turning away, Tyen walked to the very top of the stairs and gazed down at the city. When the meteor showers came, some of those left behind would survive. They must have before, or there would be no recollection of a time before the Raen came.

Could he stop the meteor showers? He had no idea how the Raen had done so, and an attempt might make things worse. Perhaps, instead, he could do something about the other groups, waiting to be transported to a new world. He would tell Baluka of this place. He couldn't imagine his friend abandoning them to the meteors out of revenge for them relying on the Raen for their survival.

Right now he needed to get back to Doum. The Claymars might respond quickly to his threat to leave. They might respond badly.

I can't help all the worlds, he reminded himself. *But I can help Doum. I can help Rielle survive when the Raen returns. In the process, I might even find a way to restore Vella.*

Even so, all he felt was a hollow in the depths of his stomach. It was an old but familiar sensation.

It's because I've been in this situation before, making a deal with a dangerous, ruthless sorcerer, knowing that I can't stop them, but hoping to reduce the harm they do.

Only this time he wouldn't be spying. He would be experimenting and building something, this time with flesh rather than machinery.

That didn't make him feel any better, so he pushed out of the world and started the journey home.

CHAPTER 10

Y*ou will need a world unusually rich in magic*, Vella wrote. *Rich enough that you can make the transformation as well as leave when you are done.*

An unpopulated world, Tyen added. *One people don't travel to or through, either. I don't want to be responsible for stranding people in a world.* A world with no or few people was unlikely to contain much magic, but occasionally one became inhospitable to humans through a disaster of some kind, leaving it unpopulated but not yet depleted in magic.

Tyen thought of the world of the meteors. It had been rich with magic, no doubt because the population had been creating treasures as payment for the Raen's assistance. He had sent a message to Baluka alerting him to that world's situation, so it may have been evacuated since his visit. However, once news of the newly depopulated world spread, other sorcerers would come to take the magic. If Tyen was there when they did, they might leave him stranded.

While you are there you will be in danger from the meteors, Vella pointed out.

Which raised another question. *How long will it take for me to learn pattern shifting?*

It could take a quarter cycle or many cycles. The process will be faster if you can spend almost all of your time concentrating on the task. The help Dahli offered was more than just the knowledge you require. You need someone to provide food, remove distractions and protect you when you are vulnerable.

I'd have to trust whoever that was. I don't trust Dahli.

Then who do you trust?

Tyen paused and slowly shook his head. *I'd trust Baluka, but he has the Restorers to look after. I might trust Rielle in future, but I don't really know her that well yet and someone should stay and watch the Emperor. Tarran would be trustworthy, I think, but he can't abandon his students for a half cycle. Do I really need someone else to be there?*

If you prepare well, you can minimise distractions. Choose a location where food is in abundance or will not spoil quickly.

An abundance of food probably means an abundance of humans. He sighed. *There has to be another way to do this. Could I gather magic and take it to the location I settle in?*

You could. It will take a long time to gather and deposit enough. In the meantime, other sorcerers might find and use that magic.

Not if it is known to be a dead, unpopulated world. How long would it take?

That depends on how much magic you take from other worlds to fill it. If you don't want the occupants to notice the depletion of their world, it may take several cycles.

He shook his head. *I thought learning pattern shifting without a teacher was going to be the hard part. Anyway, I can't start anything until these negotiations are over.* His stomach grumbled – more a sensation than a sound. *I'd better get something to eat. Goodbye, Vella.*

Until next time.

He closed her covers and slipped her back into the pouch hanging around his neck. Tucking it under his shirt, he buttoned up the vest he'd begun wearing to conceal her. It meant he was a little overdressed for Glaemar's climate, but his workers and the locals assumed he wanted to look more formal because he could be called on at any moment to negotiate with Rielle again. Some approved, while others thought he had become a little self-important since taking on the task.

A few of his employees were still in the workshop downstairs, finishing off an urgent order. He asked if they wanted him to bring them back some food, but they were nearly done and had meals to return home to. Leaving them applying the last details to the wheels, he headed to one of his favourite local eating establishments.

It was a short walk away, but the streets were busy with Glaemarans setting out for their evening meal. Before he'd reached his destination, he heard his name called by an unfamiliar voice. He sought out the source, and found a messenger hurrying towards him.

"Tyen Wheelmaker," the man said. "You are required immediately at the Claymar House to meet Rielle of Murai."

Tyen's heart skipped a beat. He nodded. "Thank you."

He glanced wistfully at the door of the restaurant before he pushed out of the world. So far, the food served at his meetings with Rielle had been good, but it did not live up to what he could buy in his neighbourhood.

Following his usual route, he skimmed across the worlds to the Island of Tiles. He found Rielle waiting on the bridge, looking as beautiful as ever. She was talking to Abler. The official radiated admiration – and regret that such an elegant woman was representing Murai rather than Doum. He found Tyen a bit insipid and untidy in comparison.

Too important to some, not enough to others, Tyen mused.

"Good evening, Rielle Lazuli," Tyen said, bowing to her as the pair turned to face him. He nodded to Abler. "Abler Tithen."

"Tyen Wheelmaker," the official replied. "I must congratulate you. The Emperor has agreed to a modified version of the terms you and Rielle of Murai presented to him."

"And the Claymars have approved it, with some changes the Emperor has conceded to," Rielle added, her eyes bright.

Tyen looked from one to the other. "Truly?"

"Yes," Rielle replied, then laughed at his surprise. "I was as startled."

"The final document will be duplicated tonight, by Doumian time," Abler told them. "Then presented for signing and stamping tomorrow." His lips widened in a formal smile. "At which point your task is complete, Tyen Wheelmaker. I and the Claymars thank you for your patience and persistence in this difficult task."

Tyen nodded. "It was the least I could do for a world and people so welcoming, and that I hope will have a stable and prosperous future."

Abler turned to Rielle. "And we extend our thanks to you, Rielle of Murai, for your common sense and fairness, and tolerance of a people you must have found stubborn and contrary at times."

Her smile was breathtaking. "I hope my efforts were of benefit to both Doum and Murai." She looked at Tyen. "I know my mentor, a man of great wisdom, will be proud."

Her gaze lingered a little long, and Tyen's heartbeat quickened. *She wants me to meet her at Tarran's house again.* He decided he would go straight there next. Even if he'd misinterpreted her look, he would still enjoy a chat with Tarran.

"If there is no other matter you wish me to discuss, I will go now," she said.

Abler shook his head. "You will, no doubt, wish to return to your world and perhaps join arrangements to celebrate your success. I wish you well."

"Thank you." She faded from sight.

The official looked at Tyen. "Is there anything you wish to convey to the Claymars?"

Tyen considered. "Only my thanks and congratulations. And . . . that with all the terrible conflicts and strife occurring in other worlds, it gives me hope to see two resolving their differences without bloodshed and destruction. I hope other worlds learn from their example."

Abler nodded. "I will tell them."

"Thank you. Is there anything else you need from me?"

The man shook his head. "You're free to go."

Tyen pushed out of the world. He retraced his steps to Glaemar, as it was what would be expected of him, but when he reached the city he did not return to his workshop. Instead he returned to the place between worlds, dove through the core of the world and left Doum.

When he reached Tarran's world, he approached the lake from a different direction than during his previous visit. It was a clear night there, the sea a rippling blanket reflecting the stars. He found his former path and travelled along it away from his destination for a while, before departing from it and carefully concealing his trail, skimming downwards until he was under the surface of the water. Then he approached the spire of rock from below. As the rock obscured all, he sensed another trail. A fresh trail. It led upwards. Tyen followed, and as he skimmed out from the spire, the walls of the courtyard where he'd met Rielle on their last visit appeared.

He emerged and paused until his lungs stopped dragging in air. Muffled voices reached him from somewhere within the house, to his left. Two lamps were burning within the courtyard. He headed for the courtyard, and his guess proved correct as he found Rielle and Tarran relaxing on a wooden bench.

"Tyen," Rielle said. "We'd given up on you."

Tyen spread his hands. "It takes time to conceal my path."

Her eyes brightened with interest. "Does it really?"

Tarran glanced at her briefly. "Welcome back, Tyen. Come join us. I've arranged for a nice meal to be brought. This is worth celebrating."

"The agreement between Murai and Doum?" Tyen asked as he walked towards the door. Rielle led the way through the house.

"Of course. What else?"

"Nothing. Just checking in case some other scheme of yours has succeeded."

The old man chuckled. "I'd let you know if it had."

They reached a room with a small table on which the beginnings of a meal had been laid out. Rielle glanced back at Tyen as she entered. "You must show me how you do that one day."

He frowned. "Do what?"

She and Tarran sat down. "Hide your path."

He raised his eyebrows, pretending to not understand as he took one of the empty chairs.

She smiled. "I know you can do it. I was intrigued by the absence of another arrival path, after you came here last time. So I checked the place where Tarran said you had appeared. I found no disturbance in the place between."

"Ah."

"Drink?" Tarran asked.

"Yes, please."

The old sorcerer poured a steaming purple liquid from a jug into a pottery mug, and handed it to Tyen. The drink was sweet and very alcoholic. Rielle made a ticking sound with her tongue.

"'Ah'?" she said. "Is that all you can say?"

Tyen considered, then nodded.

She made a noise of disgust, but then lifted her mug and smiled. "I guess we all have secrets we'd rather not share."

"Here's to small but important victories," Tarran said, raising his glass.

"Small?" Rielle's eyebrows rose.

"Yes," the old sorcerer replied. "Signing an agreement is easy. A motion of the hand and the application of ink. Sticking to the agreement is the greater challenge."

"If we wait until they've proven they can stick to it, we'll be waiting a long time to have our celebration."

"Indeed," Tarran replied. "So we drink to celebrate what milestones we reach, no matter how small."

"Or to commiserate with each other for setbacks," Rielle added.

"Which means there's always a good excuse for a drink," Tyen finished along with her.

She smiled at him. "What do you think of our little victory, Tyen?"

"I have to admit," he replied. "It was easier than I expected."

"Too easy?" Tarran asked.

"Perhaps. Does this make it more likely the agreement will fail?"

The old man shrugged. "No way to know. If it was in response to Rielle's threat to switch sides or Tyen's to leave, then perhaps not."

Tyen's heart sank a little at the old man's words. *What will happen when I leave to learn pattern shifting? If we're the cause of the two worlds cooperating, will the Emperor begin scheming again?* As servants arrived, each moving around the table carrying a large serving bowl, Tarran and Rielle began filling their plates. Caught up in his thoughts, Tyen did not notice that one servant had been standing at his elbow for some time until the man cleared his throat.

"Sorry!" Tyen grabbed the spoon and hurried to catch up.

"What is it?" Rielle asked. "Something has you lost in thought."

He glanced at her, then at his former mentor. "I have decided it is time I became ageless."

The old man's eyes brightened. "Finally!"

"Ah," Rielle said, her solemn tone in contrast to Tarran's enthusiasm.

Tarran looked at her, amused. "'Ah'?"

"He can't do it in Doum," she explained. "He must find a world rich in magic but where its loss won't be missed." She looked at him. "What changed your mind?"

Tyen looked away. "I have a promise to keep, and it looks like I can't do that without knowing how to pattern-shift."

At a knowing look from Tarran, Tyen looked deeper and saw that the old man had guessed what the promise was. *The book,* he was thinking. *He's found a way.* Tyen hid his dismay, knowing that Rielle would have seen Tarran's thought.

One of her eyebrows rose. "Do you need a teacher? I've not tried to teach anyone before, but I have a fairly good idea what is involved."

Tyen shook his head. "I know what is involved, and I'd rather not risk that anyone else be stranded in a world without magic."

"Then you must find the right world," she advised. "Do you have one in mind?"

He shook his head.

"I know of one that would suit. A desert world, unpopulated and rich in magic. The Traveller family I lived with for a while used to visit it, but it's a long way from their path now and they don't intend to return."

"A desert world."

"Yes. You would have to take enough water and food to last a quarter cycle or more. I could visit you when it is due to run out, bringing enough magic to get us both out of the world if you've depleted it."

Tyen paused to consider her offer. He could see no reason to reject it, though he ought to ask Vella for advice before he accepted.

"I'll think about it. About the world, not your help, that is. Wherever I go, your help will be most welcome." He smiled, hoping that he was hiding his apprehension well. *What will I tell her when I leave to join Dahli?* He'd thought about little else since meeting with the man. Here, in Rielle and Tarran's company, agreeing to help Dahli seemed crazy. *But if I hadn't, Dahli would be seeking another helper. If he found one, and resurrected the Raen, we wouldn't know until Valhan appeared to exact his revenge on us both. Better I have the chance to warn Rielle and Baluka and an opportunity to persuade Valhan to let Rielle live. At least this way I can prevent someone being killed in order for the Raen to have their body. If I can find another way, that is.*

She frowned. "Something worries you?"

He searched for another plausible reason for the anxiety she had detected. "Will Doum and Murai honour the agreement if I am absent? I didn't want to leave until the negotiations were over and peace was assured, but I can't help wondering how long it will last without me."

"I will still be in Murai," she reminded him. "I will make sure the Emperor knows that my threat still stands. If Murai invades Doum, I will switch sides."

Tyen nodded slowly. "That should dissuade him."

"That's a generous offer," Tarran told Rielle. "What of your determination to never interfere in a world?"

"I already have, haven't I? It would be wrong to say I'd protect a world only to abandon it."

Tarran looked at Tyen, thinking that Rielle ought to receive something in return for her efforts. Tyen considered what he could give.

"Would knowing how to hide your path be a worthy exchange for Rielle's protection?"

Tarran drew in a quick breath. "That's . . . more than I expected."

Tyen chuckled. "Not if Rielle ensures I don't become stranded in a dead world."

Her wide smile brightened the room. "You don't have to demand payment. But being able to hide my path would mean I wouldn't lead anyone to whatever world you learn pattern shifting in." She glanced at Tarran. "And I can tell you everything I remember from my lessons." She leaned forward. "Is there anything in particular you would like to know?"

"Stop! Not here! You will make me jealous! Take this." Tarran picked up the bottle and handed it to Tyen. "Then both of you go down to the lookout."

"But we can't leave you here to finish alone!" Rielle objected, though their plates were now empty. "What about dessert?"

"I'll send it down for you," Tarran said.

Rielle caught Tyen's gaze, and her mouth quirked into a familiar mischievous smile. Tyen's heart skipped a beat, then began to race. As Tyen took the bottle from Tarran, he smiled in reply.

"Well, I suppose it is well past your bedtime, Tarran," Tyen said. "I wouldn't want to keep you up late."

Tarran's brows rose in affront. "It's not sleep that I crave, but some time to myself."

Rielle grinned. "Well, then make sure you don't nod off in your armchair again, trying to prove a point. I can't always be around to heal your sore neck."

He rose and waved his arms. "Go! Out! I'll have no cheeky young things mocking me for my age in my very own house!"

She laughed, rose and held out a hand to Tyen. Taking it, he let her haul him to his feet and towards the door.

"Come on, Tyen," she said. "Tarran needs his sleep and we have a *great deal* to talk about."

As she pulled him through the doorway, Tyen glanced back to see Tarran smirking at them. At the last moment, before Tyen moved out of sight, one of the old man's eyes closed in a very deliberate wink.

PART TWO

RIELLE

CHAPTER 1

While designing mosaics demanded most of Rielle's attention, making them left her mind free to think. On a good day she found the latter relaxing, but lately the slow process of finding the next tile made her restless.

The trouble was, after the challenge of negotiating an agreement between Murai and Doum, her quiet life among the artisans now seemed a little, well, boring. Yet she needed the work. Hiding from Dahli and his friends limited her ability to earn an income. Using her remarkable strength could have earned her great wealth, but also drawn attention. She'd turned to her other talents for work, but gaining employment as an artist or weaver wasn't easy when she was a stranger and foreigner wherever she went, and when she did, it only paid a modest income at best.

Fortunately, ageless sorcerers weren't uncommon, across the worlds, so she'd paid for her tuition from Tarran with healing. It was Tarran's insistence that she learn his style of calligraphy that had led her to the mosaic-makers. With the leftover ink, she had painted small scenes on scraps of paper, which Tarran had kept. A former student visiting the old man had been impressed by them, and taken a few to his world to show Bowlen, the master of the mosaic-makers. Soon after, the group began commissioning designs from her.

The artisans were a diverse group who moved from world to

world, going wherever commissions took them. Murai was the third world she had worked in since joining them. Her official task was to paint designs, but since it was faster than mosaic-making, she'd been taught the basics and set to work on smaller, less important areas like borders and corners.

Bowlen had told her she should not get involved in local politics and strife. She'd agreed wholeheartedly. He had not been happy when the Emperor had insisted she negotiate with Doum on Murai's behalf.

If it weren't for Tyen I'd have refused. Sometimes local politics and strife gets involved with you.

Bowlen had even gone so far as to threaten to seek designs elsewhere. When she tried to use this as an excuse to avoid becoming Murai's negotiator, the Emperor had made it clear that if the group no longer gave her work, then he would find new mosaic-makers for her to work with. It saved her job, but did not endear her to the artisans. So she'd been immensely relieved when the negotiations concluded and she could start to mend her relationship with them. They'd only given her monotonous work to do since then, and no designs, to make it clear she must earn their respect again. She worked diligently, making sure her work was faultless, and reminding herself that Tyen's task was far more boring and challenging.

A quarter cycle has passed since he started, she thought as she searched through her trays of tiles. *Not long enough for him to have learned pattern shifting yet, I suspect. Dahli said it takes longer for most people, and Tyen may be handicapped by learning from a book.*

She was impatient for him to return. Impatient to resume getting to know him. Her pulse quickened when she thought of the times they'd spent together in the cave, talking and love-making.

Am I in love? she wondered.

She was not infatuated in the way she had been with Izare.

154

She wasn't sure she could be. The girl who had fallen for Izare had been inexperienced and innocent. The woman she was now was not. She wanted different things. What those things were, she wasn't completely sure of yet. All she knew was that it couldn't be the same way it had been before, least of all because she feared that going down the same path might mean it ended the same way.

She tossed the tile she'd been considering back into the tray. It was almost perfect for the gap in the design, but Bowlen would never let her progress to larger designs if he caught her making easy choices.

I like Tyen. I want to see more of him. I haven't felt that way in quite a while. It wasn't that she hadn't taken lovers since Valhan's death, but she'd chosen only those men who, like her, wanted a passing encounter and no commitment. Men who didn't want to know her life story, or even her real name. Men she didn't have to trust to keep her secrets.

But Tyen already knew about Qall. He'd helped her save the boy. Perhaps, of all people, he was one she *could* trust. And yet she hesitated. Perhaps only because not being able to read his mind made her nervous.

It was strangely exciting as well. She liked that none of her stray thoughts could bother him. They would be like ordinary people. As ordinary as two people with dangerous secrets could be.

She did wish he could be a little bit more talkative. *He may be a little reticent, but that doesn't mean he isn't attentive. For someone who can't read my mind, he's rather good at interpreting non-vocal cues.* She smiled as heat spread through her blood at the memory.

Her eyes fell on a tile of exactly the right shape and colour for the space she needed to fill. Using tweezers, she dropped it into place. It was perfect. Sometimes it was worth taking the time to find the perfect piece. It would take more careful choices before the mosaic was finished, however. Examining the design, she considered which shape to look for next, then began searching.

So far Tyen had not expressed anything more than the passion of a lover. Perhaps he never would. She believed that pining for someone who didn't love you was pointless. Having seen the pain such a situation had caused Dahli, she was determined to never fall into the same trap. She could not offer any commitment anyway. She had made a promise to protect Qall. Keeping him from Dahli was her highest priority. Tyen had his own prior commitment, too.

Tarran believed that the promise Tyen had referred to, and his reason for learning pattern shifting, was to restore the body of the woman in the book he carried, Vella. Tyen had told Rielle about her during one of their nights at the cave. She had been fascinated to learn of this woman transformed by Valhan's Predecessor, who was only conscious when held by a person, and absorbed all the knowledge of everyone she touched.

Tarran believed a bond existed between Tyen and the book. He said it was akin to the dependence a student feels towards a mentor, or the friendship that forms when two people have been through trials together. He didn't voice his suspicion that Tyen might be a little in love with the woman in the book.

Though Rielle would never discount any possibility after more than five cycles of reading minds, she didn't think Tyen had a carnal fetish for books. If it was an attraction, it wasn't physical. Yet. *Maybe he wants to restore her body so he can find out if he does love her. Maybe I'm the reason he wants to know.*

She shook her head, amused and a little ashamed at the vanity of the thought, and made herself pay more attention to her work . . . and blinked as she realised she was looking at exactly the shape and colour of tile she sought. Plucking it out of the pile, she set it in place. The odds were against her finding the perfect match twice in a row, but it was not impossible. Could she make it three? She turned to the piles again.

Her thoughts returned immediately to Vella. What intrigued Rielle most was that Tyen touched the book at all. It – she – must contain all his secrets. He made himself vulnerable so that the woman inside could be aware. It was his treasure but also a great weakness.

Would Vella lose the ability to absorb knowledge once she had a body? Would she remember everything she had stored, or would it all be lost? By restoring Vella's body, Tyen might lose everything that made the book a treasure. Tyen must have considered the possibility, yet he still wanted to do it. Perhaps because he cared more for the woman trapped inside than for her value as a rarity and tool. Perhaps because he cared about right and wrong.

Could I help him resurrect her?

Rielle frowned. *If it involved killing anyone – no.* She wanted to believe that Tyen would never do that. After all, he had helped her save Qall because he disagreed with sacrificing a person to give another life.

She looked down at the tile she was holding. Her thoughts had strayed again. She examined it, looking for flaws, then rejected it. Where it fell lay a similar tile. A better match. Placing the tile on the design, she moved it into position. The tile's colours matched the design, and the shape complemented those next to it. She slipped it into place.

She straightened and stretched her back as she considered the work that remained. Only a few more tiles were needed. The design portrayed fruits from neighbouring worlds that Muraians considered exotic. They spilled from a typical Doumian pottery bowl. The mosaic would be a corner piece, more elaborate than a simple border design but not as challenging as the picture both would frame.

In the corner of her eye, she saw Bowlen glance towards her. He was thinking that she was working slowly today. Making herself concentrate only on the mosaic, she selected the last few tiles for the border square and set them in position. After a critical look at the whole, she plucked out a few tiles that weren't working and found replacements. Only then, when she was satisfied that she could not improve it at all, did she set the tile trays aside.

In her mind she compiled a list of what she required next. A square of cloth and glue to stick it to the top of the tiles first. That would allow the mosaic to be lifted in one piece and mortared into its final position. When the mortar was dry, the cloth would be removed and caulk worked into the cracks. Yet before any of that could happen, Bowlen must approve of her work. She looked up and located him, now at the far side of the work area.

As she took a step towards him, a sound unlike anything she'd heard in this world brought everyone's heads up. It was low, but rapidly escalated to a roar.

Then everyone and everything, including Rielle, was knocked to the floor.

Pain blossomed in her shoulder, but faded quickly as her body used magic to heal. Her first thought was to still the air above the artisans in case the roof was about to fall. That done, she scrambled to her feet, wiping dust from her eyes. The pillars holding up the palace roof were intact, to her relief. Tiles cascaded from her clothes and skin and hair. A clatter and tinkle surrounded her as others rose and dusted themselves off.

A brief moment of stillness followed as the artisans took in the devastation that had replaced months of work. Only the sturdier tables remained standing, but what had been on them was scattered. The mysterious force had lifted the edges of the heavy paper Rielle had painted her design on and hurled it and the carefully arranged tiles away.

Mutters and curses cut the air, most at the mess and the loss of hundreds of days of work, but also at a multitude of small injuries.

Why didn't I think to shield us? Rielle wondered. The expressions of the other sorcerers in the group reflected the same bitter regret. *It happened too fast and we had no idea what the sound meant.*

Which had been . . . exactly *what?*

Straightening, she turned to face the direction the force had come from and searched with her eyes and mind. First, she saw movement several hundred paces away. A crowd of people was forming. They were servants, confused and frightened. They had no idea what had happened either. As she sought minds further away, her ears picked up a new noise. It was distant and varied. Not the hum of voices. More like the roll of thunder.

A breeze set her skin prickling. The palace was drafty, but this was odd. After a moment, she realised why: she had never felt any movement of air coming from the front of the vast building. Ventilation always came from the side. From the river.

Her mind's search stopped finding confused servants and started finding terrified ones. They all believed the palace was under attack.

"From what?" she muttered as she stretched further, all the way to the formal entrance to the building where, at last, she found the mind of a guards who knew what was happening. His thoughts as he fled his post sent a shock through her.

This battle is not for the likes of me to fight. Only the palace sorcerers can defend us. They had better hurry up or there'll be no palace left to save! Through his eyes, she saw groups of plainly dressed men and women drawing closer to a gaping hole in the palace wall. Their uniform was familiar . . .

"Doumians," spoke a voice close to Rielle. Startled, she brought her attention back to her surroundings. The nearest group of artisans was looking at her, making no effort to conceal disapproval and suspicion. She claimed to have negotiated peace between the two worlds. Clearly, she had failed. Perhaps this had been her goal all along. She opened her mouth to protest, then closed it again as she saw that no words would ever entirely convince them the latter was not true.

And they were right: she *had* failed. Doum was invading Murai. The Claymars had broken the agreement. She scowled. *All while Tyen is worlds away. I doubt that's a coincidence.*

She had promised to defend Doum if something happened while he was away. *No, I promised to defend Doum if Murai invaded, not the other way around.* Yet her determination to remain out of local strife wavered.

"Rielle Lazuli," a voice boomed.

She turned. An official was approaching. As she saw his intention to deliver to her the Emperor's summons, she straightened and forced her face into what she hoped was a dignified yet appropriately grim expression.

"Yes?"

"The Emperor demands your presence."

She allowed herself a small grimace. "Yes, I expect he does."

He turned on his heel and marched away, intending to force her to run to keep up. She resisted, keeping her strides long and purposeful to give herself time to consider what she would say to the Emperor. *That depends on what is behind the Doumians' attack. Is it retaliation for another Muraian attack? Or is Doum invading Murai? Either way, the Claymars must have found a way to overcome their smaller numbers and strength. Perhaps by making an alliance with another world.*

She sent her mind out, searching for the minds of Doumian sorcerers. When she found one, his thoughts were on the battle and she only managed to pick up a small amount of information. What she saw nearly made her stagger to a halt before the audience chamber.

Invasion had been the Claymars' intention all along. The four most powerful of them had begun preparations for war even before the Muraian merchants had attacked the market, knowing that when they refused to lower their prices the merchants would retaliate. Spies had told them that the Emperor had discussed expanding his empire into Doum. He just needed an excuse.

Doum's sorcerers were trained in a worldwide system that gave them basic magical education in all areas before they specialised in the fields their extended artisan families required. The Claymars kept in contact with those sorcerers in order to offer extended training in different areas, from healing to martial skills. In the wake of the attack on the market, most of Doum's sorcerers had taken up the offer of free battle training so they'd be ready in case of another strike

Tyen and Rielle's attempt at negotiation had given them the time to do it. When the Claymars had called for sorcerers to support their "solution" to the threat from Murai, nearly all of the worlds' sorcerers had volunteered, not realising that invasion was the *Claymars'* intention.

Either Tyen never looked for the Claymars, or he never found them. Rielle doubted he'd have left, if he'd known what they were planning. *At least . . . I hope he didn't know.*

Stepping into the audience room, Rielle approached the Emperor, stopping to bow when she reached the expected place and moment. All the while, her mind raced.

The Claymars had never intended to honour any agreement. They could have kept us in negotiations for as long as they needed to prepare, though the longer they did, the greater chance Tyen or I would have stumbled on the truth. They agreed to our terms as soon as they were ready.

As had the Emperor. His spies in Doum had observed sorcerers returning from battle training and warned that conquering the neighbouring world would not be as easy and quick as it had first appeared. Advisers had warned that Doum would have to be ruled from afar, forcing him to appoint someone to the task, who might then turn on him or his heirs later. It would involve endless meetings and planning – and sorcerers demanded ridiculous wages when they went to war. All to satisfy a pack of arrogant merchants wanting to squeeze a few more coins' profit out of a trade that had already made them rich.

Once he'd had time to consider it, the Emperor had proven too lazy and miserly to go to war. He hadn't anticipated that Doum might invade Murai. That he had been duped so easily would have been satisfying, if she and Tyen hadn't also been used and deceived, and the plot led to war and death.

"Emperor Izetala-Moraza," she said as she straightened.

"Rielle Lazuli," he said, baring his teeth. "Are you aware that the Doumian army is outside, destroying the city and attempting to enter my palace?"

She nodded. "I have just learned of it."

"Were you aware that they were planning this for some time?"

She shook her head. "No."

"I find that hard to believe. Did you not look into their minds once?"

"As I told you previously, only Tyen and an official were present during negotiations. He did not know where the Claymars were, just as I did not know your location."

"Did you look?"

"No. That would have violated their trust—"

"What trust?" The Emperor thrust a hand towards her. "You couldn't read his mind and you wouldn't read theirs. What use were you to us?"

Rielle drew a deep breath and let it out. "As much as any negotiator, though with the advantage that Tyen Wheelmaker could not read my mind either."

The Emperor's shoulders dropped a fraction. He put a hand to his face, then quickly drew it away.

"Then you must choose," he said. "Help me defend my world or leave."

Rielle forced her eyes to meet his. "As I have said before, killing is not a service I offer."

"Then get out of my world and never return."

She bowed again. "If that is your wish. I assure you that my efforts at negotiating peace between your worlds were done with the best intentions, and I regret that I did not succeed. I believed the Claymars as willing to honour the agreement as you, Emperor." He stared at her coldly, not in any mood to accept that she was not at fault: he had never been the type of ruler to forgive failure. She closed her mouth and turned to leave.

Two sorcerers followed as she made her way back to the mosaic-makers, pleading with her to help them. She could not reply. Sympathy and regret froze her throat. *I could try to help, but that would mean killing Doumians. It would lead to Murai seeking revenge on a weakened Doum — more deaths. If the Doumians overthrow the palace quickly, there may be less bloodshed.* Or not — Valhan's admission that he could not always predict the outcome of his interference in worlds echoed in her mind. She shook her head. *I shouldn't have meddled. I wouldn't have, if not for Tyen . . .*

"We have no chance against this sorcerer, this Tyen Wheelmaker," one of the sorcerers said.

"No," she agreed. She almost told them that Tyen wasn't there. If they feared he was a part of the invasion, they might surrender sooner, saving more lives. "I do not believe he is supporting this aggression, but I cannot be sure. I will go to Doum and find out." The two sorcerers exchanged a glance, then hurried away towards the increasing noise echoing from the front of the palace.

What if he has returned? What if he is behind this?

She had to find out. It would be dangerous for her to seek him out. His powers matched hers, so it might only take the help of a few more sorcerers to surpass her in strength. She doubted any of these Muraian sorcerers could be trusted to act as her protectors. But then, as Tarran had taught her, it wasn't always the strongest sorcerer who won, but the first to take all the available magic. She didn't have to approach Tyen either. She could read minds until she found a Doumian who knew where he stood in this conflict.

And if he is involved? She shook her head. *He can't be. He wouldn't.* The truth was, she couldn't be sure.

The mosaic-makers had returned to their workshop area. They stood around the largest table, and as she approached they all turned to face her. Few of the faces were friendly. They blamed her, she saw, for ruining the profitable arrangement they had in Murai, and for endangering their lives by bringing strife here.

"Bowlen," she said, finding the master. "The Claymars planned this invasion all along – even before the merchants attacked the Grand Market in Doum. I can assist you to flee to safety, if you wish."

Bowlen shook his head. "We can take care of ourselves." Though he approved of her offer, his resolve did not waver. His lips pressed into a firm line. "We no longer wish to use your designs."

She nodded once. "I understand. Good luck."

So that was that. What should she do now? She started towards her "rooms", making a mental list of what to pack and what to abandon. At once she thought of Timane, the servant she had helped. While Rielle had taught her to use her magical ability, it was a small one and no defence against the average Doumian sorcerer. Looking towards fabric covering the entrance, she saw it twitch. She looked closer, and caught a rapid, repetitive thought.

Take me with you. Take me with you. Take me with you.

Rielle reached the hanging and pushed inside. "I must leave this world," she told the girl as she strode through. "I may never return. But I will take you home first."

"No!" Timane shuddered. "They'll just sell me into servitude again. Take me with you."

"Is there anywhere else I could take you?"

"Nowhere. I have nowhere else to go."

It was not entirely true, but Rielle understood the girl's reasoning. Anywhere Rielle took her that was safe would mean beginning afresh in a strange place, so what would it matter if that place was in Murai or another world?

And who knew what taint the girl had now, having been the sole servant of the otherworld negotiator who'd failed to discover the Doumians' plans for invasion?

As Rielle grabbed a few personal items and her store of gemstones, Timane dragged a bulging pillow cover out from behind the column. "I found your jewellery and grabbed a change of clothes."

"Thank you."

The girl did not hand the makeshift bag over. She stared at Rielle expectantly. Rielle considered her. *What if she changes her mind? I suppose I'll have to bring her back. Well, I can do that, if I have to. It's more than I was able to do for Sesse.* If she had been able to go back to check whether her servant in the Raen's new palace was alive and safe, she would have, but she couldn't without risking her and Qall's life. Maybe this time she could make sure someone who had served her ended up in a better, not worse, place.

"Where's yours?" Rielle asked, nodding at the pillow cover.

"I don't own anything valuable."

A boom came from the direction of the front of the palace, sending a vibration through the floor. Dust trickled down from where the columns met the roof. In the corner of her eye, Rielle saw the artisans vanish. In the distance, servants were running for the river – the closest exit from the palace.

Timane remained standing, trembling with fear. Rielle held out a hand. The girl's face lit up with surprise and delight. Taking it, she closed her eyes in anticipation.

"Take a very deep breath," Rielle instructed. "There is no air between worlds."

Timane's chest expanded. Rielle drew enough magic to get her to Doum and back, and to defend them if attacked. It was tempting to draw all the magic from around the palace to slow down the invasion, but she resisted. The Emperor did not want her interference. She pushed out of the world.

All the way to Doum, she considered how she would find Tyen. Guessing that the Doumian sorcerers had travelled to Murai from Alba, as it was the city closest in alignment to Glaemar, she sought their paths. Sure enough, many of them had cut through the place between. She followed one until Alba began to resolve out of the whiteness below her. The path angled away rather than descending to the city, so she left it and plunged down towards the metropolis.

Choosing a shadowy, empty alleyway, she brought them into the world. Timane immediately exhaled then sucked in air. As the girl regained her breath, Rielle scanned the minds around her, looking for a name. It did not take long to find it.

. . . *Tyen Wheelmaker returns, he will be angry* . . .

. . . *a shame. I liked him. But he isn't in charge. The Claymars are. And if they think it's safer for us to throw him out* . . .

. . . *what they did to his house. No chance he'll be setting up here again. Forrel even destroyed his wheel. A waste, that. The Claymars said nobody is to say a word against those who worked for him, so I reckon that goes for the wheels they worked on too. I'm not* . . .

The images she saw through the eyes of these minds were of a crumbling, smoking ruin. Tyen's home and workshop. Rielle let out a little sigh of sympathy and relief. Tyen wasn't behind the invasion. When he returned he was going to be in for a shock, however. All his possessions had been burned – if they hadn't been looted first – by a people he loved and had tried to help. People who had used him badly.

I have to warn him, she thought. But that meant interrupting his attempt to learn pattern shifting. What would he do once he heard the news? *He'll want to come back and try to stop the war. It might mean he'll have to start learning pattern shifting again from scratch.* She considered leaving him ignorant, but shook her head. *It's his decision to make, not mine.*

Would she join him in trying to stop the conflict? She frowned. *Aside from threatening to strip both worlds of magic, what can we do? Perhaps Tyen will think of something.*

She looked at Timane. "Take another deep breath."

As the girl's cheeks puffed from holding her breath, Rielle pushed out of the world.

CHAPTER 2

"It is his writing," Tarran said. "And he was in a hurry."

Rielle looked down at the stone, smooth but for where glyphs had been carved into it. *I am alive. I will return.* She'd found it during a long, fruitless search after discovering that Tyen and his belongings had disappeared from the desert world. Paths in the place between worlds had led her around that world but revealed nothing, or headed away from it only to join with well-used paths leading to several nearby worlds, any one of which he could have taken. Heading back to the desert world, thinking that Tyen might have buried a message in the sand, she'd paused to search the arrival place in the neighbouring world and found the carved stone on the trunk of a recently felled tree.

She realised she was grinding her teeth, and relaxed her jaw. "What do you think it means?"

Tarran shrugged. "That whether he left willingly or not, and was successful or not, he is safe. That he will return, but when or to where he dares not reveal."

"He could mean here, the place I found the stone, or the desert world." Rielle turned away and began to pace. "We're only assuming the message was for us too. Perhaps he meant it for another." She frowned. "Perhaps I should take it back."

Tarran turned so the light touched the stone from a different direction. "No, I think it is for us."

She returned to his side. "How do you know?"

He pointed. "He's added curls to the end of these lines – a habit from the writing of his own world. I called them antennae and made him rewrite every glyph he added them to. It became a little joke between us."

"So it was meant for us. Or you, at least. But he hasn't returned." An uncomfortable sensation began in Rielle's stomach. "Can you guess how old it is?"

The old man shook his head. "How fresh was the path?"

"Not very. I assumed at first it hadn't been used since I took him there. I found signs that someone had skimmed away from his campsite, but after stopping a few times the path led out of the world. It was old, too. I suppose he could have stayed longer, then concealed his path when he left."

"Not using either route out of the world, or he'd have erased all signs of earlier use as well." Tarran put the stone on his dining table. "So either he left soon after you did using one of the two paths still detectable, or he left by a different route, which he concealed, perhaps later."

The discomfort inside Rielle was now a mix of nausea and dread. "The magic in the desert world was much diminished, but not completely removed. If he succeeded, surely he would have returned here?"

"Then why leave a message?" Tarran added. "Perhaps it wasn't safe to come here. Perhaps his enemies caught up with him and he didn't want to lead them to us."

"If they found him, then they might have interrupted before he could complete the transformation." Rielle sighed. "I thought that world was safe. Only the Travellers used it, and they had stopped visiting because the worlds on either side had become dangerous to them." She paused. "Perhaps sorcerers from those worlds were tapping the magic there, and when they found it was reducing rapidly they investigated and found him, or started taking as much as they could before it was all gone."

Tarran shook his head. "He'd have returned here before seeking

169

a new world to work in. No, something has prevented him coming here, and the simplest answer is his enemies."

She rubbed her stomach muscles as they tightened further. "Could they have followed my path? I'm not as good at hiding it as Tyen is."

"If they did, you can't blame yourself, Rielle." Tarran placed a hand on her shoulder. "You did everything you could to prevent someone tracking you. For all we know, he left for another reason."

"Then why didn't he come here and tell us? Or send a message?"

"He did: he left this." Tarran held up the stone, then as he saw her expression he squeezed her shoulder. "We'll find out when he returns. We can do nothing but hope and wait."

"Not search for him?" Rielle asked, though she knew the answer.

"And risk leading his enemies to him?" Tarran shook his head. "Tyen can take care of himself. He'll come back or find a way to send word when it is safe to do so." He chuckled. "I've now become the message service for the both of you. This –" Reaching into his jacket, the old man drew out a slightly transparent piece of paper sealed with resin. "– came for you yesterday."

Taking it, Rielle broke the seal and unfolded it. The only people who sent messages to her were Lejihk and Ankari, but Tarran didn't know that. To maintain the impression she was communicating with more than one source, the Travellers alternated between different materials and delivery methods each time they contacted her.

The paper was made of a reed or grass-like fibre fused into layers of strips. Several words and numerals had been written on it in a hard, glossy paint. She counted them to find the ones to pay attention to, decoding a date and the number "4".

The words indicated the Travellers wanted to meet, and the number told her the location. The date indicated when they would arrive at the location, where they would stay for a few days at most. Working out when a date was in the Traveller cycle meant applying mathematics too sophisticated for quick mental calculation. She headed for Tarran's timepiece.

Before she'd met Tarran, when she needed to know the precise date in the Traveller calendar she'd sought out worlds with civilisations sophisticated enough that someone would be keeping track. Here she only had to consult the timepiece, which indicated Traveller time against that of an unknown world, saved from Liftre after it had been abandoned. She walked through the house to where it stood in a wall alcove. Tarran gave a small huff of amusement as she stopped.

"Tyen made this," he said.

"What? Really?" She turned to stare at him, then looked at the timepiece again. Now that she knew, it was obvious. It had a similar look to the mechanical insect that Tyen had made.

"Is it his world this measures Traveller time against?"

"I believe so," Tarran replied.

She gazed at the hands and number, which indicated that it was night and winter in a place in Tyen's world. That told her nothing useful, however. She turned her attention to the Traveller settings.

"Five Traveller days ago." She tossed the message up in the air, which she set vibrating fast enough to produce heat. The paper burst into flame and quickly turned to a fine rain of ash. "Tell Tyen – if he returns before I do – that I'm annoyed at him for writing such a useless message. Do you mind if I leave Timane here for a few days?"

Tarran winced. "Must you? One of my students has decided he's fallen in love with her."

"Already?"

"She is rather attractive."

Rielle smiled. "I guess I've grown used to being surrounded by beauty. The Muraian Emperor expects all of his servants to be pleasant for the eyes. Does she share your student's feelings?"

Tarran's eyebrows rose. "Not surprisingly, considering her

maturity compared to his, she isn't so eager or quick to fancy herself in love."

"Very well." Rielle searched the house for Timane's mind. She found the girl in a room at the end of the corridor, where she'd been hovering in anticipation of being summoned. "Timane!" Rapid footsteps followed and the girl burst into the room.

"Welcome back, Rielle Lazuli," she said in Muraian. "Was your errand successful?"

"No, but I have something else to attend to now." Rielle paused as she realised the girl was wearing different clothing. "You changed."

"I hate that uniform!" Timane shuddered. "I told Tarran's servants to burn it."

Rielle resisted a smile. The servants' clothes had been designed to flatter, but were uncomfortable and impractical. "Just as well they had something to replace it with."

"You had lots of nice things at the palace. Will you go back for them?"

"No. I haven't the time. It's easier to travel with less, too. You will have to get used to owning only what you can carry if you want to travel with me."

Timane shrugged. "I've never owned much. Even in the palace. No point when other servants will steal it from you."

Rielle walked to the girl and held out a hand. "I will find a better home for you, where you can keep any fancy thing you acquire. For now, we only carry essentials. I'll buy us both packs and a purse for you on the way to our destination. From now on, try to speak Traveller tongue. Thanks to their trading across the worlds for thousands of years, their language has become the most common, even if it's only spoken by the traders and sorcerers of a world. I'll keep teaching you as we travel."

The girl nodded, took Rielle's hand and turned to Tarran. "It was an honour to meet you," she said. Then, recalling the need to take a deep breath and hold it when travelling between worlds, she quickly inhaled.

Not wanting to waste the girl's breath, Rielle nodded a farewell to Tarran and pushed out of the world.

Their journey, thanks to Timane, was slow. Every time they arrived in a world, Rielle waited for the girl to catch her breath. Remembering how she had once done so herself, before she had become ageless, roused memories of being taken by Valhan to see worlds he had influenced, trading favours with both the powerful and humble. She remembered his admission that he could never predict the result of his interference.

Yet he still did it. She thought back to the mind she had glimpsed during the resurrection. She had sensed no great feeling of care or nurture for the worlds – only a drive to maintain his position as ruler of them all. She had not seen anything to explain why he had wanted to rule in the first place, or if he cared whether his subjects loved or hated him. *I think he'd have preferred to be adored, though perhaps not for the sake of vanity. Willing obedience must make the job of ruling a great deal easier.*

This overall need he'd had to be in charge . . . That, she had come to see, was what made him the Raen, and her most definitely *not* the Successor. Was that the true interpretation of Millennium's Rule? Could the prophecy still be fulfilled if someone with the ambition, and the power to achieve it, rose to power?

Not much of a prophecy, she mused, *if it has to be bent and shaped to fit the actual circumstances that arise.*

A market square darkened around them. It was night, but it never closed, and the crowds were only a little thinner than what she'd seen here before, during daylight. She led Timane along an aisle, trying to remember where the bag-makers were.

Timane gazed around her in fascination. "May I ask where we are going?"

"To buy packs."

"I meant after."

Rielle paused to look into the girl's mind. Timane was curious, but she was also telling herself that she had put herself in a sorcerer's hands and must accept not knowing what lay in her future.

"I can't tell you," Rielle told her. "Not because I don't want to, or don't trust you, but because your mind can be read by sorcerers stronger than you – of which there are plenty here. We are safer if my secrets remain secrets even from you."

Timane nodded and shrugged. "As long as you don't sell me into slavery or to cannibals, I'm fine with that."

"I promise I won't do either. Also, you are not my servant now, Timane."

"What am I then?"

"A travelling companion."

"I don't get to decide where we go though, do I?"

"I have something I must do first, but afterwards . . . I suppose you might, if it isn't dangerous."

"I say we follow that man." Timane pointed.

"Ah . . . can I ask why?"

"He also wants to buy a bag. I saw it in his mind. We should follow him."

Sure enough, the man led them to a row of shops selling shoes, bags, saddles of all shapes and sizes, whips, armour and furniture. Rielle chose two light packs and a purse for Timane that could be bound to a wrist or leg, as well as hung from the waist or neck. She liked the design so much she exchanged one for the fancy purse, decorated with precious metallic thread, that she'd bought in Murai.

The bag-maker's eyes widened at the gemstones and coins she tipped from the old one to the new, and he wished he'd charged her more. Fortunately, she'd already bartered and paid for their purchases. A couple of child thieves saw as well and began following them, so she took hold of Timane's wrist, withdrew from the world and skimmed to another part of the market before resuming shopping for other necessities. Then, with them both carrying full packs, she took Timane on through the worlds.

A few worlds away from her destination, she left Timane in a quiet forest glade in a peaceful, rural country.

"I can't take you where I'm going next," she said. "I'll be back in a few hours. If I don't return, wait a day or two, then head for the road in that direction and follow it to the village. The people there are friendly and will help you."

Timane nodded, dismayed yet trusting. "Good luck."

"Thanks." Rielle smiled. "Don't worry: I'm not going anywhere dangerous."

Then, pushing out of the world, she watched the girl and her surroundings fade to white and hoped she was right about the safety of the locale she was heading to. She'd met the Travellers there before, but the worlds were changing and she could never be sure if anywhere would be the same on the next visit.

Travelling on, she took precautions to confuse anyone who might follow. A few worlds beyond where she'd left Timane, she emerged next to a sheer cliff. An ocean crashed against the wall, the foam churning a few strides below her. Skimming left a trail, so to be sure she couldn't be tracked she had to spend some time travelling within a world. Levitating was faster than walking, sailing or riding an animal, cart or other type of vehicle, so she had experimented with the method to find the fastest, most comfortable approach. Trying to stand upright on stilled air was tricky. It was easier to lie down.

Creating a disc of stilled air under her, she leaned forward so she lay parallel to the ground then propelled herself out over the ocean, heading towards a star shining faintly in the bright sky. It was the closest she had ever come to flying, and for a while she simply enjoyed the exhilaration of air rushing past.

Soon the salty air gained a sulphurous taint. A plume of black marked the horizon, and a conical peak from which the smoke belched emerged from behind the horizon. A vibration and rumble shivered through the air after each volcanic belch.

It was a spectacular sight, and she was not surprised to find the village she headed for was now abandoned. Ash coated the houses. Some of the roofs had collapsed under the weight of it. In the meeting place, squashed into the bark of the immense old tree that the villagers had held gatherings around, she found a small scrap of leather. On it was written a message.

Come to the Gathering place. The reason is urgent.

She scorched the leather to remove the message and cast it into the ocean, which foamed around the scrap. Pushing out of the world, she decided to try Tyen's method of hiding a path. Her efforts were clumsy, but the markings she left were shallower than a path, and would smooth out soon enough. With practice, she would be able to leave no trace at all.

The Gathering place was not far away. She'd not been back there since Lejihk's family had brought her to it more than five cycles ago. Instead of dozens of Traveller wagons forming circles on the hilltops and canopies atop the small plateau in the centre, one small tent greeted her. A sole figure sat before it. Ankari, Lejihk's wife. Rielle skimmed towards it and emerged in the world before the woman.

Ankari rose and came forward.

"Rielle. It has been too long this time," the woman said, drawing Rielle into a tight hug.

"It is always too long. How long is it exactly?"

Ankari stepped back and chuckled. "A quarter cycle and more."

"I assume that no messages also means no trouble."

"Not exactly." The older woman grimaced. "Come and sit with me."

Following the woman to the tent, Rielle kept her impatience in check. She resisted reading her mind, having agreed to never read the minds of anyone in Lejihk's family in case she learned something that compromised Qall's safety. Sitting on a thick

176

quilted pillow, she waited while Ankari settled. Spread around the woman were the materials and tools of the Travellers' bold and colourful style of stitching. Most of the garments were small.

"Is there another child on the way?" Rielle asked.

Ankari held up a tiny set of pants. "Jikari is expecting twins."

"Twins!"

They discussed the news of the family, Rielle asking after those she had grown to love during the time she'd lived with them. "And how is Qall?" she finally asked. She braced herself for the answer. Ankari had mentioned no other major problems facing the family, so she suspected he was the source of the trouble. The fact that the woman hadn't spoken of him yet also suggested that once they began discussing him, they might never return to more domestic subjects.

"He is fine," Ankari replied, giving Rielle a quick, reassuring smile. "The trouble is, he's old enough, by Traveller standards, to be considered an adult. He could be seeking a wife, and leaving the family to start his own, if he wished. He will soon want what we can't give him."

Rielle caught her breath. "Does he want to leave?"

"No."

"What does he want?"

Ankari chuckled. "To be able to laze about all day, like all youngsters. But beyond that . . ." Her smile faded. "He knows some of what he can't be and can't have. He thinks he can't be a Traveller unless he marries one, when the truth is we can't allow him to marry into our family because then we cannot return to the Traveller way of life. We have, by necessity, treated him a little differently because of his great magical strength too. Though we have told him our family is hiding, we haven't told him why, and he can't help but wonder if he is the cause. We have been stricter at enforcing the rule against reading minds with him as well, but to prevent him rebelling we had to promise him that the truth would be revealed when he came of age."

"Which must be soon, or he will break the rule?"

"Yes. I'd prefer you to be with him when we do, to explain what we can't."

Rielle nodded. "So it is time to tell him what was done to him, and what they tried to make him into." She had never told the Travellers whose memories were supposed to have replaced Qall's, but it had become clear as the boy grew older. His body had been changed to the same pattern as Valhan's, so now that he was an adult he looked exactly like the man. Fortunately, only Lejihk and the healer, Ulma, had seen Valhan in person. Some of the rest of the family had seen him in other people's memories, and all had seen the occasional statue. Those who saw the resemblance wondered if Qall was a relation of the Raen's – or of the same race. A few had speculated on why Qall's memories had been erased, and some had even guessed the reason, but all had complied with Lejihk's command that Qall's origins never be speculated on openly. They hadn't, which was a sign of how deeply they respected him.

Ankari met Rielle's gaze directly. "We have not yet conferred on it, but I know the minds of the family. When Lejihk and I first took him in, we all agreed that once he was of age our part was over. It is time you took on his care, Rielle."

Fear rushed through Rielle's veins. She wanted to object, to say, "But I know nothing of raising children!" but she swallowed the words. He was no child now. He was a young man. She could not expect Lejihk's family to live outside their traditional ways for his entire life.

Qall won't be content living with them if he is never truly one of them. It's amazing he hasn't succumbed to curiosity and read a few minds, and discovered who he looks similar to.

And now she must tell him. She must explain who he was, warn him of the danger he was in and teach him how to survive in the worlds. The Travellers had taught him almost everything else, so she had only to fill in the gaps in his knowledge and ensure he could use his extraordinary magical strength to defend himself. Put that way, the task didn't sound as difficult.

"Does he know who I am?" she asked.

"Only that you are a sorcerer who rescued him and brought him to us. He regards you as something akin to a mother."

Rielle winced. *This is going to be very strange.* "When do you want me to come and collect him?"

"Straightaway would be best, but I expect you need to make arrangements wherever you have settled."

"Yes and no. The world I was in is now at war, so I was already seeking a new home." She considered what this meant. She would have to take Qall somewhere he wouldn't be recognised as Valhan. That might mean travelling a very long way. Which probably meant she would not see Tarran again for many years.

At least Tyen will be able to ensure the old man stays healthy, she thought. *If Tyen is successful at learning pattern shifting, that is – and does return as he promised.*

By the time he did, she might be far, far away. Her heart sank as she realised this was the end of their time together. Though . . . perhaps once she'd found a safe place for Qall she could contact Tyen and arrange a meeting.

No. I still don't know him well enough yet to trust him with something as important as the location of the boy Valhan created to be his vessel.

Her time with Tyen had been wonderful, but it was over. Her responsibility to Qall was greater. But she wouldn't leave Tyen wondering what had happened to her, as he had done to her.

"I'd have to send a message to Tarran," she said.

And what about Timane? Should I take her with me, or find her a home now?

It might be good for Qall to have a second person, nearer to his age, around to keep him company. Would Timane see him and think he was Valhan? The Muraian Emperor had destroyed all portraits and statues of Valhan after his death, deciding it was better to not risk offending the Restorers. That had happened before Timane's arrival at the palace, so the girl probably didn't know what Valhan had looked like. *I'll check, but if she hasn't seen images of the Raen I will bring her with me.*

"I have a travelling companion, who is waiting a few worlds away. Will it be a problem for the Travellers if I bring her to your camp?" Rielle asked.

Ankari paused to consider, then shook her head. "It will be no problem. The time for secrecy is over. If anyone follows your trail back to us, they will find us gone. We will be leaving as soon as Qall does, to begin our new trading circuit."

"You have one planned out?"

"Yes. Lejihk has been working on it for the last cycle. It will be good to get back to a normal life." The woman sighed again. "We will miss Qall though. He is a good boy. I wish we did not have to send him away – and I know he won't be happy about it." She bowed her head, then wiped at an eye. "But it will be better for everyone."

"Oh, Ankari. I wish I didn't have to tear him away from you." Rielle hugged the woman. "Thank you for all that you and the family have done."

Ankari managed a smile. "I'll stay here and pack up the tent while you retrieve your friend."

"I'll look after him as best as I can," Rielle promised. She got to her feet. "I'll be back in a few hours."

Drawing magic, she pushed out of the world and started the journey back to Timane.

CHAPTER 3

When a familiar style of wagon emerged from the whiteness of the place between worlds, a wave of nostalgia and happiness washed over Rielle. Nearby, two lom, the enormous beasts that drew the wagons, grazed in a field. As she, Ankari and Timane arrived in the world, icy, dry air surrounded them.

The wagon door opened, and a familiar young woman emerged holding three long, fur-lined coats. Though Ulma was not a member of Lejihk's family, she had visited them once a cycle since they had begun hiding, to help teach Qall. Perhaps Ulma's assessment of Qall's progress had led to the Travellers deciding it was time for Rielle to take on the responsibility. That was a comforting thought, as Ulma was unlikely to advise it if Qall was not ready.

"Rielle," Ulma said, smiling. "It is good to see you again. It must be more than half a cycle."

"Ulma," Rielle replied. "How are you?"

"Well and happy," the healer replied.

"This is Timane, my travelling companion." Rielle gestured to the girl.

Ulma nodded. "Hello, brave Timane." She handed them the coats, which they donned with appreciative haste. Timane looked mystified, not familiar with the Traveller word for "brave".

"How is your daughter, Oliti?" Rielle asked.

Ulma's gaze softened. "Time claimed her, during the last cycle."

"Oh! I am sorry to hear that."

The healer sighed. "It is a strange and unnatural thing, outliving your offspring." Her mouth twisted into a sad smile. "But the time spent in love and joy outweighs the sadness. That is why I chose to bear her and the pain of her inevitable loss – and will do so with another, when I am ready to."

Rielle could only nod, all too aware that she faced that choice and its consequences as well. Ulma was the only ageless Traveller Rielle had heard of. All desire to have children had left Rielle since leaving the Travellers. The two times in her life when she had faced the prospect of motherhood, it had been a consequence of wanting something else: first because it would make Izare happy; then because it had been expected of her if she married Baluka.

Perhaps in the future, when she had no other obligations, and had found a safe place to live – and a husband – she would be ready to raise a family, if she was not put off by the thought that they might age and die while she stayed unchanged. None of Ulma's children had been powerful enough sorcerers to become ageless. Strong parents didn't guarantee strong offspring.

"Come inside and warm yourselves," Ulma invited. "I'll make you a cup of oali to drink while I harness the lom."

Once they all had a steaming mug of the spicy drink to sip, the woman disappeared outside. Rielle turned to Timane.

"Ulma is ageless," she explained in Muraian.

Timane nodded. "Ah. What did she call me?"

"Brave."

"Me? Why?"

"You left your world and everything you know," Rielle pointed out. "Most people are too afraid to do that."

"I'm not completely without fear," Timane admitted. "But I don't want to go back. Even if Murai wasn't at war. It's not a nice place."

"There are worse places. Far worse."

The girl's eyes narrowed. "Are you trying to scare me into going back?"

"No, but a little fear isn't a bad thing. It keeps you alert and wary."

Timane glanced around the wagon. "Can you tell me why we're here yet?"

Rielle and Ankari exchanged a look. The older woman nodded. "There is nothing to be gained from silence now."

"Several cycles ago I rescued a child," Rielle told the girl. "I asked the Travellers to raise him. Now that he is grown, it is my turn to look after him."

Timane's eyebrows rose. "You're accumulating travel companions."

"You could say that." Rielle chuckled.

The door opened and Ulma smiled in at them. "Ready to go. Rielle, would you join me?"

Setting aside her empty mug, Rielle rose and climbed out onto the driver's seat. Once she and Ulma had settled, the Traveller spoke a command and the lom began to walk, jerking the wagon into motion. They travelled in silence for a while, following a road that wound through gentle hills covered in a variety of plants, including one that had vertical branches shaped like corkscrews.

"While Qall lives," Ulma said, "there will always be a danger Valhan's memories will be imprinted on his mind."

Rielle glanced back at the door.

"Don't worry. They won't hear us."

Relaxing a little, Rielle looked at the healer. It was the first time Ulma had confirmed that she knew who Qall was meant to become. "So you don't think that he is too old now?"

"Age can be altered."

"Ah. Of course." Rielle grimaced and looked at the road again. "Then I should have killed him."

"Yes. As we should have. But what stays our hand is what makes us better than those who would have used him."

"Is a kindness to one person worth endangering all the worlds?"

"Yes."

Ulma's confidence was reassuring, yet Rielle's doubts lingered.

"Isn't that selfish? Aren't we endangering many people for the sake of our own sense of morality?"

"Everything we do is selfish." Ulma shrugged. "When we act to save others, we do it so we feel good about ourselves. When we make a moral decision it is because we have convinced ourselves or allowed ourselves to be convinced that *our* morality is better than others'." She glanced at Rielle. "But our selfishness is a kind of self-preservation. Killing changes a person. If you or I had killed him, what would stop the person we became then using the same reasoning to justify other deaths? You could say 'only this once', but when you live indefinitely, how long before you are faced with the same dilemma? Having reasoned that way once, it is easy to do it again. By not killing we preserve who we are now."

Rielle nodded. "I often wondered if Valhan became who he was through such justifications."

"You know that we Travellers do our best to avoid involvement in the strife of the worlds we trade in. Valhan said it was a form of selfishness; I say it is preservation. Our own survival means more to us than helping others. I told him he would do the same when his own survival was threatened. He was only able to help others because he was so powerful. That was before he had made too many deals with too many allies." She gave a low laugh. "I was proven right, I think."

Rielle turned to stare at Ulma. "You met Valhan?"

Ulma smiled. "Oh, yes. A very long time ago. We were . . . not exactly friends. He said I was the oldest ageless he'd met. He asked lots of questions."

"How old . . .?" Rielle stopped, unsure if it was polite to ask, or even her business to know exactly how old Ulma was.

The woman shrugged. "Older than Valhan was. To be honest, I don't know precisely."

"Are you the reason he allowed the Travellers to trade between worlds?"

"Yes." Ulma glanced back at the wagon. "Though only you and I know that now, and it is best kept that way. These days, people judge you badly if you've negotiated a deal with the Raen. It wasn't always that way."

"Can I . . . can I ask what he got in return?"

Ulma chuckled. "Information. Knowledge. Some long and stimulating arguments. Sometimes I made him very angry, but he always came back." Her smiled faded. "Though obviously not the last time."

"Did you part on bad terms?"

Ulma shook her head. "No, we had nothing left to offer each other. There's only so many times you can talk to someone without repeating yourself endlessly, even when you've lived for thousands of cycles."

Rielle thought of Tyen. She had wondered how long two ageless people could remain together without becoming bored with each other. Were ageless lovers doomed to eventually part? Perhaps it was better not to begin in the first place.

A gloom settled over her. The road cut between two hills ahead. Beyond, she could see wagons and people moving about among them.

"Almost there," Ulma murmured.

Rielle found herself examining each of the distant figures, trying to make out familiar Travellers, and looking in vain for a dark-haired young man with pale skin. Her stomach fluttered, then sank, then fluttered again.

"How much like Valhan does he look?"

"Physically, exactly the same."

"It must be strange for you."

Ulma chuckled. "Hmm, yes it has been. You will get used to it, as I did."

"I hope so, but not so much that I forget what others will see." Rielle frowned. "I wondered if I should have tried to alter his

185

pattern again to change his appearance, but I didn't think of it until after I left him with you."

"He was already confused and distressed," Ulma said. "It took a long time to settle him. Once we had . . . well, it could have wiped his memory all over again."

Which means I can't do it now without risking that either, Rielle realised. *The best I can do is to teach him pattern shifting so he can create and maintain a new appearance himself.*

"Is there anything you need to know before we arrive?" Ulma asked.

Rielle considered. "He has learned only three of the five applications of magic: stilling, moving and mind reading. Not world travelling. Not pattern shifting."

"That is correct."

"Have you taught him any fighting methods?"

"Enough to defend himself and others. We don't need knowledge of waging war, so it's not something we preserve or teach."

"If he was a Traveller, would you consider his training complete?"

"As much as any Traveller boy of his age – barring how to travel between worlds."

Rielle considered what else she could ask. "Where do you suggest I take him?"

"As far from the worlds the Raen ruled as possible, which may be a very long way. It may take you into the edges of the habitable worlds." A note of warning entered Ulma's voice. "You'll need to do more than gather enough magic to leave a world again. Don't trust the environment even if it looks safe. When a world is unpopulated, there's always a reason."

As Ulma's wagon emerged from between the two hills, Rielle saw that the family's wagons were arranged in a large circle beside the road. Plants had grown up around the wheels. Several of the Travellers were striding forward to greet their visitors. The foremost was Lejihk, smiling briefly as his gaze met Rielle's before returning to his customary seriousness.

"Well, we're here now and everyone can hear us," Ulma said, giving Rielle a warning look.

"Thank you for coming to meet us."

Young children ran past the adults to circle Ulma's wagon, while the older youngsters remained beside the wagons, their ages defined as much by whether they feigned indifference or were openly curious. Rielle looked at each older boy carefully, but none resembled Valhan at all.

Lejihk had reached the wagon now. He had put on a little weight, she noted. So had many in the family. No doubt it was the result of five cycles staying in one place rather than ceaseless travelling and trading. He nodded to Ulma, then offered a hand to assist Rielle in climbing to the ground.

"Welcome back, Rielle," he said. "Are you well?"

"I am," she replied. "Are you and your family?"

"Fit and healthy." He looked over her shoulder. "You have brought a friend."

"Yes." Rielle turned to see that Timane was emerging from the wagon, and introduced her. "She was my servant in the world I just left. A war has begun there. A war I tried but failed to prevent."

Lejihk grimaced in sympathy and turned to help Timane reach the ground. "It is to your credit that you tried."

The girl was taking her surroundings in with wide eyes. "I've never seen any Travellers before today," she whispered to Rielle in Muraian. "Now I meet a whole family of them."

"This is Lejihk," Rielle told her, "head of the family."

Timane began to bow, but stopped as both Lejihk and Ankari protested.

"You are our guest," he told her. "Our equal." He beckoned. "Come join us for a meal."

He led them through the gap between two of the wagons into the circle of them. A canopy stretched between them all. A raised circular platform of wood filled the space in the centre – another sign they had lived here a long time. A fire pit of stone had been built within a gap in the middle, and it flared into life as one of the Travellers used magic to light it. Firm, square pillows and blankets were brought out of the wagons, and as the adults and guests began to settle around the fire, the young women of the family were asked to bring warm drinks.

"This place is for Qall," Lejihk said, leaving the pillow between his and Rielle's empty. He looked around. The young man was nowhere in view. "Somebody find him and tell him to join us."

One of the younger adult men began to rise.

"No need," Ankari said. "He's here."

Following the woman's gaze, Rielle saw a knot of young men part, and her heart froze. Valhan stood among them, his back straight and expression aloof.

And then he looked up in her direction and became a different person. Valhan would never have allowed such doubt and longing to show. Nor would he have even felt those emotions, she suspected. At least, not towards her.

Qall was Valhan's body inhabited and animated by all the uncertainty and hope of youth. Emotions she had never seen on the Raen's face altered it to the point that he no longer looked like the ruler she had known. She almost wondered if she hadn't succeeded after all when she had changed this young man's pattern. Or that some of the information imprinted in Valhan's desiccated hand had been missing.

It was a relief, mixed with a new anxiety. He was Qall, but he was a stranger to her, and her to him. That realisation sparked even greater sympathy towards him. He was a young man with almost no memory of his life before five cycles ago, about to be taken from the only people he loved by a powerful sorceress he knew nothing about except that she had saved his life.

He was probably scared. He might also be excited. Young men were often restless, stifled by a life lacking challenges, and she could offer him a freedom and adventure that he couldn't get from the Travellers. She smiled, hoping to reassure him. His expression softened a little, then he looked away, gaze shifting to the distance, and all emotion smoothed from his face.

And suddenly he was Valhan again. Disturbed, she looked down, overwhelmed by what she was taking on. Most people, if they had ever beheld a portrait or statue or had briefly met Valhan, would believe Qall was the ruler of worlds returned from the dead yet again. They would fear him, hate him, adore him. If he was recognised before she could get him to a safe world, word of his return would spread like a windstorm through the worlds, and Dahli would come to find out if it were true.

How am I going to avoid anyone seeing him?

"Qall. Come and sit with us," Lejihk called, gesturing to an empty cushion.

Rielle watched Qall walk to the pillow and sit down. His movements were completely unlike Valhan's. They had the loose-limbed ease of youth and the awkwardness that came of being self-conscious. They way he dropped onto the cushion and hunched his shoulders hinted at resignation.

"This is Rielle Lazuli," Lejihk told him.

Qall glanced at Rielle, then fixed his eyes on the edge of her mat. "I am honoured to meet you."

"And I you," she replied, hiding her surprise. His voice was so different to Valhan's. Had it not broken yet? It wasn't the voice of a child, though. *Perhaps Valhan altered his voice. He may* not have been aware that he had. While he had used portraits and statues to remind himself of what his true appearance was, perhaps he hadn't found a way to record what he should sound like.

Lejihk looked around the group. "Most of you know Rielle." He gestured to Timane. "This is Timane, Rielle's companion."

Qall's gaze lingered a little longer on the young woman, who smiled brightly as the Travellers welcomed her. Timane haltingly spoke the polite reply Ankari had taught her.

189

"As you know, Qall," Lejihk continued. "Rielle rescued you five cycles ago from the people who erased your memories. We've raised you and taught you most of what our own children learn. The rest she will teach you."

Qall's eyes sharpened as he looked at her. "To travel between worlds?"

"Yes," Rielle replied. "But first we must find a safe place to live."

The crease between his brows deepened. He glanced around the watching Travellers, and his lips pressed together.

"You don't want to leave," Rielle guessed. "I understand. I didn't want to when I lived with Lejihk's family."

The look he sent her was piercing but brief. "You can't stay here and teach me," he guessed in return.

She looked at Lejihk. Perhaps something could be arranged. He shook his head.

"Why not?" Qall asked.

"Lejihk's family agreed to protect and heal the child I brought to them," she replied. "You are no longer a child."

"We settled here for your benefit," Lejihk continued, "but this is not our traditional way of living, and we have survived on our savings and loans from other Traveller families. We must return to our trading and pay back those loans."

As Qall absorbed that, three young women entered the circle. One carried a barrel; another a box full of ceramic mugs. The third pierced the barrel, took a cup, filled it and handed it to one of the Travellers, then moved on to serve the next.

"Why can't you start trading if I'm with you?" Qall asked.

Lejihk looked at Rielle and nodded.

My turn, she thought. *But how much do I tell him?*

"There is a danger you will be recognised by the people who hurt you," Rielle explained. "They know I spent time with Travellers, and could be looking for you among them."

His eyes widened. "They're still looking for me?"

She nodded. "Don't be afraid. I can protect you. We will find a safe place to live."

"Why are they looking for me?"

Rielle glance at Lejihk, then Ankari. She wanted to read their minds, and have some guidance to how much she should tell him. The couple nodded, as if in permission. *There is no need to avoid seeing their thoughts now*, she realised. *It can't bring Qall into any greater danger by reading their thoughts.*

So she looked. Lejihk wanted her to avoid frightening Qall needlessly, Ankari thought being truthful would help Rielle gain Qall's trust. Their opposing views did nothing to help Rielle decide. *Let's see how far his questions take us, then.* She drew a deep breath, then let it out again.

"To put someone else's memories in place of your own," she said.

"Whose?"

She shook her head. "A sorcerer. A . . . the leader of the people who harmed you."

His eyes narrowed. "A bad person."

"Yes."

An eyebrow rose. "Obviously some think otherwise, or they wouldn't follow him."

"Yes."

"Who do I believe?"

She held his gaze. "Who do you trust?"

He looked away, then his gaze flitted around the watching Travellers, and he nodded.

"I believe you," he told her. "Since you agree with my family."

My family. Something reached inside her and squeezed her heart. She had to take a few deep breaths before she could speak again.

"I wish I didn't have to take you away, or that I could stay with Lejihk's family while helping you, but neither is possible. But I hope I can be your friend as well as your protector."

The look he gave her was indecipherable. Seeing Ankari frown, she looked closer. The woman was unsure if it was wise for Rielle to propose they become friends. Qall would more likely obey Rielle without question – or at least with less questioning – if her role was more like a mother-matriarch than an equal.

"Eventually, anyway," Rielle added. "For now, I will be your protector, then your teacher when we find a place to settle."

He nodded. "When do we leave?"

She looked at Lejihk and raised an eyebrow.

"Tomorrow," the man said. His expression was controlled, but from his mind escaped a wistful thought. *It will be like losing another son.* Then he remembered that by letting Qall go, the family had a chance to reunite with Baluka, and his heart lifted a little.

Rielle braced herself for the usual pang of guilt, but it did not come. The Travellers had never blamed her for Baluka leaving them, and it seemed she had finally stopped doing so too. It helped that Baluka had not sought out his family since the Raen died. Though it was possible he was avoiding them for their benefit. Perhaps he had heard they had disappeared, guessed that they were hiding and dared not seek their location in case stronger sorcerers could read it from his mind.

Though Lejihk would prefer that his son inherited his position as leader of the family, he was also proud of him for taking the leadership of the rebellion and helping to defeat the Raen. *There are worse things an estranged son could do*, the man thought. He was smiling as he turned to Rielle. "What news do you have of the worlds?"

"It's all third-hand, but . . ." She paused to take a sip of the drink, then began to relate what she had heard.

The conversation did not shift from reports of war and disruption for the next few hours. Lejihk had been visiting cities around the neighbouring worlds, listening in the markets to gossip and rumours, so he had stories of his own to share. To her amusement, and some relief, Qall soon grew bored and was given permission to leave. She watched him rejoin the knot of young men, his posture changing to the slouch of a youth pretending relaxed nonchalance around others his age – and the young women they wanted to impress. She tried to read his mind, but found only silence. That confirmed what the Travellers had suspected: Qall had become as powerful as Valhan when she'd changed his pattern to match the Raen's.

Night came and a meal was prepared. It soon became clear it was to be no ordinary evening, but a feast to farewell Qall. He looked uncomfortable through most of it, but she caught a pleased gleam in his eyes when he lowered them at the speeches they gave towards the end.

When it was over, Ulma made up the second bed in her wagon for Timane, and Ankari rolled out the bed from under the one she shared with Lejihk for Rielle. As the activity around the wagons quietened, Rielle could almost imagine she had never left. That she'd never accepted Valhan's offer to work as an artisan in his palace. Never learned to be ageless. Never refused to resurrect Valhan and saved Qall. Never met Tyen.

Tyen. While the prospect of protecting and teaching Qall intimidated her, after talking to Lejihk and Ankari she had almost reached a state of confidence and belief that doing her best would be enough. Now a ripple of anxiety disrupted that near-calm.

Where are you, Tyen? Why did you leave the desert world? Why didn't you let me or Tarran know why you left? Have you learned to pattern-shift? Are you trapped in a dead world?

If the worst had happened, she might never have the answers to those questions. As Tarran had said: she could do nothing but wait and hope. Like Tyen, she had a promise to keep. She sighed, rolled over and resolved to think about it no more that night.

CHAPTER 4

The sun – a small greenish disc in this world – was well up when Rielle followed Lejihk and Ankari out of the wagon. She had seen glimpses of activity through the small windows, and heard the noises of the family growing more complex and numerous. Now ceaseless motion, sound and activity greeted her. Sections of the canopy over the central space were being removed and bundled up. Men, women and children hurried back and forth, calling out to each other and laughing.

Beyond the wagons, lom were lumbering in and out of sight, their rumbling a bass note behind the rest of the sounds. Nearby, a pair of the beasts were being guided backwards into the harness of a wagon. From the minds of their handlers she learned that the Travellers had regularly taken individual wagons on short journeys to prevent the lom growing unused to pulling heavy loads, and to train the younger Travellers how to drive them. The wagons had been well maintained, ready to leave in case the strife in the worlds spread to this one. They were well set up to resume their trading lifestyle.

As one of the wagons shifted, a familiar figure came into view. Shoulders hunched, Qall watched the preparations. He was wearing one of the warm coats that Ulma had presented to Rielle and Timane. A pair of Travellers passed him, placing a reassuring hand on his arm and shoulder, and he managed a small smile.

Feeling as if she was spying on him, Rielle began to look away,

194

but then a young woman approached him. His face relaxed as he saw her, then frowned as she pressed something into his hands before hurrying away. He looked down, unfolded a piece of cloth and his eyes widened. Looking in the direction she had disappeared in, he appeared to search for her.

A hand touched Rielle's shoulder.

"You and Timane can keep the coats," Ankari said. "We have hundreds of them – they are part of the stock we'll sell as we resume travelling."

"Thank you."

Ankari turned to Lejihk. "Would it be kinder for Rielle to take Qall now, rather than make him watch us packing up, knowing he won't be joining us?"

"It would," Lejihk replied. "Everyone is hurrying in the hopes it will ease the pain of parting too. We don't want to rush only to discover a cracked wheel or lame animal at an inconvenient time later." He looked at Rielle. "Are you ready to adopt your new charge?"

Rielle drew a deep breath and let it out slowly. "As ready as I can be."

Ankari took Rielle's hand and squeezed it. "Take good care of him – and yourself."

"I will," Rielle assured her. She glanced from the woman to her husband, then back again. "You be careful too. The worlds are not as welcoming as they once were – even to Travellers. If you can avoid sorcerers powerful enough to read your minds, it will reduce the chance any will learn of Qall and try to track us, or punish you for hiding him."

The couple nodded. "We'll try," Lejihk told her. "I will avoid telling the others why we were in hiding for as long as possible, but once the truth is out at least if any sorcerers do see memories of Qall in our minds, they'll also learn that he is not who he appears to be."

"They will also see that the Raen's friends seek him," Rielle reminded them. "Some might resent you for preventing them from finding him – or for protecting someone the Raen's friends value."

Lejihk shrugged. "If they want to find something in it to object about, they will. We'll deal with that if it happens."

"Then I hope your skills of persuasion have been kept in as good a condition as your wagons and lom."

Ankari chuckled. "There is always a youngster of a quarrelsome age among us to practise on. Qall has been particularly good for the task."

Rielle's stomach sank a little. "Is he very quarrelsome?"

"Only a little," Ankari assured her. "And you may find you enjoy the discussions."

"I have to confess," Rielle murmured, "I'm more afraid of trying to look after a youngster – even a grown one – than of fending off his enemies."

Ankari laughed. "Then I know I need not worry about either of you. You have the skills now to defend yourself and your companions. Qall is no child; he's an adult with very little experience of the worlds. Think of yourself as his guide, allowing him to gain that experience safely. As all parents are."

"A guide," Rielle repeated. She looked for Qall, finding him on the other side of the circle, still searching for the girl, or someone else. She drew another deep breath. "I had better find Timane."

Ankari looked around. "I'll fetch her for you." She turned to Lejihk. "Call him over before he gets distracted."

As the woman walked away, Lejihk called to Qall and beckoned. The young man's shoulders slumped. He looked around the camp once more, then shrugged and strode across to meet them.

"Is it time to go?" he asked.

"Yes, Qall," Lejihk answered. "Are you ready?"

Qall nodded to his pack. "Yes."

"That's a small pack. Do you have everything you wish to take with you?" Rielle asked.

The young man glanced around, then shrugged once more. "Everything I can."

"Rielle!" a high voice called. They turned to see Timane hurrying towards them, her own pack already on her shoulders, Ankari following. "Don't leave without me!"

Though Timane grinned to show she didn't truly think Rielle would, her thoughts betrayed her anxiety. *I could do worse than being abandoned with the Travellers, but I'd rather help Rielle.*

Rielle hid her consternation. What had she done to deserve such loyalty? She had given Timane relief from the bullying of the other servants, and taught her to use her meagre powers. That was all. At Rielle's thoughtful look, Timane grimaced.

"Sorry I held you up. Ulma tells good stories."

"She certainly does." Rielle smiled. She turned to Ankari. "Final farewells?"

The woman nodded and wordlessly turned to Qall, drawing him into an embrace, which he managed to return with the grudging stiffness of someone not old enough yet to be sure such affection didn't make him look foolish to his peers. To Rielle's surprise, Lejihk also hugged him, and suddenly Qall did not look at all embarrassed.

"Be careful," Lejihk told him. "Remember all we taught you. Above all, remember you are in charge of the kind of person you will become." He smiled. "I hope we will cross paths again, many times."

"Listen to Rielle," Ankari urged. "She knows the worlds and their dangers better than we."

Qall's gaze flickered to Rielle, then away again, and his expression made her wish she could read his mind. Was it disbelief she had seen? Or simply a measuring look?

At last, the two Travellers stepped away, gesturing as if to say, "He's all yours." Rielle slung her pack on, Qall following suit. She stepped forward and held out a hand to him. After a slight hesitation, he took it. His skin was warm and grip firm. She looked for Timane, and the girl stepped in to grab her other offered hand. Timane and Qall linked their free hands.

Without Rielle having to tell either, they both drew a deep breath. She nodded to Lejihk and Ankari, then pushed out of the world.

Qall looked around at the camp as it faded. Some of the Travellers had stopped to watch, and a few raised hands to wish him farewell. As all became white, Qall's expression went blank.

Rielle had discussed which way to travel with Lejihk and Ulma the night before. This world was just outside of those that the Travellers' trading routes covered, yet still well within what Valhan had dominated. Ulma had advised her to seek a home where nobody had ever heard of the Raen. That meant travelling a long way – further than Rielle had ever explored. It would take as much as a quarter cycle, perhaps more.

Once there, we'll have to find a world with enough magic for me to teach Qall what he needs to know and how to defend ourselves from attack. One with a society where sorcerers aren't disliked or so rare we attract attention, where people aren't so different to us in appearance that we won't fit in, where we have to find a way to earn a living, or at least hunt, gather and grow enough to eat.

She faced a similar difficulty to the one Tyen had, when searching for a world in which to become ageless. Unpopulated, hospitable worlds rich in magic were extremely rare, and often did not remain so for long. If people could live somewhere, they would. Tyen had improved his chances by selecting a world that had become inhospitable – well, she had chosen it for him. It was suitable because he did not need to stay long. She did not know how long they would have to stay, so it needed to be hospitable, which meant she could not avoid unpopulated worlds. Instead they would seek one where three strangers could make a home without attracting much notice.

It was generally believed that the further you travelled, the stranger and more hostile the worlds became. Ulma disagreed.

She said the worlds were like trees of a forest, which grew around obstacles like mountains and lakes, forming arms in fertile valleys. Some of these arms linked with other forests. If Ulma was right, Rielle could eventually find an arm that led to a forest Valhan had never visited.

Fortunately, she could begin their journey at speed. Lejihk had recommended a safe path through the neighbouring worlds. If someone followed them, she would be able to travel quickly to shake off pursuit without worrying that she would flee into an area of dead worlds.

Even if someone saw Qall and thought he was Valhan, it was unlikely they would follow them. But news of the sighting would spread quickly, and once Dahli heard, he and his supporters would rush to track her. So it would be better if nobody saw Qall. As they arrived in the next world, she turned to him.

"Put up your hood."

He paused, surprised, then reached back and pulled his coat's hood over his head. It wouldn't hide his face from anyone approaching from the front, but it would conceal him from casual glances.

Pushing away from that world, she concentrated on following Lejihk's instructions. In places, the paths between worlds were faint; in others, they were deeply tracked. Most of the time she had to skim to new locations from which to leave, but occasionally a new path led from the arrival site. Now and then she skimmed away from the arrival place and made a new path running parallel to the one Lejihk had recommended, practising using Tyen's method of concealing his path to hide the beginning and end of their journey.

After they had travelled through twenty or more worlds, she reached a thoroughfare Lejihk had told her was the main route to a great market. Assured it was safe, she was able to pass through several worlds in quick succession before stopping to allow Qall and Timane to catch their breath in a night-shadowed alcove of the market.

When they had, she gathered more power.

"Wait," Qall said.

Turning to look at him, she saw in the lamplight that his brow was furrowed.

"What's wrong?"

He let go of her and Timane's hands and pushed back his hood. "We're going too fast. Can you slow down?"

"Why?"

"So I can memorise the path."

"You don't need to, Qall."

"How will I find my way back?"

"Your family won't be there."

He looked away, his frown deepening. "How will I find them?"

"By searching through the worlds for Travellers, then asking for Lejihk. They will lead you to him."

"But . . . I . . . When will you teach me how to travel between worlds?"

"When we find somewhere safe to live."

His lips pressed firmly together. "What if we get separated before then? Wouldn't it be better – for Timane too – if I could do it now?"

Rielle shook her head. "It takes time to learn how to do it safely." A movement in the corner of her eye made her tense. "Put your hood back up."

He obeyed reluctantly. "It's not as though anyone will recognise me."

"In some worlds, people are paid to watch and memorise or record descriptions of people using arrival places. If anyone discovers that you were hiding with Lejihk's family they will try to track you using the memories and records of these observers."

"If they know you took me away from them, they'll look for you in these records."

Rielle nodded. "They might. But I need to be able to see where I'm taking us. Still, it would be wise to make some changes."

Taking a little extra magic from the world, Rielle stared at a lock of her hair lying against her chest. She concentrated her will, stripping them of colour, then spreading the change across all of her hair. The next alteration was easier, introducing a twist that made her hair shorten as it curled.

Timane was staring at her in astonishment. She tugged at her hood. "Ah . . . should I?"

Rielle shook her head. "The people we are avoiding aren't looking for a young woman of your colouring, build and age. Keep your hood down. I need you to warn me if any danger appears behind me." She held out her hand to Qall. Air hissed out of his nose as he sighed. He took hold of her hand, his mouth turning down at the corners.

She pushed out of the world.

Quickening their pace, she had only time enough to spare the occasional glance at him. His frown changed from one of annoyance to worry, then it vanished and he simply looked forlorn and a little ill. She stopped.

"Are you all right?" she asked.

He nodded, but his shoulders sagged.

"Really?" she asked, both sympathetic and disbelieving.

"So far," he said, grimacing. "I didn't think we'd go so far."

She squeezed his hand. "We have barely begun. Don't worry – you'll be able to travel like this one day. It won't seem so far then."

The tightness in his face eased a little. Timane smiled sympathetically.

They continued on. Soon after, they reached the end of the path Lejihk had recommended. Anticipating this, Rielle had taken extra magic from the last five worlds of the route. Qall's head rose the first time she did so, and as she paused to let them catch their breath, he turned to her again.

"Are you expecting trouble?" he asked.

She shook her head.

"But you've been gathering magic."

"In case we arrive in a dead world. This is as far as Lejihk's suggested path goes. I'm surprised he travelled this far actually."

"Why would you be?" He sounded defensive.

She met his gaze. "Lejihk is a strong sorcerer, but not so strong that he could easily gather enough magic to escape a dead world. Before he visits a world unknown to him, he has three options: travel around a neighbouring world drawing enough magic to escape the new world if it proves to be a dead one; glean what he can of that world from people in neighbouring ones and hope the information is still correct; or simply enter the world and hope it contains magic. Since he'd never risk being unable to return to his family, he must have been choosing the first two options, and they take time. He has spent a lot of effort, and been absent from the family a great deal to map this path – not to establish a new trade route, as this is further than the family would normally travel, but to give us a safe start to this journey."

Qall considered that, and nodded. "So what do we do now?"

"I now have plenty of magic in reserve to escape a dead world if we encounter one, so we continue on – but carefully. We will take recently used paths as they are less likely to lead to dead worlds. It is still possible they could lead to a world that has been recently drained of magic, but it is unlikely."

He shuddered. "What happens to the people in a world if that happens?"

"To most ordinary people, little changes. It depends how much they rely on sorcerers. Those sorcerers will find themselves without magic to call upon. The ageless will no longer be so. Eventually, depending on how populated and prosperous a world it is, it will recover as people generate more magic, but by then most ageless will have grown old and died."

"If the sorcerers held power over the ordinary people, the lives of all would change dramatically."

She nodded. A chill ran down her spine, but she ignored it.

Just because he can see the political implications of such a situation doesn't mean he is thinking like Valhan.

Qall looked away and she guessed from this that he had no more questions. Pushing into the place between, she turned her mind to travelling again.

With no way to measure time, and her body healing away weariness and hunger, it was impossible to judge how much was passing. From time to time, she paused to read Timane's mind. When the girl grew hungry and weary, Rielle decided to stop and look for food.

The next arrival place was in an ocean world where people lived on clusters of islands. She flitted over the minds of people as Valhan had once taught her, to judge the general character of a society. It was welcoming to visitors, used to trading with neighbouring worlds. Even so, she hid her path then skimmed to another island, in case these traders arrived and recognised Qall.

There she found a woman willing to let out the seaside hut her husband stored his boat in, currently empty because he was away fishing for a few days. They bought food from the woman as well, and ate it as the sun descended below the horizon, leaving the island lit by the blue light of a moon with a band of light around it; then Timane and Qall crawled into sling beds and fell asleep, while Rielle set her back against the wall to watch over them.

Listening to the sound of their breathing, Rielle healed away weariness. She doubted she would sleep until they were far beyond the worlds the Raen had ruled. How long that would be, she couldn't guess. But she'd reach it eventually. Only then would she rest.

CHAPTER 5

O nce dawn arrived, the hut grew unbearably warm. Timane and Qall woke and threw off the jackets that had kept the chill of night at bay. Qall moved to the door.

"Qall, stop," Rielle warned. He froze and looked back at her. She nodded at the coat at the end of his bed. "Hood up, or wait here."

He looked appalled. "But it's so hot."

"We won't be here long." She took a square of gold out of her purse and handed it to Timane. "Buy some food."

The girl nodded and slipped out of the hut.

Qall crossed his arms. "I need to pee. Do you want me to do that in here too?"

She nodded. "Wait here. I'll get a bucket."

The sun's heat made her wince. Timane was already several strides away, heading towards a fan-shaped shelter under which several locals were lounging. Rielle cast about, but found no suitable vessel nearby. She started after Timane.

A short while later, she and the girl returned carrying a bucket, a bowl full of some kind of salted and fried sea creature and a crisp, slightly slimy vegetable that looked like the pith from the centre of a reed. As Rielle reached the hut door, she froze. It was slightly open. Grabbing the handle, she pulled.

The room inside was empty. Qall's coat lay on one of the beds.

Muttering a curse, she grabbed the coat and searched the area with both eyes and mind. In the thoughts of two children, brother and sister, she found him. They were leading him towards the altar around which most of the villagers were now gathered for their daily worship. To the statue of the Hero, brought by the missionaries many generations before, worn but still recognisable.

Rielle grabbed Timane, pushed out of the world and skimmed towards them. The thick vegetation along the beach blurred past. The trees beyond whipped to either side. A cluster of huts surrounded them, all radiating out from a mound around which a crowd had gathered. Qall was less than a hundred strides away.

Skimming to a stop in front of him, Rielle returned to the world with Timane.

"What are you doing?" she hissed at Qall.

He smiled down at the children. "There's no danger here. They think I'm their saviour. The Hero they worship."

The two children repeated the word "hero" in the local language, gazing up at his face. They were holding tight to his hands.

Qall looked up at Rielle. "We could stay here. They won't hurt us. They'll—"

"You can't stay here," she snapped.

The children regarded Rielle with suspicion, not at all surprised that she had just materialised in front of them. *Familiar with sorcerous ways. That's a bad sign.*

She gently pushed the girl away and took Qall's hand. "There is danger even here," Rielle told him, keeping her tone quiet and persuasive. Timane, guessing her intention, freed his other hand from the boy child's grip.

"But they would never harm the one they worshipped."

"Others would hear about you, and come to see for themselves. Other more powerful people," Rielle told him. "People who don't worship this Hero; who would be jealous of your power or seek to gain from it. Who would harm these people in order to manipulate you."

"We wouldn't let them."

"As a living god, you would attract attention outside this world. Your enemies would eventually notice."

"And you are not who they think you are," Timane added. "You'd be deceiving these people. That's not fair."

Rielle glanced at the girl in surprise and dismay. When had Timane learned that he looked like the Raen? A quick look in the girl's mind revealed that Timane had only seen that the children thought Qall looked like their Hero, not that the Hero looked like the Raen.

Qall's shoulders fell. Pushing out of the world, Rielle took them back to the hut.

"Get our packs," she said to Timane. "I'll take us somewhere more comfortable to eat." Timane set down the bowl and hurried to obey. Qall looked down at his wrist, which Rielle was still holding. She let it go, took his coat and held it out. Reluctantly, he slipped his arms in and pulled up the hood. He stood with his back to her, which she took to be in sullen protest until she caught a movement in the direction he faced.

People were pushing through the vegetation fringing the beach several hundred paces away, and when they saw Qall and Rielle they began running towards them. Looking in their minds, she read hope and delight from those who had believed the children's claims that the Hero was on the beach, and anger from those who thought the visitors had made just a preposterous, blasphemous claim.

"Hurry, Timane," Rielle called.

The girl emerged and handed them their packs. Shouldering hers, Rielle didn't wait until the others had done the same before grabbing their arms and pushing out of the world. Immediately the heat was gone – and she saw her relief mirrored in her companions' faces. The villagers were nearly upon them. She skimmed quickly out over the water, then higher so they could see further into the distance. The island disappeared over the horizon.

Ahead, the arc of a sandbank appeared, as white as snow. Heading for that, she set them down on the grassy centre. Only then did she realise that they'd left the bowl of food back beside the hut.

Sighing, she fished out of her bag some of their dried travelling rations and handed it around. They all brought out their water flasks. Qall looked less annoyed now, Rielle was glad to see.

"So who is this man they call the Hero?" he asked suddenly. "The village elders also called him the Raen and believe he is a hero in all worlds."

Timane coughed, choking on a mouthful of water. She looked from Rielle to Qall, her eyebrows high with disbelief.

Rielle shook her head. "I don't know about the Hero, but I know about the Raen. He was a very powerful sorcerer, hated in some worlds and loved in others. You are not him either."

"He *was* a sorcerer?"

"He died."

"Well, then I don't have to fear him at least."

"No." Rielle rose and held out her hands. "Let's move on."

Qall paused. "These people we're hiding from . . . they'd have harmed my family if I'd been found with them?"

"Perhaps."

He nodded and took Rielle's hand. "Then it is good that I left."

A wary relief filled her. Was this the first sign of him accepting his new future? Linking hands with her two companions, she skimmed across the world. Hoping to avoid more encounters with worshippers of the Hero, she stopped here and there to search minds whenever they encountered small settlements. It became apparent that he was one of this world's most popular deities. Travelling away from the sun, she reached a city still in darkness and found an arrival place with an established path leading away.

From there, they barely paused in each world, only standing long enough on solid ground for the young man and woman to catch their breath and Rielle to draw enough magic to replace what she'd used. The arrival places were situated in greater and more elaborate city locations. Some were outdoors – a vast plaza or raised dais. Some were enclosed – sheltered by delicate pergolas or protected within soaring, highly decorated domes. Sometimes hundreds of uninterested citizens walked by; sometimes they were surrounded by a circle of watchful guards.

All the time, Qall kept his hood up, his face hidden in the shadows and his shoulders hunched in a manner that could be fearful or sullen. All Rielle could see of his eyes was a faint gleam now and then as he lifted his head to observe each new, increasingly grand location.

Then abruptly the spectacle changed. They arrived between two halves of an immense stone roof, split down the centre. One half sloped towards them, its far end raised on an unseen prop. The other, behind Qall, had been flung outward to rest against the pedestal of an enormous statue.

Rielle looked up and her blood froze. Qall glowered back at her, a thousand times larger than his living form. She heard Timane gasp and, looking down again, saw that the girl was staring at the statue, her mouth agape. As was Qall, his hood slipping back as his head remained tilted. He let go of Rielle's hand to catch it.

Timane tore her eyes away. Her gaze moved to Qall. He met it; then they both turned to stare at Rielle.

She bit back a curse. *What were the chances we'd pass through so many worlds without him seeing something like this?* Paths tended to end and start in important locations, and none were more important than where the ruler of worlds was worshipped.

"This Hero, this Raen . . . he is a god in many worlds, isn't he?" Qall asked.

"Yes."

"And he is dead."

"Yes."

"So a lot of people would like him to return."

"Yes, but more do not."

"But the ones who want to find me, do."

"Yes." Then she added, "You are not him, Qall. Your body was changed to look like his, but they didn't have a chance to replace your mind."

He turned away from the statue and she caught a fleeting, reproachful glance sent in her direction before he lowered his head and retreated into the hood. His voice, quiet and shaken, emerged.

"Is there anywhere he isn't known?"

"Lejihk believes so. I believe so. Nobody, in all the thousands of cycles of human existence, has ever mapped out a limit to the worlds."

He said nothing.

"We will find a safe place for you," she assured him. "I will explain more when we—"

"Just go." He sighed and shook his head.

"What is it?" she prompted.

"Just . . . go. There's no point staying." His head lowered further. His words were nearly inaudible. "I can never come back."

Her heart twisted. Timane's hand moved, squeezing his in sympathy. Which was admirable considering what the young woman had just learned about him. She looked at Rielle. "Is that true?"

"No," Rielle told them both. "Once we have found a safe place to live, I will teach Qall pattern shifting. He will be able to change his appearance, and then he can go wherever he likes."

His head rose. She caught twin flashes of reflected light within the hood. He said nothing, but nodded and extended a hand.

His grip was firm. After the others had taken a deep breath, Rielle pushed out of the world and sought the next path. Qall had somehow retreated further into the hood of his coat, so she could only see his face below his nose. He did not look up and around, or at her or Timane. For a while his withdrawal distracted her, but she resisted the urge to try to draw him out, or at least reassure him. Part of her was still shocked by the statue of Valhan. She could not help seeing him in Qall's firmly pressed lips and tense jaw. She was too conscious of the touch of his hand. It wasn't anger at Valhan that discomfited her, but the echo of the admiration and fascination she'd once felt. It would have been easier to forgive her foolish gullibility if it had been simple infatuation, but she had come to approve of him, even agree with him.

None of the Raen's memories had been imprinted in Qall's mind. Only his body had been changed and memories removed. She'd wondered who he had been before then many times since leaving Qall with the Travellers, but resisted the temptation to try to find out. If Dahli knew where Qall had come from, his people would be there watching in case someone started making enquiries about a missing boy with particularly strong magical ability.

How strong was an interesting question. Qall might be stronger than her now, but had he been before? Or had changing his body to match Valhan's pattern made him more powerful? Either possibility was significant. If it hadn't, if he had been as strong as Valhan, perhaps he was supposed to have been the Successor. If changing him to look like Valhan had made him as powerful, the implications were frightening. It meant she could do it again using Qall as the source of the pattern. She could make lesser sorcerers as powerful as the Raen had been, with the only penalty being that they would look like him until they learned to pattern-shift and change their appearance.

She could do it to herself. The thought that she might look like Valhan, no matter how briefly, was a very strange thought indeed.

So she turned her mind to traversing the worlds, and resolved not to think about it again until they had found somewhere safe to build a new home. Pushing on from world to world, looking for signs that the Raen was loved, feared, worshipped or merely known of, she must eventually find a place where they could make a home, safe and free from the danger that Qall would be recognised. A world far from his family, but also far from Dahli and his schemes.

In the meantime, she would have to watch Qall closely, in case he hadn't learned his lesson from the encounter with the islanders. The three of them would grow weary of constant movement, and the sense of danger would lessen with time and distance. The temptation to stop where the people were friendly would grow more powerful the longer and further they travelled. She could not slow their pace or compromise on the need to travel beyond the Raen's influence, however. They must, at the least, settle in a world where nobody knew who the Raen was.

CHAPTER 6

As she searched minds, Rielle felt a now-familiar dread. Every time she had thought she'd reached a place where the Raen was not known, she had heard his name in someone's mind. Though she always checked the minds of those in power, it was usually in the markets that Rielle found the evidence that propelled them onward. Twice already they had moved on from a world that looked promising. Each time she'd pushed them on for at least fifty more worlds before she stopped again. After an eighth of a cycle's travelling and passing through what felt like thousands of worlds, had they finally moved beyond the limit of the Raen's influence?

Perched on a doorstep, with a scrap of old fabric covering her head and a dirty, tattered blanket wrapped around her shoulders, she let her mind drift over the thoughts of stallholders and customers. *Ah! There!* The Traveller tongue was being used somewhat clumsily by a local merchant to communicate with an otherworld sorcerer selling exotic trinkets.

Rielle watched. When the women parted, Rielle ignored the merchant and watched the sorcerer's thoughts. People tended to reflect a little on a conversation before their next task distracted them. The woman was digesting the news the merchant had told her. A civil war. Strife in a nearby world. Prophets in the sorcerer's home world would no doubt claim a distant civil war was more proof that the strange circles of light in the sky, several cycles ago, warned of the end of the universe. They had ordered the sorcerers from their world to look for such signs. She snorted at that. They'd said nothing about looking for evidence the worlds were *not* ending. They never did.

As the sorcerer turned her mind to finding the next merchant interested in her wares, Rielle brought her full awareness back to her surroundings. The overcast sky looked no different to when she'd arrived, but the people around her knew instinctively that evening was drawing close. Watching them, she waited until nobody was looking in her direction before pushing out of the world.

White surrounded her. She retraced her steps through four worlds, circling back to the one in which she'd left Timane and Qall. As she travelled, she considered what she had learned about the worlds neighbouring their prospective home. None worshipped the Raen, and neither the general populace nor ruling elite appeared to know of him. A few traders and sorcerers had heard of him, but only as a powerful figure important to distant worlds that didn't matter to them.

They do to me. Thinking of the people she'd left behind sent a pang of sorrow through her. She had not had the chance to bid Tarran farewell properly. She hoped her message had reached him. Had Tyen come back? Was he annoyed at her for disappearing? *Well, he left me with no explanation.* She shook her head. She had no claim over him. They'd been lovers, no more. She had vanished from so many people's lives in the past that she had no right to complain when someone disappeared from hers. He probably had as good a reason as she to leave without explanation.

But she hoped he felt as guilty about it as she did.

Night shrouded ruins surrounding her as she arrived in their potential new home world. It was raining. Heavy cloud hid the stars. Once she had searched for minds nearby and found none, she created a light. Wet, blackened wood glistened like the molten iron. It lay in piles where houses had once stood.

Occasionally, a skeletal wall remained. Moving into the recently abandoned city, she made her way down to the rubble-strewn remains of one of the larger buildings. Mostly made of stone, more of it remained standing than the wooden structures, though the interior was charred. She slipped inside and made her way to a tower at the centre, and pushed through a half-burned door into a darkened stairwell.

Brightening the light, she descended.

Four hundred and sixteen steps later she emerged to find a murky dawn filtering through the clouds. Gentle hills stretched before her. Swapping the old scarf for a newer one and bundling the blanket up, she made her way down the slope. By the time she had reached the narrow muddy track that passed for a road, the hidden sun was up. She started along it.

As she walked, she searched for minds and found Timane angrily washing up dishes in the abandoned cottage they had repaired and adopted. Qall hadn't come home the night before, or the two previous. Rielle's heart skipped a beat. *So where is he?* She quickened her pace, at the same time looking for human minds in the hills around her. She found none until she reached the small village in the next valley. Nobody there was thinking about the white-faced young foreigner. The path took her out of the trees and up to the cottage door.

"He's up at the cave," Timane said from the doorway. She too had adopted the local habit of wearing a scarf tied around her head. "Been there since you left – three days now. He sneaks in for some food when I'm asleep." She scowled. "I think he must be reading my mind. Last night I sat in a chair in the hopes of catching him, but I fell asleep and when I woke up the food was gone. I guess he figures if he's not here when I'm awake, I can't tell him to do anything."

"Why do you think he's doing it?"

The girl shook her head. "If I didn't know anything about him, I'd say he was being lazy – avoiding work like the male servants his age at the palace. Which is silly when he can use magic to do it. Maybe he doesn't like taking orders from a former servant."

"He won't have learned that from the Travellers."

"No, but he's not among the Travellers now, and he's just learned that he looks like someone people will obey without question."

Rielle frowned. "Has he been officious? Cruel?"

Timane grimaced. "No. Just disobedient." She let out a long sigh. "I guess he's struggling to adjust. When I remember that he's lost his family and learned people want to kill him, I can't stay angry with him for long. I wish he'd talk to me. Maybe he'll talk to you."

"Maybe." Rielle started along the side of the cottage, where the track up to the cave began. "I'll see if I can persuade him to join us, at least."

She climbed slowly, considering what his behaviour could mean. He probably wanted time alone to think over the changes in his life. That was understandable, but they also needed to clean up the cottage and find a way to earn a living or acquire food. She had hoped being involved in making a home here might help him accept it more easily.

When she had nearly reached the cave, she looked up and stilled. The cave was more of an overhang where wind and rain had washed away the earth below rocks embedded in the hillside. Silhouetted against the clouds, Qall sat with his back hunched, his elbows on his knees and his head supported on his hands.

Every part of him expressed misery.

Taking a deep breath, she looked down and moved on, deliberately making noise to let him know someone was approaching. The shape against the clouds moved abruptly, and when she glanced up again he was sitting straight, gazing out at the darkened valley with a lofty expression.

"Qall," she said. "I hear you've been sulking."

He turned to regard her, his eyebrows rising. "Not sulking," he said defensively. "Thinking."

She sat down beside him, on a lower boulder.

"What have you been thinking about?"

He looked away. "Nothing you'd be interested in."

She crossed her arms. "Have you read my mind?"

He frowned. "No." A hint of softness in his voice sent a chill down her spine. Was he lying?

"Then how do you know whether I'd be interested?"

His frown deepened. "Because . . . I'm thinking about things that only matter to me."

"If they matter to you then I am interested."

He glanced at her then looked away.

"Is there anything I can help with?" she asked.

"No."

He'd answered reflexively, without thinking. She watched him, waiting. His eyes shifted in her direction; he pursed his lips, scratched at an ankle, then sighed.

"I don't like this world. The people here hate foreigners and otherworlders. They think we brought the plague. What if the plague returns?"

"If it does, if you and Timane catch it, I will heal you." She looked down the valley at the distant lights of the village, visible at this height. "The people will accept us, if we don't give them cause to fear us. If we trade with them, and obey their laws, they will grow used to us. Their suspicions will alert us if someone comes looking for us.

"But we need something to trade with them. Something ordinary. They don't have much use for precious metals and gemstones – and my store of those won't last for ever anyway."

"So we sow crops and raise animals?"

"Yes, and we learn useful skills. Nothing too fancy."

"Can't we go to the cities and buy things to trade with them?"

"Not yet. If that's what you'd like to do, then you can do

it once your training is finished. For now, we have to live simply."

"So when will you start training me?"

"When we . . ." *What? Have something to exchange for food?* They didn't need to wait. Crops took time to grow. Raising animals was not done in an instant. Between these tasks, she could make time to teach him. ". . . have eaten. Later today," she said. "Then tomorrow we will clear some land and plant the seeds I bought at the market. Does that suit you?"

He met her gaze, face smooth but hope shining from his eyes.

"Will you teach me how to travel between worlds?"

"It's more urgent that you learn to defend yourself," she told him. She stalled his protest with a raised hand. "I know the Travellers taught you some defensive fighting, but they can't teach you how to fend off very powerful sorcerers, or hundreds of attackers."

His mouth closed with a snap and he nodded. "Will I learn here?"

"No. It will frighten the locals. We'll have to find a suitable place. Perhaps up at the ruins. Not now, though. First I need to test your knowledge and skill, and we can do that without using much magic."

He swivelled on the rock to face her. "When?"

She shrugged. "Now, I suppose. If you're ready."

"I am."

But where to start? Her first lessons in magic after leaving her world had been with Baluka. He'd tested her reach and tried to show her how to travel between worlds. The latter had been a disaster. He hadn't been a particularly good teacher, but then he had probably taken the same approach that his teacher – most likely Lejihk – had used with young Travellers already accustomed to using magic and familiar with the concept of world travelling.

Dahli had been a better teacher. He too had tested her strength before giving her many exercises to develop her reflexes and concentration. She would do the same with Qall.

"First, let's try to establish how strong you are," she said.

As Baluka had with her, she instructed him to reach out as far as he could with his mind and tell her what he sensed. She was not surprised when his senses encompassed the whole world.

"That's amazing!" he gasped. "The world really is a globe! And magic . . . it's like a fog that can penetrate everything – even the ground."

At first, his reaction startled her. She'd assumed the Travellers would have tested his strength this way. Perhaps they had done it in a way that didn't reveal to him how powerful he was. Fortunately, his eyes were still closed so he didn't see her surprise. She smiled at the wonder in his face. *Not an expression I ever saw on Valhan's face*, she couldn't help thinking. *After living a thousand cycles, perhaps nothing could impress him any more.*

"It's denser and lighter in places," Qall said. "Why is that?"

"Most likely it's stronger around cities, where more people live and create."

He nodded. "There are two thinner parts opposite each other."

"The poles, perhaps," she said. "On some worlds they are too cold for humans to live. In others there's a central band that is too hot. Sometimes a world has a side that is too cold or hot, because one side always faces the sun or suns."

Qall opened his eyes. "I'd like to see that."

"You will one day," she told him.

He looked at the sky. "I had no idea I could do that."

"Not many people can sense all the way around the world. How far you can is called your 'reach'."

"How rare is it?"

"I know of three people who can. You, me and a friend. This is a small world though. Some worlds are too large for me to sense the entirety of." She thought back to her own world, recalling that Valhan had needed to travel from the north to the south in order to take in all the magic in it, which was proof that her world had been larger than average – and that even he had had limits.

Which meant Qall did too. She remembered, as she had many times, what she had learned from Dahli: at times Valhan hadn't been able to read her mind. She did not think that meant she had been equal to him in strength, but she might have been close. Qall should have trouble reading her mind too, though he shouldn't be trying. He ought to be sticking to the Travellers' rule of good manners that said you should respect the privacy of family members and friends – especially your elders.

"Reach out again," she instructed Qall. "Tell me where you can take magic without anyone noticing."

"At the poles," he said.

"Not necessarily. It may be cold there, but people can live in very hostile places – especially if they have magic."

"So . . . nowhere, because you'll be able to sense it."

"Discount me."

He squeezed his eyes shut. "Then . . . high in the air?"

"You could take it from there, yes. The chance that a sorcerer will notice is slim."

"And far underground?"

"Yes. People are often unaware of what is below solid ground. An absence of magic feels like darkness, and it is easier to hide darkness in a place with no light."

"If I slice an even layer off the furthest outer edge, it wouldn't be as obvious as taking a chunk somewhere."

She nodded, pleased. "Or the lowest inner edge."

"So magic doesn't extend right through the globe . . . ? Ah! I see. If I took a slice of equal thickness from the inner and outer edges, the one from the inner would contain less magic, since the area gets smaller the closer you get to the centre of the globe."

"You get the idea," she said. "Take a little magic now. You won't need much. We're going to do some skill tests."

Qall followed her instructions willingly at first, but as she worked her way through tests of his reflexes and control, he quickly grew impatient.

"I've done all this before," he grumbled as he floated effortlessly a hand span from the ground.

"Yes, but *I* don't know what you can and can't do," she replied. "I don't want to waste time devising whole lessons only to discover you already know what I want to teach you or that I miss a hole in your knowledge. I need to know the level of skill you have. Come down and sit."

He obeyed, returning to the rock.

"What do you know of the five applications of magic?"

He shook his head. "The Travellers don't divide them up into five. They have three: basic, mind reading and world travelling."

"What are the basic kinds?"

"Moving, stilling, heating and cooling." He paused. "Which are two kinds, since to heat you move, and to cool it you still."

"Correct. What do you know of mind reading?"

He shrugged. "A stronger sorcerer can read a weaker sorcerer's mind even if they are blocking. People without magical ability can't block at all."

"What else?"

He drummed his fingers on his knees. "It is impolite to read the mind of family and friends."

"Among the Travellers. In many worlds it is forbidden to read minds, so if you do you had better not be too obvious about it. Have you read Timane's mind?"

Looking away, Qall bit his lip and didn't answer for a moment. "Ah . . . she's not family."

"So you think, therefore, that she doesn't deserve to be treated with respect?"

"No."

Rielle set her elbows on her knees and steepled her fingers. "She knows you read her mind. She's no fool. You should apologise."

He nodded. "I will," he murmured.

"I understand the temptation," she told him. "We are in a

220

position where we may need to bend rules, but only when it's necessary. The only person I expect you to not read the mind of is me. For everyone else, I want you to get used to reading minds and not showing any sign that you have."

He looked up. "But what if . . .?" He stopped and shook his head.

"What?"

"What if we encounter Travellers?"

"It's unlikely we will, but if we do it's up to you to decide whether you will respect their privacy or not. I will be reading their minds, however. I won't be taking any risks."

He nodded.

Next on the list was world travelling, and she hesitated as she considered how much to tell him. She was reluctant to even talk about it in case she gave him a clue or an incentive to try to do it on his own. But if she did, she could underline the dangers, which would encourage him to wait for lessons.

"My teacher told me there are five kinds of magic. Moving and stilling were the first two, mind reading the third, world travelling the fourth," she explained. "Did you ever travel between worlds with your family?"

A light had entered his eyes. "Only when I was younger, when they were looking for a place to settle."

"What do you understand of it?"

"Not much. I know that the place between is white, and that you can't breathe while you're there so you will suffocate if you stay too long. I know about 'skimming', where you move out of a world a little so you can still see it, then change your position."

Rielle nodded. "Moving away and towards a world is a little like pushing and pulling, but not exactly. Lejihk's son tried to teach me by describing it that way, but I couldn't do it because I couldn't stop thinking of it as a physical act rather than a mental one. The place between is more accurately described as light or energy. It is like the opposite of the darkness we perceive as the absence of—"

"How did you learn to travel between worlds then?" he interrupted.

She smiled. "I read how to from a sorcerer's mind as he was doing it."

His eyebrows rose and his eyes brightened with interest.

Perhaps I shouldn't have told him that. "And if I ever catch you reading my mind while I push out of a world, I'll make you do a quarter cycle of digging in the fields before I teach you anything more."

His mouth twisted in amused defeat.

"I will teach you, once you know all of the dangers," she told him. "Suffocation is only one. Arriving inside something would be a particularly unpleasant way to die. Arriving at a dangerous orientation to the ground is another risk. Knowing exactly how to protect yourself the instant you arrive is vital. The environment you arrive in may have hidden dangers, like poisoned air, unstable ground or temperatures that could kill you."

"Why would a path lead to a place where people can't survive?"

"The last sorcerer to travel there might have made the path and died at the other end. Or they backtracked – perhaps when someone who arrived before them died. Or they arrived and left again very quickly. An ageless sorcerer might survive a brief exposure to a dangerous world when an ordinary sorcerer wouldn't.

"Something might have changed since a path was made," she continued. "A volcano explodes. Floods inundate the land. The air is poisoned, by natural or human causes. War breaks out. There are stories of worlds disappearing completely, of suns exploding or going cold, of enormous rocks falling from the sky or the land shaking apart. Then there are the dangers of dead and weak worlds." She grimaced. "Which are becoming more common, I am told."

"Why?"

She opened her mouth to explain, then shook her head. "Another time. Stories of the worlds could take up the rest of the day, and as much as I'd enjoy that, we should stick to the applications of magic. Can you guess what the fifth is?"

His brows lowered as he considered; then he shook his head.

"I don't . . . but I guess it has to be what the last four don't explain. So . . . agelessness?"

"Yes. Or rather, agelessness is only the most coveted use of the fifth application. The application is known as pattern shifting."

"'Pattern shifting'," he repeated. "Shifting patterns. What patterns?"

"The ones that make up every living thing. You. Me. The flying creature over there. Those plants."

"Only living things?"

"I honestly don't know," she admitted. "It might be possible to change those rocks to gold, but I've never heard of anyone doing it. I've only worked with the patterns of living things."

"What can it do other than making someone ageless?"

"Healing. I don't need to worry as much about breathing between worlds because my body heals the damage of suffocation as soon as I arrive in one. I can heal other people. All living things."

"Can you bring the dead back to life?"

"I don't know. I haven't tried. I think, if they hadn't been dead long, I probably could. They might have lost some memories though."

He tensed. "Is that what happened to me?"

"No," she replied. "You never died. You were put into a deep sleep, your bodily processes slowed by cold."

He swallowed and looked down at his hands. "And my memories were removed."

"Mostly. Enough remained that I could see that what was done to you was done against your will."

"Will I ever get those memories back?" His voice was barely audible.

She shook her head. "It's very unlikely at this point. If they were going to return, I think they would have by now. If I hadn't taken you away, what was left would have been erased when . . . when the Raen replaced them."

"Using pattern shifting."

"Yes."

"Is . . . is that how you became ageless?" He looked up, his gaze suddenly piercing. "Do you take over someone else's body when you get old?"

She shuddered at the thought. "No. Nothing like that. I altered my mind so that it constantly uses a little bit of magic to keep my body in the same pattern."

His eyebrows rose. "Oh. That's . . . very different to what I imagined. Much simpler."

"It is only simple once you achieve it. Achieving it takes a great deal of magic and time."

"So why did this Raen want to live in my body?"

"He knew he was going to die. In fact, he deliberately killed himself to make his enemies think they'd defeated him. Only a small part of his body survived – his hand – and he put all of his memories into it, though don't ask me how. That I don't know."

"And my enemies still have this part of him with his memories?"

"I believe so."

He looked away, his gaze fixed far beyond the valley below as he absorbed that. Then he suddenly shrugged and turned back to her.

"What is it like being ageless?"

She considered how to answer that. "I don't feel any different to how I did before, most of the time, but I don't get tired or sick. I still feel like sleeping and eating, because they're natural needs of the body. I might be able to change that, but I guess I'd eventually run out of the stuff my body needs to repair itself.

Or I'd have to change my body so it can get what it needs another way. Which would make me less human.

"That leads me to one of the dangers of pattern shifting," she added. "If you're always aware of how others see you, and keep changing to please them, you may end up forgetting how you're supposed to look. Or want to look."

"You can't return to your original pattern?"

"Perhaps only by stopping your mind automatically pattern shifting."

"So you need to pattern-shift to make any change, and that includes going back to what you were," he said, nodding. "If your body is constantly repairing itself so its pattern remains the same, why doesn't that erase new memories?"

"It only removes flaws." She smiled. "Developments are preserved. Not just memories, but muscle, so if you learn and keep practising a skill, you retain it."

Qall nodded. "I suppose you'd have never done it if that hadn't been true. Not just the memories, but the skills, because you're an artist."

Rielle winced, and he immediately straightened.

"What is it?"

"Nothing relevant to this lesson." She waved a hand dismissively.

"No? How can you be sure? Have you read my mind?"

She nearly laughed aloud at him turning her earlier words against her.

"No, but I'm sure Lejihk and Ankari would have told me if you were a Maker."

He frowned. "I'm not. But you are. Ankari told me."

"I was. Losing that was the price I paid for becoming ageless. You cannot be ageless and a Maker."

His eyebrows rose. "That was a great sacrifice."

She shrugged. "I wasn't told it would happen, so it wasn't a willing sacrifice. However, I never saw much value in generating magic. I can still draw and paint and weave. That's what matters to me."

He nodded slowly, an odd expression on his face – like the knowing look of an elder, but instead of sympathy there was a shine of satisfaction that made his efforts at appearing wise seem unconvincing.

His heart was in the right place though. She stood up. "That's enough for today, I think. You need to apologise to Timane for leaving her alone for days."

His brows lowered. "Must I?"

"Yes. She, like you, has also left behind everything that was familiar."

"She wanted to."

"Because her world was at war. She was sold into near-slavery by her parents, so she could hardly return to them." Rielle sought his gaze, but he avoided meeting her eyes. "She's a person, no better or worse than you – and not your servant."

"Or yours," he pointed out. "So why do you get to explore and buy seeds?"

"Because she can't travel between worlds," she told him, "and I needed to make sure we are safe here before you show your face anywhere."

His brow creased. "And are we?"

She nodded. "As far as I can tell."

His face relaxed. "I could do with some breakfast, I suppose."

"Me, too." Standing up, she led the way back down to the cottage. *That went well I think*, she mused. *Despite finding out some grim things about his past, he actually seems happier. All I need to do now is figure out how to teach him everything he needs to know without freaking out the locals.*

CHAPTER 7

"No, Qall!" Rielle scolded, her senses reeling at the sudden blackness. "You'll learn nothing if you strip the entire room of magic."

"But it did stop you attacking," he pointed out smugly. "And I'm sure I have more magic than you now."

"Put it back."

He sighed and let it go all at once. Magic spilled outward, intense and dazzling, and spread beyond the room into the burned city beyond.

"No more than what you took, or someone might notice." Exasperated, she drew the extra magic in.

"There's nobody here," he pointed out. "None of the locals with ability would understand what they were sensing, even if they did come up here. And they won't. They think the souls of the dead live here."

"It's not villagers we have to be careful of. It's sorcerers who might follow my path here." She cursed Qall silently. He had been in a defiant mood all day, refusing to focus on the manoeuvre she was trying to teach. Keeping up with his moods was a constant challenge. At times like this she wondered if she'd made a mistake, promising to take care of and train him. His defiance and lack of interest were so easy to interpret as ingratitude and a failure to appreciate the threat he faced if he did not learn to protect himself.

And yet at other times he was gratifying to teach – attentive and quick to learn. Sometimes she recalled what Dahli said about Valhan being good at all forms of magic, and wondered if that had been transferred to Qall when she'd changed his pattern.

"Why am I learning to fight like a weak sorcerer? I'm never going to use these moves."

"You need to understand how weaker sorcerers fight, because it's far more likely you'll face a group of them than one strong one."

"You're avoiding teaching me how to defeat you," he accused.

She began to deny it, then smiled. "That's a good idea actually. It doesn't make sense to teach one of the few people in the worlds who could defeat me how to kill me."

His eyes widened slightly as he realised his mistake. "What if your friend, Tyen, tries to kill me?"

She let her smile drop. "Let's hope it never comes to that." *How does he know about Tyen? Did he read about Tyen from Timane's mind?*

His chin rose. "Because I'd kill him?"

"No, because I like both of you. I don't want to lose either of you."

His eyes flickered away and back again. "What if another strong sorcerer – one you don't know about – attacks me?"

She crossed her arms. "It's not that I don't want to teach you how to fight someone close to you in strength, Qall. I will eventually."

Qall's eyes narrowed. "You haven't fought anyone as strong as us before, have you?"

He was too smart with his guesses sometimes. She smiled again. "No. And I'm glad of that too."

"You haven't killed someone either."

A chill ran down her spine. "Actually, I have."

His eyebrows rose. "Who?"

"I'd rather not talk about it."

"Why not?"

"It's not something I'm proud of."

"Why not?"

"Killing is never something to be proud of, Qall. I wish that I hadn't."

"Why did you, then?"

She considered whether she would answer or not. Avoiding the subject would only make him more curious. She didn't want him thinking of the deaths on her hands as victories from some glorious battle either. The truth was more brutal and shameful.

"The first was accidental," she told him. "I did not know my strength. The second . . . he gave me no choice. I killed him to save people who looked to me to protect them. Neither death was the result of fighting."

His expression was serious and he regarded her in silence for several heartbeats before he spoke again. "You've never fought in a battle, have you?" He crossed his arms, perhaps in imitation of her. "Shouldn't I be learning from someone who has?"

Her stomach sank. How could she answer without losing his respect for her as his teacher? "I'm afraid I'm all you've got, Qall. If we were to recruit a sorcerer with battle experience to teach you, we'd have to be sure we could trust them not to tell anyone about their remarkably powerful student. They'd be weaker than you too. Which raises the question, why would someone train you to fight? Would they do it out of kindness? I doubt it. They might agree if the price was right, but we don't have the sort of wealth we'd need to offer."

"What about Tyen? He's strong, and fought with the rebels."

"And we don't know where he is." She winced at the bitterness that crept into her voice. "I don't know him *that* well anyway."

"He's your friend but you don't trust him?"

She uncrossed her arms. "I'd trust him with my life, but that's mine to risk. I won't risk yours. While I believe he's trustworthy, I've learned the hard way to be cautious with people whose minds I can't read."

"So he's stronger than you."

"He can't read my mind either. We are equal in strength."

Qall's eyebrows rose. "Was he the one who taught you to be cautious?"

She drew in a deep breath and let it out again. "No. It was Valhan. The Raen."

His mouth opened in a silent "ah", then closed and his jaw tensed. "So you trusted him, and he betrayed you."

He held her gaze, and she knew she was never going to get him to learn any fighting tactics today. Sighing, she beckoned to him and walked towards a fallen column.

"Very well. I'll tell you what happened."

The chill of the stone seeped through her clothing immediately, so she warmed it with magic. Qall dropped onto one of the stone bricks nearby, too tense from anticipation to look truly as nonchalant as his pose suggested.

"I've always intended to tell you, but I wasn't ready until now," she explained. "I'll start at the start because I haven't told anyone else the full story and I don't want to miss anything relevant." She drew a deep breath, let it out, then cleared her throat. "I met Valhan in my world, which was a weak world. He had been trapped there for twenty cycles . . ."

As she continued through her story, she did not mention why she had met Valhan, since the story of her early life felt too personal and Qall didn't needed to know she had been a criminal among her people. Instead she explained why she had accepted Valhan's offer to take her to his world. She described how Inekera, Valhan's ally, had left her to die in a desert world at his bidding when he realised how powerful Rielle was, but the Travellers had found and saved her. When she told Qall she had left them to join Valhan, he was puzzled.

"But he tried to kill you."

"Yes. I know it sounds strange now. Every source of information, including the Travellers, described a man who was truthful. So I believed him when he said he still wanted me to join the artisans in his palace."

It was gratifying to see Qall's scowl when she revealed that the lessons in magic, visit to Valhan's home world and demonstrations of how he maintained order were intended to convince her to resurrect him. He shook his head when she explained Valhan's plan for the rebels and allies to fight each other so he was free from all the deals he'd made with the allies when he returned, and there'd be fewer rebels to eliminate.

"His own friends were planning to kill him?"

"Not friends," she corrected. "Allies. Powerful sorcerers he had exchanged favours with, who he allowed to retain power in their world or worlds in exchange for their support."

"So why did they want to kill him?"

"For twenty cycles they'd had a taste of the power they could have without him around. They wanted that back – permanently."

Qall nodded. "So he lured the rebels to his world, knowing that the allies would arrive too late to help him, and then the rebels and allies would finish each other off."

"Yes."

He shook his head. "Why didn't he put someone else in his place who he'd changed to look like him, instead of killing himself?"

"Someone among the rebels or allies might have been strong enough to read their mind and discover the truth. Or it's possible that changing a person to another's pattern means they also gain that other person's magical ability, so he'd be creating a potentially dangerous rival."

"Ah." Qall frowned. "So he put his memories into a piece of himself – his hand – ready to move them into a new body. A body he'd changed to look like himself."

"He didn't change the body," she corrected, then paused to swallow, her throat suddenly dry. "I did that."

His eyes widened. "You?"

"It was the first stage of the resurrection. You were in a large coffin of ice. Dahli – Valhan's most loyal friend, who was leading the resurrection – told me you did not have a mind. I didn't know otherwise until I looked at Valhan's memories. I don't think he knew I would be able to see them. He might have gambled that I would not object to destroying a person so that he could live, but not that I'd overlook the fact that he planned to kill me after I'd restored him."

"Why would he do that, when you'd helped him come back?"

"The same reason he always killed all powerful sorcerers he encountered – well, except his friends and the allies. We were a threat." She shrugged. "Though maybe he knew me better than I did. Maybe if your mind had been empty, I would have resurrected him anyway."

Qall's brows knit together. "*Why?*"

She spread her hands. "He'd convinced me that the worlds would fall into chaos and destruction without him." Qall did not look any less confused. "You've seen the effect he had on people," she reminded him. "The statue. The Hero. People loved and worshipped him."

"But more hated him. You told me that."

"Yes. Love and fear. Both gave him a means to control others – though from what he'd shown me, it often took more than that. He also ruled through an exchange of deals and favours."

Qall kicked at the rubble. "So the strife in the worlds is happening because he's not around to stop it."

She nodded. The Travellers might not have told him who he was, or much about the Raen, but they had made sure he was informed about the state of the worlds. "Partly. That doesn't mean the worlds won't eventually sort themselves out, with the help of the Restorers – what the rebels call themselves now."

"Tell me about the people who want to bring the Raen back."

"They call themselves his friends. Some do truly love him, as a follower loves a leader." *And more, in Dahli's case.* Which was why she believed the danger to Qall would not end – at least not until Dahli was dead. "Some want to be well placed when he does return."

"Why don't you kill them?"

She raised her eyebrows at him. "The same reason the Travellers didn't."

He lowered his gaze. "I wouldn't expect them to. They weren't strong enough."

"That isn't the only reason, and you know it."

"Because they don't interfere with worlds."

"No: because killing is wrong."

"So what am I supposed to do? Why shouldn't I kill them when they effectively want me dead?"

"Because *you* are strong," she told him. "If you kill people because they want to take advantage of you or they don't like you, you are as much a tyrant as they are." Then she smiled to let him know she didn't think he was a tyrant. "Once you can change your appearance, there'll be less chance you'll have to confront that dilemma."

"But . . . these people will always be out there, trying to find me."

Rielle wanted to laugh at that, though bitterly. "I don't know that anyone has ever gone through life without making enemies. Certainly not the ageless." Except maybe Ulma. "All you can do is make sure you only have enemies because you are a good person."

Qall frowned as he considered that. After a moment, he straightened. "I'm hungry."

She smiled at his sudden change of subject. He had the appetite of a growing youth. "Then go back to the cottage and get some food," she said, getting to her feet and wrapping her scarf around her head. "I'm going to see if I can find a metalworker to make some tools for us."

He rose and strode out of the room. Rielle followed soon after, but headed out of the building towards the area of the ruins from where she usually pushed out of the world. She had been arriving and leaving in two separate directions to give the impression the ruins were a place someone regularly paused to catch their breath before moving on, rather than their destination.

As she walked, she considered Qall's questions. They had covered most of what he needed to know now, but she was sure he'd come up with more questions. She ought to try to anticipate them and be ready with answers. He might want to know more about Dahli, for instance.

Reaching the open area she usually left from, she pushed out of the world and skimmed in the direction of one of the local cities along the path she had forged the last time she had visited it – and immediately stopped. The path had been freshly travelled, and she hadn't come this way in several days.

Backtracking, she moved past the point where she had pushed out of the world. The path's freshness continued on. It had been used less than a day before. Whoever had taken it had used it to pass by the ruins.

She couldn't tell if this stranger had stopped in the ruins, but if she travelled for long enough along the path she would know the direction they had been going, because their tracks would either grow more or less fresh. Moving in reverse to the direction she'd intended to travel, she kept her senses attuned to the substance of the place between. After a few hundred paces, the stranger's path split from hers.

Curious, she followed it. Soon it became clear that it was heading towards the village. The path descended towards the houses, but stopped before reaching them, instead diverting to a ridge overlooking them. Guessing that the stranger had emerged in the world there, she did so as well.

She looked around with her eyes and mind. The cottage couldn't be seen from here, she was relieved to see. The minds of the villagers were within easy reach. Lightly touching on each, she jumped from man to woman to child, finding them occupied in their usual activities. Nothing unusual. No memories of strangers visiting them in the last day.

Pushing out of the world, she found that the stranger's path continued over the village, withdrawing further into the place between worlds, then skimming closer when they reached the other side of the valley. It led to the top of the ridge between the village and the cottage, and once more descended to the ground.

Arriving in the world again, Rielle examined her surroundings once more. She looked first towards the cottage. It was shrouded by trees, so she was only able to locate it by seeking Timane's mind.

Next she scanned the area for minds. The closest was that of a young woman, Omity, who was waiting to meet someone beside a pool down in the valley. The girl's excitement made Rielle smile. Omity was full of hope that the young man she loved would appear. He never came to the village. Her parents would not approve of their meeting, nor would his mother, so they had arranged to meet halfway between the village and the cottage he lived in. He tried to visit every day in the late afternoon, but sometimes his mother found something else for him to do. *What will he show me today?* Omity wondered. A memory rose of a pale-skinned, dark-haired man making rocks hover, or magicking them to grow so warm they turned water to steam.

Rielle's heart froze. Despite the glamour the girl's infatuation had cast on his appearance, they had no doubt the young man was Qall. Air hissed out between her teeth. *How long has he been seeing her?* She, Timane and Qall had arrived less than a twelfth-cycle ago. The girl had met him several times now. Perhaps before

Rielle had started teaching him. *Hmm. Perhaps he did more than sulk that time he left Timane on her own for three days.*

The sneaky . . . what? Liar? He hadn't deceived her. He simply hadn't told her. She'd not forbidden him to meet villagers; she'd only said he shouldn't leave the area on his own. So why hadn't he said anything about Omity? *Perhaps he thinks I'll disapprove.* The girl seemed to think so. *And what's with him calling me his mother? Do I look that old? Surely he'd call me his sister . . .*

Shaking her head, she made herself consider what to do, if anything. What harm would it do if Qall made a romantic connection here? *Well, there's the girl's heart to consider. If we have to leave, she will be heartbroken. If we stay and she is right about her parents' likely disapproval, it will cause trouble with the villagers.* Was he as infatuated? He would be even more unhappy if he was forced to give up the girl, or move on.

And they might be forced, if this stranger had seen them. She considered what she had learned about the mysterious visitor, and immediately realised that it might not be a coincidence that she should stop here and detect the pair.

The girl's excitement intensified suddenly. Qall had appeared. As he reached the pool, he drew her close and kissed her. Rielle retreated from the girl's mind. Eavesdropping on such a personal moment felt intrusive, especially when she was seeing Qall through the girl's eyes.

Then flashes of light drew her gaze, followed by laughter. She sought the girl's mind again. A cloud of coloured lights was swirling around the pair, spiralling up towards the treetops.

Show-off, Rielle thought, amused. Moving along the ridge, Rielle found that she could see the couple between the tree branches. Then all her humour dissolved. *If I can see them from here, then the stranger would have been able to.*

Her blood went cold. It was possible the stranger had viewed the valley from both sides, and no more, but it was also possible they had seen Qall showing off to Omity. If they were from this world or neighbouring ones, they would not have recognised Qall. But they might report seeing a sorcerer here to a local authority, and she needed to know if that was going to attract trouble. She would have to follow their path and locate them. A mind-read would confirm or dispel her fears. In the meantime, Qall and Timane ought to be alert and ready in case they all had to flee.

That meant interrupting the entanglement below. She hesitated, and peered down at the pair. They were kissing again, and their hands were exploring in ways she was very sure the girl's parents would not approve of. Pushing out of the world, she skimmed down to the pool, arriving behind Qall.

They were so engrossed they didn't notice her, so she cleared her throat. At once, they jumped apart, the girl quickly straightening her clothes. Qall gaped at her, then his face flushed a bright red. The girl regarded Rielle with wide eyes. In her mind rose guilt, longing and a little defiance. Rielle could not quite smother her smile. Memories of her own long-forgotten infatuation with Izare reminded her of how intense and important it had seemed at the time.

"Qall," she said, then turned to nod and smile at the girl. "Omity." Looking back at Qall, she held his still-fuming gaze. "Someone skimmed to the ridge above here yesterday," she said in the Traveller tongue. "There's a chance they saw you, if you were here." She paused and glanced at the girl. "What were you doing yesterday?"

"Nothing," he replied through gritted teeth.

She held back a laugh. "I don't mean romancing this girl. What did you do with magic?"

He blinked, then his brows knit together. "Making clouds into shapes."

She winced. He'd revealed how great his reach was, and therefore his unusual strength. "Ah. Go back to the cottage. Protect Timane. I'm going to see if I can find out what this stranger saw and what he or she plans to do about it."

He nodded. Glancing at the girl, he spoke an apology in her language, then strode away. Rielle nodded at the girl again, then pushed out of the world and returned to the ridge.

She would have to travel fast. Finding the stranger's path, she propelled herself along it. She was not surprised to find they had withdrawn further from the world again, as it made them less easy to see. But they did not skim towards a local city. They continued deeper into the place between, forging a new path out of the world.

That is a bad sign, she realised. Whatever the stranger had seen, it had spurred them to leave the world immediately. She increased her speed. The stranger had a day's head start. If they had continued on through more worlds it could take longer than that to catch up, if she didn't lose their path.

The next world emerged from the whiteness. The path led to the middle of a field, then skimmed on from there. It took her to a sprawling city, to an arrival place from which two paths led away. One hadn't been used for days, so she took the other. It led to the next world, then single paths continued through two more. From the following world's arrival place three paths led away, all recently used. She selected one, which skimmed to a circle of stones, tended by a group of women seers. In the minds of two she saw a memory of the last person to appear in the circle. A man, blond, short and with the paunch and sagging skin of middle age.

Not an ageless sorcerer. That would make him easier to find, if he was the stranger. But she ought to check the other two paths first.

Returning to the world with three possible paths, she investigated the next. It led to an arrival place from which nobody had continued onwards, so either the stranger had backtracked, or he'd continued on foot or by other means. A quick scan of minds told her no sorcerers were within a day's walk. She returned to the last world and tried the third path.

This took her to the estate of a powerful, wealthy ruler. The arrival place was within a symmetrical garden. It was morning, and a fine, warm rain misted the air. Despite this, a servant stood waiting. He smiled and walked forward to greet her.

"Welcome," he said in his native language. "The Lord invites you to visit him, if you have the time. He is a man who enjoys tales from the worlds." *A woman this time*, the servant thought. Few sorcerers passed through this world. *Two in two days, and yesterday's visitor is still here. His Lordship will be delighted.*

Rielle looked towards the house. Sorting through the minds of numerous servants, she learned where the visitor was, and jumped from mind to mind until she finally found the Lord. Through his eyes she saw a well-muscled man not much older than Tyen. All his features were well-balanced and perfectly aligned, giving an impression of exaggerated masculinity.

Too perfect, she mused. *So probably ageless.*

She sought the visitor's mind.

A pity this place is so far from everything, the sorcerer was thinking. *It's been a while since I enjoyed such luxuries — and the woman he sent to my bed was surprisingly open to my requests. But Dahli will want to know I've found the lookalike . . .*

Dahli! Rielle sucked in a breath. It was worse than she had feared. As she watched the man's thoughts, nausea rose. Not long after she, Qall and Timane had left Lejihk's family, Dahli had learned that they had been protecting Qall and that Rielle had left with Qall to find a place to live far from the worlds the Raen had ruled. He even had an idea which direction Rielle had gone, thanks to Lejihk mapping a path for her, which meant he could send out trackers in a wedge-shaped wave rather than out in all directions.

I should wait a few days before heading back to make sure the messenger delivered his note, the man thought. The note contained a threat to kill Lejihk's family if Qall did not return and cooperate with Dahli's demands. *By the time I go back, the lookalike will have left, either to hurry back to stop Dahli, or to seek a new hiding place.*

And Qall would want to go back, Rielle realised. She had to get back to the cottage and take him and Timane away as soon as possible, so he didn't receive the threat. *You can't blackmail someone if you can't communicate with them.*

She would have to take them far away, this time by a more convoluted route. Once Dahli learned where they'd been hiding he would gather his hunters and set them following all paths away from it.

Unless she killed this man, to stop him returning to Dahli.

The thought paralysed her. A memory of Sa-Gest flying out over the abyss flashed through her mind, then the face of the sorcerer she'd suffocated between worlds, after he'd threatened the artisans of Valhan's palace.

Not again, she thought. *I can't do it again.* But she had to, or give Dahli a better chance of finding Qall. She took a step towards the mansion, then stopped.

But if I get Qall and Timane away before the note arrives, the messenger will tell the hunter he failed. The hunter might suspect Rielle had somehow learned of the note's contents before the messenger arrived, but he couldn't be sure. *You can't blackmail someone if you can't communicate with them. Or can't be sure you've communicated your threat to them.*

The tracker would try to follow them. She wouldn't be able to travel as fast as he, since she couldn't risk stumbling into a dead or inhospitable world, but she could hide her path. She'd practised the trick Tyen had taught her, and was much better at it now.

Tyen wouldn't kill this man. He'd never killed anyone, which was remarkable considering that he'd led the rebels and fought with them. *I told Qall only this morning, that when you are strong there is no excuse for killing. If he finds out I ignored that principle, he'll be less inclined to follow it himself.*

Drawing in a deep breath, she let it out again. Turning to the servant, she made a shallow bow and thanked him for the invitation, but she had to decline. He smiled at her good manners and nodded.

Pushing out of the world, she hurried away. Qall was going to be upset that they were leaving, but then he was partly to blame for them having to. The hunter might never have found them, if he hadn't been showing off to the girl.

Timane would accept it with her usual pragmatic cheer. *And me? I never really liked this world. Not that it matters. What matters is that we settle far enough away from here that it would take Dahli's most powerful hunters more than a cycle to reach it.*

CHAPTER 8

"We'll stop here for the night," Rielle said. "I'll have a look around. See if we could settle here."

"Here?" Timane repeated, her eyebrows rising as she looked around the crowded city street.

Rielle nodded. After another eighth of a cycle travelling, she had traded most of her jewels and precious metal, and all of her jewellery. They'd exchanged small magical favours and even menial work for food and accommodation as much as possible, hoarding their savings to help establish themselves wherever they settled. "There are people here from many parts of this world and neighbouring worlds, both living in and visiting this part of the city. Among them, we will be another group of outsiders looking for work."

The girl frowned. "But so will those who are looking for us. They'll be harder to detect, won't they?"

"Yes, that is true. The advantages are disadvantages, whether we stay among people or isolated from them. At least I have more options for making an income in a city."

"And me." Timane's expression became grim. The girl looked at Qall, and Rielle could see she was wondering if he understood how dire their financial situation was now. He did not look her way, face hidden within the hood of his coat. Sullen silence had been his demeanour for most of the journey.

"Let's find a place to stay," Rielle said, and led them out of the alley and into the busy street.

The main road was lined with the elaborate façades of buildings dedicated to entertainment. Theatres, drinking establishments, smoking rooms, gambling houses and brothels stood side by side. Most were decorated to a theme, though sometimes what that entailed could only be discovered by reading the minds of the staff, or customers familiar with the establishment. Most tended towards the ribald and lewd. Rielle began to reconsider the suitability of this world for Qall. He had no experience of places like these. Would he be tempted and easily exploited by them? Would he seek distraction from his worries to the point he didn't apply himself to lessons?

By flitting from mind to mind, Rielle was relieved to find other areas with more restrained entertainment – and one particular area where children were catered for, in which strict laws forbade establishments that offered "adult" pleasures. She headed for an area that appealed to customers with refined tastes, and was pleased to find the façades there were more beautiful and the atmosphere quieter and safer, even if a search of minds revealed that some offered the same range of services to customers as the bawdy quarter, just not as openly or cheaply.

Behind the theatres, accessed through cleverly hidden archways, were alleyways leading to accommodation for the workers of these establishments. Unfortunately, the rented rooms in the more refined area would empty Rielle's purse too quickly, so she and her companions backtracked towards the area they'd arrived in.

Before they had gone far, however, their progress was hampered by a crowd far denser than any they'd encountered before. Qall hunched further into his coat, whereas Timane was bobbing up onto her toes to look over heads. Following the girl's gaze, Rielle saw that the audience was centred before an elaborately carved stone façade with tiny balconies festooned with ribbons.

At first, Rielle thought this might be a brothel, as young women began to emerge onto the balconies to pose and wave to the crowd, but a quick look into a few minds told her that these were singers and dancers, and the building was one of the more popular theatres of the area. The attire of the women, while designed to show a little more chest than Rielle thought decent, was far more demure than that of the local prostitutes.

They had nearly made their way past the audience when it began to quieten, enabling a voice to break through the general clamour of the street. It was sweet and high, but as people fell silent in order to listen, it deepened, gaining a thrill of richness and emotion. Timane stopped, her expression rapt as the woman on the central balcony lifted her arms with each swell of melody, her mouth opening wide as she sang the next rising note. Then the other women's voices joined her, high and low tones blending with the first. The effect was beautiful, and sent a shiver down Rielle's spine. She glanced at Qall to see if he was affected at all, and found him looking at Timane, enough light penetrating the hood to reveal that he was smiling.

Turning to Timane, Rielle saw the girl's mouth moving along with the song and realised she must be reading the mind of the singer in order to anticipate each note and understand the words.

Abruptly the song ended, just as it seemed to be nearing a peak. The singer beckoned to the crowd and withdrew into the room behind the balcony. The others resumed waving and posing, as cries of good-natured protest broke from the crowd. Looking into the minds around them, Rielle read that the sudden end of the performance was designed to convince passers-by to pay for the full night's entertainment.

I'd like to hear that, Rielle thought. "We should come back and see the show."

Timane frowned. "It's expensive. And I know how the story ends. That's the bad side of reading minds in order to understand the lyrics."

"You should try to get a job there," Qall said.

Rielle hid her surprise. It had been hours since he'd spoken, and many days since he'd uttered more than a short reply to a question.

The girl glanced at him then blushed. "I'm not that good."

"You sounded good to me. How will you know if you're good enough until you try?"

Timane shook her head, but as Rielle led the way onwards she kept glancing back at the building. All of the women were gone now. Rielle sought the girl's mind.

She was thinking back to her childhood, to days when she had slipped away to the local woods to sing because her mother assumed that having breath meant Timane's chores weren't hard enough. Timane had fancied herself better than most of the young women in her neighbourhood. *Perhaps I will try for a job there*, the girl thought. Rielle hid a smile as the young woman imagined herself in place of the lead singer, luring crowds into the theatre.

Returning to the more pressing task of finding an available room for the night, she searched minds until she found one, then led them to it.

The landlord heard their unfamiliar accents and raised the price, and would not be beaten down again, so they left and sought another. This one proved to be in much worse condition than the deluded owner believed. It was starting to grow dark when they finally settled on a place. It was a dingy single room, but it had piped water and a basin and drain. Hooks had been attached to the ceiling for curtains to divide the room into private areas. A pair of mattressless bed frames leaned up against the walls.

Qall regarded it all in silence, then moved over to the single window and sat on the sill.

Rielle and Timane exchanged a look, then set to work, heating the metal bed frames with magic to kill the bugs, scouring the basin, unblocking the pipe when it refused to drain freely and washing and drying the bedding strapped to their packs. Qall's they placed on one bed; theirs they laid out on the other. When they had done all they could do, Rielle sat on a bed and searched minds in the hope of learning where the best cheap food could be bought, what kind of employment was on offer and any other information that might make settling in here easier.

The world was known as Amelya, and the city was called Deeme. The theatre district was what the city was famous for, but the world also had larger, more important cities.

As evening approached, Rielle grew aware of Timane's growing hunger. She told the girl where she could find decent fare and gave her the last of the coin she'd exchanged for a gemstone when they'd first arrived.

"He'll try to charge you more if you seem new to the area. It doesn't look like you'll be in any danger otherwise."

"Did you see anything else?" Timane asked.

"One of the local theatres needs a better props and backdrop painter. I'll look into that tomorrow."

"Anyone need a cleaner?"

Rielle shook her head. "Nobody nearby. Menial jobs are easy to fill here. Plenty of young people are drawn to this city hoping to make their fortune, but find it much harder than they expect."

"What about sorcerers?" Qall asked.

Rielle turned to the window. "A few come to see the shows," she told him. "None of great strength are living here, as far as I've seen."

Qall shook his head, tugging his hood back up when the movement threatened to dislodge it. "I meant jobs for sorcerers."

She considered how to respond. "You don't have to work," she told him. "But if you want to . . . you might need to be more flexible. I doubt there are many jobs that require magic, but there is no harm in looking."

He was silent for a long moment, then suddenly spoke again. "There are," he told her. "In the theatres. They create light and noise and . . . effects that go with the production."

She examined the shape of him, darkened by the light of the grimy window behind him. So he had been carrying out his own search of the local minds. Did he fancy living here? Had the prospect of not travelling any further lightened his spirits? Perhaps now was the time to raise some sensitive subjects.

"I'm sorry we had to leave," she told him again.

He shrugged.

"Had you and Omity—?"

"No, I didn't lie with her," he snapped, then turned back to the window.

Rielle smothered a laugh. "That's not what I was going to ask. Did you and Omity have feelings for each other?"

His shoulders rose and fell. "No," he said, so softly he was barely audible.

It was a lie, she knew, at least as far as Omity was concerned.

"So you were never in love?"

He stiffened. Intrigued, she considered whether he had lied about himself, or whether something else had upset him. *What did I ask exactly?* Whether he had ever been in love. Perhaps he has been, just not with Omity. She thought back to the Travellers, and a memory of a girl handing Qall an object surfaced.

"Was there someone among the Travellers you had feelings for?" she asked.

His head bowed, but he did not answer. She waited in the hope that if she left him enough space and time, he would offer up an explanation, but he did not speak or stir. Giving up, she sent her mind sweeping through those of the locals again, but soon wound up regarding Qall.

He had been withdrawn throughout the whole journey. She'd set a gruelling pace though. Perhaps he would brighten up when his training resumed.

Muffled footsteps drew near; then the door opened and Timane, and a delicious smell, entered the room. Pushing away from the window, Qall moved to the other bed. Timane handed out the parcels, then perched next to Rielle.

"That theatre tests new singers every ten days," Qall said. "The next is in three days. You should try."

Timane blushed. "I . . . ah . . . don't even know the language."

"It won't take long to learn it."

She glanced at Rielle. "But . . ."

"I see no harm in you trying," Rielle said.

A small smile pulled at the corner of Timane's lips. "Then I will."

Qall looked at Rielle. "There's another theatre near here in need of a better artist. It's not as popular as the one Timane's going to work for, but you can always look for a better place later."

Rielle realised her mouth was hanging open, and closed it. She nodded. "Thanks, Qall. I'll look into it tomorrow."

He nodded and turned his attention to the contents of the parcels – thick, sweet pastry surrounding a chunky mix of meat and vegetables. It was as good as the locals regarded it, and Rielle gave a little sigh of appreciation. Sometimes the simplest meals were the best.

She considered the difficulties they would encounter here. The lack of valuable possessions to trade was a worry. She couldn't train Qall here, so she would have to find another place. Otherwise this city looked very promising. She still needed to investigate the surrounding worlds though.

As she finished the last of the parcel, she stood up. Qall shifted to face her.

"You're going to scout the area," he guessed. "Can I come with you?"

She shook her head. "I will travel faster alone. Take the opportunity to rest and learn more about this world. If you have to flee, burn a message into the floor, and when you have found a safer location, send someone with a message written in Muraian to mix with the audience outside the theatre we stopped by before."

Timane nodded. Qall said nothing.

"I'll be back in a few hours." Leaving the room, Rielle made her way down to the city streets and walked for several blocks before finding a quiet corner from which to push into the place between. She travelled around Amelya first, visiting several cities and noting arrival places and the amount of traffic they received. Stopping to read the minds of sorcerers entering and leaving to find out about the neighbouring worlds, she learned that Amelyn was at peace with the closest, unified by trade.

She did not want to be gone too long, so after absorbing information for a few of the local hours she pushed out of the world and started visiting the ones closest to it. What she observed confirmed the information she'd gleaned from the sorcerers: no major conflicts or disputes plagued the local worlds. Five were part of a loose alliance. All traced their people's origins to a world that had been destroyed a few thousands of years before, so they were unified by this mutual tie despite being of greatly varied physique and appearance. Being the descendants of immigrants, most embraced visitors and migrants from other worlds.

Heading back to Deeme, she considered the journey they'd made to get to this world. A handful of worlds after the one they'd fled, they'd begun to encounter many dead and dangerous worlds. She had to backtrack from clusters of worlds contained within inhospitable ones – effectively dead-end routes. Seeking information within populated worlds, she was often able to avoid these. It often took more time to do so than to explore, but it was safer and a more efficient use of magic. Occasionally she stumbled upon someone who possessed a map of many surrounding worlds, and it was one of these people who first confirmed that the branches through to other large areas of worlds did exist.

The other disadvantage to seeking this information was that it effectively made a deep and distinct footprint in whatever trail she might be leaving. Hunters would seek out the same people, to see if anyone had asked about surrounding worlds. Though she had changed her hair again – short and curly – and darkened her skin tone, and Timane had cut her own glorious long hair to a simple bob and asked Rielle to change it to black, sorcerers seeking the information weren't common.

The hunters too could learn there were routes through the dead and dangerous worlds to areas of hospitable ones. Realising she could give them a valuable clue just by seeking information, she stopped directly visiting people with it, instead searching minds from a distance and hoping she'd find the right people and they would think about the local worlds while she watched.

At last, she'd learned of another route linking to a new area of worlds. Following it, she'd emerged into a pocket of about twenty worlds. The potential to be cornered within them worried her, so she took herself, Qall and Timane out and sought another linkage. This one led to an area of worlds that, even if it was contained within dead worlds, was so large that nobody knew they were surrounded.

Nobody had heard of the Raen, as far as she could tell. She was intrigued to learn that a string of powerful sorcerers had ruled this area – currently a relatively benign brother and sister duo were said to watch over them.

Arriving in Deeme, she emerged in the same place she'd left from, then walked back to the apartment. The landlady peered out of her door as Rielle passed, still awake despite the late hour. Timane and Qall were sitting on the beds chatting as she entered. They both looked up hopefully.

"Everything looks fine," she told them as she sat down beside Timane. "The local worlds are peaceful. I heard no thoughts of the Raen. I think we can settle here, but I'll have to find another world to train Qall in."

Timane clapped her hands. "Wonderful!" she exclaimed.

"Here," Qall said, rising and handing Rielle a small parcel.

Mystified, she unwrapped it. Small jars filled with coloured paste spilled out onto the bed. Three wooden boards remained in her hands.

"The theatres will expect you to bring samples of your work," Qall explained. "I found a supply store a few blocks away." His shoulders lifted. "I still had a few bits of gold left that my family gave me."

Rielle looked up at him, surprised and pleased. "How did you know what to . . .? Of course, you read it in someone's mind."

"Other local artists," he confirmed. "You should paint people. Plants and animals are different everywhere, but people are the same everywhere."

She nodded. "Thanks, Qall."

He shrugged.

"You must really like the look of this place."

"Not especially, but I can see staying here working for us."

She smiled. "I'm glad it's not just Timane and me. It will be a lot of work, but different to what we did at the cottage."

Timane nodded. "And perhaps better suited to all of us."

CHAPTER 9

The façade of the theatre had been painted black, but in the bright sunlight it looked grey. Daubs of what had once been white paint appeared to represent stars, and swimming among them were several men and women. All of the figures wore the same face, no matter the gender, which was a little disturbing. Cracks and peeling paint did nothing to improve the impression.

Rielle slipped through an archway to the left of the building. Ignoring a group of young men lurking in the shadows further down, she examined each of the small doors in the theatre wall until she found what she was looking for: a simply painted mask with a conical shape below it. She knocked.

A long silence followed, but as she was about to raise her hand to knock louder she detected the mind of an older woman coming to answer the door.

"I'm coming, I'm coming," the woman muttered out of habit, belatedly realising that there hadn't been a second knock, as there usually was. She considered whether the visitor had given up and gone away, and that she may not need to check the door, but she was only a few steps away so she continued towards it.

The painted mask swivelled inward. Rielle smiled at the wrinkled face that replaced it. The woman examined the visitor, noting the mousy blonde hair, light brown skin and green eyes of a people known for their artistic skills. *This ability to change my appearance would be an unfair advantage, except that it won't take long for my accent and unfamiliarity with that people's language and history to reveal I'm not from there.*

"I have heard that you need a painter."

Rielle had practised the phrase in Amelyan before setting out. Picking the right words from the minds of people could be a slow process, and made it obvious she did not speak the local language. While many workers in the city did not know the tongue, even a basic grasp of it was an advantage when looking for work.

The woman's eyebrows rose slightly. "You did? Well, then you had best speak to the manager."

The sound of metal scraping against the odd dried pulp used in place of wood in the city followed, then the door opened. The old woman beckoned Rielle inside, then led her up a staircase to a closed door. At her knock a voice called out from inside:

"Yes?!"

"A painter come to offer her services," the older woman said by way of introduction.

"Let her in."

The woman opened the door. Sitting at a table that almost completely filled the small room beyond was an elderly woman. Her white hair strained away from her face in a lively, curly halo. Her wrinkles told of many smiles and her eyes were a vivid, alert blue. Rielle instantly liked her.

"Come in," the old woman said, beckoning with both hands. As Rielle entered, the door closed behind her. "What is your name?"

"Elle," Rielle replied.

"I am Windra." The woman's eyes had dropped to the boards Rielle was carrying. "Your samples? Show me."

Rielle handed them over. Windra spread them over the items covering the table, exclaiming wordlessly as she examined each. She then arranged them in a line and leaned back to regard them all.

"Good work," she said, then looked up at Rielle. "The theme of this theatre, as you have seen, is 'Tales of the Night'. What would you do to represent that on the exterior?"

Rielle considered, then sought the right words from Windra's mind. "I would paint the entire building dark blue," she said. "And use gold paint for stars so they glitter even in daylight."

"And?"

"No more. A simple façade among so many complex façades will attract the eye. Then I would choose bright colours and designs inside, so people glimpse something interesting when the doors and windows open and close."

Windra's eyebrows rose, hovered, then lowered again. "I like how you think."

"Thank you."

Rielle looked at her hands modestly as Windra examined the samples again. *The girl can paint, that is clear*, she was thinking. *Anyone else would have suggested painting figures on the façade. Maybe she thinks that this will get her work inside as well – more work overall. But her idea has merit, and it'll be cheaper, even with the gold paint.*

"I will do it," Windra said. "When can you begin?"

"In nine or ten days," Rielle replied. Though she had no other work, now that Timane had a well-paid job, she wanted to resume Qall's training so he didn't get bored and restless. It didn't hurt to give the impression her work was already in demand too.

They came to an agreement over the fee. Rielle told the woman to choose one of the samples to keep, then retrieved the rest and left. As she walked back to the apartment, she considered the progress that she, Timane and Qall had made in the last ten days. The greatest surprise had been Timane's success at securing a role as a singer. The manager at the Quaver Theatre, where they'd seen the women performing, saw great potential in her. He had arranged training in dance, singing, theatre customs and the local language. Her income was small for a singer, but much better than the menial job she had expected to take.

This kept Timane very busy, but her lessons began at midday so Rielle had been seeking work in the mornings so that Qall had company. Once she began work, there would be no choice but to leave him alone for most of the day.

He can't hide away for ever. Timane had suggested trying some of the tricks actors used to change his appearance. He'd been amenable to bleaching his hair, or perhaps growing a beard, but rejected the idea of using skin paint.

If he could change his appearance with magic, it would make it so much easier. But it feels too soon for him to become ageless. He's barely begun living a mortal life. Only five cycles and a half, if I count from when I rescued him. He ought to know and understand the dangers of learning pattern shifting before he attempts it.

She doubted he'd turn down the chance to stop ageing though. Who wouldn't want to live as long as they wanted to, and be able to heal from most injury and disease? Still, it was important that *he* felt as if he made the decision when he was ready to. She did not want him blaming her for steering him into becoming ageless when he was too immature to understand what it truly meant.

That's what makes me hesitate, she realised. *His lack of maturity.* His sulks and mood swings suggested he wasn't yet ready to make such an important decision. *I'm not sure I was when I became ageless*, she mused. Not being told there were consequences until it was too late had been unfair to her. She didn't want him blaming him if he forgot his original appearance and lost his sense of identity.

She had changed so much since she'd learned it, but it felt natural – the normal shifts that happened through experience and time. She wasn't sure she even believed in angels now. Nothing she'd seen in all the worlds had suggested they were real. A part of her still wanted to believe, and reasoned that they, not being physical beings, could exist outside all the worlds. Plenty of religions were structured around that idea, though the actual being or beings they worshipped took on a multitude of different forms. At the same time, she couldn't escape the fact that humans simply liked to think that *something* existed greater than them, something that had a plan or reasons of some kind for the ills of the worlds, so that they did not have to take collective responsibility for all the pain and cruelty and foolishness.

Reaching the apartment building, she ignored the landlady peering out of the open door of her room and started up the stairs. Out of habit, she searched for minds above. The drunk on the second floor was asleep and caught in a nightmare; the mother of five on the third was teaching her youngest how to sew; and in the now-familiar room on the fourth, Timane was practising with the face paints the theatre manager had given her.

Reaching the door, Rielle stepped through. Timane lifted the edge of the heavy curtain that divided the girl's space from Qall and Rielle's.

"Qall's gone out," she said.

A stab of alarm halted Rielle. "For how long?"

"I don't know," Timane confessed with a grimace. "I was asleep."

Rielle took a deep breath, trying to calm her racing heart. "Did he leave a message?"

"No." Timane disappeared behind the curtain again. "He can't have gone far."

"Far enough to make it hard to find him," Rielle muttered, walking to her partition and sitting on the rickety third bed they'd bought a few days after arriving. "I'll see if I can locate him."

"We can't expect him to stay holed up here all the time," Timane said. "It isn't healthy."

"Well, I don't need to paint any more samples, so I was going to resume his training today," Rielle told her.

"You got the job!"

"I did. But I won't be starting for some days yet."

"That's wonderful."

Closing her eyes, Rielle sent her mind out and down towards the street. *Where would he go?* She had no idea. Perhaps he had been hungry and, not wanting to wake Timane, decided to fetch the food. She searched the minds of street vendors but saw no memory of him, and none were looking at anyone of Qall's appearance. She kept searching through the minds of people on the street who tended to note passing young men – like the young women at the bakery. She moved steadily further afield, but found no memory of him.

Perhaps he didn't go out on the street. She searched the alleyways and the houses nearby, but saw no sign of him. Not even the nosy landlady below had seen him leave. That might have given Rielle some idea of which direction he'd gone in. She let out a sigh of exasperation.

Then a chill went through her. *The landlady didn't see him leave?* That was odd. Nothing evaded that woman. Either he had an undiscovered talent for slipping past people or . . .

She drew magic, then hesitated. *Surely not. Even if he'd worked it out for himself, he knows it's dangerous.*

But he had all the respect for danger of most young men his age. Her brother might have been much older than her, but she could still remember a time when risky activities had a mysterious attraction to him. It was only when she'd cried hysterically after he'd returned one night bleeding from a fight that he had stopped seeking thrills so ardently.

Pushing out of the world slightly, she sought and found what she feared.

A path.

Despite the non-physical state of the place between, her mind buzzed with alarm. Had he learned how to travel between worlds, or had someone else taken him? Had one of Dahli's hunters arrived and delivered his threat to harm Lejihk's family if Qall didn't return and do as he asked?

Calm down, she told herself. *Think.* The path was recent, but not fresh enough to suggest someone had just forged it. Rushing down it would not result in her catching up with its creator before the next world. *If Qall went that far. He might have moved a short distance, and still be finding his way back.* He might have arrived within an object, becoming trapped. *No, don't think about that.*

Returning to the world, she drew a breath.

"Timane."

"Yes?"

"Someone has left this world from this room. I'm going to investigate."

"Qall?"

"He doesn't know how."

"Someone abducted him?" The girl sounded frightened. "And while I was asleep!"

"Perhaps. I will find out." Rielle's heart pounded. She drew a couple of deep breaths, willing it to slow. "Stay here . . . wait, no. Go to your lessons. It will be safer. I will fetch you once I have Qall back."

She didn't wait for Timane's answer. Pushing into the place between worlds, she relocated the path and propelled herself along it, reaching the next world in moments. Paddocks dotted with strange, stumpy animals stretched in all directions. Just before she arrived, she sensed another path leading sideways.

It was as fresh as the last, and skimmed across the world in a straight line. Following it, she found it emerged in the world several times, suggesting stops to breathe. *Not an ageless sorcerer, which suggests Qall made the path and not one of Dahli's hunters.*

The path eventually reached a small city, descending to an arrival place within an enormous octagonal hall. On each wall there was a mural depicting the eight lands of the world, but she was too distracted to admire the artistry of them. Searching the minds around her, she found that some of the people present were tasked with watching and recording who arrived and left.

She chose a young man. Her approach made him tense. Sorcerers had been known to make impossible and unpleasant demands on the watchers. She smiled and collected words from his mind.

"Did a young man arrive and leave in the last few hours, either alone or with a companion?"

Memories rose to the surface of his thoughts. He glanced down at his notebook. Three visitors met that description, including the handsomely pale, dark-haired one who had arrived and left alone, and stayed only long enough to take a deep breath and leave.

As he told her this, she almost sagged with relief. Qall was alone. That he was travelling between worlds was still worrying, but not as alarming as the alternative. She nodded and took a small slip of gold from her purse. The watcher shook his head. Taking payment was forbidden. They watched so that visitors did not seek answers in less pleasant ways.

Thanking him, she pushed out of the world. Two paths led out of the arrival place. She had no way of knowing which one he'd taken. All she could do was try one, and return to the other if her guess was wrong.

She continued on, from world to world, retracing her steps when it was clear she'd taken the wrong path. Not every world had watchers or similar, but she could often find the information she needed in the minds of children, who loved to observe mysterious strangers appearing and vanishing at arrival places. None had seen a young man of Qall's appearance recently.

She returned to the hall, trying not to imagine him getting further and further ahead of her. The other path led to a monastery where the monks recorded the rare comings and goings of sorcerers in their arrival place. She learned that Qall had been there not long before and hope burned in her again.

Two paths led away, if she ignored the one she had arrived through. One felt freshly used, and led to a world of life and water. The arrival place was a deep ravine. On all sides was a thick abundance of moss of every colour, except where thin water-falls cut through it. As Rielle arrived, the roar of the water filled her ears.

A movement caught her eye, but when she turned she saw nothing. Pushing back into the place between worlds, she felt a shadow receding.

Qall?

Propelling herself after the shadow, she drew close enough to know it. Her eyes registered him as a tiny, distant figure. He looked back, saw her gaining on him, and quickly turned away. The figure began to shrink.

"Qall!" she called. He looked back and, to her surprise, stopped.

Aware that he could be suffocating as he waited for her – unless he had taught himself pattern shifting – *oh, don't let that be the case yet!* – she hurried to catch up. Another world formed around her. Black rock appeared all around, twisted in shapes as though it had been a molten, boiling sea that had suddenly frozen in place. An arrival place had been carved from it, with a road leading away. People had been here. The path was relatively fresh. It was most likely safe to arrive.

Qall's face was tight with annoyance as she caught up with him. She took his arm and moved towards the world. Before the frozen rocks could resolve around them, a resistance pulled at her, dragging her to a halt. She looked back. His eyes gleamed with satisfaction.

"Do you want to suffocate here?" she asked.

The gleam died. He stopped resisting, and she pulled him on into the world. Sure enough, as cold air touched her skin he drew in a deep shuddering breath and had to brace his hands on his knees as he gasped for air. She let go of his arm, as he was not going anywhere like this.

"What were you thinking?" she asked. "You know it can be fatal to travel between worlds before you know all the dangers."

"I . . . know . . . them," he told her.

"How?"

"From . . . you." He straightened. "I've been . . . watching you . . . doing it since . . . we left our first . . . new home."

Her heart squeezed a warning, an instinctive fear rising. She ignored it. "You've been reading my mind."

He nodded. She held his gaze, and though he tried to meet it, his own soon slid away.

"Why?"

"Because you hide things from me."

"For your protection."

He shook his head. "I have to find my family."

"Why?"

"You know why. They are in danger because of me." His gaze rose to meet hers, blazing with anger. "You've known since you tracked down Dahli's hunter, but you didn't tell me. He's going to kill them if I don't return."

"No, he isn't. For a start, that would be stupid," she told him. "And Dahli is not stupid."

He opened his mouth to object, then closed it and shook his head. "What do you mean?"

"If you kill a hostage, you lose your bargaining power. A threat is only effective when you know the target has heard and understood the threat."

"But I have."

"He doesn't know that."

Qall's shoulders dropped and his brows knit together. He thrust his hands into his coat. The knuckles of his right hand pressed against the cloth, as if he had taken hold of something.

"What is that?" she asked, nodding to his hand. "What do you have there that worries you so much?"

He quickly removed his hand. "Nothing."

"Liar," she accused. "I can't help you if you don't tell me, Qall."

His face remained closed, but then his eyes narrowed slightly.

"If I tell you, will you help me?" he asked.

"If I can, of course."

He looked down, then reached into his coat and drew out a plaited length of coloured thread. Rielle let out an "ah". The last time she'd seen one of these, Baluka had been knotting it about her wrist, making official their engagement.

"So that's what the girl gave you."

His gaze was penetrating. "You saw her give it to me," he stated, reading her mind.

"I saw her give you something, but not what it was." She looked up, watching his face closely. "Do you love her?"

She did not expect the rapid shifts in his face. Doubt. Guilt. Confusion.

"I . . . don't know," he confessed. The honesty of the admission caught and squeezed her heart, both in sympathy and in that he trusted her with the truth. "Before she gave this to me, I'd have said 'no'."

"But you did say yes afterwards?"

"No. But . . . I do like her. Everyone said I would have to marry outside the family, so I never thought about any of the girls in that way."

"And now?"

"Since I've been gone I . . . I miss her. All of them. I don't want them to suffer because of me."

Rielle nodded. "I understand. I felt the same once. It was one of the reasons I left them." She sighed. "If you go back, Qall, you will put them in more danger than if you stay with me. Surely you see that?"

He scowled, but the anger in his face as quickly dissolved away. "Yes."

"I love them too, Qall. The only thing stopping me from rushing back to help them is the certainty that it would make their situation – and yours – worse."

His eyes became dark and intense with anguish. "How can we know if we can or can't help them if we do not know what is happening to them?"

She sighed. "We can't."

"*You* can," he said. "You could go back and see if they are alive and well."

"Your enemies might try to blackmail me, if they learned I'd come back. They might try to follow me here."

"You can travel fast, and you know how to hide your path. Only one other can do that, and he's your friend."

"But—"

"If nothing else – " He took her hand and pressed the braided strand into it. "– take this back to Givari and tell her I cannot accept." He sighed. "I will never know if we could have been together if things were different, but at least she won't be waiting for me to come back."

Rielle could not speak. Her mouth tried to form the sensible reply, to tell him that life was full of unanswered questions and the girl would have known that her hopes were misplaced when the Travellers told her who he really was. But as she looked at the braid, she found herself nodding. She could not deny his request. She dared not lose his trust now.

So she considered how she would make it happen. Finding her way back to the Travellers would be harder than travelling away from them. It meant moving towards a point, rather than simply fleeing from one. She had written down a description of their journey whenever they had stopped to rest, but they had travelled through hundreds of worlds and there were gaps where she couldn't quite remember where she had gone.

But since she had come to this area of worlds through a sequence of worlds hemmed in by dead worlds, heading back in that direction would mean she would be funnelled back through that route. From there, she could not backtrack exactly, because she had to give the world where they'd settled before a wide berth. But from there she could reverse her objective, looking for worlds where the Raen was known rather than where he was not. Eventually she would find worlds she recognised.

Without two mortals needing to breathe she could travel faster, too. However, she had no store of gems and precious metals to barter for practicalities. That would make finding food harder, and she'd have to camp outdoors whenever she stopped to rest.

What would Timane and Qall do while she was gone? Timane would be fine. The girl's employer was a good person. Qall would have to sit and wait, but he could not stray if he wanted to hear news of his foster family when she returned.

"You must look after Timane," she told him.

"I will," he promised.

"No travelling between worlds while I'm gone."

He grimaced. "Very well."

"I'll be gone a long time. Maybe a quarter cycle. Are you sure you want to delay your training that long?"

"Yes."

She placed a hand on his arm. "Then we'd best get back and let Timane know. I'm going to need my pack and plenty of supplies." And she would have to tell the theatre manager she couldn't start the painting job when she'd promised to. She suppressed a sigh. Things had been going so well. But then, as far as setbacks went, this wasn't a bad one. She might even get a chance to see Tarran and Tyen again, even if only to give them a proper farewell.

CHAPTER 10

When Rielle emerged from the ground into the familiar courtyard of Tarran's home, and air surrounded her again, she staggered a little from dizziness. She told herself it was from relief that the long journey was over, but she had begun to wonder how many times her body could heal away weariness, hunger and the effects of spending so much time in the place between. She had grown thinner, bones hard under her skin.

A shadow moved within one of the windows, then the door opened. Tarran stared at her for a moment, then grinned. "Rielle!" He strode out, smiling broadly. "You cut your hair and curled it. Ooh! And your eyes are different." He looked her over. "But I'd know you anywhere."

"Hmm," she muttered, dismayed. "Then Dahli would too."

He nodded. "Perhaps. I got your message. It sounded as though I wouldn't see you again for a long time, but here you are!"

"Sounded like? I thought I was clear about that."

He chuckled. "Yes, you were." He peered at her, and frowned. "You look a bit pale. Are you ill?"

She shook her head. "I've been travelling with scant rest for nearly an eighth of a cycle. Does this help?" Taking off the long coat she'd made the night before leaving Qall and Timane, she turned it inside out so that the tattered, patched side became the lining and the more refined fabric was on the outside. It allowed her two ways to blend into a crowd when she didn't want to be noticed.

265

"No," Tarran said as she put it on again. "You look like you've not been getting enough to eat. Am I right?"

She grimaced. "It's hard to keep track."

"I don't know much about pattern shifting, but I do know you can't make something out of nothing. If you don't give your body fuel it can't repair itself, or has to rob from itself to keep alive."

"I have no valuables left to trade with," she told him. "I foraged, mostly. I couldn't bring myself to steal from people."

"You could have looked for rich people who won't suffer if you sneak into their kitchen and take some of their food. But never mind. You are here. I still have the stash of precious objects you left with me, but in the meantime, come inside and I'll have a meal brought."

"I can't stay long."

"You can stay long enough to eat." He ushered her inside, spoke to a servant, then led the way to the dining room. "Now, if you've travelled so far to visit, you must have a good reason."

"Of course."

"Can I help?"

"Do you know where I can find some Travellers?"

He glanced back at her, his eyebrows high. "Not far from here. You may want to approach them with caution."

She frowned. "Why shouldn't I approach the Travellers?"

"They are being watched."

"All of them?" Fortunately he was still walking ahead of her, so she didn't have to feign surprise. The less he knew about her reasons for leaving the better.

"Yes."

"Who by?"

"The Raen's old friends."

"Why?"

"I don't know. I heard this from an old friend at Liftre, and not directly. It may be an exaggeration."

Rielle's stomach sank. The best way to find a particular Traveller family was to seek the nearest one and ask. By watching all families, Dahli would be warned of Rielle or Qall's approach sooner. She would have to find Lejihk's family without other Travellers' help.

They reached the dining room. Entering, Tarran ushered her to a chair on one side of the large table, then dropped into one opposite. She frowned at him as she realised that the Travellers were the only people Dahli might keep an eye on. If he or one of his students had revealed to anyone at Liftre that she occasionally visited, and Dahli had spies at the school . . .

"Are you being watched?"

"I don't think so." He shrugged. "Which means either I'm not, or whoever is watching is clever at concealing it." He drummed fingers on the table as he considered the question more seriously. "My servants and students know only that you are a former student. However, there is one visitor who knows better."

"Tyen." Rielle's heart skipped a beat. "Have you heard from him?"

"I have. He has visited only once, I'm sad to say."

"Did he succeed in learning to pattern-shift?"

Tarran nodded once.

"Did he say why he left the desert world?"

Tarran nodded again. "A former rebel arrived to take magic. They had been doing so for a while. Not as much as Tyen can, of course, but they detected what he was doing and came to investigate. They recognised him and slipped away to report his location. The first he knew about it was when sorcerers turned up to attack him. That he found time to leave any message was remarkable."

"He escaped them, or he wouldn't have been talking to you."

"Yes."

"So why didn't he come and tell us?"

"He didn't want to risk leading them to you, me or Doum. He sent other messages, but none reached me."

"Did he say where he went then, to learn pattern shifting?"

"No. I did ask." Tarran shrugged. "He only said it was an uninhabited world, but no less uncomfortable."

At that moment, two servants entered and laid out several simple dishes, including cold meat sliced thinly, a range of condiments, bread, vegetables and fruit. A bottle of wine was tucked under one servant's arm, and he presented and opened it with practised ease. Rielle waited until they had left before speaking again.

"Uncomfortable?" She frowned as she heaped food on her plate. "I suppose it would be for most people. Hot. No water. Not a good place to be stranded, if he accidentally used all the magic. Rather like my home, actually. Had he been to Doum?"

"No. I told him what happened there. He . . . he left in a bleak state of mind."

"I'm not surprised. He wanted to live there permanently."

"And he was disappointed that you had left," Tarran added.

She winced. "At least I left a message. A proper explanation."

"But that wasn't all that was bothering him," Tarran continued. "He said the ongoing wars were partly his fault – though not the one between Murai and Doum – because he'd taught people how to make machines and they'd turned them into weapons. He said he was going to try and fix that."

"Machines like the creature he made?" she asked. "Like Beetle?"

"Yes. Other inventors have created ones designed to kill, and made armies of them. They are not a great threat to sorcerers, but can be devastating to ordinary peoples."

A memory surfaced of Valhan handing her the insectoid, saying it was "*the future*". She shuddered as she imagined a great swarm of them, stinging and biting. What could Tyen do to stop people making them? How could he prevent them passing on that knowledge? It seemed an impossible task, but she admired him for tackling it, and taking responsibility for it. A pang of longing shot through her.

"I wish I could help," she said. "But I must leave again and nobody can know where I've gone."

Tarran nodded, and as she tucked into the food he grazed lightly, mostly drinking the wine. Rielle considered what she should do next. She couldn't risk asking for directions to Lejihk's family from other Travellers. The only way she could find them was to begin in the world they had settled in and track them – which might be as dangerous. Dahli would have watchers in every place the family had visited, anticipating that Rielle or Qall might seek them this way.

That turned her mind to another problem she had been wrestling with all the way from Deeme. Once Givari, the girl who had given Qall the braid, received Qall's message, a watcher was bound to read about it from her mind. Dahli would guess that Rielle or Qall were close by. He might harm one of the family in the hope that she or Qall would try to save them.

When she realised this, she nearly abandoned the task. Only the knowledge that Qall would read her mind as soon as she returned, even if she forbade it, kept her travelling. She would, in his situation. It was vital that she keep him from trying to return until he was mature enough to learn how to pattern-shift. He would stay put for nothing less than knowing the girl understood what his intentions were.

A few solutions had come to her during her infrequent rests. She could arrange for someone else to deliver the braid then report back to her, though that held the danger they would lead Dahli back to her. Or she could leave it somewhere the Travellers would visit in future, disguised somehow so watchers wouldn't know it was a message for Givari and intercept it. The advantage of the first method was that Qall would have proof it had reached Givari. The advantage of the latter was that she would be long gone before the girl received it and Dahli learned she had returned briefly from hiding.

To do either meant locating Lejihk's family, and perhaps

where they would be visiting in future. Lejihk hadn't decided what his new circuit of trading worlds would be when she'd left him. Judging by the path he'd recommended to her, he'd explored an impressively long way from their settlement. He wouldn't have sent her along the same route he was going to take, or he would have diminished her lead over any pursuit. But that left hundreds of worlds to search. Better she start from the world the family had settled in and track them from there.

It was the beginning of a workable plan. As Rielle continued to eat, she looked for weaknesses or ways it might backfire.

Dahli might have left someone watching every world Lejihk's family had visited, anticipating that she would try to find them that way. She would have to search minds wherever she went. And if a watcher did see her . . .? Could she deal with a hunter or enemy without actually killing them? Leaving them in a dead world was one possibility, though she was reluctant to even do that. However, if she only wanted to delay them delivering a message to Dahli, she could leave them in a void large enough it would take several days for them to travel out of it.

When she was too full to eat another mouthful, she apologised to Tarran for her short visit, thanked him for the food and bade him farewell as affectionately as she would have before if she'd known she'd been about to become Qall's guardian.

"Give Tyen my best wishes," she said to him as they reached the courtyard. He nodded, then made a shooing gesture.

"Go on. I know you're in a hurry. Don't let this old man hold you up any longer."

She smiled and pushed away from the world. Though the sooner she left this part of the worlds the better, she travelled slowly, making her way towards the world the Travellers had settled in by a winding, indirect route. Many of the arrival places she passed through were surrounded by signs of recent fighting. Once, she held off from arriving completely when it was clear that a battle was underway; instead she skimmed away from the conflict. Another time she arrived in a peaceful, bustling town only to find the world's magic was nearly completely depleted, her habit of carrying enough magic to leave a world again saving her from becoming stranded.

At last she approached the world where she had met up with Lejihk's family. She skimmed slowly towards the former camp; then, when close, she drew further from the world and travelled in almost total whiteness. Soon she detected an old, faint path leading away from the world. Following it until the next started to come into sight, she broke away from it and continued parallel to it.

That put her in a field outside a village. Skimming to a copse of trees, she arrived and began searching minds. It was early evening and most of the locals were absorbed in tasks like cooking and eating, while a few were asleep. Eventually a couple said goodnight to their neighbours and, as they donned coats for the walk home, the husband recalled how, three-quarters of a cycle ago, the famed Travellers had driven their carts through the village and sold them the coats.

The traders had continued north. Rielle stilled the air below her and levitated up into the sky, following roads and searching minds in the villages she passed over. The people who had bought items from the Travellers thought themselves lucky because the family wasn't intending to visit this world again.

Everywhere Rielle went, she searched but found no sorcerer keeping watch for Dahli. After Rielle found no more memories of the Travellers' visit, she began looking for paths into the place between. When she found one, old and faint, she followed it to the next world. There she sought and found more memories of the family's passing.

In this way or similar, she slowly tracked the path of Lejihk's family. After eleven worlds, she finally found one in which they'd bought goods to sell, but still with no arrangement to return in

271

future. They didn't trade in the next world, or the one after, but in the third she learned, after waiting for the locals to wake up, that a permanent arrangement had been discussed but not made.

Yet in the next few worlds, no trade had been made or proposed. She realised that it was likely they would avoid making permanent arrangements until they'd travelled the circuit a few times. If that was right, she would have to abandon her plan and find another way to get Qall's message to Givari.

In the next world, Rielle found a watcher.

He was living across the road from a merchant Lejihk's family had traded with. Rielle had stopped in the shadows of a storeroom, her cloak turned shabby side out.

. . . might never come here, the man was thinking. *But this place is comfortable enough and the food is good. Not as nice as the place Dahli is staying in though.*

An image of a room flashed into the watcher's mind. Tiles covered the floor. Steam rose from a deep, rectangular pool. Scantily-clad servants provided anything a customer needed. The thought of that stirred lust and jealousy in the man, but he quickly turned his mind away from picturing anything in more detail. What if Dahli found him too caught up in pleasure to watch the locals' minds.

Dahli, Rielle thought. From the impression she'd gained, he was only a few worlds away. *If I could get close enough to read his mind without alerting him to my presence, I might learn what his precise plans are – and find a weakness.* She might not find a way to prevent him blackmailing Qall – or her – but she could discover something else she could use against him.

Getting close enough to Dahli to read his mind was risky, however. She observed the watcher, gathering information. Dahli was in Yolin, a town in a nearby world famous for its natural springs and heated waters. When she had a clear picture of the location, she took a circuitous route through the local worlds and arrived at a distance to Yolin. She changed her appearance further, shortening her nose and narrowing her mouth. Joining a steady stream of people walking to the town, many of them sick and hoping the waters would cure them, half of one of the long, local days passed before she crested a rise and looked down on the town.

It nestled in a shallow valley, surrounded by lush vegetation and shrouded in steam. The upper slopes were covered in terraced fields. Perching on the wall of one of these as if to rest, she read the character of the place, taking information from the minds of the inhabitants.

Finding Dahli among the thousands was easier than she'd hoped. Establishments with a natural supply of water made greater profits than those who had to buy it from them. Few new sources had been found in recent times, but recently an otherworlder sorcerer had created a spring in exchange for free use of a bathhouse. Searching that establishment, a rush of cold set her skin prickling as she found the mind she sought.

Dahli was eating a meal while receiving a messenger's report. None of his watchers had noticed her, she was relieved to learn.

She's smart, Dahli was thinking. *She's not going to come back. I'm wasting my time.* The man's dark mood lightened hers, but she could see his determination to keep waiting. The sighting of the boy was the only lead he had after more than five cycles since Valhan's death. *What else is there to do while Tyen works?* Dahli asked himself.

Rielle's heart stopped. *Tyen?*

Was he lying when he said he needed to work alone with no distractions? Dahli wondered. *What would he gain from that?* While he couldn't escape the suspicion that Tyen was delaying, he couldn't see a good reason for it. *Except, perhaps, to use the information I gave him to restore the woman in the book* before *resurrecting Valhan.*

Rielle stood frozen, unable to look away from Dahli's mind.

I've seen no sign he has though, Dahli reminded himself. *I'll keep visiting, no matter what he says. I must keep the pressure on him. I'll go in a few days.* He mentally traced the path from this world to the one Tyen was working in, considering how he would avoid a few worlds that had exploded into war recently. *But if he sees my memories of the devastation there, it will emphasise the urgency. Though I doubt it'll convince him to stop insisting that we don't use a living vessel . . .*

Breath caught in Rielle's throat. Tyen was not trying to find a way to deal with the mechanical weapons. He was seeking a way to resurrect Valhan!

Why would he? Had Dahli blackmailed him? She saw no thought of it in the man's mind. As far as Dahli was concerned, Tyen was partly doing this in exchange for the knowledge of how to resurrect Vella, partly in order to save the worlds.

Dahli had finished eating. *At least I've finally convinced him that this is the only way to prevent the worlds' self-destruction,* he thought.

Rielle hissed out a breath as her frustration increased. *Didn't we agree that Valhan wasn't the solution to the worlds' troubles? That they didn't need one all-powerful leader? That they would sort themselves out in time?* Or had she assumed agreement from his lack of arguments against her opinion?

She couldn't remember. She was too angry. Then she gasped as Dahli's thoughts revealed more.

. . .Valhan warned me that Tyen must feel he has chosen the path of least harm. Tyen only continued to spy on the rebels in order to keep them alive longer – not realising this was what Valhan wanted. Dahli smiled, but his satisfaction at the success of the Raen's plan quickly withered away. *Ultimately it failed. Valhan misjudged Rielle. She did not return him to me.* Dahli ran his hands through his hair, fighting a familiar despair.

Seeing the grief within her former mentor, Rielle's anger began to wane. Though she should not sympathise with the man who wanted to kill Qall, she could not help it. *He has lost someone he loved. A man he adored and served despite receiving no love in return.*

It must have been unbearable, but there had been no escape.

Valhan had not allowed strong sorcerers to live who weren't under his control. Dahli had no choice but to stay and serve him. What sort of man would Dahli have been if he'd been free to leave and seek a person who could return his love?

Knowing that Valhan could not have been blind to his most loyal servant's pain and longing only made Rielle hate him more.

And she could see how much Dahli hated her.

And yet, I don't hate him. I think I would if he harmed Qall or the Travellers, though.

Tyen, however . . .

She scowled. She had assumed that, as long as Dahli never located her and Qall, everyone would be safe and no chance of the Raen returning remained. But nobody would be safe if Tyen succeeded in resurrecting Valhan. The Raen had allowed the Travellers to trade between worlds, but would he revoke that favour when he learned that they had actively worked against his return? If Valhan had believed he must eventually kill Rielle because she was too close to him in strength, he would not tolerate Qall's existence either.

Tyen, having resurrected him, would be spared. Had Dahli promised as much? She looked into the man's mind again.

Either way, I have no choice but to trust Tyen. Once he manages to resurrect a test subject, he'll have all the knowledge he needs to give Vella a body. If he breaks our agreement, then I can do nothing, but at least I've not had to risk trusting him with Valhan's hand. To ensure he keeps his promise, I will have to make sure he keeps seeing the increasing chaos in the worlds . . .

The hand. Valhan's hand. Rielle drew in a deep breath. Qall was only one ingredient in the recipe for a resurrection, and if Tyen was working on producing another vessel for Valhan's mind, then he wasn't vital. While the hand existed, the Raen could return.

If it didn't exist, Valhan could never come back.

It was Dahli's weakness. *It must be destroyed.* Her heart skipped a beat. She looked into Dahli's mind again, hoping that he would continue to think of it and betray its location. All she discovered was that he had hidden it and blocked his memory of its location. He would not unblock that memory until Tyen had proven himself and had a vessel ready to imprint.

She couldn't wait around until then. Qall needed protecting and training.

But she knew of someone who could wait and watch, and strike when the moment was right. Someone who would be *very* interested to know what the Spy had done, and planned to do. Someone who could deliver Qall's message.

She pushed out of the world and went in search of Baluka.

PART THREE

TYEN

CHAPTER 11

*B*y *now I ought to be used to regretting making alliances and ending up on the wrong side,* Tyen mused. Looking down on the ruins of Glaemar's palace, he watched the minds of both conqueror and conquered. The gentle Doumians, unused to subjugating others, feared those they now ruled and so kept order with an edge of wary cruelty. The Muraians, familiar with an unfair social hierarchy, were adapting to their circumstances with a remarkable acceptance.

He'd checked on his former employees before coming here. Fortunately, none of them had suffered for their association with him. Some had set themselves up as makers of magic-driven wheels, which he was happy to see. They'd told him the Claymars were insisting no acknowledgement be made of the source of the invention, claiming instead that it had been a rediscovered secret of a long-dead potter, but assured him they were recording the truth in other ways.

What did I do to the Claymars to deserve that? he wondered. *Was negotiating peace with Murai on their behalf, even when they never intended to honour any agreement, really such a great crime?*

At last, he found the mind he sought. Claymar Fursa now lived in one of the grander Glaemar homes, taken from one of the merchants who had attacked Alba's market. Tyen smiled. Despite the wrong the Claymars had done to him, he could not help enjoying a little satisfaction at that.

He pushed out of the world a little and skimmed down to the city, through walls and into the passageway Fursa was striding down. She jolted to a stop, catching sight of his form, and backed away as he arrived.

"It wasn't my idea," she blurted out.

He nodded as he read from her mind the names of the Claymars who had hatched and proposed the plan to invade Murai. *But I agreed with them*, she thought. *I guess that's just as bad.*

It was, but Tyen wasn't here for revenge, or to punish anyone. "I was honest and did everything for the benefit of Doum," he said. "In return you deceived me and robbed me of my home. So why pretend the wheels are a Doumian invention?"

Her lips pressed tightly together, but her mind answered clearly. *So nobody would have cause to respect you*, she thought. *You were meant to have failed. We told the people that the Emperor did not sign the treaty, and it was your fault.* She shivered, knowing that he was reading these thoughts but unable to stop them. *What now? Will he punish me? Will he kill all of us?*

"Are you enjoying your new role in Murai?" he asked.

She stared at him, wondering at the change of subject. As she considered the question, the self-loathing and homesickness that assailed her when she first woke up every day returned.

He shook his head. "I don't need to punish you."

Relief was etched in deep lines on her face. Lines he didn't recall seeing when they'd last met. He pushed out of the world, and as she faded from sight he wondered if being conquered by the Doumians would bring improvements to Murai. The Doumian system of electing rulers and holding artisans in greater esteem might create a fairer society. *But if you are willing to kill and dominate others to impose such changes, how do you convince those others not to kill and dominate if you give them back their freedom?*

What do you think, Vella?

"Creating laws is the most common way humans maintain a peaceful and fair society," she replied, her voice clear in his mind. *"A mix*

of incentive and punishment encourages the following of those laws. I've never encountered or heard of a society that was able to maintain them on incentive alone, though some successfully restrict their punishments to social, non-violent ones."

Doum was one of those, Tyen said, *but it took so little to change it. I must admit, I'm relieved that I can't return. I'd have to try persuading the Claymars away from violence, or else sit back and watch everything change for the worse.*

"You have more important tasks now."

He reached the next world and skimmed to the arrival place. It was a raised wooden platform inside a hall, a painted design flaking away beneath his feet. He pushed on.

Yes. Challenges against which the problems of Murai and Doum are commonplace. Keeping an eye on Dahli and stopping him pursuing Rielle, resurrecting the Raen, destroying all the weaponised insectoids, and restoring you.

"Restoring my body is not important," she reminded him. "At least not to the worlds."

It is to me. I made a promise. While I won't kill to do it, I can try to find another way.

"The price for doing so is bringing back the Raen. Is it too high?"

I don't know, he admitted. *Restoring you is not the only reason I am doing it, however. Helping Rielle and being able to warn others that he is about to return is more important.*

"Rielle is gone. She does not need you to stop Dahli chasing her."

The next world was in darkness, the stars illuminating crystalline stones thrusting up from the ground. The area he arrived on had been levelled and a narrow road led away. He pushed on.

Yes, but Baluka will also need to know. The worlds will need to know and prepare.

"How certain are you that Dahli could resurrect the Raen without your help?"

Not completely. He is, though. Given time – and he has plenty since he is ageless – he will find someone strong enough and willing to help him. I can't take that risk. As long as he has Valhan's hand, there is always that danger.

"The hand may be deteriorating, according to Dahli."

Yes. But Dahli blocked his memory of how quickly, and that makes me distrust his claim. Why hide that piece of information?

"So that you don't waste time or delay. So you are forced to make decisions without spending time in deliberation."

Did I decide too quickly?

"I don't know enough to judge."

Short, stumpy trees surrounded him in the next world. In contrast, the men and women guarding the arrival place were tall and thin. He skimmed away.

Working with Dahli bothers me but at the same time his arguments have merit, he admitted. *The Restorers aren't as effective as Valhan was at maintaining order. They didn't even know about the world of the meteors, and they have no idea how to save it. If Dahli believed I was the only one who could ever help him, I might have still agreed to try resurrecting the Raen eventually.*

"And yet you don't want to."

No.

"This way, if you change your mind, you could destroy the hand. Then there'd be no danger of the Raen ever returning."

Yes, but only after I access the information in it I need to restore you. Valhan might have seen a way to combat the war insectoids, too. He recognised that they would be a problem in the future, so perhaps he saw a solution as well.

"Perhaps you can use that reasoning to convince Dahli to show you the hand."

No. Dahli isn't going to let me near it until I've proven I can resurrect someone, and have a vessel ready for Valhan.

The next arrival place was a frozen pool within a ruin – an odd location, but perhaps the former occupants planned to deal with unwanted visitors by shattering the ice and plunging them into the water below. Tyen moved on.

If there is any chance Valhan had a solution to the insectoid problem, I have to try to access his memories. It is my fault they exist.

"You couldn't have known that the knowledge you exchanged for training at Liftre would lead to people making war insectoids," Vella said.

No, but I should have seen it coming. The Leratian empire used mechanical magic for war too. Their war aircarts and cannons enabled them to conquer most of my world.

"That only proves that humans will turn whatever they can into weapons, wherever they are. It is not your fault that the worlds did the same with mechanical magic."

Even so, if there's a solution, I must try to find it. I can't do that with no funds and no home.

A part of him was drawn to the safety of Dahli's protection. It would be a relief to not be constantly on guard. A darker part of him that he didn't like to consider too closely feared what would happen to him if he refused to help Dahli, and the man then succeeded in resurrecting the Raen. *The Raen would consider me too powerful to allow to live. I'd have to flee to the edges of the worlds, as Rielle has.* Valhan might kill Tyen anyway, once he read his mind and learned how he had helped Rielle and the Restorers. When considering that possibility, Tyen wondered if his hope to ask for Rielle's life as a reward was an overly optimistic delusion. After all, the Raen had planned to kill Rielle, even as he expected her to resurrect him.

At other times, Tyen wondered if the Raen would find it so easy to become the sole ruler of the worlds again. Most of the man's allies and friends were dead and the Restorers were well established now. If the Raen had been in such straits that he was driven to an act as risky as killing himself and trusting others to resurrect him, he clearly had a limit to his power and influence. What if the Restorers, Tyen and Rielle joined together to fight him? Could they kill him? Could they make a truce? Would Valhan agree to rule only some of the worlds?

There might be other ways to ensure a resurrected Raen wasn't as great a power in the worlds, but for the moment they were incomplete ideas hovering at the edges of Tyen's mind.

The world sharpening around him was his destination. As he arrived, he breathed in the scents of a garden, marvelling again at his body's new ability to survive the lack of air between worlds. Walking out of the circle of plants, he entered a grand labyrinth. It spread over a vast area, maintained by hundreds of residents living in little houses hidden within the walls. Visitors strolled along the pathways. Tyen could hear children laughing and calling out. He passed rooms containing a fountain, statues and even a pond with a tree-covered island at the centre, a boat tied up invitingly at the shore.

He had taken the opportunity to stop in Doum and Murai because they were on his route to this place. Somewhere to the east, in a cave, he would find Baluka. The land rose ahead of Tyen, revealing the top of a decorative stone archway set into the slope. Tyen made his way towards it.

Sure enough, the arch was the entrance to a tunnel. Exploring within, Tyen was disappointed when he emerged on the other side of the hill. It was a passage, not a cave. But as he scanned the maze below, he noted a circular hole in the centre of one clearing. Perhaps this was the cave Baluka meant. He made his way down.

Reaching it, he found there was a stairway spiralling into the darkness. He created a light and descended. At the bottom was a single seat, carved roughly into a boulder. A man was sitting in it. Baluka. He was talking to a sorcerer standing before him.

Baluka's voice drifted up to him. "You may go."

The sorcerer faded out of sight.

"You took your time." Baluka looked up and grinned. "Did you get lost?"

Tyen shrugged as he descended the last steps. "No. I made a quick detour."

"How are you?"

"Well enough. You?"

"The same as usual."

Tyen paused. He knew that Dahli had managed to get a spy near Baluka, but he didn't know how. One of Dahli's friends was arranging it and had been given strict instructions not to tell Dahli the details. So far Tyen had resisted telling Baluka, since it might make Dahli wonder how the man had come by the information.

Tyen looked around, as if searching for the other man. "Are you taking all the security precautions you can?"

"Of course."

Tyen nodded. "You should be extra careful."

Baluka's eyebrows rose. "Any particular reason?"

Tyen shrugged. "Nothing I can specify."

"I see." Baluka nodded to a large sack at the foot of the chair. "That's for you."

Tyen lifted it. The weight caused him to stagger a little. It made a metallic crunch as he set it down again. Opening the top, Tyen caught a glimpse of polished metal and hinged claws.

"Insectoids?"

"Yes."

Tyen squatted and opened the bag further, scanning the tangle of metallic limbs gleaming inside. "Thanks. There's a few here I haven't seen before."

"Would you like more?"

"Yes. Different kinds. And if you can, keep them alive."

"That won't be easy."

Tyen nodded. "Not if they're the exploding kind."

Baluka's eyebrows rose. "Exploding?"

"Designed to blow up when they reach their target."

"That *will* make them hard to catch." Baluka paused. "Any progress?"

Tyen rose. "Only research so far. It took some time to find a safe place to work."

"I could have helped you there."

"I know." Tyen waited, knowing from Baluka's thoughts that his friend had something else to tell him but was not sure how to begin. The silence stretched out between them. Tyen lifted his eyebrows. "What is it?"

Baluka smiled crookedly. "It is nice of you to pretend not to have read it from me already." His expression became serious. "Rielle has adopted a child – now a young man – that she took from the Raen's allies soon after he died. Their intentions were to bring Valhan back by replacing the boy's memories with his. She objected to them using an innocent child this way, stole him away and gave him to my family to raise."

Tyen nodded. "Yes. I know. Well, not where she took the boy, but all of the rest."

Baluka's jaw dropped, then snapped closed again. "Why didn't you *tell* me?" He sucked in a breath. "No. You don't have to defend yourself. I know why. My mind is too easily read. If I know the Raen can be brought back to life, others could find out." He sighed. "Well, I guess the secret's out now. Though I can only assume by the lack of Raens roaming the worlds that this particular boy was essential to the process."

"Perhaps." Tyen shrugged.

"Fortunately, Rielle has taken him far away," Baluka continued.

Tyen raised his eyebrows. "She will be a formidable protector."

Baluka nodded. "And a kind one." He smiled as old memories played out in his mind. Which roused newer ones in Tyen's – and an uncomfortable mix of guilt and desire. *Would he hate me if he knew Rielle and I have been lovers?*

According to Tarran, she'd been annoyed by Tyen's hurried message, left at the exit to the desert world. After he'd evaded the ex-rebels who had discovered him using up the magic of the desert world, he'd sent a few messages to Tarran. He'd been worried the rebels were still following him, so he'd made his instructions obscure and used unfamiliar message-bearing methods. Too obscure and unfamiliar. None had arrived.

Then he'd had to find a new world to learn pattern shifting in. In one of the moments his mind had wandered during his first attempt, he'd remembered the ice world where the Raen's resurrection had been attempted. It had been unpopulated and rich with magic, and because Rielle had never finished the task, there was plenty of magic left. He'd resumed his task and achieved agelessness a quarter cycle later.

He'd been looking forward to celebrating with Rielle and Tarran when he got back. Doum's invasion of Murai wasn't the only disappointment awaiting him on his return.

I doubt we'll see her again, Baluka was thinking.

Tyen nodded. *I have to hope she won't come back, but I also hope that she will. I suppose what I hope is that one day it will be safe for her to.*

"The best thing we can do for her is ensure the threat at this end is dealt with," Baluka said, pushing sadness aside and replacing it with resolve. "Dahli and his supporters." His chin rose a little. "You could join us. You could help us restore order to the worlds too. The more worlds at peace, fewer will have reason to make insectoids."

Tyen shuddered and shook his head. "No." *He wouldn't offer me that if he'd seen how badly things worked out in Doum and Murai.*

"I'm not offering you the leadership," Baluka reminded him, adding a ghost of a smile.

"I know," Tyen replied. "I appreciate the offer, but my time is better spent on what I know best – mechanical magic."

Baluka nodded. "Well, then. Good luck. I will see if I can get you some more specimens – and some live ones."

"Thanks." Tyen hoisted the bag over one shoulder, grimacing at the weight. "Take care, Baluka."

"You too."

Baluka smiled, but as Tyen pushed out of the world the smile faded. The leader of the Restorers looked grim and tired, but as determined as ever. Tyen's resolve to warn his friend of the Raen's return hardened. *I may not be any good at negotiating peace, but I am good at spying. I may as well put that skill to good use: keeping an eye on Dahli.*

CHAPTER 12

Setting the disappointingly small stack of paper aside, Tyen sighed. He'd read the Raen's notes three times since Dahli had produced them, but each reread produced no new insights. Looking around the large room – a basement under a crumbling old city mansion in a world that had once thrived under the Raen's rule – he listed the objects surrounding him. *A table large enough for a man to lie down on. Medical instruments. Medicines. Water filter. Burner. Bandages.* His gaze moved to the other side of the room. *Table. Shelving. Insectoids. Tools. Metal to forge into parts. Chemicals. Oil.*

He considered whether he needed anything else. Had he forgotten anything? He knew he was looking for an excuse to avoid starting work, and yet he looked anyway.

Perhaps I can replicate everything we gathered for the Raen's resurrection in another area, for when I restore Vella. He straightened. *Vella,* he thought. *I knew there was something I hadn't done yet – check with you.*

Lifting her pouch out from under his shirt, he removed her and opened her covers. Her elegant script appeared on the page.

What should I do next, Vella?

Stop procrastinating? appeared on her page. You know you've reached the point where Dahli will grow suspicious if you keep delaying.

He nodded. *You're right. And yet I'm honestly not sure where to start.*

So what is holding you back?

Where to begin? I wish the Raen had written down how to resurrect a person in logical steps. There are so many gaps in his notes. Sometimes he is very clear and detailed, and makes no effort to conceal important results; other times he refers to information rather than includes it.

He probably did not expect others to read them, and he was a busy man.

That is true. It's also possible Dahli left information out when translating the Raen's writing, then blocked his memory of having done so.

It would not make sense, if there's a chance the information he omitted would lead you to fail or refuse to continue, or produce an unsatisfactory result. But he did admit that the translation of the notes might not be accurate.

Because the translators' knowledge was incomplete. We're lucky that people still exist who speak the obscure language he used. Dahli had wondered if it was the language of the Raen's home. He had found the speaker by sending his followers out to the great markets and stores of knowledge in the worlds, and even to the Travellers, with a random phrase to translate. It was a scholar at Liftre who had discovered the source.

Fortunately, the phrase hadn't revealed anything Dahli wanted to remain secret. When he'd found the people who spoke the language, he had chosen three translators who did not know anything of magic, and given them pages out of order in the hope they would understand so little of what they were translating that he wouldn't have to kill them when they were done.

He wouldn't have gone to the trouble had he been working with someone less scrupulous as Tyen. Yet he was not annoyed by the inconvenience. He was strangely gladdened by it. He was pleased to discover he did not like to kill, even after hundreds of cycles of doing so for the Raen.

Dahli is a conflicted, contradictory man, Tyen mused. *Though with him blocking memories he doesn't want me to see, I can't be entirely sure that the person I see is truly his natural, whole self.*

If he held me, I might be able to access those memories.

He's never going to fall for any trick meant to achieve that. Tyen sighed. *Or allow me to delay for ever. I must proceed with something soon, but what?* It was a question for himself, not Vella, so she did not reply. He chewed on the inside of his cheek. *There are three parts to this. The challenge is to discover how Valhan had copied his memories into his hand, and replicate the process. It would help if I had the Raen's hand to study, but Dahli isn't going to produce that until I've proved I can successfully resurrect someone.*

You have me to study. I am a more complex object, but I do contain memories. Knowing how to pattern-shift will help you understand my structure.

He nodded. *I will do that. But I also need to find someone who doesn't mind having their memories copied into an object. I'm not going to volunteer, and I doubt Dahli will, so we'll have to bring in somebody.* His best idea had been to imprint the memories of a dying person into an acceptable vessel. The idea that he would be effectively saving them from death made the whole exercise much more palatable.

Except that he could heal them instead. He could now heal anyone, and extend their life. He could be doing so now, but he wasn't.

Rielle hadn't mentioned that moral dilemma of learning pattern shifting. When he thought of how he could be curing all the illness and disease in the worlds, he could see the mess it could result in. He couldn't heal everyone, so how would he choose who to help? How far should he go when he could make a human physically perfect and even reverse their age? Once it was known what he was capable of and willing to do, would the demand for healing create competition and chaos among the needy, leading to those with wealth and power pushing aside ordinary people?

He did not yet have the courage to face those questions. Fortunately he had a deal, a promise and a mistake to attend to first.

The second challenge is preparing a vessel. I'll need a body for that.

Valhan wrote that he needed an untrained sorcerer as close to him in strength as he could find, in case his magical ability didn't transfer to the vessel.

Reading that, Tyen had felt a chill. Rielle would have qualified as Valhan's vessel. As would Tyen. *But he didn't know I was so powerful, and I had already been trained in using magic.* Next to the notation had been the world "male" underlined. Perhaps that was all that had disqualified Rielle.

It would be useful to know whether Qall had acquired the Raen's full strength. If so, then magical ability was entirely physical, and it was possible to make anyone that powerful. It also would mean Tyen would have to abandon his ideas of ensuring the newly restored Raen was weaker, and therefore less of a threat to the Restorers and Rielle.

What if Qall had been nearly as strong as the Raen? It seemed a strange coincidence that two sorcerers nearly as powerful as the Raen had been born around the same time, but the idea of a third was astounding. Was this Millennium's Rule in action, producing more potential rivals every thousand cycles? He doubted a supernatural force was shaping the future, so either a natural variation in sorcerous strength occurred roughly every thousand cycles, or there had been no rivals to the Raen before his twenty-cycle absence because he had killed them. The latter was disturbing because it meant sorcerers of great strength were being born all the time and the worlds would soon be full of them. It also meant the Raen was not extraordinary in his magical strength, but for his success in maintaining power and order.

It would be a great irony if Qall became the Successor after Valhan created him in an attempt to stay in power. Especially if he fights a resurrected Raen and wins.

You're getting distracted again, Vella told him.

Tyen brought his thoughts back to the present.

I don't need a vessel of similar strength to the Raen. All I require is the body of someone who has recently died, or at least whose mind has.

292

Both options still made Tyen uneasy. A person's corpse ought to be treated respectfully, and even someone whose memories had been lost would lose the chance to live a new life if their mind was replaced.

Valhan had tried beginning with a newborn and using pattern shifting to speed its growth into an adult, but its mind and body did not develop properly, lacking the life experiences needed to learn and adapt. Memories had failed to imprint correctly. Limbs had failed to respond to unfamiliar commands from the mind. An adult mind needed an adult vessel. Tyen wondered if this also meant that a male mind needed a male body for the male organs to function properly, and female for female. He wasn't going to test that theory in his experiments, however. What he was doing already involved enough ethical dilemmas.

The third challenge he faced was to transfer the information stored in the object into the vessel. That created another dilemma. What would they do with this new person? Even if they succeeded, they would have to find a home for them. And if they didn't? Tyen shuddered. *I guess that depends on how we fail.*

For now, he should concentrate on the first challenge. That meant finding a dying man or woman who wanted the change to replicate themselves. *Which means leaving the safety of this room. Maybe that's why I'm hesitating—*

A movement at the end of the long room drew his attention. Looking up, his heart froze as he made out the shadow of a man growing clearer, but as he recognised the figure his pulse returned to a normal rhythm.

"Tyen," the man said as he arrived.

"Dahli," Tyen replied, returning Vella to her pouch.

The Raen's most loyal had changed his appearance again, removing his beard. His hair had grown a little longer and was now a pale shade of blond.

"I had something to investigate," Dahli said, weaving his way through the furniture. Looking closer, Tyen read that the man had been checking on the people he'd set watching Baluka's family. "Have you made any progress?"

Tyen ignored him. "I won't help you if you harm them."

Dahli's eyes narrowed. "If all goes well, I will never need to." Moving to a chair, he nodded at the Raen's notes. "Well?"

Tyen suppressed a sigh. "I've read them three times. For a man who lived a thousand cycles, he doesn't write very clear instructions."

Dahli's eyebrows rose. "For a man who insists Valhan went about resurrections the wrong way, you are surprisingly reliant on him for information."

Tyen shrugged. "If I knew exactly what he did, I could avoid making the same mistakes."

"If they were mistakes." Dahli waved a hand dismissively. "We must work with what we have. Is there anything I can do to help?"

Tyen began to shake his head, then paused. "Do you know someone who doesn't mind having copies made of them?"

Dahli's eyebrows rose. "Sorcerer or not?"

"Doesn't matter."

"Should I bring our volunteer here?"

"No. It may take a great deal of magic, which would weaken this world."

"Would you use them as the vessel as well?"

Tyen shook his head. "How would we tell if it worked?"

"Good point. You'll need a vessel, too."

"Yes. Someone not long dead. I'll heal their body, then change it to the volunteer's pattern. I won't need as much magic for that part, so we can do it here. I'll need a strong, unpopulated world for the resurrection though."

Dahli nodded, but his attention had strayed to the far end of the room. "Is that what I think it is?"

Tyen traced the man's gaze to the insectoids. Much larger than Beetle, their hulking bodies looked menacing in the shadows.

"Yes."

Standing up, Dahli wandered over to the machines. Tyen followed.

"Why do you have these?"

"I'm looking for a way to destroy them. Something that will work with all kinds."

"Is that possible?" Dahli asked, reaching out and poking one as if to check if it were only sleeping.

"Probably not," Tyen admitted. "But I have to try."

Dahli turned away, nodding in approval. "It would be a great benefit to the worlds if you succeeded." He frowned. "Is this the reason your work on the resurrection has been so slow?"

Tyen shook his head. "So far I am only disassembling them to look for common weaknesses. It's easy work – any of my students at Liftre could have done it – and it gives my hands something to do while I'm thinking about the resurrection."

"Why don't you find a student to do it for you?" Dahli suggested.

"I would need to supervise, and if they're here they'll see what I'm working on."

"They only need to know that you're looking for a way to replace someone's body with a younger or different one. Your experiments won't involve Valhan. When we create a body for Valhan we will send them elsewhere. Look for someone young, who doesn't understand pattern shifting or they'll wonder why we're bothering putting people's minds in new bodies when we could just heal them. If you don't find anyone suitable at Liftre I can direct you to other schools of magic, though I don't think their instruction in mechanical magic is as advanced."

Tyen nodded reluctantly. He would rather not draw anyone else into his situation, but Dahli's suggestion had become an order.

"Make sure he or she is a weaker sorcerer than me," Dahli added, "or I will have to kill them when their work is done."

"Could you, if they were stronger?"

295

"Of course." Dahli shrugged. "With experience, knowledge and loyal friends, you can overcome most adversaries."

"I'll remember that."

Dahli's gaze slid to the distance as he drew in magic from far above them. "I'll find you a volunteer while you fetch your assistant."

Tyen nodded. "What sort of wage should I offer them?"

"Whatever they want – I will arrange it. Is there anything else you need?"

"No."

"Then I will collect you when I have our volunteer." Dahli faded out of sight.

Walking past the place Dahli had vacated, Tyen picked up the Raen's notes and approached a row of cupboards that ran along one wall of the room. He'd seen the original, tiny notebook in Dahli's memory. Had the Raen hidden it, or carried it around with him? Had he kept it in a pouch beneath his shirt, like Tyen did with Vella?

Tyen smiled at that thought, but his amusement quickly faded. The day he had first encountered the Raen had been a revelation to both of them. In Vella, the Raen had seen the glimmer of a solution to his problems with the allies. She had revealed a way to store all his memories in an object, from which he could extract them later.

Tyen unlocked a cupboard door and pulled out several bundles of bandages from the lowest shelf. Once clear, he used magic to work a mechanism that lifted the shelf upwards, revealing a cavity in the base of the cabinet. As it opened, he spoke a word.

"Beetle."

From within the dark space antennae emerged, twitching eagerly.

"Come out."

The insectoid scurried up onto the underside of the shelf. Tyen slipped the notes inside. He would rather have destroyed them, now that Vella had absorbed their contents, but Dahli wanted them intact.

"Guard these, Beetle," Tyen ordered. "If anyone but me or Dahli tries to take them, burn them."

A whistle of affirmation came from the compartment. Closing it, Tyen began moving the bandages back into place. Perhaps he would find a way to destroy all of the weaponised insectoids in the worlds. Perhaps he could do so without harming the benign ones as well. But if he had to destroy them all, he would. Even Beetle.

Dahli's suggestion that he find an assistant surprised him. The man did care about the worlds, so it made sense that solving the insectoid problem appealed to him – as long as it didn't take up all of Tyen's attention. What surprised Tyen was that Dahli was willing to allow another person to be close by as Tyen undertook his experiments.

Tyen locked the cabinet door and stood. Drawing magic, he pushed out of the world and started a cautious, indirect journey to Liftre.

As he drew closer to the school, he began to worry. Tarran had said that those at the school who had known Tyen as a student and teacher had attributed the invention of insectoids to him. Unfortunately, this had led to people believing that he'd created the weaponised ones as well. While Tarran had asked his students to correct this whenever they visited Liftre, Tyen did not know how successful they'd been.

That was not his only source of anxiety, however. The rumour that Tyen had been a spy among the rebels might cause him problems. If it was believed by enough teachers and students there, they might unite to expel him. At the very least, news that the Spy was visiting Liftre would immediately go straight out into the worlds and he'd have to flee, no doubt with angry sorcerers in pursuit. So he had better find a hidden place to arrive and then search minds until he knew whether anyone there was qualified enough to be his assistant, and then make sure only they saw him.

He entered Liftre's world away from commonly used paths to avoid the risk someone would pass him in the place between. Forging a new path, he concealed its beginning and end. Keeping to the far side of the narrow ravine the school was located within, he skimmed close to one rock wall and chose a shadowed crevasse to arrive in.

He'd never seen Liftre from this vantage point before. The view was impressive. The ancient building, added to over many hundreds of cycles, grew up out of a rocky outcrop in the middle of the ravine. A steep road had been carved out of the base, winding down to the village below.

It was morning. Classes were about to begin. Searching for minds, he soon heard the buzz and clamour of many, many thoughts. It was like watching a cloud of kites, some colourful, some subdued, some dark, some bright, the closest overlaying the furthest. He jumped from one mind to the next, hoping that among the random snippets he would catch something related to mechanical magic.

One cluster of minds was focused on calculating cycles against a world's own seasons. Tyen smiled at the new students' boredom and confusion. The next group was creating sculptures by lifting water and freezing it – an exercise in control – and most were enjoying it. Another was bracing itself for a long history lecture, with more than one student lamenting that recent events were far more interesting than these old stories.

Then Tyen caught a familiar sight – cogs and other parts from insectoids. He concentrated on that one mind, finding a student building a small machine. It was not an insectoid, but a kind of lathe for carving chair legs. The girl making it looked across at another student's basket-making machine.

It's looking too much like an insect. A memory of their teacher came, speaking her oft-repeated words: *"Machines should look like machines, not creatures!"* The girl frowned. *It'd be easier if the parts we have weren't originally designed to make insectoids.*

Tyen moved to the boy's mind.

Zeke doesn't care if a machine looks like an insect, he was thinking. *He says machines should look however they need to, to do what they're meant to do. After that, they should be beautiful. What is more beautiful than a mudweaver?* An image of a multi-legged sea creature appeared in his mind, its shell an opalescent dome. Mud clutched to its belly with scoop-like arms was carefully deposited on the ground by four others as it turned in circles, creating a delicate, twisting column in which it would lay its eggs. *Like my basket-weaver*, the boy thought.

Zeke, Tyen thought. *Where have I heard that name before?* He searched the minds of the other students, then the teacher. When he heard the name again, it was in the teacher's mind when she examined the boy's invention.

Well, it's clear who has been influencing this one, she thought disapprovingly. Tyen saw that Zeke was not a teacher, though he had been until recently. When this woman had been promoted over Zeke, he'd quit teaching and now designed machines for clients who came to the school. He was perpetually broke, like all of Liftre's inventors who refused to make weapons, but he made his situation worse by taking longer than he quoted on commissions as he added features the client didn't ask for, or thought of another way of making them and started again. *His sister, Dalle, has a better grasp of how to run a business*, the teacher thought.

Dalle? Zeke and Dalle! Tyen let out a soft "ah!". He remembered the pair now. They'd been his best students in his last cycle at Liftre. They must have returned to Liftre to finish their education. *And it looks like they both specialised in mechanical magic.* An odd feeling of happiness stole over him, and he realised it was pride.

It faded quickly. What sort of a future had he given them,

when all people wanted of mechanical magic was to make weapons? What future would they have if he succeeded in destroying all magical machines?

Suddenly reluctant to continue his search for an assistant, he forced himself to look for Zeke and the rest of the inventors the teacher had thought about. If Zeke was a slow worker, perhaps it was best to not approach him, but try one of the others.

He found them all in the lower floors of the school sharing a late breakfast. In the basement, ironically. *Perhaps dark underground rooms are where we creators of magical machines all wind up*, he mused.

Scanning their minds, he saw a different view of his former student. Many of them believed Zeke was one of the best inventors there. Some disliked him, jealous of his talent or simply sure they were better – if not at invention then certainly at making money from it. A few made weapons exclusively, and were proud of it. Zeke did not like them. Tyen took note of their names.

None were especially powerful sorcerers – which was partly why they had been attracted to mechanical magic. He also noted that some had links to the Restorers. He wished he could prompt them all into thinking about him so he would know who believed he was a spy and traitor.

As the group finished their meal and chatter and separated to return to their rooms, Tyen chose who he would approach. Zeke first. The task needed genius more than speed of work or economy of design. Of course, the young man might not want to leave Liftre and assist his former teacher, even if it came with an income as high as he wished for, so Tyen had a short list of potential recruits among the others.

When Zeke had returned to his room, Tyen pushed out of the world until the school was a faint shadow in the whiteness, then skimmed down to the base of the building. Once within the walls, he could barely make out his surroundings, but that meant that he'd be difficult to see as well. He headed in the direction of Zeke's room, and when he thought he was near, drew close to the world until he could see enough to find an empty corridor to arrive in unseen. Once air surrounded him, he quickly scanned the minds around him, locating Zeke in a room reached by a corridor running parallel to this. Tyen pushed out of the world and skimmed into the room.

The young man was sitting at his desk, bent over an elaborately decorated brass box. He didn't notice Tyen's arrival, his mind wrapped up in the work. None of the boyishness of the student Tyen had taught remained. The young man was still lean, however, his straight, chin-length black hair not quite concealing high cheekbones. His skin was a paler brown than Tyen remembered, but then, he probably spent most of his time in this underground room.

Moving closer, Tyen saw that the interior of the box was filled with elaborate machinery. It was to be a rhyming machine, designed to hear the last word in a sentence and respond with another word ending in the same sound – if Zeke could work out a way to store thousands of words. He drew in a breath to speak.

Suddenly Zeke yelped and spun around. He stared at Tyen, who immediately began apologising.

"Ever heard of knocking?" the young man said in a strained voice when Tyen finally fell silent.

"Er. Yes. Sorry . . ."

Zeke frowned and narrowed his eyes. "Tyen? It really is you?"

Tyen glanced down at himself, seeing nothing odd. "Yes. Why?"

The young man shook his head. "You look different."

Remembering Rielle's warning that his appearance might change to meet others' expectations, a flash of alarm went through Tyen. "How?"

"I . . . don't know. You *look* the same but . . . not."

"That's helpful."

Zeke shrugged. "It isn't. It's not a bad change," he added. "You still have those pale, careless-about-grooming good looks."

"Er . . . thanks."

"So what brings you to my humble abode?"

Tyen drew a deep breath, let it out, then decided to get directly to the point.

"Want a job?"

Zeke's eyebrows rose. "You're kidding?"

"No. I need an assistant. I'm looking for a way to disable, if not destroy, the insectoids made for use in battle. I—"

"Yes," Zeke interrupted.

Tyen paused. "Yes?"

"I'll take the job."

"But . . . we haven't discussed a wage."

Zeke stood up. "We'll work something out. If I get to shove smashed war insectoids up those smug inventors' butt-holes, I'll work for free!" His grin was fierce, but quickly faded. "Not that I'm saying I won't take a wage. I have no other income, and I work better when not dying of starvation. I'm nicer to be around when I don't stink from lack of washing too."

Amused and surprised by Zeke's eagerness, Tyen considered what else he ought to tell the young man. "We must work in secret," he warned. "No, er, shoving of machines anywhere until they're smashed."

"Of course." Zeke shrugged. "The warmongers will get no chance to counter-attack."

"They may seek revenge."

"I'll tell them it was your idea. You tell them it was mine. Either way, as many people will be pleased and impressed with us as won't." He lifted his palms towards the ceiling. "Commissions and money will rain down on us from the sky."

"Well . . . then consider yourself hired, Zeke. Of course, if you find you're not happy working for me, I will bring you back here. You have my promise on that."

Zeke's eyebrows rose. "You're taking me away?" He looked around the room, then laughed like a madman. "You're taking me away!" His gaze snapped to Tyen's. "What's it like where you live?"

"Um . . ." Tyen looked around and shrugged. "Not much different to this, but quite a bit larger."

"But the company is better. I'd better pack a bag then."

"I can wait until you're done. I figured you'd want to finish your current job and say goodbye to—"

"No. One of the others can have this." Zeke gestured to the box. "But I will write a quick letter to the heads and my sister . . ." He moved to the desk and dug out some paper and a pen.

"How is Dalle?"

The young man winced. "We haven't spoken in four cycles. She sided with the rebels during the war. I . . . didn't. Not that I was on the Raen's side either. I don't like violence."

Zeke didn't see Tyen's wince, his attention turning to writing. The sound of pen running over paper followed. Zeke quickly finished one letter and pushed it aside, then hesitated before slowly writing another. By the time he was done, Tyen had seen most of the source of the conflict between the siblings. Dalle had joined the rebels after Baluka had become the leader. Zeke had refused to accompany her, or go to the final battle. He hadn't believed that the rebels would win, or that she would go if he didn't. Now everything was the way he had predicted it would be, adding resentment to her belief he had stayed neutral out of cowardice. The Restorers were unable to stop sorcerers behaving as badly as Valhan and the allies had. War was everywhere. Worlds had turned on their neighbours. Sorcerers sought to expand their empires. More and more worlds had been stripped of magic.

As Zeke started tossing clothes and other belongings into a sack, he wondered if destroying weaponised insectoids would please or displease her.

She'll be happy I joined Tyen, the former head of the rebels. Unless he really was a spy. Zeke paused. *If he was, do I care?* He shrugged, lifted the sack, winced at its weight, then dug inside and drew

out a few items, throwing them on the unmade bed. *I don't know.*
I guess I'll find out. He slung the sack over one shoulder, looked
around the room and nodded.

"I'm ready to go."

A *few good-quality tools, some gifts from his sister and some comfort-*
able clothes, Tyen mused, remembering his own careful packing
before leaving Liftre. *He already knows what he values most.* He
held out a hand. Zeke grinned and seized it. Tyen pushed into
the place between and started the journey back to his basement
workroom.

CHAPTER 13

"Nice place you have here."

Tyen stopped writing and looked up to see Zeke descending the stairs into the basement. The young man glanced upwards pointedly.

"Yes," Tyen agreed. "A . . . I suppose you'd call him a patron . . . found it for me."

Zeke's eyebrows rose. "Is he financing some of this?"

"Most of it." Tyen frowned as he realised that wasn't entirely true. "All of it, really."

"He has a particular interest in your experiment?"

"Yes, and he supports my wish to deal with the insectoids too." Tyen paused. "I'm sorry. I should have mentioned him earlier. Are you okay with this? If you ever feel uncomfortable with the arrangement, I can take you back."

"I guess . . ." Zeke moved to the tables where the war insectoids lay. "I'm just glad to be away from Liftre. Anyone who wants to get rid of the war insectoids already has my high opinion."

Tyen managed not to wince. As soon as they'd arrived the night before, all the ways the arrangement could go badly had occurred to him. What if Zeke learned something Dahli did not want known? Would Dahli kill the young inventor?

Zeke was now examining the large notebook Tyen had left out for him, leafing through the drawings and observations on the first few pages. "Do you need me to be as thorough as this?"

Tyen considered. "What do you think?"

"I don't normally take notes. Everything important goes in here." Zeke tapped his forehead. "But then, nobody else has had to work with me before." He gave the contents of the tables another quick scan, then looked at the shelves laden with the odd mix of tools and supplies around Tyen. "Can I ask what you're working on?"

"I am seeking a way to transfer the mind of a person into a new body," Tyen said.

Zeke's eyes widened. "Wow. That's . . . ambitious. And more biological than mechanical. Is that the direction your interests have taken now?"

"Yes and no. I spent some time in Faurio, studying to be a healer, but I wasn't very good at it. I guess this is another way I can use what I did learn."

Zeke walked up to the shelves, examining the contents. "You've not begun yet?"

"Only if you consider throwing around theories a start."

The young man chuckled. "I do. Will you be working on the insectoid destroyer? Hmm. We need to come up with a good name. The insect squasher? Bug catcher? Neutraliser?"

"'Neutraliser' is less fanciful, so more likely to be taken seriously. I'll work with you when I can," Tyen told him. "Do you have any ideas?"

"A few. It depends what you're trying to achieve." Zeke took a stool, brought it over to the other side of the table and sat down. "What is the best outcome we could achieve?"

"One where all war insectoids are destroyed and no more are made."

Zeke nodded. "Let's call them war machines, because from what I've heard they don't always take the shape of insects now."

"Very well."

"Since the war machines are in many worlds, the neutralisers must move between worlds, too," Zeke continued. "For that they need human help – unless they can be made to transport themselves between worlds?"

Tyen frowned. "If neutralisers can take themselves between worlds, the war machine creators would know it was possible and give their machines the ability."

"There's a nasty thought."

"I'm not sure it's possible though."

"*You* don't know?"

"Why would I?"

"Nobody thought machines could use magic until you came along. Surely you must know the limitations of what they can do with it."

"I've not had a reason or time to find out," Tyen admitted.

Zeke placed his hands flat on the table. "Well, if we don't, you can be sure the war machine makers will eventually. If I don't know what they might achieve, I won't be able to counteract it."

"Perhaps you had better not make those notes," Tyen said, sighing. "In case you discover something we'd rather not risk anybody finding out."

Zeke tapped his head. "Yes, sometimes it's better to keep them up here. For now the neutralisers shouldn't be able to do anything we haven't seen war machines do. You'll have to recruit a bunch of well-intentioned people to deliver them to their targets, though I don't think that will be hard. In fact, I think there are plenty of people who will do that to stop their enemies, as long as they don't have war machines of their own." He paused. "Do you still have your first one?"

Tyen blinked, surprised by the question. "Yes."

"Beetle, wasn't it?" Zeke smiled. "So simple, but elegant."

"It's been modified quite a bit since then."

"Not into a war machine?"

"Of course not. Though it has defensive features so it can protect my property."

"You won't want our neutralisers to target it." Zeke shook his head. "It's going to be very hard to make a machine that can decide what to destroy and what to ignore."

"Must it be a machine?"

"Yes." Zeke frowned. "I thought that's what you wanted? Making machines is my specialty. Why else would you hire me?"

Tyen shrugged. "The problem is mechanical. The solution may not be. Keep your mind open. A human solution may prove the best."

"If humans could hunt down and destroy every last war machine, the Restorers would have done it already."

"Not necessarily. They may simply be too busy dealing with human problems."

Zeke frowned. "War machines are essentially a human problem. They don't create themselves. Yet."

"Do you think they could be made to self-replicate?"

"If they had access to materials and were able to make parts . . . yes."

Tyen shuddered as he imagined worlds filling up with war machines. Had Valhan seen this possibility, when he had predicted that Beetle was the future? *His future, since he planned to be resurrected and resume his rule over the worlds.* The two projected futures combined in his mind, into a horrifying image of a Valhan-insectoid.

As a tingle ran down Tyen's spine he sat up straight. What was it Zeke had said? "*. . . from what I've heard they don't always take the shape of insects now.*" Had any of the machines been given the form of a human?

It probably wasn't what Valhan had meant, but it raised a very interesting possibility. In Tyen's imagination, a mechanical human formed. It shifted into a nightmare image of a gleaming, metallic human with Valhan's ancient, calculating gaze, but he pushed that side and instead conjured a feminine form, beautiful and far less frightening: Vella.

Could he give her a mechanical body? One that could be repaired and modified. It wasn't quite what he had in mind for her, but it was an idea worth exploring if his efforts at restoring her body failed. The greatest challenge would be to transfer the immense store of knowledge from her pages into the machine. *No*, he added. *The hardest part would be replacing the parts of her mind that were missing, like the ability to feel emotion.*

"Tyen?"

"Ah, sorry," Tyen muttered as he brought his attention back to the inventor. Zeke's eyes were wide and he was pointing somewhere behind Tyen. Turning, Tyen caught his breath as he recognised the figure rapidly sharpening into solidity.

Dahli.

At once his heart began to race. Everything would go badly for Zeke now if he recognised Dahli and objected to working for the Raen's most loyal friend, or if Zeke's belief that his powers weren't strong proved to be wrong and he could read Dahli's mind.

Tyen rose and beckoned to Zeke. "This is our patron."

"Ah," was all Zeke said as he moved to Tyen's side. He hadn't recognised Dahli yet . . .

Dahli, however, was regarding Zeke thoughtfully. Tyen knew the moment the man arrived because he was suddenly able to see the thoughts to accompany the expression.

. . . *very good-looking*, Dahli was thinking. *And he has no idea who I am, or he wouldn't be looking at me so boldly, thinking what he is thinking.*

. . . *hope I'm right about Tyen, because that's one less good-looking man between me and any chance of getting this one . . .*

Tyen smothered the urge to smile and stopped reading their minds. "This is Zeke, the best inventor at Liftre and a former student of mine." He opened his mouth to introduce Dahli, then paused. Zeke might not recognise Dahli, but he might know the name.

Dahli spoke. "I am Dahli."

Tyen hid his surprise, and searched Zeke's mind. The young inventor hadn't recognised the name. He bowed. "Honoured to meet you, Dahli."

"And I you," Dahli replied. He turned to Tyen. "You have an assistant; I have a volunteer."

A shiver ran down Tyen's spine. "Where?"

"Not far. I'll take you there now."

Tyen turned to Zeke. "Do you need anything?"

The young man tore his gaze from Dahli and shook his head.

"I'll be back . . . to be honest I don't know when, but I doubt it'll be more than a day or two at most," Tyen assured him.

Zeke shrugged. "I'll be fine."

Tyen walked over to Dahli, who took hold of his arm. The basement and Zeke receded into whiteness as Dahli pushed out of the world. Until they'd started working together, the only time Tyen had travelled with Dahli had been to the ice chamber where Qall had lain ready to receive Valhan's memories. Then, as now, he disliked being under another's control, even though he knew that, as the stronger sorcerer, he could easily pull away from Dahli's grip.

Maybe it's because I don't trust Dahli. I know he would do anything in order to bring Valhan back, no matter how immoral. While I respect his loyalty, knowing what he's capable of makes me uneasy around him. But he did trust that while his and Dahli's aims were in sympathy, Dahli would not act against him.

Several worlds appeared and disappeared. Tyen counted them and noted features in case he had to return alone. When they finally stopped, more than thirty worlds were between him and the basement. They stood high up the inside of an immense crater. The air stank of sulphur. Terraces curved in a great arc to either side, disappearing behind a column of steam which rose up from somewhere below the lowest.

It's a live volcano, Tyen realised with horror. *We're inside the crater of a huge, active volcano.*

310

The arrival place was a flat area carved from the black rock. A city spread around them, made of the same dark stone. Nearby, two sets of four men watched them expectantly. Their skin was pale and translucent, arteries and veins visible beneath their skin. Between each pair was a chair attached to two poles.

"Ugh," Dahli said. "I hate being carried. So slow and uncomfortable."

He still held Tyen's arm. The terraced city faded slightly, then blurred as Dahli skimmed off the arrival place and traced a path along the streets, bringing them back into the world in front of a large stone building.

"Why did you seek a volunteer here?" Tyen asked when he could draw breath again.

Dahli shrugged. "Plenty of magic."

It was true, Tyen realised as he focused on the world. The magic swelled up from the lower levels of the city. He sought the minds of the citizens there, curious to know what they were creating to generate so much magic, but before he found any, Dahli let go of his arm and stepped forward. The door to the building was open and a servant had emerged to invite them in.

The interior was opulent. Their volunteer was rich, or a friend of someone wealthy. As the servant brought them into a nearby room, the former became apparent. The man who awaited them was dressed in a sumptuous gown covered in rich embroidery and gold thread. Servants hovered nearby, ready to attend to his needs.

"This is Pieh, Patriarch of the Rivu," Dahli said when he had introduced Tyen.

The man was very old, Tyen noted. He was suffering the usual ills the elderly endured, some of which were severe. While his mind was sharp, he was in constant pain. He regarded Dahli's proposal that his mind be copied into a new body with scepticism, but saw no harm in trying it.

It won't be me, the man thought. *Someone else gets to be me.* But

311

it didn't matter. He was dying anyway, and had no heir. *Who better to inherit my wealth and power than another me?* His only condition had been that Dahli not bring the new Pieh here until the old one was dead.

"Shall we begin?" Dahli asked.

"No reason to wait." Pieh looked at Tyen. "Are you ready?"

Tyen nodded. "This may take a while, so you should be as comfortable as possible." The old man moved to a large, padded chair. Tyen glanced around, then used magic to push two smaller chairs closer to either side of the old man. Dahli settled in one, and Tyen the other.

"Give me your hand," Tyen instructed. The old man eyed him for a moment, then extended his arm. Taking the withered hand, Tyen closed his eyes and sought the state of mind that had allowed him to see the pattern within his own body. He achieved it more easily than he expected, but then it hadn't been long since he'd learned to pattern-shift.

He considered which body part he would imprint the man's memories onto. Something easy to detach and not likely to be missed. He chose the smallest finger of the left hand. It needed to be prepared for the task. He'd hoped to learn how to do so from Valhan's notes, but the lack of information in them had forced Tyen to consult Vella instead. It seemed insensitive to ask how she had been created, especially when he knew the experience had been terrible, but she had reminded him that she could not feel emotion, and then delivered the information in a matter-of-fact way that was both helpful and refreshed his anger at Roporien for what he'd done to her.

The flesh that was to hold the pattern of memories must be dried out to help preserve it. Water was removed while the information was imprinted. More information could be added later as well, but it would be more difficult. The dried flesh was imprinted with the pattern of the subject's memories, much like pressing an object into clay, but on a miniscule scale. The whole life of a person could be recorded in less than a pinch of Vella's pages. Valhan had also decided that the memories ought to be copied several times, in case the preserved body part was damaged.

Why Valhan had chosen to use an entire hand was not clear. Tyen had wondered if it was because he wanted to record his physical pattern as well as his memories – though as far as Tyen could tell, the entire pattern of a single human body was contained within every cell of their body, so the hand would be an excellent record. Perhaps it was simply that the memories of someone a thousand cycles old required more flesh to store it. Yet Vella contained the memories of many thousands of people, and had room to spare.

Tyen regarded the end of Pieh's little finger. How to copy memories into it was something even Vella hadn't been able to explain clearly. She'd suggested the method might be obvious once Tyen had a person's memory to copy. There was only one way to find out.

He focused his mind, extending and enhancing his senses by pattern shifting his own body. The flesh grew into a pattern he could understand. After blocking the pathways of pain and sensation to Pieh's finger, to which the old man grunted in surprise, he sought the man's memories. Examining the brain, he ignored the man's current thoughts, instead seeking the physical manifestation of memories and enhancing his mind's ability to sense detail.

A long stretch of concentration later, he began to see them: lightning-fast shivers of energy running along similar pathways to pain and sensation, sparking feedback where connections had previously been made. Memories, he saw, were not unlike paths between worlds. The more they were used, the stronger and more defined they became; the less, the swifter they faded. Some were created strong in the beginning, so they aged less quickly. He could see shortcuts and alterations, perhaps where less important details had been forgotten or corrected. Maybe even miscorrected.

He could see how to block them, though not how that would affect the functioning of the subjects' mind.

Now that he had a way of comprehending Pieh's memories as a physical structure, he could replicate them. When Rielle had accessed Valhan's memories for the resurrection, she had shaped magic into a complex pattern. He guessed that he would have to do this now before impressing that pattern into the flesh of Pieh's finger. However, doing so for an entire person would take a great deal of magic. It would weaken this world considerably. Tyen opened his eyes and looked at Dahli.

"I can do it, but we should move to a strong, uninhabited world."

Dahli shook his head, but it was Pieh who answered. "This one will recover."

Tyen looked at the old man, reading his mind. Dahli had already explained that it might drain much of the magic of Pieh's world. The old man didn't care. The workers in the Lower Rings would eventually replace what was lost, he reasoned.

"It is his decision," Dahli said.

Tyen looked from one to the other, then shrugged and closed his eyes again. Drawing magic from as far from the city as possible, he started to work.

He focused on a memory and replicated its pattern in the nearby magic of the world, then moved on to the next. He did not try reading and writing memories at the same time. Dahli's instructions to Rielle from the failed resurrection of the Raen had been to copy the memories to magic first, then imprint them on the boy afterwards. Valhan must have had a reason to do it that way.

Tyen became immersed in the task, losing all sense of time. When he finally had all of Pieh's memories written into magic, he could not tell if hours or minutes had passed. He did not pause or rest. Holding the pattern took concentration and he feared if he was distracted he'd lose part or all of it. Turning his mind to the man's finger, he began altering its composition and pattern, bit by bit, to record the great mass of complex pathways written into the magic.

It took as long as it had to write the pattern into magic. When all was done, he checked that the finger was now devoid of water and nothing else would endanger its state of preservation, then severed the finger from Pieh's hand and quickly healed the living end.

The old man yelped in surprise and yanked back his hand.

"What have you done?!"

Tyen looked at Dahli. "You didn't tell him?"

"No . . ." Dahli turned to face Pieh. "Do you want him to put it back?"

The old man looked down at the withered finger in Tyen's palm, then shook his head. "It's done now."

"I could grow—" Tyen began.

No, Dahli thought, turning to hold his gaze. *If he sees that you can grow a new finger, he will realise you can heal him young again, and he will be of no use to us at all.*

Tyen looked down at the finger. He suppressed a shudder, closed his hand over it and stood up.

"Thank you," he said to Pieh. "I will take very good care of this."

The old man's expression softened a fraction. His eyes never left Tyen as Dahli thanked him and bade him farewell, reminding him that this was the first attempt they'd made to copy a mind into another body, and they could make no guarantees of success. As a servant escorted them out of the house, Tyen slipped the finger into a pocket.

He had achieved the first part of a resurrection. But he suspected it would prove to be the easiest.

CHAPTER 14

"Tyen."

Looking up, Tyen found Zeke standing beside him, holding a tray. The smell of fresh bread and spicy sauces hit him like a gust of wind, and his stomach growled.

"You were out of the present," Zeke said, smiling as he sought a clear space on a table.

"I was," Tyen agreed. He lifted a box of parts and set it down on the floor, then drew his chair over as Zeke placed the tray in the empty space. He hadn't been so lost in a creation since the last time he'd worked on an insectoid. Which had been back in his house in Doum. That felt like a lifetime ago now. He wondered if anyone had taken the unfinished toy before the house was destroyed.

Taking a disc of bread, he broke off a piece and dipped it in one of the sauces. As he ate, he examined his work so far. He'd made most of the humanoid machine body but it had no brain or mechanical version of most internal organs yet. He'd started by acquiring a human skeleton to copy, and begun shaping metal bones and joints. From there, he'd examined his own body to work out where muscles and ligaments attached, finding mechanical equivalents for each. Now he was making a system of control out of tubes and wires, all linking back to the humanoid's polished but empty skull.

"You're making good progress," Zeke commented.

Tyen shook his head. "I've barely begun."

Eventually he'd have to work out what to use for skin, but the brain would be the greatest challenge – to create memory storage and a feedback system many times larger than an insectoid's to fit into such a small space.

Magical storage wasn't as great a challenge, as he had most of the chest to store it in. Certain metals, when prepared correctly, drew magic to them. How that happened was not entirely understood by the scientists at his world's famous Academy of Belton. Magic heated and vibrated the specially prepared metal, which was shaped into wires to deliver the energy, or coiled to form an isolated loop that could store a small amount of heat and vibration for a short time.

In the great engines of his home world, magically created heat was used to boil water to make steam, which moved the pistons in machines. In insectoids, heat and vibrations flipped switches or turned cogs. A simple command like "Beetle, fly in a circle" involved a multitude of such mechanisms – first the sensors that heard and recognised sounds, which released energy to the wings, as well as a chain of systems that recognised obstacles and steered to avoid them. It was so complicated that it had taken centuries for inventors in his world to develop mechanical magic to this level of refinement – and more than a few years for him to work out how to adapt it to make insectoids.

In comparison to Beetle, the humanoid was a thousand times more complicated. He would have to find a way to reduce the size of the parts, or Vella's memory store would be as large as a house. It might take him many cycles, maybe tens of cycles, to work it all out. Fortunately, he could now take hundreds of cycles if he needed to.

The task was not urgent, however, and he ought to be helping Zeke.

He turned to the young man. "How is your work going? Is there anything you need?"

Zeke finished chewing, then swallowed. "I could do with more war machines to study."

Tyen nodded. "I'll see if my source has caught any more. Any ideas on how to destroy them?"

"Plenty, but it depends on what we target – all machines, or all *war* machines."

"All war machines would be better. It would be a shame to destroy machines which benefit and help people."

"And it would put me out of a job," Zeke added.

"There are always other ways to earn a living," Tyen told him. "Magical or not. I never thought I'd be anything but a machine operator, which in my world was low-paid drudge work."

Are the machines of my world still working? Tyen wondered. Eleven cycles ago, his world had been running out of magic because machines used more magic than they generated. The idea that creativity generated magic was considered superstition, and with machines making many objects that were once created by hand fewer people were generating magic.

"Wiping out all machines would be easier, but if we leave anything behind, including the neutralisers, people will work out how to make war machines again," Zeke pointed out.

"We'd have to destroy all knowledge of mechanical magic too. Even the idea of it."

"Can we do that?"

"No." Tyen frowned. "Unless we found a way to make the neutralisers wipe people's memories . . . and the neutralisers could travel between worlds as quickly as sorcerers can."

Zeke's eyes had widened. "Wipe . . .? It's possible to wipe memories?" His eyes narrowed. "You haven't wiped my memory have you?"

"No," Tyen assured him. But had Dahli? "Do you have any suspicious gaps in your memory?"

"No." The young man let out an inheld breath. "Promise me you'll try not to let me learn anything you'd have to remove later.

The idea of having someone messing with my memories gives me chills."

Tyen couldn't help smiling at the request. "I promise."

"Good." Zeke finished his meal with a last few rapid bites. "I be'er g' ba' to w'rk," he said with his mouth still full. Pouring a glass of the local mildly alcoholic herbal concoction, he carried it back to his desk.

Tyen filled his own glass and drank slowly, eyeing his humanoid. If destroying all magic-fuelled machines as well as all knowledge of mechanical magic was possible, and the only way to deal with the war machines, would he do it? The humanoid would be destroyed too. His only alternative body for Vella would be lost. So would Beetle.

They hadn't explored any alternatives. He looked over to Zeke.

"So if we can't destroy all knowledge of mechanical magic, how do we get rid of the war machines?"

"Spread the knowledge of how to neutralise them?" Zeke suggested, from the other side of the room. "Once we work out what that is. Of course, warmongers will use that knowledge to defeat their enemy's war machines. Perhaps they'll get rid of all the war machines for us."

"They'll give their own machines a defence against it. It could become a war of adaptation." Tyen drummed his fingers on the table. "Perhaps it's better to keep the knowledge of how to neutralise war machines a secret, and make the neutralisers destroy themselves once their task is complete, or if someone meddles with them."

"That's achievable." Zeke rose and started back towards Tyen. "Our patron is back."

Tyen followed Zeke's gaze. A shadow of a familiar stature was rapidly darkening into full focus, but it was an odd shape. As it grew more distinct, Tyen could see that Dahli was carrying a person. A man, limp and pale. His heart skipped a beat.

Time to return to my true purpose for being here, he mused.

As Dahli arrived he took the few steps to the nearest table and lay the unconscious man down. He straightened and looked at Tyen. "Your vessel."

Not unconscious, Tyen corrected as he saw the man's glazed eyes. *Dead. And not for very long, judging by the colour still in the lips and fingertips.* Patches of the man's face were red, and the hair of one temple was matted with blood.

"He's damaged."

Dahli shrugged. "If you want someone young who hasn't died of disease, the chances are they'll have expired thanks to violence."

He had a point. Tyen moved closer and examined the body. He would have to act quickly if this corpse was to be a viable vessel for Pieh's memories. Fetching the box holding Pieh's fingertip from a cupboard, he set it down next to the dead man.

"Who's this?" Zeke asked, a note of wariness in his tone as he regarded the corpse.

"A beggar," Dahli answered. "Beaten up and left to die." He turned to Tyen. "Let me know if you need more magic than this world offers."

Tyen nodded. As Dahli moved away, saying something to Zeke, Tyen ignored the pair and settled into a chair beside the table. While healing the beggar was well within Dahli's abilities, and he could even tackle changing the body to Pieh's pattern, Tyen had told the man he wanted to perform all the stages of resurrection, to be sure he knew exactly what had been done. If he was going to delay the return of the Raen as long as possible to give Rielle the chance to find a safe place to live, having control of all parts of the process would help him do that.

He closed his eyes and sought the state of mind he needed in order to perform pattern shifting. It came easily – faster each time he used the skill – and soon he was correcting the errors in the corpse where it had sustained damage. The man's injuries were worse than they appeared. Ribs were broken. One had punctured a lung. A strike to the back of the head had been the killing blow. This meant damage to the brain. Tyen had hoped to not have to work on a brain until he was ready to imprint memories.

Restoring circulation to the brain was the most urgent task, but it would do no good if all the man's blood pumped out of his wounds. Tyen concentrated on the punctured lung first, removing the rib and sealing the hole. When it was healed, he persuaded the heart to resume pumping and the lungs to work. At once he had his hands full, fixing the head wounds and repairing ribs. Restoring the skull was easy enough, but once he started healing the brain it began to wake, fragments of thoughts and memories stirring.

Valhan had made notes of the kinds of memories he had removed or blocked in his test subjects, but not the final combination he'd used on Qall. Having no experience in removing or blocking memories, only Vella and Dahli's description of how it was done, Tyen paused to consider how to proceed.

He decided to quell everything that wasn't vital to the body functioning. Concentrating, he was both worried and relieved by the many blank patches he encountered. Worried because he did not know if this would cause the resurrection to fail. Relieved because if his healing had restored the man completely, he would have had to stop and tell Dahli to return the man to his world. The state the beggar was in meant he was essentially a broken and unviable version of what he'd been before he'd died. Tyen could still consider him irretrievably "dead".

Removing memories, it turned out, was like smoothing patterns in sand or concealing his pathway between worlds. He worked slowly and carefully, and when he eventually decided that he was done, the memories left were merely the simple ones – feelings and knowledge of the physical body.

When he finally opened his eyes, he could not guess how much time had passed. Nothing in the room indicated the time of day. Zeke and Dahli were standing before the humanoid. Reading their minds, he saw that not much time had passed at all.

". . . even so, it's quite ugly," Dahli was saying.

A little pang of disappointment rose in Tyen. He sought Dahli's mind. The man was contemplating the possibility of placing Valhan's mind within the machine. He found the idea distasteful. *I'm surprised he's pursuing this idea for Vella*, Dahli thought. *Wouldn't it be better for his great love to have a proper, warm body?*

"Great love"? Tyen hadn't realised that Dahli assumed love was his reason for wanting to restore Vella's body. *But then, maybe it is. It's not a romantic love – not like I was hoping would grow between Rielle and me . . .* As regret and disappointment rose, he shook his head. *Forget about Rielle. Rielle is gone.* She had promises to keep. Qall to protect.

He picked up the box containing Pieh's fingertip. Time to see if he could alter the corpse's pattern to the old man's. He drew in more magic.

This task was simpler than wiping memories, once he got the hang of it. It was like healing, but instead of using the beggar's pattern to correct a damaged part of the body, he imposed Pieh's pattern onto all of it. Yet because he was changing every part of the body except the mind, it took more magic and – to his perception – time. He began at the feet and worked his way slowly up to the head, noting how the old parts of the body rebelled against the parts that had changed until they were also altered.

When he reached the brain, he paused, remembering how Valhan had described in his notes how he'd changed a vessel's mind to the pattern of the subject's brain, thinking that it would imprint all of the subject's memories as well, but the experiment failed. He'd concluded that the subject's memories must be added after the brain's pattern was changed and the vessel's memories removed.

Tyen saw that if he didn't alter the vessel's brain quickly, it would reject the body. Working fast, he altered it to match Pieh's pattern, then examined the result. An echo of Pieh's memories had been laid down, but what remained of the beggar's remained, too. The two were muddled together. Tyen carefully quelled all memories until there was no sign of either man's. Uncertain, but hopeful, he left the body in a deep sleep and brought his awareness back to the room.

The beggar was gone, and in his place lay an old man – Pieh, but with a blankness of expression even more vacant than that of sleep.

His heart sank. This would not satisfy the old man. He wanted an heir, not an exact copy of himself. Drawing in a little more magic, Tyen set to work again, repairing the damage of old age. Slowly the bones grew stronger, the skin smoothed and muscles firmed. When he stopped, the body before him looked not much older than Tyen's, if he ignored the grey hair.

At last the work was done. He looked around. Zeke and Dahli were still sitting where they had been, but had swapped places. Empty dishes and glasses lingered on a table nearby. Signs that more time had passed than before.

A laugh from Dahli brought his attention back to the pair. He realised he'd never heard the man laugh before. At least, not without a good lacing of dark humour or bitterness. Zeke glanced at Dahli, then quickly looked away. Amused, Tyen wished he could see Dahli's expression for himself, not through Zeke's besotted eyes. The young inventor was trying to decide if Dahli's smile showed interest, or he just wished for it so much that he was only seeing what he wanted.

If he knew where Dahli's heart truly lay, he'd save himself a lot of disappointment, Tyen mused. *I can't tell him the man is still in love with the Raen, but maybe there's a way to let him know Dahli is never going to be interested in him that way.*

"I'm done," Tyen said, rising and stretching.

Dahli turned, his eyes moving from Tyen to the body before he stood and strode over to examine it. Zeke followed slowly, his eyes widening as he drew near.

"You changed him!"

"In all but mind."

"And that's the next step? Will you do that next?"

Tyen nodded.

"Not here," Dahli explained. "It takes a great deal of magic to copy a person's memories. Enough to strip a world." He turned to Tyen. "When do you want to tackle it?"

I ought to delay the next step, Tyen thought. That would mean keeping Pieh's double asleep and working out a way to feed him, however. He could not think of a good enough excuse to go to that trouble. "The sooner the better."

"Then we should go now. Worlds with enough magic to transfer memories are growing fewer every day as more sorcerers attempt to become ageless. If we wait, we might arrive in the one I have found, only to discover it weakened."

Tyen hesitated, then nodded reluctantly. "Let's go then."

Dahli turned and nodded to Zeke. "It was a pleasure talking to you." With one hand he grasped the ankle of Pieh's duplicate, with the other he took hold of Tyen's arm. Pocketing the finger, Tyen grabbed the corner of the table in case it didn't move into the place between worlds with the body, then nodded to show he was ready.

At once, the basement faded into white.

CHAPTER 15

T he route Dahli took was convoluted, with many loops and
reverses. Two sorcerers travelling with a table occupied by
an unconscious man was a memorable sight, so he kept mainly
to rarely used paths and unpopulated arrival places. Tyen concentrated most of his attention on Pieh's duplicate, since it could
not draw a deep breath between worlds to avoid running out of
air, alerting Dahli when the body began to suffocate.

Now and then, Dahli travelled quickly through several worlds,
not trying to hide his tracks and taking well-used paths. At the
end of the first of these dashes, when they stopped to allow Pieh's
duplicate to breathe, Tyen sought the man's mind to learn the
reason.

They were clusters of worlds embroiled in conflict. The chances
were, if a sorcerer saw Tyen and Dahli, they'd be too busy with
the local strife to investigate, so the worlds provided a useful,
if grim, shortcut. At the end of the third cluster, Tyen read
that it was the last such crossing they had to make. They were
still far from their destination though, so they did not pause
for long.

The lips and fingers of Pieh's duplicate began to gain a bluish
tinge despite them stopping to allow it to breathe. Though its
chest heaved whenever they reached a world, instinctively
attempting to gain more air, it could not draw in a deep breath
in preparation before they left a world so it was slowly being

robbed of air. Dahli had noticed as well, and his brow was creased by a deepening line. Yet he did not slow his pace.

He had begun peering into the whiteness between worlds, so Tyen looked closer and immediately he sensed what Dahli had glimpsed: there was another sorcerer in the place between. When Tyen detected that person again three worlds later, he caught Dahli's gaze and nodded in the direction of the shadow.

"What do you want to do?" Tyen asked when they stopped in the next world.

Dahli let go of the body and Tyen's hand. "Split up and meet again. Read the route and location from my mind."

Tyen concentrated, memorising what he saw as Dahli quickly visualised the path in his thoughts.

"Got it?" Dahli asked.

"Yes."

"I'll see you there."

"Good luck."

The sorcerer did not reply, as he'd already started to fade. Taking hold of the body with his free hand, Tyen pushed out of the world and travelled rapidly away. He searched the place between as he travelled but sensed no other sorcerers, apart from a single instance: a fleeting, distant presence moving in the opposite direction.

At last he reached the world Dahli had selected for their experiment. The arrival place was a smooth white bowl, the sides pierced by tunnel entrances. Hot sunlight radiated from the ground and the air tasted salty. He found no minds of people nearby, so he lifted the table with magic and moved it into one of the tunnels. The walls were a dirty white. A closer look revealed they were carved from salt.

Turning to the body, he examined it closely. More time to breathe meant it was recovering well. Once he was satisfied that Pieh's duplicate was healthy again, he pushed out of the world a little and skimmed up through the earth above him to the surface, then arrived again. Instead of skimming on to look for the tower, he sat on the table and lifted it upwards.

The white bowl shrank below him. Many more came into view, each dotted with tunnel entrances. In some areas, they were smaller and flatter; in others, the sides were so high they sat proud of the earth and began to curve inward, the outer edge shadowing the interior. It was as if many, many air bubbles had risen up through the salt, freezing at different moments of reaching the air.

Following the instructions, Tyen sped in a widening spiral. Dahli had pictured a temple with a white tower, a gaping hole in one side. Sure enough, a spire appeared at the horizon. He propelled the table towards it.

Looking down again, Tyen caught a movement below. He slowed and looked closer. People were walking across the surface of some of the bowls, entering and leaving tunnels. A search for minds revealed hundreds of minds, and perhaps thousands further afield.

This world is populated! Dahli lied!

But he couldn't have. Tyen would have seen it. *Either he has wiped his memory of them from his mind, or they've arrived here since he checked this world, or he doesn't believe the people here count as occupants.*

Annoyed and worried, he continued to the tower. The area around it was empty of people, the houses surrounding it a shambles of burned ruins. He moved through a gaping hole in the side of the tower and descended into a great hall. It was clear it had been filled with entwined columns once, but whatever power had blasted the side of the tower open had shattered half of them. The rubble glittered white: everything here was also made of salt.

Once he had satisfied himself that Pieh's duplicate was unharmed, he looked for the minds of the locals. Flitting from one to the other, he learned that they had a history which went back thousands of their years, so they couldn't be recent arrivals. They were not a technically sophisticated people, however. Their knowledge of metal working was basic, learned from another race that had dominated this world and forced the religion of the nearby temple upon them. The dominant race had been killed or driven away recently, by people who claimed to come from other worlds.

The light from the entrance flickered. He sensed Dahli's mind. Looking up, Tyen scowled as Dahli strode into the hall.

"This is *not* an empty world," he growled as the man arrived.

Dahli nodded. "The locals didn't know other worlds existed until recently, and have no interest in exploring them. Their sorcerers are weak and untrained. They will barely notice when the magic of their worlds lessens."

"They will, if we take it all. What give us the right to rob them of the chance to use it?"

Dahli crossed his arms, his mouth tightening with amusement. "Do we have the time to argue over this?"

Tyen looked at Pieh's vessel. The body's chest was rising and falling slowly. He straightened his shoulders.

"We must find another world. An unoccupied one."

Dahli let out a short, sharp breath. "Unoccupied worlds rich in magic have always been rare. All the ones I knew of have been drained." *If we have to search for the perfect world every time we attempt a resurrection, it will take us hundreds of cycles to bring the Raen back,* Dahli thought. *I may as well break my deal with Tyen and search for someone else as powerful as he but less scrupulous. It might actually take less time, in the long run.*

Tyen looked at Pieh's duplicate. He was not going to win this argument. *But I can make sure a little magic remains here for the local sorcerers.*

"Very well," he said. "Are you holding enough magic to get us both out of this world again?"

"Of course."

"Then make yourself comfortable. I have no idea how long this will take."

Dahli nodded. "I will keep watch."

The table from the basement looked out of place in the temple. He moved it next to a large chunk of fallen masonry and sat down. Taking Pieh's fingertip out of his pocket, he set it next to the body.

Staring at it, he sought the state of mind needed to access the information imprinted within it. He took a little magic from the world to enhance his mind and senses. Glimpses of a pattern began to form, but it was the wrong one – the pattern of Pieh's body repeated over and over countless times in his flesh.

No, I need the other pattern now, he thought. *The memories.* His concentration deepened and his awareness shifted. Markings of a different kind emerged, and as his mind sought understanding, their meaning slowly grew clear. Tyen saw the image of a young woman, dressed in finery, smiling politely at him. Not him, but Pieh, who was pleased that the wife his family had chosen was good-looking, and that she was intimidated by him. The wife who bore him four daughters and one spoilt, foolish son who got himself killed on his first trading mission. Pieh had been more relieved than regretful, though it had left him with an awkward issue of inheritance.

Not a particularly nice man, Tyen thought. *But I didn't need to see his memories to know that.*

Tyen resigned himself to seeing every one of Pieh's memories – to live the old man's life – in order to copy them into the body. To do that, he had to first translate them into magic. Taking a deep breath, he began to draw and shape magic. There being no obvious place to start, he began at the memory of the wedding and let the connections from there take him in whatever direction they led. It was slow work, but as he grew used to it he realised he didn't need to see every memory in order to translate it to magic. His mind adapted to the process and it became a reflex, and soon he was channelling memories too fast to comprehend them.

Free of that distraction, he grew aware of how much magic he was using. He now sat within a void that already extended far beyond the house – the lack of magic as dark to his senses as the charred beams of the houses around the tower. Though magic rushed in to fill the space, he was using so much that the void was steadily growing.

How long before it reached populated areas? What would the local sorcerers do? *Dahli had better be right about their limited abilities*, he thought. *Or we'll have irate visitors very soon.* If the locals did not know how to travel between worlds, they would never reach the house before Tyen was finished. They were simply too far away.

He wouldn't easily forgive himself for what he was doing to this world. It was another wrong added to the long list of lies and deceptions. He worried, too, if Dahli would run out of sparsely populated worlds to drain, and insist Tyen started ruining ones where the people relied on magic.

The area around him was now intensely rich with magic shaped to record the memories. When at last all the memories stored in Pieh's fingertip had been translated to magic, Tyen turned his attention to the duplicate's mind. He wasn't sure where to start, or how to go about imprinting it on the new mind, so he spent some time concentrating on the brain, seeking information. Slowly, a sense of where and how to imprint the memories began to grow. No corresponding memories in the duplicate told him where the new ones would fit, so he let memories imprint where they seemed to want to be. He did not rush. This was his first attempt. He needed to be careful – and learn from observation.

Gradually the magic shaped into memory dwindled to nothing, and the brain of the vessel filled. When the last of Pieh's recollections had been transferred, Tyen drew his attention back to his surroundings. Dahli sat on another old chair by the door, his gaze fixed on a place far away. His mind, Tyen was amused to see, was on Zeke. Dahli had decided he liked the inventor, and he was worried what the Zeke would think of him, once he learned who Dahli was. *He already knows too much for me to let him go free. I'm going to have to set a guard to make sure he doesn't wander off while Tyen is attempting resurrections, and someone reads his mind and finds out what Tyen and I are doing.*

"Dahli," Tyen murmured.

The man's head snapped around; then he leapt to his feet and hurried over to the bed.

"It's done?"

"Yes."

"Has it worked?"

"I don't know yet."

"Wake him."

Tyen focused his attention on Pieh's heir again. What should they call him? Pieh Two? He gave the man a mental nudge. *Wake up!*

The man's eyes opened. He stared at the roof of the temple, blinked and frowned. Confusion filled his eyes. Tyen read a wordless fear blossom and grow in his mind.

Dahli reached out towards the man's shoulder.

"You are safe," he began, but as his hand met flesh, the man flinched, raising arms in an instinctive gesture of defence. He stared at Dahli without comprehension; then a memory stirred. Information came: this was someone powerful. And dangerous.

Pieh Two scrambled off the table. When his legs met the floor they wobbled and he collapsed. Tyen moved around the table to help him, while Dahli approached from the other side. The man looked from Tyen to Dahli, his mouth opened and he began to wail in terror.

They both backed away.

"What's wrong with him?" Dahli asked.

"I don't now," Tyen replied. "He's scared of you. Stay back and let me approach him."

331

Dahli moved away. Watching Pieh Two's mind, Tyen dropped into a squat, hoping this looked less threatening, and crept forward.

"Pieh," he said. "Do you remember me?"

The man's screams diminished to a whimper. His gaze fixed on Tyen, but he did not recognise this stranger. Perhaps memories of the sorcerer who had copied his finger had been too new to linger.

Was that the problem? Had only the oldest, most often accessed of Pieh's memories been those that had successfully transferred? Tyen began speaking, asking questions that should rouse memories both recent and old, but they might as well have been gibberish for all that Pieh Two comprehended of them. Then one made the squirming man pause. His mind ran down the path of memory, but it confused him. It felt wrong. He knew things, but they were wrong. They did not belong. Or he did not belong.

Pieh Two pressed his hands to his head and groaned.

"Tyen . . ." Dahli began.

Tyen lifted a hand to stall him. He inched a little closer.

"Pieh," he said. "We've put your mind in a new body. It will probably take time for it to feel right. Relax. Give yourself time to adjust."

"You did this to me?" Pieh Two said, the words slurred, his eyes bulging as he stared at Tyen.

"Yes. At your request."

Suddenly the man was on his feet. He threw himself across the room, grabbing Tyen's shoulders and dragged them both to the ground. Tyen resisted the urge to push the man away.

"Who am I?!" Pieh Two shrieked. "What am I? What was I? No! This isn't me!" He rolled off Tyen and his head knocked into a wall. He stared at the salt bricks. Rising to his knees, he began to slam his forehead against them. "Get it out! Get it out!"

Tyen rose and reached out to stop him, but the man suddenly twisted to one side. A crack echoed in the room and Pieh Two fell to the floor. Bending over him, Tyen sought the cause of the collapse and was shocked to see his neck was broken. Pieh Two's crazed mind slowly faded to silence.

Tyen looked up at Dahli in surprise and horror. "What did . . .? You killed him!"

"Yes." Dahli crossed his arms. "He was mad. It clearly hadn't worked."

"You don't know that! He might only have needed time."

"You don't know that either," Dahli pointed out. "We don't have time to waste nursing an invalid." He spread his hands. "Surely you didn't expect to get it right the first time?"

Tyen looked at the corpse. "Maybe. Valhan did. He expected Rielle to, that is."

"Which makes it likely that the fault with this one was in the earlier stages, and waiting would gain us nothing."

That did make sense, Tyen had to admit. Though he still could not dismiss the possibility that the transfer had worked and the disorientation Pieh Two had experienced was to be expected. As Dahli regarded the corpse with disgust, another possibility occurred to Tyen.

Dahli won't want Valhan coming back as a madman, even if it was for a short time. Not only would it be unpleasant, it would be dangerous. Tyen wasn't going to give in so easily though. He was appalled at how casually Dahli had killed. "How am I meant to work out what part went wrong now he's dead?"

"You have the body and the fingertip. We'll take them back with us." Dahli walked over and placed a hand on Tyen's shoulder. "I know it's shocking to you. I would not have done it if I didn't think it was necessary." He walked over to the body. "I had misgivings when I selected the beggar. There was no way to know what he was like alive. Maybe he was already mad."

That was a possibility too. Tyen sought magic, finding a little still lingered in the world, but then remembered his intention to leave some for the local sorcerers.

"You'll have to transport us back," he told Dahli.

333

Dahli nodded. Tyen lifted the corpse with magic and placed it on the table. They linked as they had before, this time with Tyen's hand gripping the corpse and Dahli's holding the table. The room faded to white.

The journey home was as convoluted as the one that had brought them there, though this time with no pursuers to shake off. All the while, Tyen retraced every step of the experiment in his mind, seeking clues as to what had gone wrong. His guesses were vague and he was thoroughly dispirited when the basement finally began to take shape. As air surrounded him, he staggered forward and let go of the corpse's arm.

"What happened here?" Dahli asked, his voice low with anger.

Surprised, Tyen looked up. The sorcerer's gaze wasn't on him or the body, however. It was fixed on Zeke, who was limping towards them.

"A woman came here," the young man said, his voice shaking. "She was angry. Really angry. She kept asking where Tyen was . . . and . . . for the Raen's hand."

Zeke paused to step over something. Looking down, Tyen saw that mechanical parts were strewn across the room. Familiar parts. He drew in a sharp breath and turned to the humanoid.

It was gone. The parts were what it had become. Among them were other fragments. The contents of the shelving and cabinets. Turning full circle, he took in the destruction he had been too preoccupied to notice as they'd arrived. The only things not smashed in the room were the insectoids Zeke had been studying. Among them, he saw with relief, was Beetle – missing a leg but otherwise whole. Zeke picked it up.

"I've been fixing it," Zeke said, noting the direction of Tyen's gaze. "I—"

"What did you tell her?" Dahli cut in.

"Nothing." Zeke shrugged. "Not that it made any difference. I couldn't read her mind."

Looking in the inventor's mind, Tyen saw a face. His heart lifted.

Rielle! She's back.

Then it plunged deep into his belly. *She knows I'm working with Dahli. To resurrect somebody. She'll have guessed who that is . . .*

"We had better leave," Dahli said. He was looking down at a pile of ash – from the location they must be Valhan's notes, Tyen realised. Beetle had done his job. "I'll send others back to fetch anything you need here. I'll just check which way she went."

Dahli vanished.

And in the next moment reappeared.

"Are you in the habit of hiding your path when you come and go from here?" he asked Tyen.

Tyen shrugged. "I did at first, but not for a while."

Dahli pursed his lips, then without offering an explanation, took hold of Tyen and Zeke's arms. The room faded from sight.

PART FOUR

RIELLE

CHAPTER 11

H e had changed so much.

Yet Rielle recognised Baluka the moment he stepped into sight. In that instant, she was paralysed by doubt and regret. *Of all people, I am the worst person to tell him of the betrayal of his friend. Me, who promised to marry him then left in the company of his enemy.*

Baluka hadn't seen her yet, his attention captured by the view. Massive trees stretched overhead and into the distance, lit by a thousand sunbeams breaking through the leafy canopy above. Hanging from them were hundreds of globes woven from vines, clustered together to form houses of varying sizes. These were connected by vine bridges to tree branch thoroughfares wide enough for two people to pass each other easily.

He looked down, then froze at glimpses of the abyss below, visible through the woven platform that was the arrival place. Taking a deep breath, he looked away.

She hadn't known he was afraid of heights. If she had, she would have chosen another world to meet in. She'd only seen an advantage in being among a people whose skin tone and stature were similar to hers and Baluka's. Locals with pale skin like Tyen and Dahli lived in the poorer levels below. If anyone of their appearance appeared in the upper levels the locals would object loudly, providing Rielle with a warning of sorts.

Baluka appeared calm, his fear only apparent to those who

could read his mind. She scanned the minds around her again and found a few sorcerers she hadn't noted before. All had travelled here with Baluka: his protectors.

As she moved into the opening of the globe she had occupied, Baluka's attention snapped to her.

It's her, he thought. *It really is. She hasn't changed at all. Though I suppose that's because she's ageless now.*

The wariness that followed hit her like a punch in the stomach. He believed she had become another kind of human. Transformed. Different. Unreachable. *I suppose he's right*, she thought. *We ageless are a different sort of human.* Realising this didn't make her feel any better.

It didn't help that the reality of his mortality was painfully obvious. He had aged in both body and mind – more than he ought to have in five cycles. Gone was the cheerful, boyish youth who had helped Rielle adjust to a new life outside her world.

The man he had become had a hard-won confidence and humility that was equally as appealing, however. He traced a path to her: along the bridge from the arrival place to a branch, then down to a ladder, up to a higher branch, turn right on a side branch, then climb across the bridge that connected to the doorway she stood within. He squared his shoulders and started the journey.

She retreated into the room. It was the last of a cluster of abandoned globes. The vines had been damaged by a falling branch, and the weave was slowly dying. From locals she'd learned that dead rooms were adopted by the poorer citizens living in lower levels, but they always waited until nightfall before climbing up to scavenge them.

The bridge was also dying. As Baluka made his way across, the vines creaked alarmingly. He told himself that if the bridge broke, and he was too panicked to levitate, Rielle would catch him. His trust in her soothed away the hurt at his view of her agelessness.

As he reached the doorway, he let out a long sigh of relief.

"Baluka," she said. "I'm sorry. If I'd known this place would make you so uncomfortable, I'd have chosen another."

"I'd endure worse to talk to you again," he told her. Slipping a hand into the old, worn jacket he wore, he brought out a silvery object the length of her little finger, a chain sliding between his fingers. "I believe this is yours."

She took it and looped the chain over her neck. Taking the pendant by the ends, she twisted to unlock it, and pulled it apart to show the brush within. She had sent it to him with a message curled up inside. The message was gone now. She looked up.

Baluka was gripping the edges of the entrance tightly, tensing whenever their movements made the globe swing.

"Let's sit," she suggested. Dropping to her knees, she tucked her legs to one side and sat down on the woven floor. Baluka followed suit, folding into an untidy, tense version of her own pose.

His mouth quirked to one side. "Is this a reunion only, or is there something you want to discuss?"

"Both, I guess, since we can't have the second without the first."

"No, I suppose we can't."

"How are you?"

He opened his mouth, closed it again, then spread his hands. "Still alive. You?"

"A long way from where I should be." She grimaced at the thought of the distance between herself and Qall.

"I see." He ignored the temptation to ask where that was. "Then . . . why are you here?"

"Trying to do a favour I should not have agreed to. Can you get a message to your family?"

His expression became grave. "They have told me not to approach them – that if I do I will put them in danger."

She sighed and nodded. "Dahli, the Raen's most loyal friend, intends to blackmail me and . . ." She broke off, as she read from

Baluka's mind that he knew already what she was about to tell him. He had met up with his parents after they'd resumed their trade. They'd told him Rielle had brought them a boy with no memories to look after. A boy who grew up to look identical to the Raen. He knew she'd taken Qall away to the edges of the worlds, to hide and protect him from those who would replace Qall's memories with Valhan's.

"And Qall," he finished for her. "Dahli intends to threaten to harm them, to persuade Qall to obey him. I suspected as much." He frowned. "Qall isn't here, is he?"

"No. He persuaded me to take a message to his family."

"Is it important?"

She slowly shook her head. "It is personal, and not worth endangering his family for. However . . ." She met his gaze and grimaced. "When I tried to reach them, I discovered something far more disturbing than Dahli's watchers. Something you must know."

His eyebrows rose. "Which is?"

She drew in a deep breath, then let it out again, all the while trying to decide which of the approaches she'd practised was best. *Just get to the point. We might be interrupted. Every moment that passes, Tyen gets a little closer to achieving his goals, and the possibility of Valhan returning grows.*

"Tyen is, and has always been, working for the Raen."

Baluka smiled. "You heard the rumour."

"No. Well, yes, I've known about the rumour for some time." She paused to reconsider her approach. "When I tried to find your family, I learned from a watcher where Dahli was. So I got close enough to read his mind. I discovered that Tyen really was spying for the Raen, when he was with the rebels, in exchange for Valhan finding a way to restore the woman in Tyen's book."

Baluka's amusement vanished. "Tyen has been spying on Dahli for me since the Raen died. He may have told Dahli this to convince him to trust him."

"Tyen was spying on the rebels from the moment he joined them. And he has been spying on you for Dahli for the same time."

"Playing both sides." Baluka's voice was quiet with worry, as the possible consequences of that sank in.

"That's not the worst of it," Rielle told him. "Tyen is not just spying for Dahli: he has agreed to resurrect the Raen. He's working on it right now."

Baluka's eyes widened. "But . . . he doesn't have Qall."

"He believes he can find another way to do it. Using a corpse rather than destroying a living person."

Baluka's mouth opened, closed, then opened again. "Why would he do that?"

"Again, for the knowledge of how to give Vella a body." She gritted her teeth. "And Dahli has convinced him that the Restorers aren't capable of restoring order to the worlds. He thinks only Valhan can end chaos and war."

"I know he feels bad about the war insectoids . . ." Baluka began.

"Don't believe anything he told you," she advised. "He let me think he agreed with me, that the worlds would sort themselves out eventually. I thought we were . . . friends."

He looked up. "You were seeing him often?"

"Up until around half a cycle ago. He was living in Doum, and I in Murai. We tried to get the two worlds to negotiate a peace agreement, but it went badly."

"Rumours say your strength is almost equal to what the Raen's was." His eyes narrowed. "If you didn't read the truth from his mind, he must be stronger than you."

"No," she corrected. "We're equal in strength. Unless . . . unless he lied about that too." She started thinking back, trying to remember all the clues that had convinced her that Tyen couldn't read her mind, but Baluka interrupted.

"If Tyen is stronger than you, maybe the Raen couldn't read

343

his mind. Maybe Tyen was deceiving him from the start when he agreed to spy on the rebels. But surely if the Raen couldn't read Tyen's mind, he would have known Tyen was powerful and killed him. Unless he needed something from Tyen." Baluka tapped on his knees. "Vella – or something she contained. But why wouldn't he just take her? Ah! She absorbs the knowledge of everyone she touches. The Raen needed Tyen to communicate with her for him. But why not kill him and get someone less dangerous to read her?"

Rielle drew in a sharp breath. "Because he needed someone to resurrect him, if I failed."

Baluka's eyebrows rose, and he nodded. "It makes you wonder if he saw his death coming."

"He did," she told him. "He planned it all. His allies had enjoyed the twenty cycles they'd had without him meddling in their affairs, and wanted to kill him. He encouraged the rebels to grow strong, and then imprinted his memories into his hand and killed himself, so that the two sides would meet and destroy each other. When he retur—"

"Wait!" Baluka interrupted. "Valhan *meant* to die?"

"Yes. Dahli and I were supposed to resurrect him."

"That was an enormous risk." He shook his head. "The allies must have been a greater force than I thought."

"Or Valhan wasn't as strong as he appeared. I've wondered about that more than a few times. Bear that in mind, if Tyen succeeds in resurrecting the Raen."

Baluka shook his head. "I can't help trying to think of an explanation, to find an excuse for him, but I'm not sure I can this time and my advisers have been warning me not to trust him for the last ten cycles." His face hardened as anger and determination stirred. "Can Tyen do it?"

"I don't know." She grimaced and looked away. "I thought that by taking Qall away and teaching him to defend himself, nobody would be able to resurrect the Raen. But from what I've learned from Dahli, Qall isn't the vital ingredient. The hand is. Valhan's hand, which he copied all his memories into."

"And yet if that were true, why is Dahli watching my family?"

"As a second option if Tyen fails? As insurance against you, me and Qall trying to stop Tyen?" She looked up at Baluka. "The Restorers must find the hand, Baluka. You must destroy it."

His brows knit together. "Getting it away from Tyen will not be easy."

"Tyen doesn't have it. Dahli doesn't trust him, and has hidden it and blocked his memory of its location. He won't unblock that memory until Tyen proves he can resurrect a person successfully and has a vessel ready for Valhan's memories." She rubbed at her forehead. "Unfortunately, I only found this out after I revealed to Tyen and Dahli that I know about their little project," she added bitterly.

She paused as she recalled what she found in the basement where Tyen had been working, and wondered how much to tell Baluka. Dismantled insectoids had covered the tables at one side of the room. Between them and the bare tables at the other side, a human-shaped machine had hung from a chain suspended from the ceiling. A suspicion had crawled over her: not only had Tyen lied about finding a solution to the insectoid war machines, but he was developing a greater weapon – a mechanical warrior.

It wasn't until the noise of her destroying it attracted Tyen's assistant that she learned her suspicion was wrong. The humanoid was an optional vessel for Vella, if Tyen could not work out how to transfer her into a flesh and bone body.

If he can put Vella into a machine, why not Valhan?

"Are you going to kill me?" Zeke had asked. He suspected that Dahli had been one of the Raen's friends. *I'm not going to get the chance to find out if I'm right now*, he'd been thinking, as Rielle realised that she must either kill Zeke or allow Dahli to know she had returned.

She'd left before reason had time to overcome her conscience. Left and hidden her path, then stopped in a nearby world to rethink her decision. She could not bring herself to go back and deal with him.

I should have killed him. She sighed. *But I'm glad I didn't.*

"They'll expect me to tell you what I discovered, and for the Restorers to try to stop them," she told Baluka. "But it'll be harder for Dahli to stop you than me. He will threaten to harm your family not just to prevent me acting against him, but to force me to assist him. My only choice is to leave before he gets the chance – and that is the other reason why I arranged this meeting. You must make it widely known that I have returned to my hiding place, so Dahli will learn of it. He can't try to blackmail me if he can't find me."

Baluka looked at her intently. "Or you could stay, help us find the hand and deal with Dahli and Tyen."

"What about your family?"

He looked away, a deep crease forming between his brows. "Preventing the Raen returning is more important than saving my family."

She looked into his mind and saw the struggle within. His heart fluttered in panic and denial, yet his mind knew this was the cold truth. *Am I really willing to sacrifice them for the sake of the worlds?* he asked himself.

"No," she told him. "Qall will never forgive me if I knowingly choose to let your family – his family – die."

And what would he do to me, if I do? Baluka wondered. "I haven't given up on finding a way to protect them. If I can, would you bring Qall here? We could train him together."

She shook her head. "The rebels would never accept anyone who looks like the Raen among them – especially once they know he could easily *become* Valhan. If I return, it will only be once Qall is strong enough to change his appearance and defend himself."

What kind of man will he be then? Baluka wondered. *If he is as strong as Valhan, will he become another Raen anyway?*

"Your family raised him," she reminded him. "He's had all the encouragement a young man could have to become a good person."

His expression softened. "They do regard him fondly. I look forward to meeting him one day." His gaze moved away as he wondered how hard it would be to see beyond the familiar, hated face to the person beneath.

"By then he will look completely different," she assured him. "I don't think he'll choose to look like Valhan." She hadn't given much thought to what Qall would want to do once his training was over. He couldn't rejoin Lejihk's family, unless he married a Traveller. Perhaps he'd join the Restorers.

"I should go." Baluka told her. Shadows darkened his eyes, yet his back was straight. "The Restorers need to prepare – for the hunt for Tyen and the hand, and for another confrontation with the Raen if it comes to that. Is there anything else you need to tell me?" he asked.

"No. You?"

He shook his head. They both got to their feet, setting the room swaying. He paused to catch his balance.

"It is good to see you, Rielle," he said. As he said it, something loosened inside him, as if a burden had been cut away. *She is free. That's all I wanted to achieve when I joined the rebels. In that, I succeeded, even if the friend who released her has turned out to be a traitor.*

"Good luck," Rielle replied. "I am sorry to have ruined your friendship."

Baluka's face darkened. "You didn't. It wasn't real." A part of him still didn't want to believe it had been. *He was so convincing . . .*

She squeezed his shoulder. "He deceived us both, Baluka. Be careful he doesn't again."

He nodded. "I will. And you have a safe journey back to your charge. Take care nobody follows you."

She smiled. "You may not believe it, considering how well I did at your lessons, but I'm quite good at travelling between worlds now."

His eyebrows rose. "I admit I do find that rather hard to believe."

She let go of his shoulder and poked him in the side with a finger. Then before he could respond, she pushed out of the world and pulled the substance of the place between behind her to hide her path. *Let him wonder at that*, she thought as the whiteness surrounded her. Turning away, she started the long journey back to Qall and Timane.

CHAPTER 12

The closer Rielle got to Amelya, the more precautions she took. Instead of hiding her path only as she left and arrived in a world, she erased it all the way to the next. Where possible, she made physical journeys, on sledges, boats, levitating and even arriving in the sky and letting herself fall for several heartbeats before pushing out of a world again.

Extra effort took extra time, however, and she began to wonder if she was delaying her return deliberately. *Delaying having to tell Qall that I couldn't talk to his family and the girl he loves. Delaying having to admit I was wrong about Tyen.* She didn't have to tell anyone about the latter, however, or that in her pursuit of Valhan's hand she had revealed herself to Dahli and Tyen. Neither would do more than needlessly worry Timane and Qall.

Dahli can't blackmail me if I'm not there, she told herself. *His spies watching the Restorers will have learned that I left for my hiding place straight after talking to Baluka.*

They might also report that the Restorers knew Dahli and Tyen were attempting to resurrect the Raen. It depended on how close Dahli's spies could get to Baluka, or how widely Baluka had allowed that fact to become known. Dahli would have expected her to tell the Restorers anyway. He would be taking extra precautions to hide Valhan's hand, which would make it harder for Baluka to find it. Yet enemies of Valhan everywhere would be on the watch for Dahli and Tyen now. *As well as those who believe*

349

that the worlds need Valhan, or who profited from their alliance with the Raen before. They'll want to help them.

She could do nothing about any of that. Her task was to protect Qall. Let the Restorers take care of Dahli and his friends. At least this way she didn't have to speak to Tyen again.

Coming out of the place between worlds into damp air and near-darkness, she created a spark and looked around. She was in the city drains of Deeme. The rungs of a ladder gleamed invitingly in the light filtering from a drain nearby, but she ignored it. Before she'd left, she'd learned that it was possible to cross the city using these underground waterways. Walking through them, she not only avoided leaving a path to the apartment, she didn't have to push her way through the crowded streets.

Taking off her coat, she turned it inside out so that the patched and threadbare side was on the outside, and shrugged it back on. No matter whether she showed the "good" side or the shabby side, she didn't belong here, but the patchy side was darker and blended with the surroundings. By keeping a watch for the workers' minds, she should be able to avoid them.

She soon discovered that her shoes weren't as waterproof as they'd been when she'd bought them. Blackened from when she had arrived in a burning city of a world at war, they now allowed moisture to seep in. After walking through countless puddles, she couldn't help but squelch at each step.

She made it across the city without being seen or heard by drain workers. Reading the minds of the closest people above, she found an alleyway in which she could emerge with no witnesses. A pair of old women in threadbare clothes strode into sight as Rielle closed the hatch, but they concluded she was one of the local young homeless sizing up the drains as possible shelter for the night.

"Not down there," one advised as they passed. "Drainies will find you."

Rielle nodded and slunk away. She wound through more back alleys until she found a dark, empty corner in which to reverse her coat again. With the finer fabric showing, though with a few stains, rips and a charred hem from the journey marring it, she strode confidently through the main streets, taking a circular route towards the apartment she'd left Qall and Timane in. She sought out familiar minds in the room's direction, and found none. Ignoring the landlady, she climbed the stairs and pushed through into the room.

The dividers were gone. One of the beds had been pushed into a corner, but nothing else familiar remained. She froze, her heart suddenly racing, eyes searching for some clue to the reason for their absence. *Where are they?*

"They moved," a voice declared from behind Rielle.

"Where?" Rielle asked, turning to face the landlady.

The façade of a theatre Rielle recognised ran through the woman's mind, but her face creased into a calculating expression. "They didn't pay their last week's rent," she lied.

"Well, I have no money for you," Rielle replied. The landlady was eyeing her shoes, noting the dark water oozing from them. Pushing past the woman, Rielle descended the stairs two at a time, and emerged into the alleyway.

She could not remember the way exactly, only the general direction. Night had pressed in as best it could against the bright lights of the theatre district by the time she reached her destination. Much of the water in her shoes had worked its way out too, leaving her feet merely damp.

The façade of the theatre was as gaudy and bright as the woman had pictured. Painted wrought-metal vines appeared to climb up the wall. Tendrils twined around brightly coloured glass flowers, each lit by a spark. With no evidence of fuel or flame, Rielle concluded the illumination must be magical.

Late arrivals for that night's performance were hurrying into the building. Joining them, Rielle found herself in a crowded

351

foyer. Attendants were selling last-moment tickets and ushering the audience through doors.

"Ticket?" a voice said at Rielle's elbow. She turned to find a pretty young woman with a very dark, heart-shaped face and green eyes regarding her.

"I am here to join my friend, Timane," Rielle told her. "My name is Elle."

"Ah!" the girl exclaimed. "Imani said you would arrive soon."

"Imani" was Timane's new stage name, Rielle read. The girl beckoned and led Rielle through the crowd to a side door that, though ordinary, was being watched expectantly by several men and a few women. Seeking their thoughts, Rielle was amused to see Timane's image in their minds, romanticised to improbable beauty. They were hoping for a glimpse of her, or a chance to sneak through the door and find her. Some did not know what they would do then; others had detailed plans – a few which Rielle was sure Timane would not like at all.

The girl produced a key hanging on a chain around her neck, unlocked the door then secured it again when they had passed through, much to the fans' disappointment. Through the wooden walls, Rielle heard the muffled sound of a bell signalling the beginning of the performance. Looking for minds in the audience, she learned that an act was walking onto the stage. The collective minds in the theatre move into a sympathetic, listening state as they absorbed the performance.

The girl had taken Rielle up two narrow flights of stairs now. She climbed a third, panting slightly as they reached the top, then strode down a corridor to a door set into a curved wall. As she tapped on the door, Rielle sought minds beyond and found none.

The door opened. Valhan stared balefully out at them both, but as he saw Rielle his expression brightened and Rielle wondered how she could have ever seen anyone but Qall.

"Rielle!" he exclaimed, then quickly corrected himself. "Elle."

Rielle turned to her guide. The girl's eyebrows had risen at Qall's use of the different name, but she suspected nothing more than that "Elle" was a shortened version or a nickname.

"Thank you," Rielle told her. "I expect Timane is preparing for her performance."

"I'll tell her you're here during the first break," the girl assured her. "Won't be long."

As she walked away, Rielle turned to Qall, who stepped back and held the door open. The room inside was small and round, holding only a few chairs, a table and a shelf built into the curved wall. A circular staircase led up to the next level.

"Our bedrooms are up there," he told her. "Mine's at the top," he added smugly.

She couldn't help smiling. *Valhan would have expected to have the highest one too.* But Qall could not have inherited that from Valhan, she reminded herself.

"Is there one for me?" she asked.

"You'll have to share with Imani. I mean Timane." He grimaced. "When everyone calls and thinks of her by that name, it's easy to forget to use her real one."

Rielle moved to one of the chairs and collapsed into it, then began to peel off her shoes. "Do you have any food?"

His expression became serious. "Yes. You've come a long way – and been gone a long time. Timane doesn't eat beforehand. She gets too nervous." He waved towards the shelf on which a few covered bowls were arranged, then moved to the door. "I have to help with the lighting for the show." He opened the door then paused, bit his lip and drew in a quick breath. "Did you find her?"

Rielle frowned, then a pang of guilt came as she realised he meant the Traveller girl she had left to find.

"No," she said truthfully. "I tried, but it was too dangerous to approach her. I asked Baluka to forward a message, but he could not do so either. In the end, it was a choice between delivering

your message and risk bringing harm to them, or leave her ignorant but safe. I chose the latter."

"So they are safe?"

"Yes."

She could say so truthfully. Dahli would not destroy what he
might use to blackmail her or Qall. If Tyen succeeded in resurrecting Valhan, Dahli would not need to threaten the Travellers
at all. *At least, until he learns they protected Qall. But he won't get
the chance if Baluka manages to prevent the resurrection, or the Restorers
defeat the Raen if he returns.*

Qall frowned then turned away and left the room, the door
closing firmly behind him. Rielle paused, then opened the door
and called after him.

"Did you just read my mind?"

He checked his stride, and didn't turn. "No."

"Look at me." He didn't turn, so she started after him. "You
did, didn't you?"

He stopped and though he turned he did not meet her gaze.
"You would, if you were in my position."

"Qall . . ." she began. *So much for saving him and Timane from
needlessly worrying.* She sighed and shook her head. "They are safe,"
she insisted. "You can see that I believe it. As long as we don't
return. If Tyen succeeds the Restorers will deal with . . . the
situation. From what I've heard, they would have won, previously."

He nodded. "I have to go." Not waiting for an answer, he
turned away and hurried down the corridor.

Returning to their room, Rielle sat quietly, thinking over the
whole fruitless journey. *No, not entirely fruitless.* Better that she
knew the truth about Tyen. And Baluka. The Restorers couldn't
prevent another resurrection of Valhan if they didn't know about
it.

She thought of Baluka's request that she join them. *I'd have
agreed, if it wasn't more important to make sure Qall is safe and becomes
strong enough to defend himself.* Though if Valhan did return, Qall

might be better off remaining in hiding. They might be equal in strength, but Valhan had a thousand more cycles of experience. Together, she and Qall might defeat him. Not that she had any intention of confronting and fighting Valhan, but it was reassuring, at least, to know they could defend themselves if he found them.

Rising, she went to the shelf and helped herself to some fruit and pastries. Though she'd taken Tarran's advice, stopping to rest and eat more during her return journey, she had begun it already worn out from travelling and the tension of tracking Dahli to Tyen's workshop. She ate hungrily.

Not long after she had finished, muffled steps sounded beyond the door, then it opened and Timane strode in. Rielle rose in time to be wrapped in the sleeves and skirt of a voluminous dress, and received a kiss on her cheek from a head that emerged from beneath a feathered headdress.

"Elle!" Timane exclaimed. "You're back at last!"

"Yes," Rielle agreed, backing out of the tiers of fabric carefully so as to not tear them. "I'm sorry it took me so long."

Timane dropped into a chair and began fanning herself. "What happened? Qall has gone monosyllabic again and he nearly mistimed the lights, so I'm assuming you brought news that he isn't happy about."

Rielle grimaced. "I couldn't reach his family. They were being watched. It was too dangerous to approach them."

"Ah."

"I learned that Dahli is trying to resurrect the Raen using a new body. Or rather, Tyen is. They're working together."

"Oh! Tyen? But you and he . . .?"

"Yes." Rielle gritted her teeth. "He let me think he agreed with me that the worlds were better off without Valhan. He knows Valhan wanted me dead too." She shook her head. "I wonder why he bothered to help me rescue Qall when he was a boy, when he was on their side after all."

"Perhaps he changed his mind."

"Something must have."

"We are a long way from the worlds that knew of the Raen," Timane pointed out. "If they use another body, Qall will be safe, won't he?"

Rielle shook her head. "Do you think Valhan would be content knowing a sorcerer as powerful as he, who looks like him, still lives?"

Timane's mouth formed an "o". She shook her head vigorously. The gesture was so uncharacteristically dramatic, Rielle couldn't help but smile. She thought of the girl's bouncing steps as she'd entered the room. Life as an actor and singer was shaping her into a more expressive, confident person.

"What can we do?" Timane asked.

"Stay far away from the Raen's worlds," Rielle told her. "Train Qall so that if Valhan finds us, we can unite to fend him off."

"Or kill him."

Rielle paused, then nodded. "If he forces us to."

Timane looked down at the floor, her gaze far behind the boards.

"Qall has to start training again."

"Yes." Rielle drummed her fingers on her knee. *The sooner Qall can change his appearance, the better.* She must put aside her worries that he was too young to become ageless. To the Travellers, he was an adult, ready to be trusted with adult responsibilities. If he did something foolish out of youthful ignorance? She gave a mental shrug. If he did, it was unlikely to kill him. He was strong enough to make mistakes and survive them.

However, learning to pattern-shift took a long time and required isolation. She'd have to find a world rich in magic with no occupants who would be affected if all magic was used in the process. She'd have to hope no hunters came upon them in the middle of—

"Rielle?"

Looking up at Timane, Rielle realised she'd been silent and lost in thought for quite some time. "Yes?"

"What can I do?"

"Nothing. Just . . . enjoy your new career," she told the girl.

Timane's smile was wide and delighted. "Dell says I'll probably move on to a bigger theatre in a few years," she said. "Maybe even tour the local worlds."

Rielle smiled. Timane's fame might eventually draw too much attention, but they would decide what to do about that when, and if, the time came. "If Tyen doesn't succeed or the Restorers defeat the Raen, then one day you will tour all the worlds, singing to the most powerful leaders and tastemakers everywhere – including Murai."

"Oh!" Timane's eyes widened, and she relaxed back in her seat, her gaze fixed on a distant future full of possibilities. "That would be wonderful!"

CHAPTER 13

Rielle was trying not to take it personally. Timane had observed that Qall had, slowly at first, then with growing confidence, become less reticent and more cheerful since Rielle had left. He'd been good company, helpful and even funny at times. Now, however, he was back to his old black moods and sullenness.

Perhaps it was the training, Rielle reflected. She pushed him constantly. She pushed herself too. It was a challenge to recall Tarran's lessons when she'd had little reason to use his battle training. She had never taken on the role of instructor of fighting techniques before, except to teach Timane some simple uses of magic for self-defence. If that wasn't enough, Qall did not respond to lessons the same way she had, and she could not read his mind to help work out how he would best absorb what he needed to learn.

It also did not help when he didn't bother telling her that he had already learned a particular point from the Travellers. Or he found the solution to a conundrum immediately, then grew impatient as she paused to consider how to make the exercise more challenging. Sometimes – like now – she made him go through the motions anyway, to prove that he did indeed understand the point of the lesson, as well as, she had to admit, to wipe the superior look from his face.

"Again," she said, restarting the sequence of attacks that had just defeated him.

"Why?" he complained as he repeated the exercise. "I *know* this."

"There's value in practice," she replied. "Repetition allows us to act instinctively, without wasting time in analysis. Knowing something isn't as useful as experiencing it. By running through an exercise several times, you may discover weaknesses or alternatives that you hadn't foreseen." She caught and held his gaze. "Dahli may be weaker than you, but he has experience gained over hundreds of cycles."

"It's not always true that experience is better than knowledge," he told her.

"No? How so?"

"It's better to know of death than experience it."

She laughed. "Obviously." As his defence failed again, he muttered a curse. "Again," she said. He rolled his eyes.

"So experiencing isn't better than knowing," he said as she started the sequence again.

"I never said it was better. Just different. Are you smart enough to judge when it is better to know than experience?"

"Yes."

"Is it better now, in this lesson?"

He paused, and a crease appeared between his brows. "Maybe. I wouldn't know for sure until I needed the knowledge."

"And then you'd learn by experience, wouldn't you? Particularly if you fail."

He didn't answer. Didn't even curse when his defence crumbled.

She continued. "Sometimes you can only judge what it is better to experience than know—"

"I can't judge if I'm dead," he interrupted.

She started the exercise again. "Working out which . . . well, most of the time it's a matter of common sense. No matter how much knowledge you have, there will be times you don't have a suitable pre-considered plan, or you'll be in a situation where you don't have enough time to think. Dealing with the first involves taking a risk; when dealing with the second, it helps if you have good instincts and reflexes honed through practice."

He said nothing. His reactions were sloppy with annoyance now. She stopped midway through the sequence. "Is there a way out of this?"

He began shaking his head, then paused. "I suppose there might be."

"Let's start again."

She didn't think defeat could be avoided in the exercise, but it was worth giving him the chance to try just to get him to engage with the lesson. He tried three more times. In the first, he tried a different, riskier tactic. In the second, he tried confusing her with rapid responses. In the third, he moved out of the world, skimmed into her barrier and nearly scored a hit on her inner shield, only failing because her instinct to protect herself was faster than his attack.

"You're supposed to be limiting your access to magic for this exercise," she reminded him. "You'd have used most of your strength leaving the world."

"Yes, but I wouldn't need much to kill you if I was fast enough."

She nodded. "That is true. It would be a great risk."

"A risk worth taking, if I knew trying nothing would mean losing. Working that out takes time. Time I don't . . . have . . ." His voice faded as his gaze shifted away, fixing on the distance as he realised what he was saying.

"But now that we've practised this, you may work that out straightaway, should you ever end up in this position," she finished. She smiled. "We've achieved something today."

He nodded slowly, still distracted by his thoughts.

"What is it?" She followed his gaze, seeing only the labyrinth of dark, twisted rock and soft sand that made up this part of the world they were in.

"I thought I heard something."

She listened. Sometimes the wind filled the passages and tunnels with unearthly sounds, but today it was so quiet she could hear his breathing, and the growl of his stomach.

"Time to go home," she decided.

He nodded, his gaze moving back to her. Now that the lesson was over, the withdrawn, brooding look had returned. She smothered a sigh and led the way out into a nearby cave.

They retraced their path through the rocky landscape to the place they'd arrived at. All the way, Rielle searched constantly for other minds, and found none. Despite the tall boots they'd purchased for visits to this world, sand always found its way into their shoes, so they paused to shake it out. Once they were done, she held out a hand to Qall. Once he'd taken it, she pushed into the place between worlds, moving slowly at first as she concealed their path.

As the dark rocks and sand faded, it became difficult to tell where one met the other. This was one reason she had chosen the location for their lessons – on approaching it from the place between, it looked like solid rock. Sorcerers would skim higher to ensure they found a clear space to emerge, and they would not see her and Qall, hidden within the great maze of passages and caves.

With Qall unable to go without breathing for long, she couldn't spare the time to smooth the signs of their passing all the way to the next world. After counting to thirty, she stopped and sought the end of the path they had made on arrival. She found the end, where it started abruptly at the place she'd begun concealing it, and followed it further into the place between.

She would have preferred to not travel far from Amelya, or even leave the city, but the dense population that made it a great place to hide in also meant it would be impossible to teach Qall without drawing attention. The constant traffic from other worlds also meant her journeys were lost among many others, at least until she moved further away from Amelya. Once out of the busy thoroughfares, she relied on her ability to hide her path to prevent them leaving a trail.

Complete whiteness passed, then the green ocean and sky of the next world coloured their surroundings. Creating a floor of solidified air at the moment of arrival kept them from falling. They sat down to make balancing easier as she propelled them both across the sky.

This world had plenty of arrival places, but since most of the people in it lived on huge slabs of buoyant rocks floating in the ocean, it was only ever a matter of luck if one of these natural rafts and an arrival place happened to be in the same location. Sorcerers here must skim or levitate to find "land". Rielle was not seeking solid ground, however, just adding a stage to their journey home that did not leave a path a sorcerer could track. She wasn't looking for an arrival place either, since she had forged a new path to this world. The hard part was finding where that new path had ended.

Reaching an area where the ocean was shallow enough to see the rippled floor, she sought a familiar configuration of shapes – a place where the stripes blended in an unusual way. It was not a unique feature, however, and it wasn't until she had found a familiar shipwreck that she knew she'd reached the end of her previous path.

As soon as she began following it, she sensed that someone else had recently travelled along it. Had she not been between worlds, her heart would have lurched in her chest. Qall looked at her and frowned, sensing the same thing.

"How long—?"

"Don't speak," she replied quickly. *"If there's someone in the place between, they might hear you."*

He scowled, his lips pressing together. She did not have the time to mollify him, and turned her attention to the path again. It had been used recently, but not moments ago. Probably before the time she and Qall had left the training place. Whoever it was, they were most likely long gone.

They had been following the path she had forged to get here.

How a stranger had found it when she had hidden the start, she couldn't guess. Perhaps they had stumbled upon it. Where they had gone once they'd arrived in the ocean world was not clear. Either they had retreated back to where they'd joined the path, or they'd arrived in the ocean world and levitated away. Or fallen into the water.

She proceeded along the path cautiously. They passed through the midpoint and continued towards the next world. All the way, she kept watching for the place where this stranger had come across her path and followed it. Instead, not far from the next world, their own path abruptly became less travelled. Puzzled, she continued on for a moment before she realised what this meant.

We're following their *path. They must have crossed the section between the next world and where I stopped concealing our path. But how did they know which way to go, to find the exact place once I had stopped hiding it?*

The next world grew more distinct. A thin forest of odd trees surrounded them. Single-trunked, with a mass of fine branches forming a ball at intervals, they looked like a child's idea of a tree. Below them, patches of spiny plants grew everywhere except where sheets of glittering stone broke through the ground. As they arrived, she heard Qall suck in a deep breath. She ignored the sudden pounding of her heart, as her body expressed the anxiety it couldn't feel between worlds, and created a barrier of stilled air around them as she searched for minds.

The only humans nearby were those living in farms and one tiny village. None were aware of her or Qall. She looked at him, expecting questions, but he remained hunched and silent.

"Someone found our path," she said, her breath misting in the cold air. "That doesn't mean they were looking for us though."

His expression told her he knew she wasn't as confident of that as she sounded.

"What do we do now?" he asked.

363

What indeed? she thought. "Continue home."

When coming from the other direction, she'd skimmed to this forest from a nearby arrival place in an old quarry. She decided to take a different route, then as she opened her mouth to tell Qall to hold his breath she changed her mind. *Let's see how long this nosy sorcerer was following us.*

Qall took a deep breath, reading her intention in her expression. She nodded in approval and pushed out of the world. Though she had hidden the end of her path from the quarry, she knew roughly where it was and started in that direction. Immediately she sensed a new path, used recently, connecting the gap between the arrival place and where she had previously started hiding her own.

Continuing, both curiosity and worry grew as she neared the end of the path. It changed, once again becoming the less defined trace of a single journey. It did not meander, but continued directly towards the quarry, where she emerged again to contemplate what she had just learned.

A stranger had somehow located the beginning and end of two of her paths, despite her hiding them. One for a journey between worlds, the other for a skim across a world. Was this coincidence, or something more sinister?

Perhaps it was obvious which direction she had skimmed in. She put herself in the position of the stranger. If they had been following Rielle and Qall, they'd have arrived at the quarry and found no continuing path. They would conclude that she'd either retraced her steps, travelled on from the quarry by non-magical means or hidden her path. If they'd suspected the first option, they'd have retreated, but not before eliminating the second option by skimming higher to see if they could see her, and skimming in circles to find the place where she'd stopped walking and moved into the place between worlds again.

She slipped out of the world a little, looking for evidence of the latter, and found none. The stranger had skimmed directly from the arrival place to where her path started. As if they knew she could hide it.

No! As if they could sense where I'd hidden my path!

Qall squeezed her hand. Looking up, she saw his strained expression and realised that she had slowed almost to a stop between worlds. Returning to the quarry, she emerged. Qall immediately began gasping for air.

"Sorry," she said. As he recovered, she looked around, searching for minds, and found none.

Another possibility occurred to her then. Since a sorcerer skimming close to a world could be seen as a ghostly figure, it was reasonable to think the stranger might have seen her, and the direction she was travelling in. He or she would have needed to be close to the world as well.

If they noticed me moving slowly at first, then faster, they might have investigated and discovered I can conceal my path. Maybe they followed because they want to ask me how it is done, then lost me in the ocean world. Or they could be one of Dahli's trackers.

She decided to find another way home, then changed her mind. If one of Dahli's searchers had found her, she needed to know how long they had been following her. If they had tracked her as far back as Amelya, they might have found Timane.

Qall straightened, his brows lowering in a frown of concern, and she knew he'd read her mind again. As she opened her mouth to scold him, he dragged in a very deep breath. Holding back the words, she pushed out of the world.

Coming from the other direction, she'd used well-used paths to pass through the next two worlds, so she had no way to detect if the stranger had followed her. For the next journey, not far from Amelya, she had forged a new path through the centre of a world. Taking inspiration from Tyen's approach to leaving Doum, she'd created a path that plunged straight down into the earth. At a point she thought most mortal sorcerers would baulk, she'd started hiding her path, changing direction at the same time, then travelled normally to the surface in another part of the world. This would be an opportunity to see if they could detect where she'd hidden her path.

She would need to travel slowly. Too slowly for Qall, as he'd run out of breath. As she reached the crumbling stone tower from which the path through the world would begin, Qall's expression changed to dismay.

"You're going to leave me here." A slight quaver in his voice betrayed his fear.

"Yes," she told him. "It will take longer than you can hold your breath for."

"What if they find me here?"

"Go down the tower and stay out of sight. If anyone appears, read their mind to see if they are hunting us, but don't reveal yourself."

He nodded. "Be careful."

"I will." Drawing magic from the outer edge of the world, she pushed into the place between, found her former path and plunged down into the ground.

At once she sensed that the path had been used by another sorcerer. Only by mentally counting did she know when the path was about to end and the gap began. She slowed when she was close to the end, but the path continued on longer than she expected. Anxiety had made her count faster.

At the gap, she slowed. Only the stranger's path continued, turning where she had changed direction while hiding her path.

And then she was back on her original path.

She stopped and headed back, anger growing inside.

Tyen. The liar! He made me think I was hiding my path when what I was really doing was laying a very distinctive trail.

Moving in another direction, she smoothed the substance of the place between as she had done so many times before. Reversing direction, she searched for signs of her passing. Knowing what she was looking for made it easier to detect a faint roughness in the substance of the place between. It was like how, no matter how carefully one might smooth wet sand, it never quite regained the evenness that the ebb and flow of water left. Most people wouldn't sense the roughness, but someone who knew what to look for would sense it. Someone who had been told what to look for.

Conscious that she had been in the place between for a long time now, she sought out the path to the tower. She sped towards the surface, mind racing. Would the roughness smooth out in time, or was every step of her journey to Amelya visible to Dahli's hunters?

It doesn't matter, she told herself. *What matters is that someone who can detect where I've been hiding my path is following me.* As she emerged from within the world and arrived in the tower, her head swam with implications. If the tracker had seen Rielle and Qall, they would have started the journey back to Dahli. Unless they tried to deliver a message from Dahli, threatening Lejihk's family. But she doubted they'd do the latter, because they must know she would stop them returning to tell Dahli they'd delivered it. *You can't blackmail someone you can't communicate with.*

Either way, she needed to get back to Amelya and make sure Timane was fine.

And then they once again would have to set out to find a new place to hide.

CHAPTER 14

"You could stay." Rielle told Timane. "You should move to another city though. We'd be sad to leave you behind, but happy to know you were prospering here."

"No." Timane shook her head, her face solemn and her back straight. She hid her disappointment well. "The worlds are infinite, as my ma's ma used to say. If I can sing here, I can sing somewhere else."

"It might be safer if you stay," Rielle added. "As long as you move to another city . . ."

"No," Timane corrected. "It won't be safer here than with you. If they find their way here they'll learn about me, then they'll hunt me down to ask questions about you."

"She's right," Qall said.

Rielle looked at him. He'd been scowling and silent since she'd returned from investigating the path.

"See?" Timane said. She forced a tight, determined smile. "And now that's decided, I can't see why we must delay any longer than we need to. I will go tell Dell." Rising from her chair, she slipped out of the room.

How did I earn such loyalty? Rielle wondered. *But I am glad she's coming with us. She gets along with Qall better than I do.* She turned to Qall. He had been staring at her. Now he looked away. "I'll get our packs and see if we need to replace anything," he said.

She smiled. "Thanks."

She watched him climb the stairs. She'd used the gems she'd stashed at Tarran's house getting back to Amelya: they had nothing to trade this time. *Only Timane and Qall's savings.* Conflicting guilt and gratitude rose. It didn't seem fair to use the pair's income, but without it, travelling through worlds would be much more difficult.

What to do now? She searched the surrounding minds – of which there were many since a performance was underway in the theatre downstairs. Her senses found a familiar mind: Timane. The girl was bartering fiercely with the theatre owner. Timane's mind reading advantage was countered by her not wanting to leave the woman who had hired and trained her too much out of pocket. When they were done, they touched palms in a gesture of respect, then hugged and wiped away tears. The affection and admiration Dell had for the girl was genuine.

Rielle left the room, meeting a more composed Timane halfway down the stairs. The girl pressed the bag of coins into Rielle's hands.

"Take it," she said.

"Are you sure?"

"Of course. Just don't make me shop for supplies. You're a much better bargainer anyway, and know what we'll need for the journey. I need to decide which of my belongings I have to give up. That's not something I had to do before."

Rielle hugged her. "Thank you. Qall's getting our packs ready, so you'll have an idea how much room you've got."

Timane groaned in mock horror. "You let a man barely out of childhood pack for two grown women?"

"You'd better get up there and supervise. I think he'd accept guidance from you better than from me."

The girl hurried up the stairs. Turning away, Rielle continued down. As she passed Dell's office, she stopped to thank the woman, who accepted it with a grave nod. Timane hadn't told her what she, Qall and Rielle were fleeing from, but she knew too many

369

women who had escaped powerful families or cruel husbands to resent one for abandoning her in the midst of her most successful season.

It took longer than Rielle hoped to exchange the local coins for supplies and small, precious items that she could exchange in other worlds. Gemstones and precious metals were in demand and therefore expensive in Amelya, so she stocked up on dried spices, fine cloth and perfume. She avoided seeds, following the Travellers' rule against bringing plants or other living things into another world that might destroy local crops and wilderness.

All the while she scanned the minds around her, looking for her own name, or thoughts about searching. Local children hired to watch competitors in the market were a distraction, and when she finally returned to the theatre, she chanced upon a new employee who was spying for another theatre. Seeking out Dell to inform her of this delayed her return further. It was only right to warn the woman since Rielle was about to steal away her best singer.

So it was only when she was climbing the stairs that she sought Timane's mind and found the girl in a state of anxiety.

Qall was gone.

He'd vanished after saying something about Rielle being too soft, and that he would kill the searcher himself. Timane had wanted to race after Rielle, but she wasn't sure where to look, and searching might take longer than simply staying put.

Breaking into a run, Rielle raced up the stairs and burst into the room. Timane whirled around to face her.

"He's—"

"Gone. How long ago?"

"I don't know. Not long after you left."

"Wait here."

Rielle pressed the bag of valuables into the girl's hands, then pushed out of the world.

She found his path in moments and raced along it. He'd made

no effort to confuse anyone who might trace it back to the room. *Certain that he would find and deal with the searcher, therefore removing the need for caution*, she guessed. *Foolish boy. He doesn't realise that killing is not so easy. Or rather, easy to do but hard to live with. I should have told him about the people I killed, and how the guilt and horror has never left me.*

The path took her out of Amelya to the next world, where he had skimmed to a well-used path. From there she could only guess that he'd headed towards the next world – the one where she had realised the searcher could detect where she had hidden her path – to try and pick up the searcher's trail. But when she reached there, the paths had not been travelled recently. Qall had not been this way. So where had he gone?

Straight to the first place I noticed someone had followed us, where the tracker had been most recently, she thought, and headed towards the ocean world. As she reached the world of the strange forest, she sensed a freshly used path. It didn't continue on to the ocean world, but skimmed around the arrival place in ever-widening circles. A few hundred paces from the arrival place, the path turned sharply and skimmed away, then suddenly plunged into the place between, heading to the next world. The hunter had walked away from the arrival place before continuing their journey – a simple way to hide tracks.

The path led to a temple, where most of the residents were asleep. One drowsy watcher guarded the arrival place, and as she arrived he snapped awake, thinking that God's Doorway was busy tonight. She recognised Qall in his mind, and a woman who had passed through earlier. A woman whose face was familiar.

Inekera! A chill ran down Rielle's spine as she recalled the woman leaving her to die in a desert world, not long after Valhan had taken Rielle from her home world. The thought of Qall at the mercy of Inekera filled her with horror.

Qall must have seen the woman in the watcher's mind too. It would make it easier for him to track her. As Rielle left the watcher wondering who these gods were who visited so briefly, a fresh path pulled her towards the next world, then through several more. Qall was making no attempt to hide his path. Not having to search for it meant it should be easier to catch up.

From time to time, his path skimmed in a spiral out from an arrival place or he backtracked, and she guessed that he had lost Inekera's trail. Every time, though, he found it again. Using a physical method of travelling to hide her tracks was slowing the woman down, and Rielle's hope that she would catch up before Qall did weakened.

When his path led to a world with little magic, she stopped, searching the moss-covered plain of cracked stone around her. Her habit of continually gathering and holding enough magic to travel through several worlds saved her from stranding, but would Qall have remembered to do the same? He'd been impatient during her lessons, not always paying attention.

If he had become stranded here, she would never be able to locate him by his mind. He would be able to find hers, however. As long as a little magic remained.

Fortunately, his path led onwards. It led to a dry, cold world also weak in magic. Knowing that inhospitable worlds often bordered dead worlds, she was uneasy as Qall's path continued.

To her relief, the next world was rich in magic. Officials guarded the arrival place, taking note of visitors. She realised it was a world she had visited previously, before finding Amelya. From the officials, she learned that she was not far behind Qall now. His path continued straight, with no spiralling to find Inekera's path or backtracking when he lost it.

Is Inekera no longer making the effort to hide her tracks? Is that because she has realised she is being hunted and had no time to employ evasive tactics?

Rielle quickened her own pace. A few worlds on she sensed what might be a presence in the place between. A few more and she was certain of it, before it faded away when her quarry arrived in a world. Knowing she wouldn't sense them again until she started on the next path, she hurried on without taking magic, sought another fresh path leading away and found herself skimming across a misty world of many tiny islands.

Against the white mist she saw a shadow far ahead. Though she propelled herself ever faster, it was travelling quickly, and she did not even halve the distance before it disappeared. The path turned abruptly and led into the place between without stopping in the world. She raced along it. If Qall hadn't had a chance to breathe, he was going to have to stop in the next world.

The mist faded to white, then was replaced by a weathered landscape of red earth and twisted trees. A weak world. Four black-skinned watchers squatted, two men and two women, at the edge of a circle of dusty ground. As Rielle arrived, she sought their minds. She saw Qall. She saw Inekera.

In the watchers' minds, the two were together, hands linked. *But they were not "together"*, the older woman thought. *Not by the way they regarded each other, all wary and tense, the man gasping for breath. Perhaps this one is a lover, chasing one of the others.*

Afraid to linger and lose the trail, Rielle pushed on. Qall and Inekera were travelling fast now. Qall would have to stop and breathe for more than a moment, and then Rielle would catch up. Sure enough, when the next world emerged from the whiteness of the place between, two familiar figures stood within it. Qall was bent forward, hands on his knees as he dragged in air. Inekera squinted in Rielle's direction and, seeing a shadow appearing, grabbed his wrist and yanked him out of the world.

His expression was pained, but as Rielle arrived and pushed straight on after him, he saw her and frowned. Yet he did not resist Inekera's pull. He faded, but did not completely disappear as Rielle kept close behind them. It did not make sense. He was stronger than Inekera, so he could have pulled her to a halt, or taken her back towards Rielle.

Why is he cooperating with her?

At once, Rielle thought of his fears for his family. Had Inekera delivered Dahli's threat to harm them? *Of course she has!*

"*Qall!*" Rielle called with her mind. "*You don't have to go with her.*"

Qall looked back and shook his head. His voice sounded faintly in her head, while his mouth remained closed.

"*Stop following me. Please. I don't want to hurt you.*"

Then he faded from her senses. Another world was forming. The pair was standing in a simple dirt circle surrounded by a fence of woven branches. Inekera spoke but Rielle, not yet in the world, could not hear or make out the words. Qall nodded, his shoulders hunching. He took a deep breath and grasped the woman's arm.

By the time Rielle arrived, the pair were gone. She gave chase.

Qall raced ahead, faster than she had taken him between worlds, faster than he had ever travelled. Reckless. Driven. She followed, determined that she would catch up when he stopped to breathe again. Worlds flashed by. She had no time to draw in magic, but then neither did he nor Inekera. She could only hope he would run out of breath before she ran out of magic.

Then, at last, she arrived in a world an instant after he had, and he did not move on. Instead he turned to face her, dragging in deep breaths.

"I . . . must . . . do . . . this," he gasped. "It's . . . the only way . . ."

"Qall—" she began.

Darkness surrounded her. He and Inekera vanished.

Reaching out for the magic to follow, she found none.

PART FIVE

TYEN

CHAPTER 16

T yen's new workroom was similar to the last. Another underground basement of a mansion, it was lined with shelving
and tables occupied the centre. The bodies of dismantled insectoids
covered tables at one end, and the shelving at the other was full
of the same equipment Tyen had ignored before. The only physical difference was that the stairs entered the room at the centre.

A more recent change was that he was alone. Zeke had disappeared several days ago, which was frustrating because the young
inventor had been pursuing a promising idea. Dahli hadn't visited
since Rielle's attack on the old workroom, sending a lackey to
guide Tyen to new volunteers, bring corpses, take Tyen to a world
rich enough in magic to attempt a resurrection and remove the
volunteers' duplicates so Dahli could assess how successful Tyen
had been.

Tyen had met three new subjects willing to lose a finger for
the chance of their mind living on in a youthful body. All of
them had been younger than Pieh. He'd varied his method of
copying a person's pattern into their finger, tried different
approaches to changing the patterns of the corpses Dahli brought
and tweaked the final process of imprinting the stored memories
into them. None of the resurrections he'd attempted had succeeded
– at least, not to Dahli's standards.

The lackeys did not know what Dahli did to the duplicates.
Tyen suspected the worst. He ought to be relieved when each

resurrection failed, as it meant he didn't have to pretend to be making slow progress. Until now he'd hoped he was giving Dahli a reason to not hunt for Rielle, allowing Rielle time to find a place to hide. Dahli had still sent hunters out to seek her, and Rielle clearly wasn't hiding so far away that she couldn't discover what Tyen was doing.

The thought of her believing that he had betrayed her made him feel ill. She'd met up with Baluka too. He'd read that from Dahli's mind. He'd also read that she had gone back to her hiding place, leaving the Restorers to prepare for a possible confrontation with a resurrected Raen.

The delays would help them, Tyen knew. The Raen might forgive Tyen helping Rielle, but he would not look favourably on providing an advantage for his enemy. In truth, Tyen knew he was doing neither. He was as likely to stumble upon the right process as find it deliberately. And right now he was making no progress because none of Dahli's lackeys had appeared for some time.

This had left Tyen at a loose end. He couldn't work on the insectoids in case he muddled Zeke's work method. Most details of what Zeke had learned and prepared remained in his memory.

All Tyen could do was continue rebuilding the humanoid Rielle had destroyed. In some ways he was grateful to her for forcing him to start again, because his second attempt was much more refined than the first. Partly that was because the world he was in now was technologically sophisticated, though not as developed as his home world. It was easier to obtain and commission the parts he needed, or source quality raw materials.

It also helped that a few businesses in this world were doing a strong trade in mechanical magic. Most of the creations were not warlike. Some were elegant solutions to urban challenges like supplying adequate water and lighting, and if this world had been the rule rather than the exception, Tyen wouldn't have felt so guilty about introducing mechanical magic to the worlds.

From time to time, he brought out Vella to discuss his progress. It was a very efficient way to keep a record of what he'd done. If their conversation meandered away from the subject, at least it filled in the hours.

The machines they've made here are very efficient in using magic, he told Vella. *It makes me wonder . . . the inventors in my world knew that magic was finite, even if they didn't believe that creativity generated it. Why weren't they motivated to make more efficient machines?*

Professor Kilraker was told by the Academy that discussing whether magic was finite was too close to broaching the subject of whether magic was generated by creativity. Professors must ignore both ideas or be labelled "radicals" and be in danger of losing their positions.

I wonder if there is any magic left at home. More than ten years have passed since I left.

They would have to consume a great deal of it to deplete the world completely. More likely the magic is now thinly spread.

Perhaps too thinly to be of use. The machines won't work. Aircarts and carriages will be grounded. Railsledges won't run. Without machines, will society be able to continue as it was?

The failing of such systems often leads to rebellion and war. That might lead to a breaking out of radical ideas.

Tyen sighed at the words that had appeared on her pages. *War. Another war. Is there anywhere in the worlds where people aren't killing each other? Don't answer that, Vella. I know there are worlds not at war – this one included – but it just doesn't seem like there are many of them. Let's change the subject.*

He glanced up at the humanoid. *What do you think of this, Vella?*

It is well made, she replied. You have not solved the problem of fitting an entire mind in it though.

No. But if I did, will it be a suitable vessel for you?

If it allows me to be truly conscious without relying on the touch of a human, and gives me limbs with which to transport myself and manipulate objects, it will be an improvement on my current state. But I will still be incomplete.

379

With no ability to feel emotions. He nodded. *It would be better if I could get these resurrections to work so you can have a real human body.*

And yet, I would be mortal. I wasn't strong enough to become ageless.

I could try putting you in a vessel that is.

They would have to have either died without having learned pattern shifting, or their brain be badly injured, or their body will heal itself.

What were the chances of finding a newly dead sorcerer of great strength who hadn't learned to become ageless yet, especially now when no Raen was controlling the spread of magical knowledge? Tyen shook his head. It didn't seem likely.

It might not be as unlikely as you fear. While the worlds are at war, the chances are better. Young, untrained sorcerers are more likely to become caught up in fighting.

That's true. He sighed. *All options seem like a risk. I don't know if I'll get a second chance. Valhan claimed that you would be destroyed by the process of resurrection. Though I don't know why he said that. As far as I can tell, there is no need to destroy the piece of flesh in which memories are stored. I tried copying Pieh three times before Dahli gave up.*

Perhaps there was a clue in that to why he kept failing. Yet he could not see how destroying the finger or hand or book used for storage made implanting memories in a vessel more effective. At times, he suspected Valhan had lied in order to keep Tyen willing to spy for him. Yet it was also possible that, when he'd made the claim, Valhan hadn't realised he was wrong. If only Tyen could be sure Valhan *had* been wrong.

He looked up at the empty tables. *The longer Dahli is away, the more I'm convinced he has gone after Rielle. If I'm to keep him from chasing after her and Qall, I need to make progress.* He had several fingers to work with now. All he needed was corpses to use as vessels.

Fetching corpses wasn't such a specialist task that only Dahli's lackeys could do it, though. Tyen could fetch them himself. He looked down at Vella's pages.

You've considered this before, but hesitated — and for good reason, she pointed out. *The Restorers will be watching for you.*

Yes, it's a risk, but I've got to do something. I will be careful, Vella. I'm always careful.

Closing her, Tyen put her back inside her pouch and tucked the book inside his shirt. He stood up and stretched, then looked around the room. The silence made him shiver. Or was it the cold air? This place was a lot colder than the last. It smelled vaguely musty, which was better than it did when he was working on a body. When Dahli brought corpses, he usually chose people whose body wouldn't be missed. People from the forgotten end of societies, who had no loved ones. Or soldiers, covered in the gore of warfare.

Soldiers were better, as they were usually younger and if they had fallen at the beginning of a war they were in reasonable shape. He wasn't sure how Dahli ensured soldiers didn't have loved ones who would want to bury their body, however. *I'll have to look into the minds of their fellow soldiers to find out. Which means I'll have to get close to a battlefield.*

His jacket hung over the back of a nearby chair. As it settled around his shoulders, a faint vibration came from one of the internal pockets. Since Rielle's trashing of the last laboratory, he didn't go anywhere without Beetle. It wasn't needed to guard Valhan's notes now. Keeping the insectoid with him was oddly comforting.

Reaching out to the far extent of the world, he took magic and pushed into the place between worlds. The neighbouring ones were familiar to him, as he had visited them once back when he was a student at Liftre. Some, like the world he was living in, had changed a great deal in the five cycles after the Raen had died, others were still in a state of upheaval. He wouldn't have to travel far to find a battlefield.

Keeping to well-used paths, he travelled through a few worlds then began to gather information. Whenever he arrived in a city, he skimmed to somewhere quiet so he could read the minds of the locals. Much discussion was occurring between regional leaders over tackling the conflict in Thot, which had once been a world of sophisticated, peaceful societies. Tyen was dismayed to learn that one had recently gained the upper hand through the use of mechanical magic weaponry. Nobody knew exactly what form the insectoids took, but something new and devastating about them had tipped the conflict in their favour. Tyen's first thought was to avoid that place, but it did present the opportunity to seize one of these new insectoids for Zeke to investigate.

Straightening his shoulders and bracing himself for sights he may wish he'd never seen, he travelled to Thot. A well-used path took him to a city of broken walls and scorched roof beams curving up like blackened ribs. A search for minds told him that only scavengers remained. The battle that had destroyed this place was long past, and the wounded had either recovered or died long ago. Disease had run its course. Most fields and wells had been poisoned by war machines, so the few survivors were perishing from starvation. He could wait until one died, then restore their body, but it was harder to heal someone whose body was emaciated than a person who had died of their wounds. Sickened, he moved on.

He skimmed across the world. Plumes of smoke rising above the horizon led him to the next city. The battle that had reduced this one to ruin was some days in the past. He found a makeshift hospital full of promising vessels, but could not bring himself to appear in the middle of the wounded to take away one of the newly dead, especially after he saw insectoids enlarged by terror in their memories.

It would be easier to snatch a fresh corpse unnoticed in a battlefield. Continuing on, he eventually reached a sprawling temple city still burning from an attack that morning. He stopped in the farmland outside to scan for minds. The realisation that some priests were likely to be people who had no family sent a flash of excitement through him, followed by a shudder of horror at himself for feeling any kind of enthusiasm under the circumstances.

I have to take someone, he told himself. *If they're already dead and nobody cares what happens to the body that's better, right? Though am I denying them the rituals of their people? Perhaps I could find out what those are and ensure that, if I fail, I take them back here for the priests to deal with their body as they'd wished.*

But what if he succeeded?

Before he could begin to consider the implications, a noise several hundred paces to the right drew his attention. A great dome began to rise from behind a nearby hill. A familiar sound drifted to him, more of a hum than a noise.

The dome grew larger and became a great ball the size of a house, lifted by hinged stilts.

No. Not stilts. Legs. Eight enormous legs.

Tyen gaped at the giant contraption. It was an overgrown insectoid. A smaller sphere, ringed with tiny windows, was attached to the main ball. The silhouette of a driver could be seen within.

The creature lurched forward. Tyen looked towards its destination and, as it altered course, realised it was chasing people. They ran with the speed of terror, but they had no hope of outpacing it. From some kind of protrusion, a liquid sprayed out, sweeping back and forth, and the people fell. Tyen sought the driver's mind . . . and nausea twisted his stomach. The sorcerer inside crowed with victory as he doused his quarry with the poison, achieving two aims with one spray: kill the locals and poison the fields so that the enemy would never challenge his people's right to rule again.

Tyen recoiled. He was breathing in short, shuddering breaths, holding back the need to retch. Before he could recover, the machine began to fade, and in a few heartbeats had disappeared.

383

He stared at the place it had been, wishing that he had imagined it. The ground still steamed. Minds maddened with agony whispered at the edge of his senses. *I thought my own people were despicable for creating war aircarts and spear and arrow throwers in order to conquer and subdue the colonies, but this is so much more ruthless. This never occurred to the worst of the sorcerers of my world.* Something tightened within him. *I can't be held completely responsible for* this. *It has as much to do with my insectoids as a kettle has to do with railsledges! This is a product of* the worlds. *Not my world. Not me.*

And yet they blamed him.

Anger boiled up inside him, leaving him shaking. He wanted to chase after the machine and its driver and destroy both.

No. Not the driver. The machine, yes. Destroying it may be one small, futile act, but if it prevents a few deaths or gives potential victims time to flee or hide, then it is worth doing.

Pushing a little way out of the world, he skimmed to the place the machine had stood when it disappeared. His stomach turned as he saw the bodies of the sorcerer's victims curled up on the ground, their tongues protruding, eyes staring and blood-shot. Whatever poison the man had used, the death was not pleasant.

A path led away, and he followed it. The sorcerer had skimmed across the world, taking his monstrous weapon away from the temple, past cities and over rivers and mountains. He was not ageless, Tyen guessed, noting that the man had stopped several times for no obvious reason except perhaps to breathe.

The path descended into a valley, the bottom of which was darkened by the shapes of men, all the usual features of an organised, army encampment, and several machines. Tyen counted forty-one of the monsters. *Do I destroy one, or all of them?*

Stupid question really.

He let the poisoner's trail take him down into the midst of the encampment, to where the man was climbing down a slim ladder from a hatch in his machine's belly. As Tyen arrived, he stilled air around himself to form a shield. The man stepped off the ladder, looked around and saw him. Tyen met his surprised gaze.

The sorcerer took a step backwards, his eyes moving up and down as he registered that this stranger with a silent mind wore no familiar uniform, nor looked like any race of his world. This stranger with murder in his eyes. He pushed out of the world and fled.

Tyen resisted the temptation to follow. He drew magic from the valley, leaving it darkened to all sorcerous senses, then stilled the air either side of the machine above him and drove it inwards.

The double spheres of the hull crumpled with a satisfying, deafening crunch. Tyen stepped back out of the way as the machine crashed to the ground.

Silence followed.

He looked around, ignoring the many eyes and minds that were fixing on him, and chose another machine to crush. The driver dove out of the belly just in time as it collapsed.

A new noise replaced the silence. The noise of many voices shouting in anger and warning. Tyen moved to the next machine, then the next, and added the sound of metal tearing and crumpling and glass shattering to the protests.

More than a quarter of the monstrosities lay squashed and useless when Tyen heard a new kind of shout. This one was an order. He smiled as the attack came. It was stronger than he'd expected. The attackers had arranged themselves into a small arc to one side of him. They must have used the little power they had left to skim out of the valley in order to collect magic. Either that or they'd held plenty of magic in reserve. He resisted the temptation to rid the world of them, walking away in order to get closer to more machines.

Crushing them was exhilarating. His determination to never kill so often restricted what justice he could seek. Having something non-human to strike against was immensely satisfying. The fact that he was also punishing people who had corrupted mechanical magic made vengeance extra sweet.

Walking between the lines of machines, he rejoiced as each crumpled, and cheered silently as the sorcerers shifted their defence to protecting the machines and failed. He laughed softly as, after the last of them crashed to the ground, another materialised. He let the driver leap clear before he destroyed the giant insectoid.

No more appeared. He turned to look back at the defenders. They staggered backwards, breaking formation as they realised that together they were one easy target. He took a step towards them, and they disappeared as they fled into the place between worlds.

Silence remained. He looked around at the mounds of broken metal. Smaller objects lay between the machines. Looking closer, his mouth went dry as he realised they were bodies.

But I . . . His feet took him towards one. The man's face was contorted in the same way the poison victims' had been. The stink of the liquid filled Tyen's nostrils. *Did some of the poison spray out when I crushed a machine?*

The jubilation and anger in him died. He looked around, noting three other corpses nearby. *How did I not notice?* The unwelcome answer came. He'd been too focused on what towered above him to see the few people who hadn't had the time to run clear of the spray.

I tried not to kill anyone, he reminded himself. *That's better than they deserve.* Yet he felt no better as he pushed out of the world.

As he returned to the temple he forced himself to see the destruction around it, and remember who was to blame. He searched the minds around him, seeing their recollection of the monstrous machines and their poison. *They did far worse than I,* he told himself, but he felt no easing of his conscience.

Several priests huddled in a secret room below ground, the entrance blocked. Their minds were full of concern for the priests who hadn't made it back in time to join them. He found one of the latecomers sprawled in the middle of a street, half crushed by a fallen wall, mind blank but body still warm. Moving away the rubble, Tyen lifted the bloodied corpse and pushed out of the world.

He couldn't retrace his steps exactly. If he took a corpse along well-travelled paths it would attract notice. Someone might see the body and, having heard that the Spy was trying to resurrect the Raen, wonder if this was the traitor. So Tyen forged new paths and then hid them. It was slower, but he did not want to attract any more attention than he must.

He was a few worlds from his new home when he sensed another shadow in the place between. It was behind him, and when he changed direction it followed. Stopping, he turned back to scan the whiteness. A figure emerged, and recognition came even before the man's features were fully visible.

Baluka.

His friend's eyes full of accusation and challenge. Several shadows appeared, joining the Restorers' leader. Though Baluka's mouth did not move, his voice sounded clear in Tyen's mind.

"So. Tyen. Is that to be Valhan's new body, or Vella's?"

CHAPTER 17

Tyen paused. He knew he ought to flee, but something made him hesitate. *Am I foolish enough to think I can explain myself to him?* he wondered. Then a sense of something approaching drew his attention back in the direction he had been travelling. Several more shadows crowded the place between, blocking his path. How many sorcerers surrounded him was hard to tell. More importantly, he had no clue as to their strength while he was in the place between. No doubt Baluka hoped or believed they were strong enough to win if Tyen chose to attack or tried to escape.

Tyen made himself meet and hold Baluka's gaze.

"*Neither*," he replied. "*Which way, then? The last or next world?*"

"*Next.*"

Tyen turned to the sorcerers behind him. They retreated, watching him warily. He followed them to a rocky landscape of interlocking columns as big as mountains. The arrival place was on the flat top of one of these. As Tyen glanced down to make sure the ground was clear of obstacles, he noticed a crystalline lacework of cracks in the surface.

Air surrounded him, and the whine of a restless wind. He stilled it in a protective shield around himself. The sorcerers behind Baluka moved forward to flank their leader as he arrived. They did not suck in a deep breath as they reached the world. Only Baluka began breathing deeply. Only Baluka was not ageless.

Looking around, Tyen counted fifty sorcerers and gauged their strength by what he could read from their minds. They were the strongest of the Restorers, and all had gathered magic in anticipation of a fight.

Destroying the machines had depleted Tyen's store of magic. He had more than enough to leave this world. Enough to put up a good fight too. Whether he had enough for both was doubtful. If he left now, and the next world turned out to have been stripped of magic, he'd be defenceless and trapped.

He reached out to the magic of this world and was not surprised to find that it was patchy and thin. The unevenness hinted at a deliberate draining, as if many sorcerers had travelled around the world taking as much magic as they could. That they hadn't stripped the world completely hinted it was done in a hurry.

A hastily made trap, he concluded. *What if I had tried to retreat to the last world?* He might have forced his way through, and escaped. He might have found the previous world as depleted. There was no point wondering. He was here.

The only chance I have is to talk my way out of this.

Fortunately Baluka wanted to question Tyen. The Restorers would not strike until he ordered it. They were eagerly awaiting that moment, when they could finally deal with the Spy permanently.

Who spotted me travelling between worlds? Tyen wondered. He let out a huff as he read the answer from Baluka's mind. news of Tyen's attack on the machines had spread quickly and the Restorers had been prepared to respond quickly. Tyen might have returned to the workroom safely if he hadn't taken the corpse from the temple. By stopping, he'd given the messenger time to reach Baluka and for the Restorers to catch up with him.

The corpse was a heavy weight in his arms now that he was in a world. He gently set it down on the ground.

"So," Baluka said as he caught his breath. "Why are you carrying a body?"

Tyen glanced around at the sorcerers again. "Can we have a little privacy?"

"You expect me to talk to you alone?"

"If you want answers, you will. I'd do it myself, except I doubt your friends will react well if *I* create a noise shield around *you*." Though it would be pointless if anyone could read lips. He did a quick scan, and was relieved to find none had that skill.

Baluka frowned, then took a step forward. One of his companions made a low noise, but he silenced the man with a raised hand. After another step, Baluka stopped. The sound of wind ceased.

"Speak," the man ordered.

Tyen turned his palms upwards. "What would you like to know?"

Baluka looked down at the corpse. "If this is not for Valhan or Vella, what is it for?"

"A rich merchant with a terminal disease," Tyen told him truthfully. He was not yet sure how much Baluka knew, so it was safer to tell the truth. If he was caught lying, it would make the man distrust everything he said. But that didn't mean he couldn't avoid telling some truths.

The rebel's eyebrows rose. "So you are not, as Rielle claims, attempting to resurrect Valhan?"

Tyen lifted his shoulders. "I am."

Baluka's mouth opened, then closed again. "You admit that?"

"I won't say I never lie, but I avoid it unless doing so will protect others from harm."

"You could justify a great deal, saying that." Baluka crossed his arms. "Like spying on the rebels you claimed to be supporting – and then leading."

Tyen spread his hands. "I am sorry, Baluka. Sorry that I deceived you. But I am not sorry that I tried to keep the rebels from attacking the Raen, or that I minimised the damage when they did. My intention was to save lives – and yes, that included my own. If the Raen hadn't intended to die, the rebels would all have been slaughtered before I became leader."

"Or we may have survived and won," Baluka pointed out.

Tyen nodded. "I actually thought you would, at the end. I wanted you to, even as I hoped the only person who could help Vella wasn't about to perish."

Baluka said nothing as he considered Tyen's words. Watching the man's thoughts, Tyen saw that Baluka was disturbed to find Tyen was neither pretending to be the same man he'd thought he'd known, nor had he transformed into a different person once confronted with the truth. He was seeing the man he had glimpsed the one time Tyen had laid bare his mind.

But Baluka's anger was deep, and he wasn't ready to forgive Tyen yet.

"Is that why you're trying to resurrect him?" Baluka asked. "To give Vella a body?"

"No. If I can resurrect him, I can resurrect Vella."

"Then why do you want to bring him back?"

How much can I risk telling him? Tyen wondered. *As much as I have to, to safe my life.*

"I don't. Dahli does. He believes the Raen is the only one who can end the chaos and wars in the worlds—"

"Chaos? Wars?" Baluka let out a disbelieving huff. "Do you mean the chaos and wars in which your invention wreaks the worst damage?"

"I'm working on a solution, Baluka. We've made excellent progress." Here, Tyen hoped, was a reason for Baluka to let him live. "If I can't get rid of them, Baluka, who can?"

"Valhan is not the solution to everything!" Baluka exclaimed. He drew a deep breath and let it out slowly. "There are countless people in the worlds. Given the freedom to learn and teach and move about, the chances are that solutions will be found for many – if not all – of the worlds' problems. Besides, there are more worlds at peace than at war now – and more joining them every cycle. Chaos was inevitable after the Raen died, but it will not last. There will always be wars somewhere, but only local conflicts, more easily resolved with the help of the Restorers."

He believed it, Tyen saw. While Tyen could dismiss Baluka's optimism, he could not overlook the man's knowledge of the state of the worlds. It wasn't entirely based on the information given by the men and women who reported to him. Baluka regularly ventured out to gauge the state of the worlds for himself, at no small risk to himself.

Yet I have seen war and chaos in the worlds, Tyen thought. Worlds Dahli had shown him. Worlds he'd passed through on the way to find volunteers for resurrection, or to attempt a resurrection. Worlds like the ones poisoned by the machines he'd just destroyed. He'd seen Dahli's mind, and knew the man believed the worlds were descending into chaos as much as Baluka was sure they were not. *But perhaps he sees what he expects.*

Perhaps Baluka saw what he expected too.

"The war machines are a small problem compared to the cost in human lives if you bring back the Raen, Tyen. Is freeing Vella worth that? One human life in exchange for countless others?"

"Rielle thought the same when she saved Qall," Tyen pointed out.

"Yet she asked me to stop you resurrecting the Raen. She understands he is the greater danger." Baluka frowned. "She said you knew that the Raen intended to kill her. Do you want her dead?"

"No, of course not. But she was far away, and I assumed she would be as safe there from Valhan as from Dahli." Tyen frowned. "Why did she return?"

"That is not for me to say," Baluka replied, though the truth was clear in his mind – she had tried to get a message to Qall's adoptive family, and in doing so had stumbled upon Dahli and the news Tyen was trying to resurrect the Raen. She had told Baluka what she'd learned, then returned to her place of hiding.

Tyen paused. How much of his plans could he trust to Baluka, and the many sorcerers who could read the man's mind? Did he have any choice? "Dahli would much prefer to use Qall than another vessel. I am giving him an alternative. As long as Rielle and Qall stay in hiding, they are safe. It's likely to take me some time to work out how to resurrect someone, which should give her time to get as far away as possible."

Baluka's lips parted, but he did not speak. *So if I eliminate Tyen, I give Dahli a greater incentive to search for her. Is Tyen hinting that he is doing this to help Rielle? He said he didn't want to resurrect the Raen. Is he being forced to, or is he intending to fail? Should the Restorers try harder to find and eliminate Dahli instead? Rielle said we had to find the hand, not kill Tyen.* Letting Tyen go would weaken him in the eyes of the Restorers . . . or would it? His closest followers trusted his instincts, sometimes more than he did.

As the other man considered these questions, Tyen's hopes grew. Baluka was realising that, if Tyen was telling the truth, he had to let him go. If he killed Tyen, Dahli would redouble his efforts to find Qall and Rielle. If he found them, it would be partly Baluka's fault.

Tyen looked down at the corpse. The longer he waited to shift the body to the volunteer's pattern, the less chance he would be able to repair the deterioration. If Baluka let him go, he'd be a fool to go straight back to the workshop. He'd have to take a longer way home, using all the methods of concealing his path that he could.

"You have two options," Tyen said. "Kill me and put Rielle and Qall in greater danger – and lose a chance of ridding the worlds of war machines, or let me continue with all my experiments while you prepare the worlds to face the Raen again." He lifted his eyebrows in a challenge. "How sure are you that the rebels would have defeated him if he hadn't killed himself, Baluka?"

"Sure enough," Baluka murmured, holding back the doubts that threatened the certainty he'd held on to since the battle.

Tyen nodded. "As am I." He managed a wan smile. "I can't tell you how long you have to prepare. Killing me will give you more time only if Dahli doesn't find Qall. Letting me live at least has the added possible consequence of ridding the worlds of the war machines."

Baluka's mind swirled with choices and imagined consequences. His instincts told him to trust Tyen, but then they had been wrong before. Or had they been right all along?

"Very well." The whistling wind split the air again as Baluka let the noise shield go. "Go." *But if you do care about Rielle, Qall and the worlds*, he thought at Tyen, *don't resurrect the Raen. Destroy the hand.*

Tyen did not wait for the surprise and disbelief on the other sorcerers' faces to turn to anger and rebellion. Leaving the corpse, he pushed out of the world and fled.

CHAPTER 18

*D*estroy *the hand.*

Tyen paced the workroom. He'd taken a long, circuitous route back, using as many precautions as he could incorporate into the journey. Baluka had let him go, intending to order the Restorers to leave Tyen alone, but it was always possible that he would change his mind, or that his followers might rebel against the order. As far as Tyen could tell, nobody had tracked him to here. Several days had passed and no pack of vengeful sorcerers had appeared.

Neither had Dahli nor Zeke. Tyen dared not attempt finding another corpse. Unable to continue with resurrection experiments and having had no new ideas for how to deal with memory storage in the humanoid, he'd turned his mind to the war machine problem instead, taking over Zeke's work.

But it was hard to concentrate. His mind kept returning to the bodies on the field of smashed war machines. *I didn't kill them deliberately or directly, yet if it wasn't for me they'd be alive. Whether they deserved to die or not doesn't matter. They were people, with lives and loved ones. Fathers and mothers, maybe wives and children. For all I know, they were servants, or did not want to kill but were forced to fight in that war.*

It sickened him, and hardened his resolve to avoid killing. That only made him more nervous about working with Dahli. The man had been pushing at Tyen's discomfort and scruples, forcing him to concede a little here and a little there. One day, the man was going to bring the corpse of someone he'd killed, and argue that the situation of the murder made it acceptable. Perhaps the victim had attacked him. Perhaps they had attacked someone else. Perhaps they had made war machines and used them on innocent, defenceless people.

The prospect of that filled him with horror and dread, so he fixed his mind instead on Baluka's request. Destroying Valhan's hand *was* the only sure way to prevent the Raen's return. Another vessel could always be found – or at least Tyen believed so – but lose the store of memories and you lose the person.

It wasn't that he hadn't thought of it before, but Dahli had gone to extreme efforts to keep the hand safe. He would not produce it until Tyen had proven he could resurrect someone, and had a vessel ready for Valhan. Even then, Dahli would not simply trust Tyen with the hand without ensuring his cooperation. Most likely he'd demand Tyen give him something he valued, that he'd threaten to destroy if Tyen betrayed him.

Probably Vella.

A chill ran down Tyen's spine. He was not willing to sacrifice Vella in order to get hold of the hand. She was a person, albeit not a complete one. If he went ahead and resurrected the Raen, there was a chance he'd not get Vella back anyway. Valhan might not approve of Tyen's intention to work slowly, to give Rielle time to get to safety. Tyen had made up his mind to send Vella somewhere safe, before he resurrected Valhan, in case the ruler punished him. At least she would get away safely.

I have to give Dahli something else to hold on to as a guarantee of my cooperation. Something I appear to value more. He considered what he owned. *Beetle?* He shook his head. *I don't think Dahli would believe that it was as valuable to me as Vella is. Besides, I could easily have made and given him an identical insectoid – or make a new Beetle if the old one is destroyed.*

Another obstacle lay in the way of getting hold of Valhan's hand. Tyen would have to succeed in his experiments. Instead of delaying, he'd need to speed up his efforts. A part of him had begun to worry that Dahli was right: Valhan had ensured somehow that only Qall could be the vessel of his memories. If he had, his memory of doing so would be in the hand. Though surely Dahli would have looked for that information in the hand, and not recruited Tyen if he knew there was no alternative to using Qall.

Was there another way to persuade Dahli to produce the hand? *Perhaps by convincing him that I need more information.* It would still require Tyen to produce something he valued for Dahli to hold as insurance.

What else did he value? He owned no other objects of value. That only left people.

Tarran. Baluka. Or Rielle.

Tyen's chest tightened as he remembered what he had seen in Baluka's mind. Rielle's fury. Her belief that Tyen had deceived her. *I don't want her hurt, and I certainly don't want her to die.* He wished he could explain to her why he had chosen to help Dahli. *And tell her to stay away.* He sighed. *How did I get to the point where I want the woman I desire as far away from me as possible?*

He'd wondered many times how events could have worked out differently. It had occurred to him a few days ago that, if Rielle hadn't left to protect Qall, they might have joined together to tackle Dahli. He wasn't sure what they could have done once they discovered Dahli had blocked his memory of the hand's location though. He doubted killing Dahli would have solved the problem. The man was too smart to not have left instructions in place to protect the hand and put it in the hands of people who could continue his quest to resurrect the Raen.

Besides, Tyen wasn't sure he could bring himself to kill him. Perhaps Rielle would. She had Qall to protect.

The trouble is, there is no right side or wrong side in this. No unquestionable good and pure evil. The Raen helped the worlds as much as he harmed them. Dahli believes the worlds need Valhan. He wants to keep the promise he made to the man he loves and is loyal to. He has lived longer than Baluka and can see the chaos in the worlds is worse than it has ever been in his lifetimes. Rielle and Baluka believe as strongly that the worlds will settle down given the chance — are already settling down — and have a right to live free from the control of an all-powerful ruler. Which is something Dahli cannot prove wrong since he has never seen the worlds not controlled by the—

A throat cleared behind him.

He jumped and spun around. Zeke stood in the centre of the room, one eyebrow rising.

"Heh," he said. "*I* managed to spook *you* for once."

"Zeke," Tyen said. "Where have you been? Is Dahli . . .?"

The answer was clear in Zeke's mind, and the young man knew it, but he explained anyway.

"Qall has joined us. Willingly. He wants to meet you. I'm to take you there."

Tyen realised his mouth was hanging open, and closed it quickly. Mind spinning with the news, he stood, donned his jacket, walked over to the young inventor and held out his hand.

As soon as Tyen took it, the room began to fade. The journey was slow, as they had to stop in each world for Zeke to catch his breath and gather more magic, but Tyen held back from offering to transport them. He needed time to absorb what he'd just learned.

Qall had *joined* Dahli. Sought him out, if Zeke was right. If Qall was as powerful as Valhan, he must have seen into Dahli's mind and learned what the man wanted to do to him. Why would he submit to that?

The answer was obvious, especially when Tyen had seen the plan in Dahli's mind, and glimpsed the efforts he'd been going to in order to keep track of the Traveller family that had protected Qall. Dahli must be threatening to harm the family if Qall didn't do as he ordered.

Zeke doesn't know about it, Tyen guessed. Zeke did not know why Qall wanted to meet Tyen, and believed Dahli didn't either. *If he's right, that proves Qall is stronger than Dahli.*

Sooner than Tyen expected, Zeke stopped. "We're nearly there. The next world is a dead one. The one after contains the base." He paused, wondering if Dahli expected him to accompany Tyen from here, or flee.

To Tyen's surprise, the young inventor knew the true purpose of Tyen's experiments. Dahli had given in to Zeke's demands to explain, warning him that if he did, Zeke couldn't roam the worlds alone in case anyone read his mind. Zeke was neither aghast at nor gladdened by the prospect of the Raen's return, but when Qall appeared he'd realised Dahli's plan had changed, and he suspected he wouldn't like it.

When Qall had explained what Dahli meant to do to him, Zeke had been appalled. He had argued with Dahli, who had reminded him of his warning. *I knew I couldn't leave*, Zeke thought. *I didn't want to leave. So if Dahli was worried someone would read of his plan from my mind, why did he trust me to fetch Tyen? Was he giving me a chance to leave?*

Zeke looked at Tyen and, knowing that his thoughts would have been read, he spoke his question aloud. "Do you think it's a test of my loyalty?"

Tyen shrugged. "I have no idea." *Yet.*

The young inventor looked at Tyen's face closely, trying to read his expression. He was telling himself that Tyen had no reason to dump him in one of the dead worlds that surrounded Dahli's location, or abandon him here now, but the possibility still lurked at the edge of his mind.

"What's the base world like?" Tyen asked.

"A world rich in power," Zeke replied.

"A fortification," Tyen guessed. Like Valhan's palace had been, it was surrounded by dead worlds. If attacked, Dahli and his allies could strip the base world so that invaders must hold back enough magic to retreat through several dead worlds, or risk being stranded. No sorcerer was likely to stumble upon Dahli's hideout either. They'd retreat from the dead worlds, not daring to go further in case the next one was dead as well, and they didn't have enough magic to return.

"We're to arrive within the lamps," Zeke added, an image of a hall appearing in his mind. "I don't know why."

A trap? "Tell me what the dead world between here and the base is like."

Zeke shrugged. "Nothing exciting. Rural. Peaceful."

It was hard to believe after the strange and dangerous worlds that had surrounded Valhan's palace, but perhaps Dahli had not been able to find an arrangement of worlds as suitable for a hidden fortification. Tyen questioned Zeke about Dahli's hideout, but the inventor hadn't seen much. It was an abandoned palace, the arrival place in the hall with the lamps. Dahli had ordered Qall to stay there, and had beds and furniture brought in.

"That's all I can tell you," Zeke said.

Tyen nodded. "Do you want to return?"

Zeke sighed. Despite everything, he still wanted to be with Dahli. "Yes."

Tyen took hold of Zeke's arm, moved into the place between worlds and started following the path he found there. They passed through the benign but dead world Zeke had described and continued on. The huge, square hall built of black marble he'd seen in Zeke's mind emerged from the paleness of the place between. *It will not be easy to see the shadows of approaching sorcerers here*, Tyen mused. Torches set in black iron stands no higher than his hip outlined a raised square in the centre of the room, and he moved to a position within them. Within the square of torches stood a low bed and several gold chairs with padded seats and backs. Two of the chairs were occupied.

The first occupant was Dahli, and Tyen felt a twinge of anticipation as he prepared to read the man's thoughts, but the moment he saw the other, his mind froze.

The Raen! He's already resurrected the Raen! As he arrived, his heart lurched and began racing, even as he told himself: *No. This must be Qall.*

At once he began searching for differences. Valhan had looked older, he decided, though he couldn't pinpoint why. He detected no thoughts, and was immediately aware that his own were available to this man — who had risen and was now walking towards him, smiling in a way that made him no longer resemble Valhan at all.

Did I ever see Valhan smile? he wondered. *Perhaps, but not like this.*

Dahli followed a few steps behind. Tyen met the man's eyes as he searched his mind. He saw that Dahli was watching his reaction closely, and had noted a flash of fear in Tyen's face. He was pleased to have seen no dislike. He imagined Tyen was now a bit disorientated, and felt sympathy, though he doubted the resemblance affected Tyen as much as it did him. Every hint that an inexperienced young man lived within the familiar body brought Dahli pain and discomfort. Qall was not the man Dahli desired, so every flash of longing his appearance sparked brought embarrassment and guilt.

Disturbed by the glimpse of Dahli's inner turmoil, Tyen shifted his attention to Zeke. Like Dahli, Zeke's calm exterior hid roiling emotions. Jealousy, anger, admiration and hope seized him in turns. Until Qall had arrived, Zeke had seen his chances of gaining Dahli's full attention growing more promising each day. He didn't hate Qall for spoiling that, knowing enough of the situation to see the young man was blameless, but he was dismayed to learn Dahli was still pining for a dead man — who he intended to resurrect. While he sympathised, he didn't think it was likely anyone could bring someone back from the dead, so he figured his prospects were good if he hung around long enough.

You have to admire his optimism, Tyen thought, turning his attention back to Qall.

Qall's lips had curled up at the sides a little, but as he stopped and Dahli reached his side his expression smoothed.

"Tyen," he said. "It is good to finally meet you. I have been looking forward to it."

"And I you, Qall," Tyen replied. "How is Rielle?"

"Alive and well last time I saw her." Qall's eyebrows rose. "Though *very* angry with you."

Tyen winced. "I expect so. Where is she?"

"Don't worry: she won't be bothering you for some time." The young man's eyes gleamed with amusement.

Alarmed, Tyen looked at Dahli.

"Don't look at me that way," Dahli said, raising both hands. "I wasn't even there."

Nor did he know where Rielle was. Qall had said he'd trapped Rielle in a world by stripping it of power when he knew she had too few reserves of magic to leave it. Though it had been Inekera's idea, the young man had done it willingly to stop Rielle following him.

"You left her in a world without magic?" Tyen hissed, turning back to Qall. "Don't you realise what that means?" The young man's eyes flickered and his face froze, and suddenly he looked like Valhan again. And yet . . . a hint of doubt and worry in his eyes betrayed him, and gave Tyen the courage to go on. "She will no longer be ageless. Or be able to protect herself."

"I'll send someone back to free her when I'm ready," Qall replied. "In the meantime, she can look after herself."

"With what?" Tyen demanded. Conscious that Dahli was watching, he moderated his voice to sound more persuasive than angry. "Her strength? Without magic, she is just a young woman, defenceless and homeless, unable to read minds. Her looks will attract the worst kind of attention. As a stranger from another world, she may be blamed for the loss of magic. I'm surprised you would do that to her, after the kindness she has shown you."

Qall's face was stiff, but his eyes were wide. "It . . . it won't be for long, I'm sure," he assured Tyen.

"How long?" Tyen asked. He took a step closer to Qall. "Tell me where she is and I will make sure she is in no danger."

The young man began to look at Dahli, then stopped. His brows lowered and shoulders straightened.

"No." He drew in a deep breath. "The place I left her was fertile, civilised and peaceful." He paused. "You can't trick me into telling you so you can find and kill her."

Tyen blinked in surprise, then immediately he understood the young man's words. Qall's voice and manner were all determination now, and yet his eyes were pleading.

He's trying to stop me from leaving and revealing I am not truly on Dahli's side. He needs me.

Tyen itched to leave and search for Rielle, but he could see how impossible the task would be. He could seek out worlds recently stripped of magic, but searching for one person within just one world could take many cycles, and hundreds of dead worlds existed now.

He drew in a deep breath. *Why am I so angry?* It wasn't anger so much as alarm and concern. *I was fine knowing Rielle hated me so long as she was alive and safe. Now . . . I might never see her again. Might never get the chance to explain my plan . . .*

His plan. His brilliant plan to distract Dahli in order to give Rielle time to find a safe place to hide, and so he could warn Baluka if the Raen was likely to return. *It's all ruined. First Rielle finds out what I'm doing and tells Baluka; then Qall leaves her stranded and joins Dahli.*

That was why he was angry. Qall had spoiled everything.

Why? Why give himself up when he had been safe at the edges of the worlds?

Perhaps because he wasn't safe. Perhaps Dahli had found them. Tyen looked at Dahli for confirmation, but the man was distracted. He and Zeke had moved away a few steps and were arguing in low tones. He couldn't make out what they were saying, though they stood close by.

"That's because I've created a noise shield that warps sounds, so while we can hear them and they can hear us, the sounds are unintelligible," Qall said. "We don't have long before they notice, however." He met and held Tyen's gaze. "Rielle believed that as long as Dahli couldn't communicate his threats to us, the Travellers would be safe. Inekera told me that Dahli's next step would be to kill them, one by one, and send the news of each death out in all directions in the hope it found me. Staying away was not going to save them." He grimaced. "He has people in place, ready to kill if he gives the order, or news arrives that he is dead. And he isn't just threatening to kill my family, but all Travellers."

Tyen nodded to show he understood. "What will you do?"

"I . . . haven't decided. That's why I asked for you to join us. I needed to know where you stood. Now that I do, I am more hopeful."

"But my plan is worthless."

"Yes, but you are smart. You'll come up with another." Qall smiled faintly. "Dahli isn't as ruthless as I expected either. He doesn't want to—" He stopped, and Tyen grew aware that Dahli and Zeke had stopped talking. Qall turned to Dahli as the man moved to his side. "Can we sit and chat?"

"Of course," Dahli replied. He gestured towards the chairs and looked at Tyen. "Shall we?"

Tyen nodded. "I'd be honoured."

The four of them strolled back to the golden seats, all polite and smiling, as if one of them did not expect another to help him destroy a third's mind and replace it with the memories of a thousand-cycle-old ruler.

PART SIX

RIELLE

CHAPTER 15

O n the morning of the fifth day, the pickers weren't given baskets and sent out into a field. Instead, a few coins were pressed into their hands, and they were escorted to the road.

Rielle looked down at the four small squares of tarnished copper, then up at the other workers. None were protesting, though they didn't look happy. None looked surprised either. Only resigned. They formed several small groups and one larger one that Rielle had guessed was an extended family; then began leaving, setting off in either direction along the road.

The three women Rielle had grown most friendly with had not moved yet. They were murmuring in low voices, frowning and looking at their coins. One said something, and the others glanced at Rielle. After a moment, the one named Bel beckoned. Grateful to be included, Rielle wandered over to stand with them. They didn't step back to include her in their circle but, after another short discussion, they gave her reassuring smiles and started walking. She fell into step with them.

They were of about the age Rielle had been when she'd met Baluka and the Travellers, and clearly were very familiar with picking. Like all the locals, they were wiry and short, and surprisingly strong for their size. They'd shown Rielle how to best strap on the enormous baskets the field workers used, and avoid the fluff full of tiny spines that grew from the stalks of the strange bulbous plant they'd been harvesting. When Rielle all but collapsed, trembling with exhaustion, during each inadequately short rest break, they'd been sympathetic.

Now they walked slowly but with purpose. They chatted quietly, two walking ahead and two behind. Mai was the most talkative, and she enjoyed teaching Rielle words of the local language. None of them spoke the Traveller tongue. Only the foreman of the farm had, and then very badly. He'd been surprised that Rielle had known the language. She'd made up a story of learning it from a Traveller, and though he'd frowned in disbelief he'd still hired her. Since the farm owner had decided to harvest early, he needed more pickers but had no more money to pay them, so hiring a foreigner not only gained him an extra pair of hands but quietened the grumbling from the workers about the cut in their pay, fearful that more foreign workers would be brought in to fill the jobs.

For the same reason, most of the pickers had been wary of her at first, but it was soon obvious that if she represented these foreigners, they weren't going to be much of a threat. She was too slight for the heavy work and unused to long days of exertion.

It was not what she'd have chosen to do, but she had little choice. Nobody in these parts had any use for a painter, weaver or mosaic designer. The nearest city was still a few days' walk away, she had been hungry and tired, and the foreman had warned her that the city was a dangerous place for a lone, foreign woman.

The sun had passed the zenith and was sinking towards the distant hills when the road met a larger thoroughfare. Not far along this, a faint noise behind them drew their attention to an approaching four-wheeled cart full of the same crop they'd been harvesting. It was pulled by a squat beast with a stumpy tail that waddled dramatically as it walked. Mai called out to the driver, and a long exchange followed, the girls quickening their pace to keep up. Then all three women stepped up to the wagon and each pressed one of the coins into his hand. Rielle did the same, her stomach sinking as a third of her wealth disappeared. She thought wistfully of the gemstones and spices she had pressed into Timane's hands before setting off after Qall.

At least Timane will be fine if I never escape this world and come back for her. Rielle missed the girl, who had become the closest thing to a friend she'd had for over five cycles.

The wagon did not slow as the girls hurried to the back and scrambled aboard. Each rearranged the crop to form a hollow, then covered it with their shawl to avoid the fluff. Not having such a garment, Rielle perched on top so as little of her skin or clothing was in contact with the spines as possible.

Though the wagon moved slowly, it was a faster mode of transport than walking. Rielle's body now ached not just from the picking, but from the day's journey as well. She concentrated on keeping her balance, taking reassurance from the cheerful talk of the girls.

The sun was setting and the wagon had crested the side of a hill when Bel exclaimed and pointed. Following her gesture, Rielle saw a great delta spread below. The threads of the river were different colours, combining to form an oily grey spilling out into a distant sea. A closer look revealed that these colours leaked from buildings crowding all of the land between. Memories of Rielle's childhood flashed into her mind, full of vivid shades and hues. They were so powerful she could almost smell the dyes and mordants.

Then she realised she *could* smell dyes and mordants. A breeze had set the girls' hair fluttering – and their noses wrinkling. They made disgusted sounds, exchanged a few words and laughed.

Looking out towards the sea, Rielle traced the oily slick to the horizon. She couldn't see the end of it. Her parents' dyeworks had released wastes into the local river, downstream of the city. People complained from time to time, and bribes had been made to quieten them.

Mother said if they want their clothes and awnings coloured, they have to put up with the consequences. I have no idea where the wastes

411

went, downriver from Fyre. She couldn't see many boats, either on the river or sea below. Even so, she would avoid eating anything that looked as if it had swum or grown in water.

It was fully dark when the wagon reached the city gates, and cold enough to set Rielle shivering. The girls hopped off, carefully shaking and picking spiny fluff off their shawls. Bel helped Rielle clean it off her clothing, then produced a piece of string and tied Rielle's hair into a bun at the back of her neck, in the same way they wore theirs. They examined each other's fingers and cleaned their nails. This attention to appearance made Rielle even more conscious of the fact that she hadn't bathed since Qall had abandoned her in this world, and no doubt stank.

Once satisfied with their appearance, the women straightened their backs and strode towards the gates.

Guards questioned them, eyeing Rielle suspiciously, but the confidence of the talkative women and another round of coins got them through the gate. Then the women's expressions became grim and determined. Sticking close together, and gesturing for Rielle to do the same, they dodged drains overflowing with excrement and rubbish and the advances of the multitude of men crowding the narrow streets. The latter were a constant source of calls and harassment, and once they had to break into a run to avoid a small gang of them. Another time they had to pull Vil away from a man who had stepped out of an alley and grabbed her hair. These men hesitated when they saw Rielle, however. A foreigner clearly made them wary.

I will always be the stranger, she thought. *In the only place I am a local – my home city – I am not welcome either. Will I ever find a place to call home again? Will I even survive being stranded in this world?*

At least it was warmer in the city. Eventually they reached a quieter part, Mai sacrificing a single coin in order to pass through a gate. The rest of their coin was pooled in order to purchase sleeping space on the floor of a room with one side open to the

street, and a meagre meal of some kind of grain and a gritty
sauce. They ate huddled between men and women sitting cross-
legged, their hands rapidly rising and falling as they stitched
decoration onto clothing.

It was still dark when Rielle was shaken awake by Bel. The
girl led Rielle out of the room and down the street to where a
tributary of the river replaced the buildings on one side. The air
stank of human waste and worse. On the riverside, flimsy, dirty
rooms barely large enough for one person had been made out of
old cloth, and outside each was a queue of men and women. Bel
and Rielle joined one, and it wasn't long before it was clear the
awnings were the local version of a toilet. All they contained
inside was a stretch of the wall, but it was evident from the muck
coating the outer side that users were meant to squat over it to
relieve themselves while not overbalancing and ending up in the
river. So many locals had been more concerned about falling than
aiming correctly that the top of the wall was almost as soiled.

When they returned to the room, the other two girls were
awake and the sun was rising. They took turns to hold up shawls
for privacy as they washed with a rag soaked in a bucket of cloudy
water, standing in the tiny space between a different set of men
and women bent over their sewing. After attending to their appearance again, they set off back towards the gate.

Tired, sore and still feeling filthy, all too aware that she now
had no money and would still be stranded out in the country if
not for the help of these girls, Rielle followed passively. When
they reached the gate, they did not pass through it out into the
menacing streets. Instead they entered a large building beside it,
the façade marred by an ineffectual attempt to repair a crack that
ran all the way to the roof with some kind of crumbling mortar.

Inside were hundreds of people sitting on the floor, shoulders
hunched, sewing rapidly. Beside them were precarious stacks of
cloth of various sizes and shapes. Nobody looked up as they
entered. Small, oddly subdued children sat beside the piles, or

lay on the floor sleeping. In one corner, a group of older children hunched over, tiny fingers moving with uncanny dexterity and speed. More men and women were walking back and forth across the room watching the workers closely, or leaning over them in an intimidating way.

Mai led them into a small room. Behind a table – the first Rielle had seen anywhere – sat a grim-faced man. He eyed them all, his frown deepening as he saw Rielle. At a question from him, Mai reached over to Rielle and grabbed her wrist, turning Rielle's hands palms up. The man examined them briefly and looked dissatisfied. He gave what sounded like instructions, scribbled on a scrap of cloth and handed it to Mai.

They returned to the main room, where Mai approached one of the men examining the sewers' work. He asked questions, to which the girls supplied quick answers. When he got to Rielle, Mai answered for her. A frown that was growing all too familiar creased his forehead. Turning away, he gestured for them to follow, then wove through the seated workers and towers of cloth at a pace Rielle had difficulty keeping up with. At one point, she grew a little dizzy, lost her balance and had to grab a tower of fabric to prevent herself from slipping over, earning a savage scowl from the worker beside it. Finding she had fallen behind, she hurried to catch up again.

Fortunately, the examiner had stopped to speak to a man with a plaited beard. He gestured in a way that made it clear they were to join this man, but as Rielle went to follow, he caught her arm. Dragging her away, he guided her to a corner where mounds of fabric had been piled up to the ceiling. It was much warmer here – uncomfortably so. He called out to a woman with greasy hair and, his tone turning disparaging, gestured to his mouth. The woman's shoulders sagged, but she nodded and beckoned. The man pushed Rielle towards the woman, then strode away.

Rubbing her arm, Rielle approached the woman, who ushered her to the edge of one of the mounds. Looking closer, Rielle saw they weren't made up of fabric but of completed garments. Workers were picking up enormous armfuls of these and carrying them away. The woman's gestures implied that Rielle should do the same. Gathering as much fabric as she could, Rielle staggered as the woman added even more. Rielle's tired arms and aching shoulders trembled, but she did not object.

Who'd have guessed clothing weighed so much? she mused as she followed the other workers into a dimly lit room. At once, an unbearable humidity pressed in around her, carrying a sickly sweet odour. Vents at floor level pumped this pungent steam into the room. There was a queue; those in line waited while the worker in front dropped his or her bundle of clothing into a huge basket, then began arranging each piece onto hangers swinging from racks filling the right side of the room. More workers were removing clothing from racks on the left side, folding them with precise and practised speed.

All of the workers in the room were coughing, and Rielle soon joined them. One of the folders paused to cough into a scrap of cloth, and before he tucked it away in his sleeve, she saw dots of red. The man was shouted at by an examiner hovering by the door, and his movements became hurried.

The ache in Rielle's arms turned to pain. She hugged the bundle closer, but it made no difference. When it was the turn of the worker in front of Rielle to drop his bundle of clothing into the basket, one piece slipped off onto the floor. Out of the steam stepped another examiner, screaming at him as he snatched the soiled garment off the floor. Rielle shifted her grip on her burden again, half dizzy from breathing the steam, and watched how the man in front arranged the clothing on the racks. The pieces were all some kind of tunic top, with slanted shoulders and a collar that was awkward to hang neatly.

How did I get here? she wondered. Her past seemed like someone else's life. She suspected that if she told anyone here her story, it would sound like a fantastic tale made up to entertain children.

Maybe it *was* just a story. Or a dream. Maybe she'd woken up from a fanciful dream about magic to a living nightmare. If the nightmare hadn't been as different to her childhood as the dream, she might have believed it.

Suddenly it was her turn to deposit the bundle of clothes into the basket. She took care not to drop any, catching one tunic just before it reached the floor. Next she turned her attention to the hanging, and earned several shouted reprimands from the examiner before she got it right. By the time she was done, the length of the line behind her had tripled, and she passed several annoyed and worried faces as she returned to the mounds of clothing outside.

With each load she grew faster at the job, though never as deft as her co-workers. Time crawled by, and she had lost count of the trips she'd made to the steam room when a bell rang and all work ceased. Relief washed over her in a dizzying rush. Most of the sewers set aside their work and rose, but many gathered up more fabric and carried it with them. Rielle guessed that they needed extra money, or else hadn't made up their quota yet.

All of the garment hangers looked to the woman who had instructed Rielle on the task, then each hurried away when the woman nodded at them. When the woman looked at Rielle, her lips thinned and she shook her head, but then a young voice spoke out, and Mai stepped out from the milling crowd of workers to join Rielle. The woman pursed her lips, then nodded reluctantly. Mai smiled at Rielle and pulled her away.

She rescued me, though I'm not sure exactly what from. Most likely I didn't do as much work as I should have, and Mai told her I would make up for it tomorrow.

She wasn't sure she *could* make up for it. As she followed Mai out of the building, she could not stop coughing. Thinking of the man in the steam room who had hacked up blood, a panicky feeling began to steal over her.

I can't do this. I'll die before Qall comes back to free me. I'll certainly never last until this world recovers enough magic for me to leave it.

416

She had to find another way to survive. As Mai joined Vil and Bel, a plan began to form in Rielle's mind. She would take the money she'd earned here today and make her way to better parts of the city to seek out artisans. If she had to use some of her remaining magic to get there safely, she would.

But none of the workers were given coins as they left. Rielle tried to ask Mai about it, tracing squares on her palm and miming the swapping of them for food. The girl shook her head and mimed sewing, flashed eight fingers four times, then drew a square on her palm and indicated four fingers.

Four coins for thirty-two days' work. Rielle's legs grew weak. Mai saw her sway, slipped an arm around her shoulders and helped her negotiate the filthy gutters as they returned to their room. Vil and Bel at once began to work on the bundles of garments they'd brought with them. Mai plucked a needle from within the seam of her clothing, measured a length of thread and began helping them. Rielle held out her hands, indicating she would help, but Mai shook her head, pointing to her needle, then Rielle.

No needle. Rielle hoped her relief wasn't obvious. With no way to help these wonderful, generous women, she curled up on the floor and fell asleep, only waking for a brief time when Mai roused her to eat another tiny meal.

CHAPTER 16

S ince her stranding had begun, Rielle had thought of only three ways she could escape the world.

Her first option was to do as Valhan had done to free himself from her home world: wait until enough magic had been generated. He'd been stranded for over twenty cycles – and had to travel from one side of her world to the other in order to gather enough to leave. This world was small enough that she could reach all the magic in it, so she would not have to travel. How quickly the people would generate enough magic for her to leave was difficult to guess. It depended on how large the population was. A greater population meant a higher percentage of people undertaking creative activities and a better chance that one or more Makers existed, creating magic in greater quantities than the average person. No matter how many Makers there were, or how many people were creating, it was still likely to take many cycles for enough magic to be generated to allow her to escape.

Her second option had been simply to hope that Qall would return for her. She had given up on guessing what the chances of that were. Waiting depended on him being alive, willing to retrieve her and free to do so. She refused to think that he would never come back if he was able to, but would he be able to relocate the world and find her within it? Here, among the multitudes of locals, her mind would be one among thousands. She would have been easier to find in the farm, as one among hundreds.

It would be easier to find her if she gained employment with artisans, because Qall would look for her among them first.

Her third option was to find an arrival place and hope someone would visit this world with enough stored magic to leave again – then persuade them to take her out. She would need to find one soon, before warnings were posted in neighbouring worlds that this one no longer contained any magic. She also needed a sure way to convince the visitor to help her. It was likely that otherworlders were hurrying to arrival places with the same idea in mind, and sorcerers outside this world might even be visiting it with a view to exploiting the situation, demanding payment from those they transported out.

She had nothing of value to offer them, but who she was might make a difference – though that had the potential to go badly. If they were an ally of Dahli, they'd leave her trapped so Dahli could return and kill her while she was helpless. If they were an ally of the Restorers, they would take her to Baluka. She could use some of her remaining magic to read their mind before she approached them, however.

A hand touched Rielle's shoulder, so she opened her eyes and pushed her aching body upright. This time Vil accompanied her to the toilets. Rielle went first, then, when the young woman was inside, hurried away. Using the shadows cast by the morning sun to orientate herself, she continued in one direction, but soon had to retrace her steps when all the streets she found came to a dead end or doubled back. Setting out in the opposite direction, Rielle found she couldn't find a way out of the area that way either.

By then the narrow streets weren't as busy. Small children followed her, staring and laughing, until older ones called them back. She would have stood out among them even if she hadn't been taller and lacking the shawl that all the local women wore, because almost no adults were about.

Deciding to always take left-hand turns, she made her way up and down streets, avoiding only the ones leading to the factory.

Most of the buildings were old and shabby, two- and three-storey boxes facing out into the street, with no front walls. Only a few houses near the factory had fronts and doors, and these were guarded.

Inside the open houses, children and the occasional heavily pregnant woman huddled, sewing all manner of decorations onto the garments Rielle had seen workers making the day before. The woefully inadequate drains running down every street were choked with refuse. Small animals lurked in the shadows, scurrying out to investigate whenever a fresh pail of rubbish was dumped. Most of the children were barefoot, feet stained black from the grime.

By the time she had returned to where she started, she had already guessed the truth: there was no way out of the area except by the gate she'd entered, which was at the far end of the street that led to the factory. She had no choice but to try to leave that way, or see if she could climb up a wall and escape via the rooftops. When she considered the state of the roof material, she concluded that she would use far less magic zapping a gate guard than healing broken bones.

Taking a deep breath, she straightened her back and headed for the factory.

The guards watched her coming. When Rielle was twenty steps away, one of them whistled. Hearing hurried footsteps coming from the factory door, Rielle turned in time to face the examiner running towards her. His face was dark with anger. She dodged as he made a grab for her arm, but collided with something solid – one of the guards. He seized her arms from behind, giving the examiner time to get a grip on her. She nearly reached for magic, but at the last moment decided against it.

What if the girls were punished for bringing a sorcerer into the factory? She did not want to cause them trouble after all the kindness they had shown her.

If I refuse to work, they'll throw me out, she reasoned.

The examiner dragged her into the factory. A murmur went

420

through the workers, but most kept their heads down. One of those who didn't was Mai, who looked relieved. She gave Rielle a sympathetic yet puzzled smile and a shake of the head.

Dragging Rielle to the steam room, the examiner left her with the woman who had watched over the hanging of clothes the previous day. The woman shouted at Rielle, but the anger in her eyes was soon replaced by a calculating look as Rielle stared back at her impassively. She did not seem surprised when Rielle refused to pick up an armload of clothing.

A warning tone came into the woman's voice then. Rielle waited, refusing to heed the fear that crept over her in response. The woman's voice grew gentler briefly, then hardened again. She called out to an examiner, who nodded and hurried away.

Now a trio of men appeared, their gazes searching the factory, then stopping as the steam room manager waved towards Rielle. They marched over to surround Rielle. Two grabbed Rielle's arms and forced her to walk into the steam room to one of the internal doors. As the third opened it, the smell of the steam room intensified a hundred times. The others shoved her inside. A brief glimpse of a small room lined with shelving imprinted on her eyes before darkness replaced it.

She cursed, then regretted opening her mouth. The next mistake was to take a deep breath in order to sigh. Coughing it out again, she drew a little of her precious store of magic and created a light.

The shelving was strewn with glistening mounds of wet vegetation. Steaming water dripped onto it from pipes jutting out from the walls, seeping through the mess onto the floor, which was coated with slime and muck. Mould covered the walls, and there even appeared to be the roots of a plant fanning out in one corner from a wide crack.

No surface was clean. There was nowhere to sit but the floor. Her eyes were steaming and her lungs spasmed into a coughing fit.

I should have fought my way out of the gates when I had the chance. But once again, she thought of the girls who had helped her, and the possibility that they would be punished for bringing a sorcerer into the factory. *No, I can endure this. It is strange that they are so determined to make me work for them when I don't want to and they haven't even paid me anything, but I'll just have to keep refusing until they let me go.*

Unless . . . The plant growing through the crack suggested that the far wall was an exterior one. She briefly considered pushing through with magic, but when she thought about the badly mended cracks in the rest of the building, she realised she could not be sure only this corner would fall down. The whole side might collapse, killing many inside.

She closed her eyes, extinguished the light and tried to take shallow breaths without coughing. *Just wait*, she told herself.

To distract herself from the smell, she concentrated on sounds. A constant dripping came from the shelving, and a high-pitched animal squeak occasionally came from one corner, but the rest of the noises she could hear originated from outside. Few voices were audible beyond the walls – regular shouted orders from the examiners mostly. She'd never heard the sewers talking. There was none of the chatter and singing that she remembered so fondly from her years among the tapestry weavers.

The garments they were making were all the same – hardly an enjoyable activity, but at least they would be making magic while they sewed. Focusing on the magic of the world, she sought the signs of new magic spreading from their direction, and was disturbed to find very little of it.

Why isn't it happening? she wondered. *Are these people unable to generate much magic? Perhaps they can't. If Makers exist, able to make more magic than usual, people who generate almost nothing must exist too.* A stab of panic went through her. *I am never going to escape this world!*

Then a different possibility occurred to her. The sewers were not really being creative. They were producing the same thing over and over, taking no part in the design and little pleasure in the creation. No wonder they generated so little magic.

A pair of voices caught her attention, growing louder. They stopped right outside the steam room door and she turned, ready to leave as soon as it opened.

It didn't.

". . . started yesterday. A foreigner. Doesn't speak our language."

Rielle started. The voices were male, and speaking Traveller tongue.

"Could she be from outside this world? The Delmegardi wants all otherworlders handed over for questioning."

"No . . . she's tall, but not otherworld-like. She's just a foreigner."

"Then what will you do?"

"A beating will get some sense in her. And it's what they expect. We can't start treating one worker differently just because she's new. Especially not now. We need every pair of hands."

The voices dropped too low to hear. Rielle turned and pressed her ear against the door, shuddering as it met the moist and sticky surface.

". . . wants the order five days earlier or he won't pay. We can do it if they work the next two nights, then keep half of them here for the one after. They won't like it. Which is extra reason why we don't need a foreigner defying us right now."

"Throw her out."

"No, we need to make an example. Show them that magic isn't the reason the Gellim are in charge."

"Now?"

"No. Tonight, after we lock the doors for the night shift. Let her steam in there for a while, and feel her lungs start to rot."

The footsteps began again, fading towards the manager's room. Rielle moved away from the door and wiped her ear on her sleeve. Unless she was willing to risk the whole building collapsing when she broke through the wall, she had no choice but to wait until they let her out. She was not going to submit herself to a beating though. Avoiding that justified using a little magic. Though . . . if she shielded herself carefully and reacted as they expected, it wouldn't be obvious she was using magic, and the girls wouldn't get into trouble because of her.

Time crawled by. Boredom set in, and she wished she could do something to distract herself from worrying. Her feet began to ache, so she began to slowly pace the room, avoiding the shelving and walls by keeping her hands out in front.

After a few rounds, she found she could make out some details. She stopped, alarmed. Was she pattern shifting subconsciously to adapt her eyesight, unable to avoid using up the last of her precious magic?

A brightness appeared above. Looking up, she realised that sunlight was filtering through the crack in the wall, which was a lot larger than it had appeared during her quick survey of the room. She resisted the urge to sigh with relief. Her body wasn't altering itself, the sun happened to be in the right place to penetrate the room. The sunlight would not hit that section of wall for long, however.

Looking around, she noticed objects she'd not seen the first time: a pail and a long stick. Walking over to them, she curled her fingers around the stick. It was a mop, the handle damp, but not sticky or slimy.

Perhaps she could clean a large enough space to sit down. Lifting the broom, she swept the head over the floor, but all it did was create swirls in the muck. The pattern was interesting, however. Rielle swished it back and forth to create swirls and circles in the grime, then made simple waves and clouds – a seascape emerging from filth. Her mood lightened. She could entertain herself during part of the long wait, and create a little magic at the same time.

And then the head fell off the broom.

Sagging, she went to put the handle aside, then paused. Drawing with it would produce a single line and allow for finer work. She started doodling aimlessly. It felt good to be making marks. She paused to touch the pendant hanging at her throat, hidden under the high neckline of her dress. It had drawn some interest from the girls at first, but once they'd seen that the capsule only contained a brush they'd lost interest. She considered painting with it instead, but the idea of soiling it with the muck was too awful.

As she sketched out a picture of the girls and the strange beast that hauled the wagon they'd arrived in, her mind kept sliding away from an uncomfortable thought. She started coughing and, suddenly concerned for her health again, made herself face it. She could use the pendant to bribe her way out of here. It was worth something for the metal, surely. She would be sad to lose Ankari's gift, but she was sure the woman would rather Rielle lived without it than died with it.

Memories of the Travellers rose. She wondered if Baluka had found Valhan's hand. The last time she had seen him, he had changed so much. He'd thought that she looked different too, and blamed it on her agelessness. She wasn't ageless now. There had been no sudden shift or change to make it obvious. All she'd consciously done was lock down the magic she held so that it wouldn't be used up in automatic pattern shifting.

It meant she was ageing again. As far as she could tell, her body wasn't changing to her real age, or returning to what it had been before she had become ageless. It simply stopped repairing itself. Which meant she hadn't actually lost the ability to pattern-shift. If she reached a world containing magic, she would stop ageing once again.

What if my body did *return to its original form? Would I go back to being a Maker?*

If it did, she could generate more magic and escape this world sooner. Her heart skipped a beat. She *could* restore her original pattern deliberately. Pattern shifting didn't take a great deal of magic. Only the initial process of using magic to enhance the mind's ability to comprehend pattern shifting did.

She might not have enough magic to change herself back to her original Maker self, however. Failure would mean using up her magic for no benefit. Was attempting to do it worth risking that?

Even if she succeeded and became a Maker again, it would still take her a long time to generate enough magic to escape this world.

Yet as a Maker, she would be valuable to the people of this world. They might protect her.

There are far too many "mights" and "ifs" for my liking, she mused. *Better I try convincing a sorcerer to take me out of this world. Once I get myself out of here.*

She'd covered all the floor with lines now. Pausing, she concentrated on the magic around her. In what had been a near void, a glow now spread around the room.

Interesting. She'd never sensed herself making magic before. To be fully immersed in a creative activity meant she had no attention to spare for detecting magic. She was probably able to now because this world was nearly empty of it.

As she drew the magic in, the world around her darkened again. It wasn't a lot, but every little bit could make a difference. Determined to spend as much time as she had left in the room being useful, she grabbed the mop head, shoved the stick into the top and scuffed out the patterns she'd made. Kicking off the head again, she began drawing, only this time depicting a tree. As each branch formed, she paused to search for and take the magic she was producing. A prickle of excitement ran over her skin each time her store of magic grew a little. Where before she had been desperate to leave the cloying damp of the room, now she hoped she had plenty of time before they came to release her.

If it's true that you can't be both a Maker and ageless, it's likely I'll lose the ability to pattern-shift. So I'll only get one chance, because if I lose the pattern shifting ability before I've regained my Maker ability, I won't be able to try it again. The risks in attempting it were even greater than she had first thought, and her determination to try faltered.

But the sooner she escaped, the greater the chance she could save Qall.

A faint sound reached her. A bell. Her heart began racing. It was the shift change signal. They would be coming for her soon.

What if she used all her remaining magic protecting herself from the beating?

It won't use magic to look within and see what needs to be altered. Closing her eyes, she forced herself to concentrate. She used her understanding of pattern shifting to probe her own mind. Since she was not creating magic, she could not pinpoint which part needed restoring to its original state. Opening her eyes, she began drawing again. It was hard – almost impossible – to concentrate on both, but by switching rapidly from one task to the other, she gradually began to hone in on the part of her mind generating magic.

It would not take much magic to change it. No more than what she had generated here, drawing on the floor. She tried a subtle alteration. It barely depleted her store. Another bit of sketching led to a portion of magic generated and gathered, and more insight into what part of her mind was involved.

I can do this.

She resisted the urge to take a deep breath and began to shift her pattern. At first, the changes made no difference; then one shrank her production of magic down to almost nothing. Alarmed, she undid the change . . . and saw that she could reverse it yet further. She returned to drawing on the floor to test the result, and a sensation shivered through in her mind. It was familiar. Something missed, but not forgotten.

That's it! She sought magic and found it rapidly spreading out in all directions. Gathering it, she revelled in the flood of power.

427

It was tempting to return to drawing and generate more magic, but she concentrated on that part of her mind she had changed. Could this ability be enhanced further? She applied more magic, shifting the pattern more.

The door opened. Rielle extended a hand towards it and stilled the air within the opening. Ignoring the grunts and exclamations of surprise, she kept her attention on the floor. The broomstick appeared to move on its own as she seized it with magic so she could draw faster. Lines appeared . . .

 . . . and the world turned white.

It was not truly white, of course. No more than that the blackness of magic's absence was truly black. She stretched her senses out to find a great explosion of magic flooding outwards to cover the entire compound.

But . . . that's more than I ever created before! Many, many times more!

She turned her attention inwards again. Could she enhance her ability even further? Was it possible to go too far? Perhaps she should try another tiny change, and see what happened.

Except . . . she was not sure what she had done. Her attempt was an aimless floundering, and she soon stopped for fear of doing damage to herself. Puzzled, she stared blankly at her surroundings as she tried to work out why.

How could I understand it one moment, then not the next? She drew in a sharp breath as she realised what she'd done. *It's true! Before I was ageless, I wasn't able to comprehend pattern shifting. Now I can't again.*

The part of her mind that had been altered so she could understand how to change patterns now generated magic.

The same part. I can do one or the other. Never both.

The loss of agelessness brought a rush of fear, but she did not fight it. She let it wash over her and it soon faded away. Perhaps one day she would change herself back to an ageless sorcerer again, but for now being mortal was her route to freedom. In the meantime, being a Maker again filled her with joy . . . and surprise.

Losing her Maker ability had not mattered to her before. She had still been able to create – once she'd got past her initial fear of losing that ability as well – and that mattered more to her than whether she could generate a little magic or a great deal. In exchange, she could live as long as she wanted, if she wasn't killed by somebody or something. She could also heal herself and others, which she had come to value even more.

And yet, this felt right. It felt as if something that had been stolen had been returned. It felt like she was her full self again.

Well, then. I hope being my natural self is worth getting old and dying for.

But not today.

She had made a great deal of magic in her previous moments of drawing, but she needed more to escape the world – and the sooner the better. Turning her attention to the room again, she swept away the mould and muck on a wall then started a new picture, this time carving lines with magic. She did not bother to pause and take in the magic she made. She just drew.

She drew the factory workers. Not hunched over their work, but standing. Not burdened with piles of clothing, but dressed in finery, surrounded by children wearing shoes, eating a feast, and living in houses that did not open into the street. She drew the delta waterways filled with boats, fishermen and women hauling in nets, the water clean.

When she was done, she sent her mind out, smiling as she sensed plentiful magic spreading across the world. She searched for the furthest edge of it, and the longer her mind travelled, the more astonished she grew. When she finally reached the limit, a multitude of minds prickled her senses. The entire city. Holes were forming as other sorcerers gathered in as much as they could. At the centre of each void, she found the minds of men and women, puzzled by the return of magic but relieved that their control over the workers would not slip any further into revolution.

Rielle's stomach sank. Before Qall had stripped the world, magic had helped to keep workers like these sewers in bondage. With her new ability, she could escape the world *and* leave it restored, but now she saw that this would only leave in place the societal structure that oppressed these and many, many other workers.

Who am I to judge them? she thought. *Valhan said you can never predict the result of your meddling.*

But whether she restored the magic of this world or not, she was still meddling. Qall, by stripping it, had already upset the balance of power. Even if she restored the magic, the idea of revolution would not easily fade.

And I have a foolish young sorcerer to rescue. Again.

She could not leave without doing one more thing, however. She turned to the opposite wall and drew the foremen kneeling on the ground before the workers, handing out coins. Then she wrote: "Rise before the magic returns."

Done, she took all of the magic she had generated, drew a deep breath and pushed out of the world.

CHAPTER 17

Having to stop and catch her breath slowed Rielle's journey through the worlds more than she liked. Added to that, she soon had to give into hunger and weariness, taking time to sleep. Finding something to eat was the hardest. She followed Tarran's advice, skimming to the kitchen of palaces and mansions and taking food from people who clearly wouldn't starve as a result, though she hated to think of the punishment kitchen workers might be suffering as a result of her theft.

She had been trapped for several days, and enough time had passed since Inekera and Qall had travelled on from the factory workers' world for their trail to have gone cold. It would take far longer for Inekera and Qall to reach Dahli, and it was an extra source of frustration to know that they were still travelling towards him as she set out after them, and yet she could not possibly catch up. Even if she could have, she did not know where Dahli was. When she reached worlds she recognised, she had to conclude that, unless something had delayed Inekera and Qall, they would have reached Dahli by now.

What can I do? If only she knew where Qall was she could try to rescue him. Though she might not be ageless any more or be able to heal any wounds she might sustain, if she gathered enough magic, she was still one of the most powerful sorcerers in the worlds. Nearly as strong as Valhan, and it would have taken an army to defeat him. *Though I've almost no experience in fighting – just Tarran's lessons to call upon.*

Where might Dahli be hiding? Who would know?

Tyen.

But he wasn't likely to give her that information, if she could even find him in the first place. Nor was he likely to tell Tarran.

The Travellers?

It was possible that Qall had insisted that Inekera let him visit his family before joining Dahli, to ensure they were unharmed. He might have demanded for them to be given a way to contact him, and he to communicate with them. As Rielle had reasoned before, blackmail depended on the blackmailed person being able to see if threats were or could be carried out. If Rielle followed a message from them to Qall, she might find Dahli.

But if Rielle was seen near the Travellers, it might be mistaken as a rescue attempt. By approaching them, she might trigger the attack Dahli was threatening.

If Qall had been seen during his journey to meet Dahli – and he hadn't been making any attempt to hide his face when he'd left her stranded – the news that the Raen was back would spread faster than gossip. She might be able to track Qall by these sightings.

But she doubted Dahli would allow such an obvious trail to exist. He'd make Qall hide his face and conceal him somewhere.

Such rumours would surely reach Baluka. So would any sightings of Dahli. He might have found Valhan's hand since she'd met up with him, or already dealt with Dahli. Even if he hadn't, he would have been gathering information and preparing for a battle with the Raen since she'd left.

He was the most useful person to seek out. *That's what I'll do.*

Contacting Baluka was easy. Previously, she had sent a message from one of the many worlds that supported the Restorers, as she had wanted their meeting to be private. She could not think of any reason to meet him in secret this time – at least, none that were worth the delay anyway – so she would approach the Restorers openly.

It did not take long to find a group of them. They sent a message to Baluka and she waited among them, listening to local news of the worlds, until the reply came. The messenger asked a few questions to confirm that she really was who she said she was, then took her on the first leg of a convoluted journey to meet Baluka.

The third guide left her with instructions that took her to a city bustling with countless people. Despite this, it was a clean and ordered place. Bright sunlight set the local white stone spar-kling and brightened carefully tended gardens. Looking into the minds of the closest people, she read of small, ordinary anxieties like whether a person had forgotten an item on their shopping list or if the loaves in the oven were burning.

She had been instructed to enter the tallest building in the city. This turned out to be a large, square building three stories tall in the centre of the city. The locals thought it boring, and she had to agree. As she made her way down the path to the entrance, she searched the many minds within: Most were occupied in admin-istrative tasks, but she chanced upon a group considering how to tackle worlds where war and opposition to the Restorers' laws against torture and slavery still continued. Surprised, she checked her stride. This was the Restorers' base. She had expected Baluka to arrange a meeting, not bring her here.

Finding Baluka's mind among all the rest would take more time than she had to spare, so she headed for the main doors. Guards watched from discrete positions. They had been told to expect a woman of her description to approach, and to let her pass.

A thin young man was waiting in the hall inside.

"Rielle Lazuli?"

She nodded. "Yes."

"Follow me."

He led her through a small door into a narrow central stairway that descended to the lower floors, having only been told to take her to a particular corridor to meet another Restorer. As she followed, she let her mind touch lightly on all those around her, taking in the general mood of the place. Baluka had ordered for a review of their assets, strength and alliances. Many wondered if this was in reaction to a threat. Perhaps from the Spy – or delivered by the Spy.

The guide brought her to another, who took Rielle down more staircases. From this woman she learned that the true height of the structure was almost triple what it appeared to be. And more: beneath the ground, away from the bright sunlight that drenched the rest of the city, Baluka spent most of his days. The sorcerers who protected him were loyal and much stronger than him, and had insisted he should not leave to meet Rielle. They could – and had – gathered in large enough numbers that they could step in and allow him to flee if her intentions were murderous – or if she wasn't who she claimed to be.

With these clues, she was finally able to locate Baluka's mind. He was pacing his rooms, worrying. He had recognised her face in the mind of the messenger, but memory could be unreliable. He'd told only the stronger and most loyal of his generals who he'd learned of Tyen's betrayal from, but it wasn't impossible that their minds had been read and someone was taking advantage of Baluka's willingness to meet Rielle to get close to him.

He was also worried about her reasons for returning, and for approaching him openly rather than in secret. *Has Dahli found Qall?* he was wondering. *Has he resurrected Valhan?*

She knew then that he hadn't found Valhan's hand. Nor had he heard whether Qall was in Dahli's control. Slowing, she considered whether she still needed to see him or would do better on her own, then quickened her strides again. With his network of Restorers and supporters, he was the best chance she had of finding and freeing Qall.

At last, the guide stopped outside a door. She knocked, then stepped back and nodded to Rielle.

The door opened. Baluka gazed at her for a moment, then smiled and stepped aside.

"Rielle. It *is* you. Come in."

As she entered, he closed the door. He ushered her to a set of large, cushioned chairs surrounding a low table covered in plates and bowls of food, and a range of liquids in bottles and jugs.

"Are you hungry? Thirsty?"

"Both," she admitted. "It's not easy travelling between worlds with nothing to trade. At least, not easy to do it quickly." As she settled in one of the chairs, she sensed his anxiety rising. She did not reach for the food, instead waiting until he sat down.

"Not long after I reached Qall," she began, "I discovered that one of Dahli's searchers had been in our area. Before I could move us away, Qall disappeared. I followed him, and got close enough to discover that he was in the company of a sorcerer named Inekera – one of Valhan's old allies. He told me to stop following him and managed to slip away."

Baluka frowned. "He joined her willingly?" Then he shook his head. "Ah, no – she blackmailed him as you feared."

"Probably. I've lost his trail, so I came here. I figured you would have heard if anyone had seen someone looking like Valhan."

He nodded. "I probably would, but I haven't. However, my watchers tell me Dahli has gathered together a large group of powerful allies and set up a base within a world surrounded by dead worlds. We're worried that this means Tyen is close to succeeding in resurrecting the Raen."

"So you know where he is?"

"Yes. A world surrounded by dead worlds would work to keep sorcerers in as much as out," he pointed out.

She sighed. "It's a prison. Qall is there."

"He might not be—"

"Has anything happened to your family?"

Baluka sighed and massaged his temples. "Dahli has sorcerers in place, ready to attack if Qall, you or any Restorer approaches them." She could see his frustration and fear for them. "Dahli has allowed them to keep trading, so I do get information from the people they have visited. So far nobody has been harmed."

"Can you get a message to them?"

"If I do, Dahli's watchers will read their minds and know I have."

"Hmm. He won't destroy his only means of persuading Qall just because you contacted them. Ulma might be strong enough to shield her mind from being read, too."

"She is strong enough to be ageless, but not as strong as Dahli and his more powerful allies."

Rielle drummed her fingers on her knees. "If I can get Qall away—"

"Dahli will retaliate," Baluka cut in. "He knows you love them as much as Qall does."

"I can't abandon Qall," she told him.

He drew in a deep breath and nodded as he let it out. "I figured as much. What are you planning?"

She looked away. "I have no plan, yet."

He crossed his arms. "You're not going into Dahli's base alone. For a start, what if that is what he wants? What if Qall isn't there and it's a trap, designed to strand you there?"

Rielle opened her mouth to tell him about her new ability to generate extraordinary amounts of magic, then hesitated. She hadn't had time to consider all the consequences yet. Better to keep that fact to herself for now.

"You can send someone to fetch me," she replied.

Baluka considered her in silence. She watched his thoughts shift, weighing risks and possible gains, and what she might do. Finally, he took a breath and shaped those thoughts into words.

"The Restorers are ready for a fight. We've tried to find Valhan's hand, but none of us is surprised that we haven't. We've been focusing on the next best thing: to kill the only person who knows where it is."

Rielle winced. "Dahli."

"Surely you do not object to that."

She shifted in her chair. "No."

"And yet?"

She sighed. "Dahli is acting out of grief and loyalty. He truly believes that the worlds need Valhan. It would be easier to kill him if he was motivated by greed and lust for power. I've met rebels far worse than he." *I killed a rebel far worse than Dahli, and that still bothers me*, she wanted to say, but she closed her mouth and let the confession remain unspoken.

Baluka's expression softened, then grew hard again.

"And yet he has done terrible things, and would kill people we love."

"I know." Rielle grimaced. "I'm not excusing him. I will kill him to protect them, if I have to."

"But you hesitate to." Baluka leaned forward. "So you definitely can't confront him alone. If he senses the slightest reluctance, he'll exploit it. Let me gather an army and we will enter the base together."

She bowed her head. "I would appreciate your help. I admit I need it."

"You will have to become one of my generals."

She opened a mouth to object, but he continued on. "You are too ambiguous a figure to expect help from the Restorers without question. They know you lived with Valhan for a time. They know you left me in order to serve him. They have only recently learned that you rescued Qall to prevent Valhan returning. They are not sure what to make of you, so you need to make your position clear. You need to tell them Qall's story, or when we fight through to him they will mistake him for Valhan, and try to kill him."

Closing her mouth, she nodded. "Very well."

"You also need to decide what to do about Tyen."

All her muscles went rigid. She did not want to even think about Tyen.

"Must I?" Her voice sounded like another person's: it was so cold.

"I met him recently," Baluka told her. "In fact, we managed to ambush him, and I think we might have been able to eliminate him if we'd tried."

Rielle's heart shrank at the thought of Tyen dying. *Don't be a fool*, she told it. *He betrayed you.* "Why didn't you?"

Baluka smiled faintly. "He admitted to everything, then he hinted that he was doing it all for you. If Dahli could find another way to resurrect Valhan, he might not spend as much energy and time searching for you."

"But . . . what if he succeeded?"

"He believes the Restorers could deal with Valhan."

She let out a bark of laughter. "How nice of him to have such confidence in you that he'd arrange a battle to prove it! How did you react to that?"

Baluka shrugged. "I don't know whether to be flattered that he thinks we could or terrified that he feels he has no choice but to hope we can."

"So you believe him?"

Baluka hesitated, then nodded. "I admit my trust is as much instinctive as reasoned. However, this was before Qall joined Dahli. That will have made Tyen's efforts to find another way to resurrect Valhan redundant."

"Dahli wouldn't need him," Rielle said. Then she shivered as she realised she was wrong. "Oh. Yes, he would. To perform the resurrection."

"Will he do it?"

"I . . . I don't know," Rielle admitted. If Tyen had been lying to Baluka about his reasons for joining Dahli, then she had no doubt he would. If he hadn't been, then perhaps he would refuse to. Unless Dahli found a way to blackmail him too. "I think we have to act as if he would. We can't afford to hope otherwise."

"I agree." Baluka paused. "You're already sounding like a general. So will you help me lead the army?"

Rielle nodded.

Baluka smiled. "Welcome to the ranks of the Restorers, Rielle."

PART SEVEN

TYEN

CHAPTER 19

The clock in the hall measured Traveller time. Though it was small in comparison, it reminded Tyen of the enormous timepiece that had dominated the hall of Valhan's palace. The light within the black marble room never changed, and the local days were short compared to most worlds', so Dahli used the clock to decide when they would eat and sleep. He had arranged for another bed to be brought in for Tyen. Dahli did not appear to sleep, though it was possible he did during the rare times he was absent. Zeke had taken a room within the palace.

Servants brought food at regular intervals, topped up the lamp oil and emptied the portable cabinet that served as a toilet – a local invention that Tyen thought was crude and ridiculous, but both Dahli and Qall did not appear to mind. Sorcerers stood guard beside the doors and in each corner of the room, watching Qall.

The torch flames were reflected in both the glossy floor and low ceiling, and those reflections replicated in turn, which made the space seem larger. Yet it felt claustrophobic. Perhaps only because Tyen knew it was a prison.

Whenever Tyen read minds beyond the room, he saw images of a sprawling, neglected palace bathed in the unvarying glow of a purple sky. He had learned that the civilisation here was a shadow of one that had once thrived for centuries. It was in decline now, mirroring the fading of the sky's light. Crops no longer grew well. Animals sickened easily. The Diminishing had been predicted hundreds of years before, when scholars venturing offworld had stumbled upon tales about their world which described the long, relentless cycles that took it from prosperity to poverty. Some had left; some hoped their descendants would survive the Diminishing; some stayed because they refused to believe in it.

Dahli had chosen this world because it was still a rich source of magic. Once the people's fortunes had begun to fail, otherworld traders had stopped coming. Along with the general population's caution with resources, local sorcerers became frugal in their use of magic, predicting that it too would decline.

"I've created a noise-distorting shield again," Qall said, then sighed. "It is a relief when Dahli leaves, as it gives us a chance to talk, but I worry what he's up to."

Tyen nodded. "It gives him a chance to unblock his memories and progress with his plans."

Qall had taken advantage of all Dahli's absences to talk openly with Tyen. In the first conversation, he'd assured Tyen that Dahli couldn't blackmail him by threatening to send Inekera to kill Rielle. "I left her in the same world," a glint of dark humour lighting his eyes. "But on the other side so she can't cause Rielle any trouble."

Then he'd asked Tyen to teach him about fighting with magic. Tyen had pointed out that the guards would report if they began sparring, so he could only tell Qall what he knew.

In the first few sessions, he'd described battles he'd seen and heard about. Qall listened to all with rapt attention. Soon Qall began asking questions, and now their time together was mainly filled with discussion of battle strategy.

"Rielle was teaching me ways to fight a large group of weaker sorcerers," Qall began, "but she didn't think I'd need to know how to deal with one strong one."

"That makes sense," Tyen replied. "The conflict you are most likely to face will be a battle against many."

"But I *could* end up fighting a single, strong sorcerer."

"There are only two who come close to you in strength. I don't think Rielle will want to fight you, and I certainly don't."

"What about the Raen?"

"But that would mean that you . . . oh, do you mean if Dahli decided I should go back to my experiments?"

Qall nodded.

"If the Raen returns exactly how he was before, I'd advise you get as far away from him as you can. He has a thousand cycles of experience and – unlike Rielle and me – will kill without hesitation or regret."

The young man considered that for a moment, then his head tilted sideways a little.

"What a strange coincidence it is that you and Rielle are the same strength, and you ran into each other."

Tyen shrugged. "It is not strange that the strongest of sorcerers should meet when the worlds are in upheaval – and it could be that our powers aren't exactly the same, just close enough to prevent mind reading."

"I suppose it is not strange that the strongest of sorcerers should meet when the dominance of the worlds is challenged," Qall agreed. "Which is why I need to know how to deal with a single powerful sorcerer. What if there are more of you?"

Tyen nodded. "It is possible there are more. The Raen, and probably the Predecessors before him, killed off anyone who could become a threat. For all we know, sorcerers of my and Rielle's strength are normally more common."

"If they killed them off before they could become a threat, then they rarely faced an adversary who could truly challenge them. Perhaps the only reason they were defeated is because they got lazy or forgot how to fight anyone close to them in strength."

It was Tyen's turn to sit in silent contemplation. *Just how strange is it that Rielle and I exist at the same time? Are there more sorcerers of our strength out there?*

445

"I—" he began.

"Wait . . ." Qall looked towards the door. "A servant is coming."

Sure enough, a door opened and a servant entered into the room. He hurried towards them, resisting the temptation to glance around the room. He knew it was dangerous in here, and had heard how his great-grandfather had once assisted in cleaning it of hundreds of mutilated bodies back when neighbouring worlds had looked upon this one with envy. Everyone had supposed that, now the Diminishing had started, having no riches for outsiders to covet meant they were in no danger of invasion. Then these otherworlders had arrived, demanding occupation of it and part of the palace. *At least they bring food in*, the man thought, *and are generous about sharing it.*

Ten paces away, the servant paused to bow, then scurried forward to place the tray on a table. It was covered in several small bowls filled with different kinds of food and liquids. Bowing again, he waited to see if they would give him further orders. When they didn't, he bowed a third time and retreated from the room.

"What is it exactly that is so dangerous about this room?" Tyen asked.

"Only Dahli knows, and he has blocked his memory of it. If we're attacked, he'll access the memory so that he can trigger the trap."

"Another blocked memory, eh?" Tyen shook his head. "His mind must be full of them."

Qall selected one of the bowls of liquid and sipped. "This is good. Sweet, but not too much so," he murmured. Tyen moved another bowl closer, but he was more hungry than thirsty and helped himself to the food.

"What do you think would happen if I accessed the memories in Valhan's hand," Qall asked.

Surprised by the question, Tyen swallowed a little too soon. He coughed, reached for the bowl and considered his answer as he rinsed away the food lodged in his throat.

"If you merely read them, then nothing."

"That would take a long time, wouldn't it? He lived a thousand years. What do you think would happen if I imprinted them on my own mind?"

"I don't know," Tyen admitted.

Qall snorted softly. "I didn't ask what would happen, but what you *think* might happen. What did your experiments tell you?"

Wiping his mouth, Tyen considered Qall carefully. A glint of something in the young man's eyes reminded Tyen of Valhan when they'd discussed his efforts to find a way to give Vella a human form. It had been a colder kind of eagerness than what was in Qall's eyes, however.

Tyen puffed out his cheeks, then deflated them. "In my experiments, I attempted to place someone's memories in the blank mind of a revived corpse. While I am sure I erased all previous memories, and that the new ones were imprinted as best as I could manage, the subject, once awakened, was always confused and disorientated. At best, they became distressed; at worst, the result brought about physical convulsions." He looked at Qall. "I did not try imprinting the memories on a mind that had not been mostly wiped clean."

"What do you think would have happened if you had?"

"More conflict," Tyen replied.

"Is it possible, though, that the original mind would remain in charge, and the memories would simply be like a book they could read when they wanted to?"

"It's possible. I can't tell you how likely though."

Qall's mouth twitched and he turned his attention to the food again. A chill ran over Tyen's skin. *Why would he want to take that risk?* The answer came a moment later. *He wants to know who he was before his memories were blocked. Who his parents were, and if he has siblings. Valhan's hand might not hold all that information, but it could tell Qall where he had come from.*

This might be a way to get hold of the hand. If Qall agreed

to sacrifice himself in exchange for knowing who he had been before . . . *No, Dahli would never fall for that.*

"It would be very dangerous," Tyen warned. "You could lose your new identity. Rielle didn't save you at great risk to herself only for your memories to be wiped again."

"Rielle didn't save anyone," Qall corrected. He looked up and met Tyen's eyes. "My original self was already gone."

Tyen had to look away. *Has he said as much to Rielle? Or has it occurred to her already?*

Qall looked down at Tyen's chest. "The same is true for Vella."

The statement sent a shock through Tyen. "Vella? That's not . . . Her memories weren't wiped," he protested. "They were retained and stored."

"Yet she isn't whole." Qall shrugged. "Whether or not to risk my life is my decision, isn't it?"

Tyen resisted the urge to press his fingers against Vella, resting against his chest, as he considered what Qall had implied. *It should be her choice whether to be given a body, but she can't feel emotion so she can't desire to be transformed or not. I can't know if she will be happy to have a body again until I give her one.* What if it made her unhappy? What if he made her situation worse? It was a risk for her too.

"There is a great deal I could gain if I have Valhan's memories," Qall continued. He picked up the bowl of liquid again. "Perhaps I could even learn how to right some of the wrongs the Raen has done. Or at least stop the chaos."

"There may not be as much chaos as Dahli wants you to believe," Tyen warned.

"Dahli can't lie to me."

"No, but he can block all evidence in his mind contrary to what he wants you to see. He can be wrong. Others believe that the worlds are starting to settle down. People who can't block memories.

"Baluka."

"Yes. Dahli has never known a time when the worlds weren't under the Raen's rule. He can't predict what it will lead to."

"He has the last five cycles to judge them by."

"Not long enough to know anything for sure."

Qall frowned. "I suppose it seems like a long time because it's all of my life," he said quietly. He lifted the bowl to his mouth.

Tyen watched the young man drink. "Be careful, Qall. Dahli may be weaker than you and his mind may be readable, but he is clever. He may be able to force you to submit to being Valhan's vessel, but if he can persuade you to submit willingly instead his task will be easier."

"He's not suggesting I absorb Valhan's memories."

"No? Then why are you thinking about it?"

Qall put down the bowl. "I'm exploring all ideas. If Dahli would prefer me to submit willingly, then perhaps I can make a deal in which he lets me seek my true identity in the hand before I die."

Tyen poured more of the drink. "He won't produce the hand unless he has guarantees we will not destroy it. He is no fool, Qall."

They sat in silence for a while; then the sound of a door opening drew their attention. Zeke strolled into the room and across to their table.

"My, you two are quiet." Zeke's mind was aglow with satis-faction. Something to do with winning over Dahli, and Tyen retreated a little from the young inventor's mind as he realised the details were more intimate than he wanted to see.

"I have news for you." Zeke opened his mouth to say more, but froze and let out a low cry of delight. "Ah! Those spicy little berries! I love those!" He leaned over the table, selecting the small round fruit that Tyen had found unpalatably salty. Taking a bite, he closed his eyes as he chewed, savouring the sharpness that had repelled Tyen, Then he glanced down at Tyen and realised he had become distracted. "Oh, Dahli sent me ahead to let you know: Baluka is raising an army. Rielle has joined him."

"Rielle?" Qall and Tyen repeated in unison, both straightening in their chairs. "Someone must have found her," Qall murmured.

"Something like that." Zeke spat pips out into his hand. "They mean to attack us."

"Here?" Qall asked.

Zeke nodded. "Dahli thinks so anyway. I don't know how they found out where this place is."

"He knew they'd find out," Qall told him.

"You read that from him?" Tyen asked. He'd seen no such expectation.

Qall shook his head. "You don't have to be hundreds of years old to see that when a sorcerer strips the magic from worlds around a central location, people are going to pay attention. It won't have been long before the Restorers learned of it and investigated."

Tyen frowned. Why would Dahli allow the Restorers to know where he was hiding? Was he *that* confident that he could defend this place? Or was he hoping that a confrontation would force Qall into doing something foolish? Qall glanced at Tyen and his chin dropped slightly, then rose again.

"What is Dahli doing now?" Qall asked Zeke.

"Rounding up his followers." Zeke went to take another berry, hesitated, then shrugged and grabbed three. "He says you're safe here. They won't attack for several days. We've got plenty of time. Ah! Here he is."

The same door opened, admitting Dahli to the hall. The man strode over to the chairs, then settled in the one next to Qall.

"So you've heard the news. Is there anything you'd like me to do for you?" he asked the young man.

Qall turned to stare at Dahli, his face turning pale, then he slowly straightened.

"Yes. I want Tyen to take a message to my family. To Givari, Lejihk's cousin's niece."

At Dahli's smile. Tyen tensed. He'd not seen the young man attempt to defy Dahli before.

"I'll allow that," Dahli replied.

It took a great effort for Tyen not to gape at Dahli. Even so, when the pair turned to look at Tyen, he was so startled that he could not speak.

"Will you do that?" Dahli asked.

Tyen looked into the man's mind, and saw only that Dahli knew he was to let Tyen do it if Qall asked, but he could not remember why. Not for the first time, Tyen wished that mind reading allowed a person to see another's memories rather than just their thoughts, and that he could somehow reach beyond Dahli's blocks.

"Of course," Tyen replied. "Where will I find them?"

Dahli told him. Tyen repeated the instructions, then turned to ask what Qall wanted him to say.

"Just give her this." The young man reached into his jacket and when he withdrew his hand his fingers were curled around whatever he held. Dahli's brow creased in a frown as Qall dropped it into Tyen's hand. It was something light and soft, and it was not hard for Tyen to keep it concealed as he deposited it in his pocket.

"Be careful," Qall warned.

Dahli looked like he wanted to ask to see the item, but was resisting. Tyen nodded at Qall, who tossed his head as if to say, "Hurry up and go before he thinks about it!" Rising, Tyen drew magic from the furthest extents of the world, and pushed into the place between.

CHAPTER 20

D ahli's directions to Qall's adoptive family's location were vague, since the Travellers were always on the move. He had suggested Tyen look for signs of their passing in markets around the worlds Dahli knew they'd been in, and track them from there. Knowing that the Restorers might still want to get hold of him, Tyen took a convoluted route through worlds he knew weren't frequently visited, but were still getting enough regular traffic to assure him they hadn't been stripped of magic recently.

As Tyen moved between worlds, he pressed a hand against the familiar weight under his shirt. *What do you think Dahli is up to, Vella?*

The sound of her voice in his mind instantly raised his spirits.

"The prospect of other people dying for him might force Qall into making a hasty decision. But it is a risk on Dahli's part. Qall might reason that more people will be harmed by the Raen returning, and turn on him. The Restorers might win. There may be other reasons for haste. You know Dahli is worried that the hand will degrade, for a start."

Dahli might be deceiving us about the hand's condition. In fact, the Restorers might not be planning to attack at all. Tyen considered other ways he could discover the truth. He could seek out a Restorer and read their mind, but it might be dangerous if he stumbled upon a larger group and would delay his return to Qall. A nagging feeling that some unspoken communication had been taking place between Dahli and Qall had bothered him since he had left. Qall had paled when Dahli ask if he could do anything for him, which suggested it meant something more than the simple question implied. As if it was a code or signal. At that moment he'd wished he could see into Qall's mind as easily as Dahli's.

A dimly lit world was resolving around him. An odd impression of thick, shifting air came to him. He hesitated, then pushed on. As he arrived, he realised the air was full of tiny particles, all gently falling downwards. Looking up, he saw they were descending from beneath weird, fungi-like trees. He didn't like the prospect of breathing them in, so he did not draw breath and pushed out immediately.

Do you think blackmail is the only reason Qall left Rielle to join Dahli? he asked Vella as the mushroom world faded from sight.

"*You suspect something else,*" Vella stated.

I do wonder if Qall is the impatient one. That he's not willing to wait for someone else to deal with Dahli or destroy the hand, so he's trying to do it himself.

"*That would explain why he asked about the effect of absorbing Valhan's memories.*"

Grass-covered hills were emerging now, the arrival place atop one of them. Yet it was not a gentle landscape. Each hill bulged upwards dramatically, like hundreds of furry balls embedded in the ground. As Tyen arrived, the ground sank under his weight. Disturbed, he moved out of the world again.

Perhaps he is only hoping to persuade Dahli to bring him the hand.

"*Could Dahli believe that if Qall absorbed Valhan's memories he will turn him into Valhan?*"

I doubt it. In his notes, Valhan was very specific about first removing memories in the vessel.

"*He could have been wrong – and told Dahli, but not mentioned it in his notes.*"

Tyen considered that as he arrived in yet another ruined city, this one covered in a spiny, purple creeper. The plant twitched as his shoe settled on it, and started moving towards his foot, so he pushed out quickly.

I suppose we'll know if Dahli agrees to letting Qall access the hand.

"*Dahli might hope that Qall won't want to destroy the hand once he knows more about Valhan – and might even help him resurrect Valhan using another vessel.*"

Tyen hesitated outside a world so he could continue talking to her. *If that is Dahli's plan, what is my part in it? Will he still need me, if Qall can perform a resurrection? I guess he's only keeping me around in case the hand doesn't contain enough information.*

"*Or Qall refuses to cooperate if you're not there.*"

Qall doesn't have much room to bargain. Dahli will threaten to harm his family if he makes too many demands.

"*He still doesn't have anything to blackmail you with.*"

Perhaps he believes I want the Raen back. Tyen shook his head. *No, more likely he's afraid I'll switch sides if he forces Qall to become Valhan's vessel unwillingly.*

"*Would you intervene if Qall agreed to sacrifice himself?*"

I don't know. If he chose it freely, rather than through coercion . . . what gives me the right to decide it's the wrong decision? Though that's like allowing someone to commit suicide.

Moving into the world, he paused to allow his body to recover from the lack of air supply before pushing on. The arrival place was on top of several wide, flat circular rock pinnacles in the middle of a heaving body of water. It looked like the foundations of some kind of giant pier. When his body had healed, he moved on.

"*If Qall could absorb Valhan's memories without harm, would you let him?*" Vella asked.

If I could be sure it was completely harmless . . . I'd encourage him to. He'd learn who he was before Valhan cleared his memories. He could benefit enormously from the knowledge Valhan held, as would the worlds.

"*And he'd learn things he will wish he didn't know.*"

Yes. That is the price for the knowledge he needs. Maybe there's always a price and you have to choose what and how much you're willing to pay.

The world that was now emerging from the place between looked familiar. By the time it had resolved to near sharpness, Tyen had worked out where he had seen it before. He arrived and pushed away again, skimming across it to another arrival place before heading into the whiteness again. Soon he was on well-used paths, and travelled so quickly that the occasional sorcerers he passed had no more than a glimpse of him.

At last he neared the group of worlds where Qall's Travellers had last been seen. Taking Dahli's advice, he sought out markets where merchants from other worlds gathered to sell their wares. In the first, nobody had seen Travellers for a long time; in the second, they were visited regularly by a family that was not Qall's.

In the third, he caught a fleeting thought of a local regretting that she had missed the new Traveller family to visit the market, as her cousin had an embroidered shawl from them that was the envy of all the merchants' wives. Tyen sought out one of the market organisers who told him that a family of Travellers headed by a man named Lejihk had indeed visited several days ago.

Once on the trail, it was not hard to trace the family's path. In each world, he searched minds until he found a confirmation of their visit. He also searched for Dahli's watchers but found none. The closer he drew to the family, the more the absence of the watchers began to bother him. Had Dahli called them away to help defend his new base? Or was Tyen simply not finding them?

Then between one world and the next he sensed a faint presence in the whiteness. Following it at a distance, he tracked the stranger back to the previous world, to a small house they were renting. Standing outside the house, he watched as the man reported to several others that Lejihk's family were still at the Gathering.

The word was familiar. The men knew it was some kind of once-a-cycle meeting of Travellers. Memories rose of Baluka telling

455

Tyen how his people gathered in pre-arranged locations to dance, sing, perform and arrange marriages, and exchange news and details of trade. The watchers knew they were no match for the many hundred Travellers gathered there, so they took turns checking on them, the rest waiting in the neighbouring world.

They were arguing about whose turn it was now. Tyen pushed back into the place between and skimmed into the middle of their room. They started out of their chairs. He spoke the code words Dahli had given him, and they relaxed.

"I'm to deliver a message," he told them. "When I am done you are to continue your watching."

He pushed out of the world and continued on to the next. He did not want to alarm the Travellers, so his plan was to keep out of sight and only approach the girl the "message" was for. Fortunately, it was night and he was barely able to make out the gully he was arriving in. He nearly fell over as he emerged onto uneven ground. Once he'd caught his balance, he sought nearby minds.

Hundreds were gathered not far away. He cautiously began to climb the hill. From somewhere in the distance came the sound of drums, and he could not help matching his steps to the beat. As he reached the summit, lights came into sight. His eyes adjusted as he strained to make out details. Canopies sheltered hundreds of people, some moving to the rhythm of the drums, others standing or sitting.

Tyen sat cross-legged on the ground and began to watch.

A multitude of thoughts greeted him. Minds caught up in the dance and the excitement and of moving in time with a desired man or woman. Minds assessing the pairings, approving, disapproving, judging the advantages or disadvantages of marital alliances. Minds caught up in memories of youth. Minds missing wives and husbands, absent due to death or the important new trade deal that many of the family leaders had left to negotiate. Minds considering news of the worlds exchanged earlier that day.

The stories the families had shared told of improvements in the worlds – of less strife and new opportunities. The number of wars to avoid had diminished, but the number of new dead worlds was still growing. One old woman mused that the ageless allies that had followed the Raen into death would soon be outnumbered by the new ageless. These newcomers had killed worlds in order to cheat death, which suggested they were as ruthless as those who had died. Tyen winced at that. While he had chosen unpopulated worlds in which to become ageless, Dahli had not when he'd selected places to attempt resurrections. These Travellers would be horrified to know the true reason some worlds had been drained.

A name caught his attention. Givari. He sought it again, finding it in the mind of a middle-aged woman watching her niece accept a dance with a young man of another family. Shifting to the girl's mind, Tyen found dizzying excitement. Givari had been hoping the boy would invite her to dance. She was hoping for a lot more than that.

Feeling too much like he was invading her privacy, Tyen shifted back to the aunt's perspective. The woman was worried about this development. She knew Givari's mother would not approve. The girl was too young to be marrying, and it wasn't fair to be dragging another Traveller family into the dangerous situation Lejihk's family faced. The boy's parents, oblivious to the danger, were pleased with the possible match, unaware of the situation their son might become involved in.

The dance finished, and the boy dragged Givari into the crowd before her aunt could separate them. He whispered a question in her ear. She spoke two words: *Ulma's wagon.* Then she pulled away and returned to her aunt's side, playing the demure and obedient niece.

Tyen could see her struggling to not think about the meeting lest her aunt put aside convention out of concern and read her mind. She made herself accept two more dance invitations from other boys, and when her aunt decided it was time to retire for the night she protested as much as she would be expected to.

Givari and her aunt joined several other women of Lejihk's family, returning to their camp as a group. The older listened with fond amusement to the chatter of the younger as they descended into a gully. They all quietened as they puffed up the slope of another hill. Once among their wagons, they bade each other good night. The girl headed to the wagon she was minding for one of the matriarchs of the family.

As she did, Tyen learned that Ulma was no ordinary Traveller. She was ageless, and a healer. The girl thought of Ulma's daughter, an old woman in her memory. Since Oliti had died, Givari had been looking after Ulma, and slept in her wagon whenever Ulma was away. Ulma was currently helping Lejihk and Ankari establish a new trading circuit.

Entering Ulma's wagon, the girl created a magical flame. She looked around, wondering what the boy would think of all the dolls. Each looked as Ulma had done at a time in her past, and it was a very, very long past. Some said she had been born before the Raen. Perhaps even before his Predecessor, Roporien.

Tyen started at that name. *Can this ageless Traveller really be two thousand cycles old?* The Raen had survived a thousand cycles, and there had been plenty of people who wanted to kill him. Ulma may simply have lived longer because she lived a quiet life among people who had few enemies. It was reassuring to think that it was possible. *Maybe the secret to a long and happy life isn't to settle in a world and hope it does not become embroiled in a war, but to travel wherever there is peace. Maybe when* people *are your home and not a place,* people *are what you defend, not the land or possessions.*

As the girl sat down on the end of the bed to wait, Tyen took out the object Qall had pressed into his hands and he created a tiny light. It was a length of string woven of many colours. He debated whether to approach Givari now or wait. A quick search of the area surrounding the camp revealed the young man creeping up the hill, giving the huge beasts grazing around him a wide berth. Wait it was then.

Moving to the minds of the other family members, he read anxiety in many of them. With Lejihk and Ankari away, they felt more vulnerable, but the couple had assured them that, with so many other Traveller families nearby, they were safer here than they usually were.

They have no idea Dahli is threatening to destroy all Travellers if Qall resists.

It had seemed like overkill to Tyen, but as he considered what it meant he shivered. Had only Lejihk's family been in danger, Baluka could have sent in powerful sorcerers to overcome Dahli's watchers, and take his relatives away somewhere safe. Which would free Qall to resist Dahli.

If Baluka had thought this was possible he'd have done it already. He must know Dahli's threat included all Travellers. Dahli would have made sure he knew. Baluka couldn't rescue or protect *all* the Travellers in the worlds.

Neither could I. And if I tried and failed, I couldn't go back to Qall. The watchers would report it, and Dahli would know he can't trust me. Qall has hinted that he needs me there . . . and here I am, delivering this "message" . . . and Dahli is letting me.

Perhaps because he wanted to talk to Qall alone.

A chill went down Tyen's spine. He'd assumed that it had been Qall's idea to send Tyen to the Travellers with a message, but what if it had been Dahli's? What if Dahli had told Qall that if he was to ask if he could do anything, it was a signal for Qall to send Tyen away?

I have to finish this quickly, hurry back and . . . then what?

Kill Dahli? Rescue Qall? Either way, Dahli's followers would set about killing all the Travellers. Tyen would be responsible for countless deaths.

If he told Dahli he wouldn't help him, he'd lose access to Qall.

He couldn't help Qall if he wasn't there. And he wanted to help Qall. But how?

Perhaps, if he was persuasive enough, he could talk Dahli into resuming the experiments – this time with Qall's help.

He would try when he returned. For now he had best deliver this message as quickly as possible.

He sought the girl's mind again and found she had company. She did not for long, however, as the aunt had guessed her intentions and soon came knocking on the door, chasing the young man away. Disappointed and angry, the girl sat on the end of the bed, lost in her thoughts.

When Tyen skimmed into the wagon to appear in front of her, she didn't notice until he had nearly arrived. Then she jumped and let out a squeal of surprise.

"Don't be afraid," he told her soothingly. "I am only here to deliver this."

He held out the braid. Seeing it, she caught her breath, and Tyen immediately understood its significance. She had given it to Qall as a marriage proposal of sorts. Guilt filled her, as well as sadness. She'd done it with some misgivings. Though she liked Qall a great deal, she would not have chosen him for a husband. At the time, she'd thought it was the only way he could stay in the family. Later she had learned the truth. He could never have remained among them. Not without endangering them all. Though it seemed that the family's worst fears had come to pass anyway.

Gingerly taking the braid, she looked up at Tyen. "Is he alive?"

"Yes."

"Does Dahli have him?"

Tyen hesitated, then saw that by doing so he'd confirmed her worst fears. "Yes," he admitted. "Is there anything you would like me to tell him?"

She nodded, and the words for an apology sprang to mind, and an assurance that she did not mind him returning the braid. But maybe it was better that he didn't know why she had given it to him. "Tell him I'm . . ." she began, then sighed. "Just tell him to be careful. And that we're all alive and well."

Tyen smiled. "I will."

"And thank you for bringing it to me."

He nodded. Satisfied that he'd completed his task, Tyen pushed out of the world and headed back towards Dahli's world.

PART EIGHT

RIELLE

CHAPTER 18

The two sorcerers paused at the doorway.

"I don't want to leave your worlds vulnerable to attack," Baluka said.

"Risks must be taken," the other replied. "Better that than a return to the old days." He bowed his head, then turned to walk down the hallway, the gold stitching on his long robes glimmering in the lamplight. Rielle had already forgotten which world he ruled. There had been so many leaders. So many sorcerers. All of them promising to support the Restorers when they attacked Dahli. All of them willing to die to stop the Raen returning.

Baluka closed the door and smiled at Rielle as he walked back and sat beside her again. "So far it's all going well," he said.

"Yes," she replied. "He *is* worried that the neighbouring worlds will take advantage of the absence of his forces though."

"I'll have to make sure someone keeps an eye on things – and that the neighbours know we are."

"Will that deter them?"

Baluka nodded, a glint of rare satisfaction in his eyes. "We do have a powerful reputation now," he said. Then he grimaced. "Which is one advantage to balance the few mistakes we've made, supporting the wrong side in a dispute, or trusting another force to mete out punishment."

"At least you admitted when you're wrong and made reparations."

He felt a flash of annoyance that she had read his mind, but it was fleeting. *After all these years, I still react as if I'm a Traveller. I'm not. If I was strong enough, I would read everyone's minds without hesitation – even the Travellers'. Understanding what people are thinking helps us do our job. Especially now, when the fate of all the worlds was at stake. What would I not give to read Dahli's mind right now?*

Rielle would have given a small fortune to be able to read Tyen's. *Is he really doing this for me?* A part of her wanted it to be, but another screamed a warning. *Don't be a fool!* it said. *Tyen was trying to save his skin. He would have said anything to convince Baluka to let him go.*

Baluka's willingness to trust Tyen surprised her. Though "trust" was not the best description. *He feels he understands Tyen's decisions and motives in the same way I do Dahli's. That doesn't mean we approve of them.* What Baluka had told her had disrupted the anger she had felt towards Tyen, and that made her feel weaker – and made her feel annoyed at herself that she might be resisting the possibility Tyen hadn't betrayed her only because her anger made her feel stronger.

She shook her head. *No more thinking about Tyen. Qall is more important.*

"What next?" she asked.

Baluka leaned forward to flip over a sheet of paper and read the schedule written on it.

"Strategic discussions with our generals."

"As a whole group for the first time. That's going to be interesting."

He chuckled at her wry tone as he got to his feet. "Yes. Let's see who got here early."

Rising, she followed him out of the room and up to the next level. The sound of two voices in heated discussion led them to the room the meeting would be held in. As Baluka stepped inside, they instantly ceased. Three men and one woman stood within. She had not met them before.

"Thank you for coming," Baluka said. "This is Rielle Lazuli."

Eyebrows rose and gazes sharpened as the four inspected Rielle. Their thoughts revealed that they knew more about her than she expected, though they had dismissed some of the rumours.

They knew that she had been betrothed to Baluka, but left him to join Valhan in his palace. They knew that she had rescued the boy intended to become Valhan's new body. They had heard speculation that she was almost as powerful as Valhan had been, and had been seduced by Tyen.

Seduced! As if I'm some naïve girl who couldn't possibly have had any choice in the matter? Wait . . . where did they even get the idea we were lovers?

Unfortunately, none of them were thinking about the source of the speculation, and she wanted their first impression of her to be of someone calm and determined, not distracted and offended by rumours. Frustrated, she nodded politely to each as they were introduced.

"Hapre, Pather, Fornt and Scith," Baluka said. The four were all Restorers, he explained, two having participated in the rebel attack on Valhan. The woman, Hapre, had been a general at that battle. The men ranged from Baluka's age to old enough to be her grandfather.

"Let's sit down," Baluka suggested, gesturing to a set of large chairs, all identical and arranged in a circle. He chose the furthest so that he would have a clear view of the room's main entrance. In the corners of the far wall were two smaller closed doors, and Rielle would have assumed they allowed access from servants, if not for Baluka's brief thought, as she noticed them, that they both led to escape routes from the building.

Rielle took the chair to his left; Hapre to the right. The others occupied seats beside Hapre, reasoning that the place next to Rielle ought to be left free in case an ally or friend of hers was going to join them. Though they admitted to themselves that they didn't want to sit next to someone looking so tense, when she was as powerful as the Raen had been.

So much for me giving an impression of calm and determination, she mused.

"I heard you talking as we arrived," Baluka said. "What were you discussing?"

Looks were exchanged, then Hapre drew a deep breath. "Dahli's defences."

"How many sorcerers have been identified," the younger man named Scith elaborated. "And their known strength. In particular Tyen."

A chill ran over Rielle's skin. She controlled her expression, even more determined to keep her reactions hidden now that she'd seen what they'd picked up from her.

"The Spy," the old man, Pather, growled. He was thinking that Baluka was a fool. They should have killed Tyen when they had the chance. How many would die thanks to Baluka's moment of weakness?

"Tyen will not be a threat," Baluka assured them.

The four did not look convinced. "How can you know?" Hapre asked. "He is a master of deceit."

The third man, Fornt nodded. "And the inventor of insectoids, which—"

"Tyen never intended for them to be turned into war machines. He abhors violence," Baluka told them. "After Rielle told me the truth about his role in the war of rebellion – " He paused to nod at her. "– I gathered all the information I could about him. I considered everything he did while among the rebels." Now he looked at Hapre, but no smile crinkled his eyes. "I realised that he behaved very oddly for someone who was supposed to be our enemy. When he first joined the rebellion, when it was disorganised and vulnerable, he pushed for changes that only made members and their families safer. When Yira was leader, he held the rebels back, advising caution and taking time to train recruits. When he was leader, he was criticised for being too protective and holding us back. Then he handed control to me. He could have had us destroyed so many times, but he didn't."

"Because Valhan planned for us to grow strong enough to wipe out the allies he didn't like," Scith replied.

Baluka turned to him. "I don't believe Tyen knew about that. If he had, he would have tried to urge us towards sending as many of our fighters to the battle so more would be killed, not giving strength to just a hundred."

"What do you think, Rielle?" Hapre asked.

Rielle regarded the woman, considering how she should reply. She did not want to contradict Baluka, but on the other hand she did not trust Tyen, and feared he would be a danger to them all.

"I don't believe we can risk that Baluka is right," she said. "Tyen is too powerful to underestimate. We must plan as if we believe Tyen will side with Dahli."

The others – even Baluka – nodded. *She is right, though I wish it were not so*, Baluka thought.

"Tyen is as powerful as Rielle," Pather said. "They neutralise the threat of the other."

"Their equal ability is irrelevant because what will matter in the end is how much magic they are able to gather," Hapre reminded him. "There is only so much magic in the worlds around Dahli's base. If we surround Dahli's fighters we'll restrict how much they have access to."

"Tyen can break through," Rielle warned. "Between worlds, he can overcome attempts to control his movements and travel so fast you won't have time to gather support and intercept him."

"Then you must go after him," Fornt said. "If you keep him occupied we will be free to deal with Dahli and the rest of his fighters."

Rielle opened her mouth to protest, then closed it again. It was a reasonable expectation. It made sense. But it filled her with dread. *And who will make sure Qall is safe while I'm keeping Tyen occupied?*

A discussion began about the sorcerers known to be in Dahli's forces. Before they had delved far into the known facts and rumours, a movement in the doorway drew Rielle's attention away. Two women were entering, one dressed in a long padded shift of an undyed woven fabric, the other dressed in a fine robe heavy with colourful beading. Even as Rielle read their identities and intentions from their minds, the four generals sprang to their feet, exclaiming and protesting.

"What are *they* doing here?" Scith spat.

"I invited them," Baluka replied.

"No, Baluka." Hapre turned to him and shook her head. "You risk losing more support than you gain."

He ignored her and turned to Rielle. "This is Ambaru and Tamtee, formerly allies of Valhan, now eager to stop the Raen returning." As he introduced Rielle, the pair straightened in interest and looked at her closely.

"How can you be sure they won't turn on us at the worst moment?" Scith demanded.

Looking at the women, Rielle saw that Ambaru, the humbly dressed one, had never liked working with Valhan, but to refuse would have meant death. Guilt at the terrible deeds she had done for him lay heavily, and she hoped that helping the Restorers would encourage the gods to forgive her.

The other, Tamtee, had not been able to get to the battle with the rebels in time, so she had sent her brother, who had died. She wanted revenge. Ruining Valhan's plans to return was as good as killing him, in her opinion – an opportunity she hadn't thought she'd get.

Both women did not want Valhan back. Each, in their own way, had found life without him was better.

Redemption and revenge, Rielle thought. *Both aims that will see them loyal to this cause.* She spoke over the voices arguing around her.

"They can be trusted."

Silence fell. Looking around at the generals, she was surprised and pleased to read that they believed her. Sullenly, reluctantly, but with no doubts in their mind that she spoke the truth. Despite what they thought they knew about her – *because* of what they knew about her – they respected her. That, more than anything, was unexpected.

But when she turned her attention back to the former allies, she saw that they did not trust her. Both were powerful, ageless sorcerers. They could read the minds of all these youthful, inexperienced mortals – picking up the remnant wistful admiration for Rielle in the magically weak leader of the Restorers – but not Rielle's. That alone would have made them fear and distrust her. What they did know made them wary.

They knew Rielle had been the last new sorcerer that Valhan had taken under his wing, and that Dahli had taught her. Valhan's newest recruits tended to be the most devoted.

They did not know that Rielle had stopped the resurrection and saved Qall.

Give them time, Rielle thought. *They'll soon learn this from the minds of the generals.*

Hurried footsteps echoed in the corridor behind them. A young man rushed into the room.

"Baluka," he panted. "You have . . . visitors. They . . . won't wait . . . They're . . . here." He turned to the door and backed away as several footsteps heralded the newcomers' arrival. Rielle sought minds, then drew in a sharp breath of surprise and delight. She turned to Baluka and found him now surrounded by the four generals.

"It's all right," she told them. "They're on our side. They've come to join us."

"It's true," Baluka confirmed. He had read the messenger's mind. His eyes were bright with delight. Smiling in anticipation, Rielle turned back to the doorway as the first of the Travellers arrived.

"I hear you need some help," Ulma said. "A small problem with a Predecessor that won't stay dead."

The woman's gaze flickered around the room and settled on Rielle. She smiled, then opened her arms and came forward to envelop Rielle in a hug.

"Ulma," Rielle said, hugging her back. "Thank you for coming."

"Father," Baluka said.

Pushing Ulma away gently, Rielle watched as Baluka came forward to meet the Travellers now filing into the room. Lejihk looked worn and old, his brow creased with ever more worry lines.

"Son," Lejihk replied. "We heard you're planning for war. We figured you might need a few extra sorcerers."

"How did you get away from Dahli's watchers?"

Lejihk's smile was humourless but full of satisfaction. "They think we're investigating a trade deal. Half of us remained at the Gathering. Another quarter are actually negotiating a deal, which allowed those I've brought to slip away."

"But . . . you don't take sides," Baluka told him.

"We do now." This came from Ankari, who stepped around her husband to hug her son. "We can't have all your work and sacrifice go to waste."

"The agreements we made with the Raen ended with his death. We intend for things to stay that way. And, of course, we want to help Qall," Lejihk added. As he turned to Rielle, her stomach clenched with guilt. "Though I hear he joined Dahli of his own volition."

Rielle nodded. "You did warn me that he had a mind of his own."

He took her hands. "He wouldn't have done so without good reason."

She grimaced. "I'm afraid your safety may be that reason." She looked from Lejihk to Ankari to Ulma. The ageless Traveller gave Rielle a very direct look that suggested she wanted to say something, but not here and now.

"But now that you are here, Dahli can't blackmail him," Tamtee pointed out.

Lejihk shook his head. "Other Travellers are being watched. Messages between groups have been intercepted and some families have been prevented from reaching the Gathering. We think Dahli has threatened to kill all Travellers if Qall doesn't obey him."

"It is true," Baluka said. "I would have warned you – I tried to – but I dared not risk Dahli's watchers would know I'd contacted you and deter further communication by killing Travellers."

"It does not matter, since knowing or not didn't substantially alter the danger we were in." Lejihk glanced around. "However, what we are doing now *is* a great risk. If Dahli finds out we have joined the Restorer army, he will retaliate."

"But we cannot sit and do nothing," Ankari added.

Several other Travellers had entered the room now, and it had become quite crowded. Some of them Rielle recognised from the Gathering so many cycles ago. Most she did not.

Baluka began introducing them. The two former allies were staring at Ulma, eyes bright with curiosity, as they had picked up that the woman was an ageless Traveller and very old. The messenger still stood by the door, paralysed but for his eyes roaming around the room, slowing coming to the conclusion that everything was fine and he could slip away. As another group of visitors arrived he joined their guide and left.

Rielle reached out and plucked at Hapre's sleeve. The woman turned to regard her.

"So how many more generals were you expecting?"

Hapre shrugged. "Not this many . . ." She peered around the room, noting the newcomers. "I think everyone we invited is here."

Rielle headed for the corridor and caught up with the guide. "Could you bring more chairs?" she asked him. "And quickly?"

He nodded, then raced off in another direction.

That taken care of, Rielle caught Ulma's arm and led her over to the chairs she and Baluka had vacated. She glanced around, pleased this time to see that nobody appeared to want to approach her. Creating a wall of stilled air around her and Ulma to muffle the sound of their voices, she leaned closer to the woman.

"Tell me," she said, "before we all start making war plans, what exactly do you think Qall is up to?"

CHAPTER 19

"Dahli's world has five neighbours," Baluka told the gathered generals and fighters. "Each one is devoid of magic. They're all safe to arrive in, though a few are too barren to support populations. My scouts found Dahli's followers in four of them. The fifth we are assuming is also well guarded, as the scouts didn't return and there are no local threats that could detain two reasonably powerful sorcerers. Those who did return reported that several of Dahli's followers are patrolling the place between around at least two of the neighbouring worlds and I suspect they are doing so around all of them.

"It is likely Dahli is expecting an attack." Baluka grimaced. "When I heard Dahli had established a base, I knew we would have to act quickly, and it's not possible to secretly send a call for assistance through the worlds at short notice.

"We've estimated that Dahli has more than a hundred sorcerers working for him. This is based on the traffic our watchers noted was headed towards the base these last few days. Restorers have reported that more than forty sorcerers we suspected were secretly working on Dahli's behalf have disappeared from their homes. We have some idea of these sorcerers' strength, at least. For the rest we have only scant information."

"You didn't stop them joining Dahli?" Tamtee injected.

Baluka shook his head. "Reports of the disappearances came

after those of increased traffic, and it all came about the time we learned Qall had joined Dahli."

"What if this Qall has willingly joined the most loyal?" Ambaru asked. "What if he wants to become the Raen?"

"I doubt he wants his mind replaced by another's," Rielle replied.

Ambaru shrugged. "That depends on his state of mind. For some, death is a welcome release."

"Qall is not suicidal," Rielle told him.

"Perhaps he wants to be the Successor and sees this as a short cut?"

"He's never shown that sort of ambition," Lejihk said.

Rielle nodded in agreement. "If he wanted to be the Successor, he doesn't have to become the Raen. He's already powerful enough."

"But he's inexperienced," Tamtee added. "He knows he'll need support. Maybe he sought that from Dahli."

"Then why is Dahli threatening to kill the Travellers?" Hapre pointed out. "Wouldn't it be better to find true supporters, rather than seek out the man who wants to replace his mind with the Raen's?"

"He'd find support among the Restorers," Baluka added.

"Stop this!" Ankari cried. She looked at her son. "All of you. There does not need to be a Successor. Don't be so eager to lay that burden on a person. Especially someone so young!"

Baluka lowered his gaze. "I do not want to, but if Qall joins us and claims the title of Successor, we could more easily create peace in the worlds."

Ankari opened her mouth to say more, then closed it and shook her head. In her mind her anger simmered, yet she understood why Baluka might welcome the idea of making Qall a leader, whether on his own or of the Restorers. *It will allow him to step down from his own position and responsibilities. Still, that does not justify forcing them onto a fragile young man like Qall.*

A short silence followed into which Ulma cleared her throat. "Let's return to discussing the strength of Dahli's forces."

The gathered generals and sorcerers exchanged glances, many nodding and a few smiling ruefully.

Baluka drew a deep breath. "I was going to conclude that while we can't know exactly how strong Dahli's forces are, his defence strategy choices appear to be straightforward. His forces will probably engage us in the dead worlds. If we arrive as one group, they will send out messages to the others to join them. If we spread our attack over all five worlds, they'll engage each of our forces separately, stopping any from reaching the base world. If we overcome them, the survivors will retreat to the base world and unite. By then the base world will contain little magic, so we must be careful to retain enough magic to transport ourselves away whether we win or lose, or we risk becoming trapped."

Rielle opened her mouth to reassure him that she could restore the magic in Dahli's world if needed, but paused as she realised that everyone here would then know she was no longer ageless. Though she knew that the two former allies of Valhan fully supported the fight to prevent his return, she would not reveal her vulnerabilities unless she had no choice. She could now suffocate between worlds, and couldn't heal her own injuries. She closed her mouth. The movement had caught Baluka's gaze and, as he raised his eyebrows, she shook her head.

When should I reveal I am a Maker again? The most obvious reason to was to prevent the fighters abandoning the fight because they needed to retain enough magic to escape the base world. She would not want to lose Qall because she was reluctant to reveal her new ability to quickly generate magic. *But there are dangers in telling them too. They might use all their magic only to be trapped if I am killed.*

As the discussion dragged on, with the more experienced fighters debating attack strategies, she made up her mind to tell Baluka . . .

477

but in private. The former allies might read it from his mind later, but it was worth the risk.

An all too familiar name brought her attention back to the conversation.

". . . will use insectoids?"

"I doubt it," Baluka replied. "War machines are not as effective against sorcerers as they are against ordinary people, except perhaps to force us to use more magic."

"But he may have invented a way to make them more effective," Ambaru pointed out.

Baluka shook his head. "Tyen has never been happy that his invention has been twisted for use in warfare. The last time we spoke, he was working on a way to destroy them all."

"You only have his word to go by," Hapre muttered.

"I believe him," Baluka said, turning to meet her stare. Her lips pressed into a thin line, but she nodded and looked away. "In any case, they aren't a threat to sorcerers."

"It would be a shame if they were all destroyed," Tamtee murmured. "They can be beneficial too. I've seen them used as an alarm against intruders or thieves, or for protection. Or to carry messages. Or simply as delightful toys."

"Should we use them?" Pather asked. All turned to the old Restorer, some with a scowl, others with eyebrows raised in consideration.

"No," Baluka replied. "For the same reason I gave before: war machines are less of a threat to sorcerers than to ordinary people. I doubt we'd have time to construct them anyway. But if anyone can suggest a way they might be used to our advantage, I am willing to consider it." He looked around. Nobody spoke, and many shook their heads. Baluka nodded. "Shall we move on?"

As the discussion shifted to discussing how to find out more about Dahli's base, Rielle wondered how Tyen would feel about his invention being dismissed so easily. *He'd be relieved*, she thought. She frowned at the certainty she felt. *Is Baluka's belief that Tyen is not a violent man having an effect on me? He might be right, but that doesn't mean Tyen isn't a deceiver and a spy. He's still sided with those who want to kill me and replace Qall's mind with Valhan's.*

Anger stirred but she held it back and forced her attention back to the meeting. When it ended a long while later, the generals rose and automatically formed four groups: Tamtee and Ambaru joining a handful of other former allies, the Restorers and Travellers seeking their own kind, and the spokesmen and leaders of worlds who had answered the call to arms gathering together. Rielle returned to Ulma's side, and when Baluka suggested they and his parents retreat to his private rooms until he could join them, she readily agreed on their behalf.

By the time the three Travellers had settled into the chairs in Baluka's room, they were in the midst of a heated discussion about how being considered the Successor would cause no end of trouble for Qall. Ankari was particularly angry, saying he would never get the chance to have a proper life at this rate – if he survived Dahli's plots. They didn't stop until Baluka entered the room some time later, when they politely changed the subject.

"I have to say it again: thank you for coming," Baluka said, looking from one face to the other. "I know it's mostly for Qall's sake – and the family's – but—"

"More than Qall's," Lejihk interrupted. "I meant what I said before. Now that the Raen is dead, the Travellers are no longer forbidden to alter a world's affairs. Not that we will meddle without a great deal of caution. In matters like this, which affect all worlds, we are willing to involve ourselves again."

Baluka gazed at his father. "So much has changed since I left you."

Indeed it has, Rielle thought. Her belief that it was better not to meddle with worlds was based in part on the Travellers' philosophy of non-interference. Valhan's admission that he could not always predict outcomes strengthened that belief. *Tyen and my disastrous attempt to negotiate peace between Doum and Murai convinced me it was right. Maybe it depends on the world, and the kind of inter-ference.* She thought of the world of the factory workers. The drawing she had left them with was meant to encourage the workers to rebel. *I guess I can't help interfering. I can only hope I haven't made things worse there, and that the ultimate result will be a fairer society.*

The Travellers had fallen silent. Now was as good a time as ever to tell Baluka her secret. She shifted her weight to the front of her chair. "Baluka . . ." she began, then the doubts crowded in and she could not continue.

His gaze shifted to her. "Rielle . . . you looked like you wanted to say something earlier."

"Yes." She bit her lip, then pressed on. "Something else has changed. You won't have to worry about having enough magic to leave after the battle. I . . . I am a Maker again."

Three sets of eyebrows rose, but Ulma's dropped into a frown.

Baluka nodded slowly. "It would still take some time for you to—"

"It won't," she told him. "I can make a great deal of magic now. Perhaps more than any Maker ever has been able to. When I was chasing Qall, I caught up with him. He took all the magic from the world we were in and left me stranded. After a few days, I decided to use the magic I had left to pattern-shift myself back to being a Maker. It worked, and better than I intended. Watch this . . ."

She cast about and found the sheets of paper Baluka had brought to write ideas and reminders on and the reed-wrapped blackstick he used to write with. Taking a blank page, she began to draw.

It was awkward at first. She was all too conscious of the others watching her. Taking a deep breath, she pushed all thoughts of them away and concentrated, refining the outline of the Traveller wagon that she'd been trying to draw from memory. When it was roughly outlined, she paused and concentrated on the world's magic. Sure enough, all around her was rich with power.

Looking up, she found four people staring at her in astonishment, and one in horror.

"Oh no," Ulma whispered.

Baluka, Ankari and Lejihk turned to her. "What is it?" Ankari asked.

"Some call it Maker's Curse, others Maker's Ruin," the ancient Traveller said. "It's a prophecy much older than Millennium's Rule. It predicts that if ever a Maker became ageless, a disaster will befall the worlds. In some versions, it says the worlds will all be destroyed. When Rielle lost her Maker ability after becoming ageless, I assumed it meant that nobody could be both."

"But we Travellers don't believe in prophecies," Lejihk reminded her.

"No . . . but there is always a grain of truth in them," Ulma told him. "A warning." She looked up at Rielle. "I guess we'll find out what that is soon enough."

Rielle smiled. "No, you won't. I am no longer ageless. When I restored my Maker ability, it changed the part of my mind that understood pattern shifting."

Ulma's eyebrows rose, and she let out a long sigh. Now it was the others' turn to frown.

"Could you become ageless again?" Baluka asked.

"I don't see why not." Rielle shrugged. "And at least I can fill a world with enough magic to do it, rather than turn one into a dead world."

"Would it take as long?" Ulma wondered aloud. "Now that you know what you did. Did the memory of learning pattern shifting disappear too?"

Rielle shook her head. She hadn't considered that becoming ageless again might be faster the second time. "But if I do it, I lose the ability to generate magic. If I stay a Maker I could restore all the dead worlds."

"That's quite a sacrifice," Lejihk observed.

"Heal yourself or heal worlds." Ulma pursed her lips. "Mortality or magic. Though I guess you could wait until you'd lived a full lifetime, then become ageless again. Could you switch back and forth as needed?"

"I guess so."

"Or work out how to retain both abilities?" Baluka spread his hands as Ulma frowned at him. "Prophecies aren't real, right? Can you see how being ageless and a Maker could destroy the worlds?"

Ulma shook her head. "People considered it seriously enough when I was a young girl that laws existed in many worlds forbidding Makers attempting to become ageless. I never learned why, but perhaps that information has survived somewhere."

"If we survive this battle, we should look into it. In the meantime —" Baluka turned to Rielle and smiled. "— as I have discovered, if you have plenty of ageless friends willing to heal you, you can live as long as they do."

Lejihk turned to Ulma, his eyes narrowing in thought. The ageless Traveller's gaze met his, then flitted away. "So when does the meeting resume?" she asked.

Baluka straightened. "Probably about now."

Ulma stood. "Then let's go before we get too caught up in this. I would like to know how we plan to coordinate our efforts during the actual battle."

PART NINE

TYEN

CHAPTER 21

The place between worlds was full of shadows. All kept their distance, but their constant presence put Tyen on edge as he approached Dahli's base. The shadows were most likely Dahli's followers keeping watch for sorcerers approaching, but Tyen couldn't help worrying that the Restorers had attacked while he was absent, won the day and he would arrive to find them waiting for him. Just in case, he'd gathered power in every world he stopped in.

When he finally approached one of the dead worlds surrounding the base, he sensed a shadow following. At once he turned and raced back towards it. The tracker came to a halt but did not flee.

"*Tyen?*"

Tyen knew the voice. He approached the shadow, and it resolved to become a familiar young inventor.

"*Zeke? What are you doing following me?*"

Zeke's mouth remained closed, his mental voice sounding as clear in Tyen's mind as speech. "*I want to talk to you, before you join Dahli.*"

Tyen took Zeke's arm and pulled him back to the previous world. As they arrived, Zeke sucked in air, panting as he tried to catch his breath enough to talk.

"You," Zeke gasped. "You can . . . read Dahli's mind . . . I want . . . to know . . . why is he . . . so set on . . . bringing . . . Valhan back? It's . . . more than . . . loyalty."

Tyen's heart sank a little. "I think you know."

"I suspect. I guess." Zeke sighed. "I'm done with suspecting and guessing. I want to know for sure. Were they . . . ? Did they . . . ?"

Tyen weighed the possible consequences of confirming the truth, and found none that would change anything greatly. At least, not for Qall. "No, but Dahli wishes it was otherwise. He has been in love with the Raen for hundreds of cycles."

"And the Raen?"

"Did not reciprocate. At least, I can only assume he felt nothing for Dahli based on Dahli's belief that he didn't. Except for the appreciation and affection for a good and loyal servant."

Zeke nodded. "Ah. Dahli seems like a good person, or he wouldn't be so concerned for the worlds, and he has firm ideas about right and wrong, but when I question some of the things the Raen did he gets angry. He admits some of what the Raen did was wrong. He says he did many terrible things for the Raen. Things he didn't want to." Zeke sighed. "Dahli doesn't want pity, but I can't understand why he did them. Or why he stayed when he wasn't loved in return."

"He had nowhere else to go," Tyen explained. "During the Raen's rule, if you were a powerful sorcerer you either hid, served the Raen or you were killed."

"Then why bring him back?"

"Other than love and grief?" Tyen sighed. "Loyalty. He made a promise."

The inventor's frown deepened. Tyen could see what the young man was too afraid to voice. *If he can't bring the Raen back, Dahli can no longer defer responsibility for all the terrible things he's done,* Zeke thought. *This determination to resurrect the man is as much about fear as grief. But I'd rather help him face that than lose him completely.* He shook his head. "What a mess. Either we lose and die, or we win and Dahli becomes the Raen's most loyal friend again and everyone else dies."

"Everyone?" Tyen raised his eyebrows.

Zeke's shoulder's rose. "Well, I suppose you and I will keep breathing if Valhan finds us useful. But Qall isn't going to survive, is he?"

As Tyen shook his head he watched Zeke closely. Could he and Zeke both pressure Dahli to let Qall live? The young inventor's shoulders dropped.

"It's hard enough liking Dahli when I know a little bit of what he's done in the past. I don't think I could continue to if he harms that young man." He met Tyen's gaze, searching for any hint that Tyen might agree. "Would you?"

"Liking Dahli has never been necessary," Tyen admitted.

"Then why are you working with him?"

"We . . . made a deal." Tyen could not tell Zeke that he had intended to keep Dahli from looking for Rielle and Qall, or that he now simply hoped he could help Qall in some way. "And as you say, if Valhan returns it is wiser to be an ally than an enemy."

"So you don't care what happens to Qall?"

"I do," Tyen assured him. "I tried to find another way to bring the Raen back, so Qall need not be harmed."

"Then Qall turned up." Zeke grimaced. "Why do you stay by his side and not join Dahli's followers preparing for battle?"

"Dahli hasn't asked me to. Qall wants me close, and Dahli thinks me being friendly with Qall keeps Qall cooperative. Why do you stay?"

"I thought I could help Dahli." Zeke bowed his head. "I'm beginning to think I'm a fool for thinking I could." He shrugged. "But we keep trying, don't we? Thank you for answering my questions, Tyen."

"Don't give up, Zeke. Perhaps between us we can persuade Dahli not to harm Qall. I doubt we can talk him out of resurrecting the Raen though."

Zeke shook his head. "No. I don't dare suggest it, but I will try to persuade him to let you resume your experiments."

"Thank you. I can take you through to the base if you want to save your strength."

"Yes. Please. I can only just gather enough magic to travel through to the base, and that means if Dahli's world is drained I'll never be able to leave without help."

Tyen took hold of Zeke's arm again and pushed out of the world.

The arrival place in the dead world was guarded by Dahli's followers. They recognised Tyen and Zeke, and did not approach. Tyen only paused long enough for Zeke to catch his breath before moving on. The place between the dead world and Dahli's base was riddled with new pathways, all leading to the black marble hall. In the safe area between the lamps, Dahli and Qall lounged on seats. Dahli leaned forward, placing his elbows on the arms of his chair, and steepled his fingers as Tyen and Zeke arrived.

"So, Tyen . . ." he began, intending to ask where Tyen had been, but then Zeke's thoughts caught his attention. The young man was all but radiating guilt at having questioned Tyen about Dahli.

While Dahli was distracted, Tyen looked at Qall. *I found your family*, he thought. *They are well.*

Qall's face relaxed a little, but as Tyen thought of the girl and her reaction to receiving the braid – and how infatuated she was with the young man from another family – Qall's shoulders sank and his gaze slid away. A moment later, he straightened, his mouth pressed into a firm line.

Tyen looked away. He'd assumed that Qall had sent the braid back in order to release the girl from any obligations she might have to him, but perhaps Qall had genuine feelings for her. Perhaps he'd only given the braid back in the hope that she would be in less danger if she wasn't betrothed to him.

Zeke, all too conscious of Dahli's stare, glanced at Tyen and rubbed his hands together.

"So has anything interesting happened while I was away?"

"Depends what you consider interesting," Dahli replied. His gaze shifted to Tyen, then to Qall. "I've been occupied in preparations for the Restorers' attack. Qall has been studying."

Knowing that Tyen would be watching his thoughts, Dahli turned to look at something in Qall's hands. It was the kind of box a bottle of expensive liqueur would be stored in. Reading from Dahli's mind what it actually contained, Tyen's body went cold.

Valhan's hand.

It was here, almost within his reach. He thought of all the people who wanted it destroyed. Rielle. Baluka. All of the Restorers. The Travellers. Maybe even Zeke, if he knew its significance. *And me*, Tyen added. *But not straightaway.* If he could possess it for just a little while, he might discover everything Valhan knew about resurrection. He might learn how to restore Vella.

Qall ought to be topmost on the list of people wanting to destroy it, yet here he was, holding the box in his lap as if it were a gift. That Dahli had trusted Qall with the hand was extraordinary. That the young man had not destroyed it was worrying.

"Qall?" Tyen said.

The young man looked up. "Dahli and I have come to an agreement: he'll let me access the information in it in exchange for me resurrecting Valhan." Qall smiled. "I'd appreciate your help in the latter, of course."

"Ah . . . yes," was all Tyen could think to say. With great difficulty, he pushed aside his astonishment and gathered his thoughts. He looked at Dahli. "So you no longer need to threaten the Travellers."

Dahli's smile became cold. "Of course I do. There's plenty of scope for betrayal. If the hand is harmed or I die, the Travellers perish. But if all goes well, nobody needs to die. That's a much better arrangement."

Tyen nodded. *If Dahli wants to get rid of me now, he can. He has*

489

made me redundant. Has he guessed I was only helping him to help Rielle and Qall? Perhaps he'll keep me around if he is still willing to honour our deal. "Is the work I have done enough to gain whatever information I need to resurrect Vella?"

A fleeting expression of smugness came and went as Dahli nodded. "If you stay and help Qall resurrect Valhan, yes. Will you?"

Tyen looked at Qall and nodded.

"Even if it means destroying the person who becomes the vessel."

"I will leave that choice to Qall."

The young man's eyes widened slightly, then he nodded once. "Thank you," he said, though to what wasn't clear. Perhaps only that Tyen had agreed to help.

Dahli straightened. "In the meantime . . . both of you come and sit with us. It is time you knew our defence strategy."

Tyen and Zeke did so, turning their chairs so they faced Dahli and Qall.

"As you know," Dahli began, "the six neighbouring worlds to this one are now dead worlds. Most of my followers are waiting in them, having gathered plenty of magic over the last few days. The Restorers will have to pass through at least one of those worlds to get here and, when they do, our people will try to stop them."

"Will we fight with them?" Qall asked.

"No," Dahli said firmly. "We will stay here. If the Restorers make it through to us, I will awaken my memory of the trap in this room. All I recall is that it can be very effective, and we will be safe if we remain within the lamps." Dahli glanced around, but no inkling came to him of the trap's location or nature.

He turned to Qall. "When they begin to arrive, you must remove all of the magic in this world."

Qall nodded. "So they have nothing to use against us."

"Yes."

"So what do I use it for?"

"Our defence, of course." Dahli turned to Tyen. "As for Tyen . . . well, I suppose I must ask him what he is willing to do."

"I will shield us," Tyen said holding Dahli's gaze. "But I will not kill." He met Qall's gaze. "Not even for you." The young man's eyebrows rose slightly.

Dahli nodded, unsurprised. "Valhan respected your determination to avoid resorting to violence, Tyen, as do I. You no doubt see that I've been unsure how useful you would be in this confrontation. Are you also willing to transport us out if we must flee?"

"Yes."

Qall's eyebrows had risen even higher, but now they lowered as Dahli turned to him.

"Rielle is among and possibly leading the Restorers," Dahli told the young man. "You will have to decide if you are willing to let her die."

Tyen's throat froze and his heart began to race. And yet he felt oddly reassured. Qall wouldn't kill Rielle. *Or would he? He'd known her less than a cycle.*

Qall frowned and nodded, but said nothing.

"It is not me who forces you to choose," Dahli reminded him, lowering his voice. "They don't have to attack us."

"I know," Qall muttered.

"You did try to protect her by leaving her somewhere safe."

Qall's lips paled as he pressed them together. "I might not be able to . . . make the final blow."

"Then give the magic to me and I will do it."

Unable to breathe, Tyen fought to hide the shudder Dahli's words sent through him. *Qall won't let Dahli do it. Surely, at the last moment . . .*

"I promise I will not do so unless it is necessary," Dahli assured the young man. "Remember, she was my student. I liked her. I still respect her."

As Dahli began to turn back, Tyen forced his facial muscles to relax, sending the anger and horror and fear deep inside himself, to gather within a hollow in his stomach.

If Dahli knew that I care for Rielle, would it save her? Tyen wondered. *He wouldn't destroy a means to blackmail me, surely.* But Dahli didn't need to blackmail Tyen now that Qall was willing to resurrect the Raen. *I can't help Rielle without abandoning Qall, and she would not forgive me if I did. Either way, I lose her.*

Dahli was watching Tyen now, his gaze sharp as he searched for clues of Tyen's mood. "Any questions?"

"I have one," Zeke replied.

Dahli turned to the young inventor, his initial irritation fading as Zeke smiled. "Yes?"

"How can I help?"

"You'll stay here with us," Dahli replied. *Out of danger*, he added silently. *Maybe I should have tried to do what Qall did to Rielle, and leave him in a dead world for his own protection, but then what would happen to him if I die and can't retrieve him?* "In the beginning, there will be plenty of messages arriving and leaving," he added, knowing that giving the inventor a purpose would ensure he didn't find something more dangerous to do. "I'll need help receiving and sending them."

"Message wrangler," Zeke said, then pursed his lips. "I can do that." He frowned. "Do you think the Restorers will bring war machines?"

A small shock went through Tyen, but it quickly faded as he realised how unlikely it was.

"No. They would be a nuisance, but ultimately not a threat," Dahli replied, in agreement with Tyen's thoughts. "Still, if you think of a way they may be effectively used on sorcerers, do tell me. And find a way to counter them."

Zeke nodded. "I will."

"I have a question," Tyen said. "Why don't we just leave? Why must there be a battle?"

"I doubt we'd get far," Dahli replied. "The Restorers are

watching. They probably let you back in here because they're not ready for battle, and their leader is convinced your pacifist views mean you are no threat. If we try to leave with all our followers supporting us, they'd engage us in battle anyway. If you, Qall, Zeke and I try to slip away unnoticed and fail, we'll be outnumbered and lose." Dahli shrugged, though his expression was grim. "This way, if we lose, our enemy will be in disarray when we flee."

"Will we win?" Zeke asked.

"Yes." Dahli's smile was full of confidence. "With two of the strongest sorcerers in the worlds with us, even with one only defending, how can we lose?"

PART TEN

RIELLE

The time for planning and discussion was over. The time to act had arrived at last. While Rielle knew that the attack must be carefully planned in order to give them the best chance of rescuing Qall, she'd spent the last few days gritting her teeth to hold back her impatience.

Even now, the wait seemed unbearable. They stood within the same meeting room they'd occupied when the Travellers had first joined the effort. *A small room for an army*, she mused. *But that is what magic allows. Thousands of volunteers gather magic for a hundred fighters, so that only those hundred need risk their lives.*

Though Rielle had been generating magic, she'd produced little compared to what would be used in the battle. It was hard to concentrate on drawing when her mind kept turning to the coming fight, whether Qall was still himself or they were about to attack a restored Valhan.

If Valhan is back, he'll find the worlds have changed in ways he may not have anticipated. It won't be so easy to take control. We won't be the only ones to fight him.

Volunteers had travelled as far as possible to gather magic so that the worlds around the Restorers' base weren't depleted. The generals were also worried about the state of magic in all of the worlds. They'd gathered for a fight, but in the process had discovered all were making the same observations about the worlds in general. The number of dead worlds was increasing, and where wars had

497

been fought, strong worlds were now so weak it would take hundreds of cycles for them to recover. Conflicts were decreasing, not just because they had been resolved by a victory, but as the result of the depletion of magic – whether because that made fighting harder, or because it had become a motivation for seeking peace.

The cause of magical depletion was twofold. In war, people created less, and when many people died there were fewer creators around to generate magic. While the creating of weapons might increase magic, battles used more than went into their making.

While magical machines were only a minor threat to sorcerers, they, too, used magic. This was exacerbated by the fact that war machines were usually introduced when a side in a conflict was desperate – and often that coincided with the supply of magic running low, by which time they made little difference to the conclusion. Baluka was hoping that war machines might eventually go out of favour for these reasons.

Rielle looked up as a few more fighters entered the room, this time a trio of ageless sorcerers representing a set of worlds allied with the Restorers. Baluka greeted them, talking rapidly. He had been going over all the details with everyone who arrived, despite the fact that none of the battle plans had changed.

He's nervous, Rielle mused. *He channels it into checking that everyone is ready and informed, which makes him appear well prepared and in control of every detail rather than relying on underlings to ferry information back and give orders.*

"He's a natural leader."

Rielle jumped and turned to face the speaker. Lejihk stood beside her, watching his son. His expression was serious, but he radiated pride. Yet she could see in his mind the regret that his observation had stirred. While the worlds had gained by Baluka taking charge of the rebels, the Travellers had lost.

"Everyone respects him, despite the fact he's a weaker sorcerer than all of them," Lejihk added.

"He would have been a good family head," she replied.

He shook his head. "No, he'd have always been restless and unfulfilled, like I was in my youth. My son inherited an even stronger version of that trait."

She looked back to see that Baluka had turned to greet more arrivals. "He will tire of being the Restorers' leader," she predicted. "He's halfway there already. Perhaps when he leaves, he'll start his own trading family."

"He won't." Lejihk shook his head. "He'll either exchange his role for the leadership of a smaller cause, or his enemies will force him to disappear entirely."

"Perhaps, if we win, he'll have fewer enemies to hide from," Ankari said, joining him.

"Perhaps," Lejihk echoed, but he did not sound convinced.

The room was filling quickly. Most, if not all, of the Restorers' fighters were present now. They made up over half of the army. Another thirty-seven represented allies of the Restorers. Seven were Travellers, the five other than Lejihk and Ankari being the strongest of their people. Nearly half of the fighters were ageless and most of those were newly changed. That made for an army with little experience compared to Dahli's five hundred cycles. Of Dahli's followers, at least those that the Restorers knew had joined him, several had lived more than a lifetime.

In the corner of her eye, Rielle saw someone approaching from her right. She turned to find Ulma drawing near. Since hearing that Rielle had become a Maker again, the ageless Traveller had looked worried, and her anxiety seemed to infect Rielle. Now Ulma smiled with her more usual calmness.

"Rielle," she said. "I have thought a great deal about your situation, and I have come to a decision. When you are free to, if you wish to, I will help you search the worlds for information about Maker's Curse. I know of a few ancient stores of knowledge, both accessible to outsiders and in private collections that we can visit. There must be others I do not know of, perhaps kept in secret by the Raen's allies."

"That would be wonderful," Rielle replied. She had been relieved to hear that Ulma would be transporting the non-fighting Travellers back to the Gathering after the army had left. Not only would it be a tragic loss to the Travellers if their only ageless sorcerer was to perish, but she liked the woman. The prospect of exploring the worlds with Ulma appealed a great deal. Perhaps they could become friends. That reminded her of poor Timane, left behind. "I'll first have to retrieve a friend from where we were hiding at the edge of the worlds."

"I'll come with you," Ulma offered. "We may find a few sources of ancient knowledge out at the edge of the worlds." She smiled. "It has been a long time since I was free to roam where whim and curiosity took me. Ah, here's Baluka."

Rielle blinked in surprise as she saw him coming towards them: he'd made his way around the room as she had been talking to Lejihk and Ulma. Baluka smiled at her, his parents and Ulma, looking calm and confident despite the anticipation and fear simmering inside.

"There's still no word from the scouts we sent to discover more about Dahli's base and the world it is in," Baluka told them. "I have decided we will not wait for them to return."

"It will be a risk to enter it then," Lejihk pointed out.

"Yes," Baluka agreed. "We know the air is breathable, at least. We'll approach slowly and shield the moment we arrive. The three of you, General Hapre and I will travel a little ahead of the army, at the centre and a little higher so we can see all around us. Once the layout of Dahli's base is in sight we will reposition ourselves so that we are between our fighters and the enemy when we arrive."

"And in sight of Qall," Ulma added. "So that he will hesitate to strike."

Seeing Ankari wince, Rielle looked over and shared a look of sympathy with her. She couldn't imagine Qall striking at anyone either, but who knew what Dahli could force him to do under the threat of harming his foster family? Still, it didn't make sense for Dahli to force Qall into killing two of the people he was threatening to harm if Qall didn't obey him.

Would Qall strike at me? she wondered. She didn't think so, but then he *had* stranded her in a dead world. If faced with the choice between protecting her or the people who had raised him, he'd probably choose the latter. Though Rielle had saved him, he didn't know her as well.

Baluka turned to her. "It's unlikely you'll find time to generate magic during the fighting," he said. "If you do, make sure sorcerers from our side are ready to take it. We don't want to give the enemy more power."

She resisted the urge to remind him that they'd already discussed this, and nodded.

"At the end, when we face Dahli," he continued, "hold back enough power to get us out of there. But if you know that last bit of magic will defeat him, use it. We can always have you create enough to leave later."

"Yes, Baluka," she said. A hint of amusement made it into her voice, despite her best effort.

He paused, then his eyebrows rose. "I'm making sure everyone's memories of their instructions are as fresh as possible."

"I know," she replied. "And ensuring that *you* know exactly what everyone will do as well, if all goes to plan."

"Trouble is, battles almost never go to plan." His smile faded. "Hopefully only a few parts of the plan will change, not everything."

"They're not so rigid that we can't adapt as we fight."

"No." His expression grew brighter again.

General Hapre approached, her expression taut and grim. "Everyone's here and ready."

Baluka looked at his family, Ulma and Rielle as he thought of all the things he'd like to say. Expressions of love and gratitude and warnings against doing anything foolish crossed his mind,

501

but an expectant hush had settled over the room, and all needed his attention.

"It's time," he said, then turned and strode into the centre of the room.

The army quietened. As it did, Baluka turned full circle, acknowledging all who were present.

"Welcome," he said, when the last voice faltered to silence. "And thank you." He paused and nodded in approval and satisfaction, then straightened his back. "We are united here today to prevent the return of the Raen. But that is not all. By doing so, we will save both the worlds and an innocent young man.

"I have explained the situation to you already, but I will now summarise it to ensure there is no confusion." He turned to the painting Rielle had made of Dahli. "This is our enemy: Dahli, formerly known as the Raen's most loyal. He seeks to resurrect the Raen using this young man." Baluka moved to Rielle's painting of Qall dressed in Traveller garb. "Who, contrary to appearances, is not the Raen. He is an innocent young man who was abducted, whose memories were removed and body changed in readiness to receive the Raen's mind. Rielle Lazuli rescued him, and he has been raised by Lejihk and Ankari of the Travellers. Though his memories did not return, he has become a new person. A good person. Recently, he was blackmailed into joining Dahli and, we fear, agreeing to become the vessel of the Raen's memories. Blackmailed with the threat of killing all Travellers."

Baluka paused to look around the room.

"We must prevent this."

An anxious silence followed. Baluka took a deep breath before continuing.

"This is a smaller army than that which I led to face the Raen five cycles ago, but it is better prepared. We have General Rielle Lazuli with us, a sorcerer of near equal strength to the Raen." Baluka gestured towards her. "We have the support of the Travellers." He nodded towards Ulma and her companions. "And we have the support of many, many worlds, represented by all who are here, and all who have gathered magic for the cause."

Baluka's expression and tone hardened. "Dahli's followers are of no small number, but they are spread thin in the worlds around his base. If we strike quickly and surprise them, we may make it through to him before those in the furthest worlds can reach us. Even if we do, however, it is likely they will join Dahli in facing us at his base, but perhaps by then the matter will be settled one way or the other.

"If we do not surprise them, we will likely have to defeat all of Dahli's supporters before we can move on to his base. We have prepared for that eventuality too.

"Our generals, of which there is one in every group of ten, will transport you in. When approaching Dahli's world, my group will travel in the centre and slightly above you, so you can all observe our signals and we can see our destination before we arrive. Before arriving, I will reposition us between you and the enemy. You know the signal to retreat." He raised a hand, fingers spread, thumb tucked in. "General Rielle Lazuli will transport us away from the scene of battle if our strength is depleted, whether we must retreat or are victorious. Be ready to link with her if she calls out 'join'."

He dropped his arm. "Are there any questions?"

A different sort of silence followed as the fighters exchanged glances and looked around the room. Rielle focused on their thoughts. Some were wondering if they'd achieved agelessness only to die in battle soon after, but their determination strengthened once they considered what would happen if the Raen returned. She wasn't surprised to find that many considered rescuing Qall to be secondary to preventing Valhan's return. Some even thought that they would try to kill Qall if it looked like they would not win the battle. That sent a chill through her, and she took note of which fighters they were, reassuring herself that Dahli was more likely to fall before Qall did.

503

But then strength did not always dictate who won or lost, died or survived in magical battles.

"Then let us begin," Baluka concluded. "Follow me."

He turned and beckoned to Rielle and his parents. As they stepped forward to join him, General Hapre moved to Baluka's side and the six of them grasped the hands of whoever stood beside them. The fighters formed tight groups of ten, all connected by linked hands. Baluka waited until everyone stood still and ready, then nodded to his parents.

"Breathe," he murmured.

They did. Rielle hastily followed suit. It was so easy to forget she could no longer survive longer than a held breath between worlds. The room faded to white, but the fighters remained visible, appearing to float with no obvious ground beneath their feet.

The path Baluka chose was indirect, designed to approach Dahli's world from a different direction than straight from the Restorers' base. The need to pause long enough in each world to allow breathing time meant their journey seemed slow. The generals had considered splitting up and regrouping closer to Dahli's world, but then each group would be weaker and more vulnerable to attack. They hadn't forgotten the general Volk, or the hundreds of sorcerers who perished with him before they could join the last rebel attack on the Raen. More groups meant more chances that Dahli's spies would notice one, and guess its purpose, too. If they travelled together as quickly as possible, they might get close to Dahli's world before he was alerted.

The first sign that this last ploy might have failed came when they arrived in a near-drained world which had previously been full of power. Rielle could sense the unevenness of the remaining magic. The sorcerers who'd taken it had stripped it in great spheres, leaving patches of magic between. Baluka nodded to her, and she transported them to the next world. All of the fighters were able to follow, using their reserves of magic. Baluka paused to order one sorcerer of each group to shield their companions as soon as they arrived in each new world. He selected Rielle as the shielder of his group, before ordering the army to follow him into the place between again.

More newly drained worlds slowed their journey. In the fifth, the arrival place was nestled among huge, grass-like plants which gave Rielle the strange impression that she and the others had shrunk to the size of children's toys. From between the enormous leaves came a magical attack – invisible concussions of stilled air bouncing off shields. Baluka did not order a counter-attack, instead telling Rielle to move them on, but slowly at first so he could make sure that all groups had been able to follow.

No shadows followed them, and all of the groups were present. They continued through several worlds unmolested. Then, with no indication as to why the attempts to slow them had stopped, they resumed. Every time they encountered a dead world, sorcerers attacked from concealed locations; in every instance, Baluka ignored the enemy and moved on.

It meant they were moving through fewer worlds with available magic, using up their reserves. Baluka now ordered Rielle to take charge of transportation for all, moving the army as quickly as she could towards Dahli's world. The ambushes stopped. In a pause between worlds, Baluka muttered that the culprits were most likely gathering for a confrontation in the worlds around Dahli's base.

"The chances were slim that we'd surprise them," he said.

"Do you still wish to continue?" Lejilik asked.

Baluka nodded. "The advantage we've lost is small. We've prepared for the possibility we would face all of Dahli's forces."

Rielle could see his disappointment fade under the force of his resolve, and was aware that all of the fighters would be reading it from him as well, and watching her and the Travellers for any sign of flagging confidence.

"We are three worlds from the dead ones," Rielle told him.

"Get us into the first dead world, then we'll travel separately again. Let's go."

He drew in a deep breath. The others followed suit. Pushing out of the world, Rielle travelled quickly. Though she shielded as soon as they arrived in the next world, no attack came. Nor were they ambushed in the following. The third had been recently emptied of magic – and more thoroughly than the previous drainings. Dahli had widened his defences, she guessed. A city was visible in the distance. Rielle wondered how the people there were reacting to the sudden magical death of their world.

I could restore it for them, but will I get the chance?

She looked at Baluka. "On to the last world then?"

He nodded. "On to the battle."

She pushed out of the world. After glancing around to make sure all of the groups were following, she continued on.

Past the midpoint where everything was white but for the sorcerers.

Into the darkening shadows of a battleground of Dahli's choosing.

Which was a grey and black battleground of smoke and ash. Whatever had surrounded the arrival site had been burned to the ground. And in its place stood rings of men and women.

They were arriving in the middle of Dahli's army.

TYEN

The hall had been emptied of all furniture except four chairs. Tyen and Qall occupied two of them. Dahli and Zeke stood at the corner of the square outlined by the lamps, receiving and sending a steady stream of messengers. This was keeping them constantly distracted and out of earshot.

Now is the time, Tyen thought. Turning to Qall, he opened his mouth to speak, trusting that the young man would distort the sound of their voices as he had done before.

"Yes, I have shielded us. No, I'm not going to destroy the hand," the young man said, meeting Tyen's gaze.

"But if you do, Dahli has no reason to blackmail you."

"And every reason to carry out his threat to kill all of the Travellers."

Tyen bit his lip. "Then let me destroy it."

"I doubt he'd see any difference in me doing it or letting you do it."

He was right, of course.

"Besides, destroying it would mean we'd lose more than a millennia's accumulated knowledge," Qall continued. "I would have thought you would appreciate its value."

Tyen frowned. "Because of Vella?"

Qall's gaze lowered to Tyen's chest. "And because you're an academic. You would lament the loss of knowledge whether you needed it for Vella or not. Who is another source of knowledge. How would you feel if I asked you to destroy Vella?"

"That's different. Vella is a person."

"Not a whole person," Qall pointed out.

Tyen could not help scowling at that. "She is more of a person than that hand is."

The young man's shoulder's lifted and fell. "That is true." His gaze lifted to meet Tyen's again. "Could you ask her a question for me?"

Surprised, Tyen placed a hand on his chest, against the firmness of the pouch. "Now?"

Qall nodded. "It is relevant to our current situation."

A glance in Dahli's direction told Tyen that the man was still well occupied instructing the men and women who kept appearing and disappearing before him. He took the strap of the pouch and lifted it out from under his shirt. Taking Vella out, he turned his chair so that she was not in Dahli's line of sight, but Qall could see her pages.

Her cover was warm. The leather was soft and fragile, the pages thin. As the book opened, delicate words appeared.

Hello, Qall. What would you like to know?

Tyen looked at the young man, seeking a sign of understanding that this was more than just a book. That it was a person. A woman, unfairly trapped. And that Tyen's efforts to free her were justified.

Qall stared at the words in fascination.

"If I imprint the memories in Valhan's hand on my mind, will they overwhelm my own?" the young man asked quietly.

I do not have enough information to answer that question, she replied. *However, I can tell you that everything a person knows is part of who they are. Absorbing the memories will change you, whether they replace yours or not.*

Qall nodded. "But we all change as we grow and learn and experience the world. How is that different?"

Who we already are shapes how we change. What we learn and experience is filtered by the morals and values we have learned and hold to. Another person's memories would be filtered by who they were at the time, and then again each time they recall and think about them. They may clash with your morals and values, causing distress.

"Turn the page," Qall murmured.

Tyen blinked in surprise; then, hearing approaching steps, did as instructed. He glanced over his shoulder to see Dahli approaching.

"No," Qall murmured as Tyen went to close Vella. "He knows you have her. I have more questions."

Reluctantly, Tyen left Vella open.

"How could Rielle have escaped the world I left her in?" Qall asked.

Someone may have rescued her.

"But nobody knew where she was."

"She may have been helped by sorcerers rescuing other stranded otherworlders," Dahli said from behind Tyen's chair.

"Could that world have recovered in such a short time?" Qall asked.

It is unlikely.

"Unlikely is not the same thing as impossible," Qall pointed out. "How could it happen?"

If the world contained many Makers, and all of them worked without pause but to sleep and eat.

"Rielle was a powerful Maker," Dahli said. "Until she became ageless. It is possible she regained that ability."

Tyen's skin prickled as he read Vella's reply.

Yes, but she would no longer be ageless. Though there is a prophecy that warns of such an occurrence, claiming that if a Maker became ageless it would lead to the worlds being torn asunder.

Dahli made a low noise. "What does this prophecy say exactly?"

I do not contain that information. The person I learned about it from only knew as much as I have told you.

"Prophecies are propaganda and nonsense." Dahli shook his head and walked away. Looking up at Qall, Tyen noted how the young man was frowning at the older sorcerer.

"He's blocking his memory of that," he said, his eyebrows rising. "He doesn't want to be influenced by it."

Tyen turned his attention to the retreating man, but Dahli had finished and was meeting another messenger. Qall's fingers drummed on the lid of the box, reminding Tyen once again that the object so many people would like to destroy lay within it, then leaned over to stare at Vella gain.

"Vella. Do you want to be restored to a living body?"

I neither want to nor do not want to. I cannot feel desire or other emotions.

"But you know what was done to you was wrong," Tyen reminded her.

Indeed.

"If you became a living person again, you would be able to feel emotions," Qall pointed out. "You may then regret becoming human, especially if you felt what was done to achieve it was wrong."

That is possible.

"Is Tyen in love with you?"

Tyen drew a breath to object.

No.

"Was he ever in love with you?"

Yes, though not in a physical way. It is not uncommon with my owners.

"What changed?"

"Qall!" Tyen protested. "This is none of your—"

He met Rielle.

All the breath went out of Tyen. He stared at Rielle's name, written so elegantly on the page. *It is true*, he thought. *I do love her. I knew I cared what happened to her, but I wasn't sure if I actually loved her. I didn't dare ask myself. I didn't want the answer to be "yes". After all, she left and took herself far away. And now I can't see any way I won't lose her. Either I abandon Qall to save her and she hates me, or she dies.*

"You can put Vella away now," Qall said.

As Tyen did, the young man watched him thoughtfully. "It is

fascinating watching you communicate with Vella," he said. "It is like you're talking to yourself."

Tyen frowned. "What do you mean?"

"She uses your mind to be conscious. Her responses, if they do not contain information she has stored, are the creation of your own mind. When you talk to her, it's usually in order to help you think through something, right?"

"Some of the time," Tyen admitted, not sure why this made him feel uncomfortable.

"I'm not saying there is nothing left of the person she was," Qall assured him. "What survives of her is as permanent as the knowledge she gathers. Her memories, personality and knowledge of right and wrong are unchangeable." His lips twisted into a brief, wry smile. "In this state, she could never be imprinted with Valhan's personality by absorbing his memories. If you were to place those unchangeable parts of her within a new mind, or a sufficiently complex mechanical one, she *would* change. Just as she believes me absorbing Valhan's memories would alter me, so her transformation would make her a different person, even to who she was originally."

Tyen stared at Qall. "Then her warning to you applies to her as well."

Qall nodded.

Would I lose the Vella I know? Tyen wondered. *Is it worth giving her a body if it destroys the person I like and admire? But surely it is selfish of me to want her to stay the same for fear of losing her?*

He looked down at her cover and realised that what he had promised her might achieve the opposite to what he intended. It could free the remnants of the woman, only to destroy them.

Was this what Valhan had meant when he said that the process of placing Vella in a body would destroy her?

511

RIELLE

L ooking past the fighters, Rielle saw a twilight scene. She made out a pale, undulating wall – a natural but steep slope. A smooth surface unbroken by footprints lay below her feet. They were about to arrive in a small, dried-out lake bed.

The enemy had formed a line around the top of the wall, effectively surrounding the Restorers' army. Rielle estimated they numbered around a half of Baluka's fighters. Good odds, perhaps, unless every one of the dead worlds held as many of Dahli's followers.

"I suspect the ground is not stable," she warned.

Baluka turned to Rielle. *"I'll move us from here."*

She nodded, and a moment later felt Baluka now propelling the entire army closer to the world. He skimmed towards the top of the lake bank. Dahli's fighters followed. Once above the bank, a landscape riddled with similar depressions appeared. Baluka skimmed towards one of the few upper areas large enough to hold the Restorers' army.

Dahli's fighters immediately moved into a single mass. Since no command had sounded in the place between worlds, the reaction must have been planned, perhaps even rehearsed. The enemy blurred as it shot forward, reaching the area Baluka was heading towards before him.

Rielle cursed silently as the Restorers stopped moving. Whoever was controlling the enemy's movements was stronger and therefore faster than Baluka. Baluka could head for another patch of high ground, but he would never get there before Dahli's fighters – and he and the other non-ageless in the Restorers' army were bound to be running out of air.

She turned to find him looking at her. His expression was grim as he nodded.

"*Take over*," he said.

A quick glance told her two more sites large enough for the army were close by. She chose one and started for it – fast, but not as quick as she could be. As she'd hoped, the enemy immediately streaked towards it. She sped up to match their pace, then at the last moment darted away and shot to the other site. The world vanished into streaks of grey. She wasted no time bringing them into the world, lowering Baluka's group to the same level as the rest of the army, and immediately created a shield to protect them. The sound of air being sucked into lungs broke the silence as the non-ageless among them caught their breath.

Baluka glanced at her, his eyes wide, then turned away to watch the enemy. Dahli's fighters were now forced to separate into three groups, hemmed in by the precipices of sunken lake beds. The general leading each group of the Restorers' army moved to the centre so they could consult with Baluka.

"Do you want to move to a position between our army and theirs?" Rielle asked.

"No. Levitate us a little so we can see clearly."

She hardened the air and soil beneath the feet of Baluka's group and the generals and lifted it so they could see over the heads of the rest of the fighters. Dahli's followers stood still, watching but making no sound or movement.

"Are the lake beds really unsafe, or was that a delaying tactic," General Hapre asked.

"Most probably a delaying tactic," Baluka replied. "Gaining time to get messages to the rest of Dahli's forces. I'd rather not wait for those forces to arrive."

"No." Hapre agreed.

After checking that all of the groups had erected shields Rielle shrank hers to encompass only Baluka's. She could have continued protecting them all, but Baluka wanted to be able to skim around the battlefield at any moment and if Rielle went with him the other groups would be left vulnerable.

"Why aren't they attacking?" Ankari asked.

"We're the invaders," Baluka replied. "We go first."

Hapre made a small noise of disagreement. "Another delaying tactic."

"Then we'd best get started," Baluka murmured. He drew a deep breath. "Let's give them no more time to prepare against us," he called out. "Attack!"

At once, the air hummed and flashed. Stilled and heated air met invisible barriers covering the three enemy forces. Dahli's fighters didn't respond except to ward off the attack, convincing Rielle that they were indeed waiting for reinforcements.

"Those not fighting, watch for arrivals," Baluka ordered, then added in a quiet voice. "Perhaps we can kill a few before they shield."

A chill ran down Rielle's spine at the word "kill". All through the preparations, she had refused to think about what this rescue of Qall might force her to do, but the few times she'd slept, her dreams had been full of reminders of the price her conscience had paid for the two murders she'd committed.

Both were in my defence, but Sa-Gest was not attacking me directly and I could have found another way to make sure Gabeme didn't come back to harass the artisans in Valhan's new palace. Both had been situations she'd been ill prepared for. Now, however, she was deliberately aiming to kill Dahli's followers at any opportunity. It ought to feel justified, but she could not help seeing the situation from the perspective of the enemy. *They believe the worlds need Valhan. Perhaps some have selfish motivations, but they are strong enough they're willing to risk their lives for Dahli's cause.*

Right now, she didn't care if the Raen returned. She wasn't sure if she would have joined the army if its only mission had been to prevent Valhan's resurrection. It wasn't even her promise to protect Qall that had overcome her determination to never kill again. *It's Qall. Despite his moods and occasional selfish moments, I like him. Though I can't read his mind, I know he is good natured. He deserves a chance to grow into whatever unique person his messed-up life has shaped him into. Or whoever he is despite the things that have been done to him.*

"Shadows!" Ankari warned.

Rielle did not waste time looking to see where the woman indicated. She read the information from Ankari's mind. Sure enough, a pattern of human shapes was emerging within the ever-darkening twilight, a few paces behind one of the enemy's forces. There was no time to judge how quickly the newcomers were arriving and how long it would take for a strike to reach them. Rielle drew from her store of magic, hardened the air beyond her shield into missiles, then sent them towards the group.

For a few heartbeats, she remained frozen, heart racing. Striking before a sorcerer arrived in a world was a tactic Tarran had taught her. Given no warning, defence was faster than offence. Creating shields required only as much time as a sorcerer needed to call up magic, reach out and still the air. Missiles of air were formed as quickly, since they were made in the same way, but it took extra time to propel them to their destination, even if the missile was formed close to the target.

But given warning – the sight of a target coming out of the place between – a sorcerer could create and project a missile *before* they arrived. Or heat the air to a high temperature in the place they were appearing in. Or remove all air, so any non-ageless sorcerers would suffocate.

The latter options were more brutal, but also more reliable as they didn't rely on exact timing, but she couldn't bring herself to be so cruel. Even so, part of her did not want to know if her strikes were effective or wasted. It wanted to look away. But before she could, the newcomers arrived . . .

. . . and at once six or seven of them fell.

Her heart sank, and it did not rise again when two of the fallen got up, having only been knocked down by a victim standing before them. *I can't be happy to kill, but neither can I be happy that people survive who support Dahli's aim to kill Qall and all who oppose the Raen.*

"Well done!" Baluka said, squeezing her shoulder. Then he cursed as he noticed that two of the Restorers had fallen. Dahli's fighters had begun striking at the Restorers' army while the new arrivals had provided a distraction. The sound of air humming with power and impacts grew abruptly louder.

"That must be who they were waiting for," Hapre said.

"No. Here comes another lot!" Lejihk shouted. "Ah! Too late."

Sure enough, a group of Dahli's followers had appeared beyond one of the other fighting forces. It immediately joined them. Yet at the same time, sorcerers within the enemy began retreating from the front. They gathered at the back and, as Rielle watched, four joined together and disappeared.

"They've depleted their magic," she noted, reading the information from other enemy fighter's minds.

"Leaving in small groups wastes magic," Hapre said. "They know it too. Dahli ordered they do it this way, but they don't know why. The newcomers only know that they're to take exhausted fighters to meet Dahli." She shook her head. "It doesn't make sense. It takes as much magic to transport forty as four. Better to wait until more are exhausted before fleeing."

"Are they gathering more power?"

"Perhaps. But from where? Several of the worlds leading to this have already been drained."

"Unless they left a few intact. An escape route as well as a source of strength."

"That would be a risk." Hapre frowned. "What if we found and stripped them?"

"Could one of us investigate?" Rielle looked at Baluka.

His brow wrinkled as he considered. She could see he was tempted. This escape route would be guarded, if it existed. He couldn't send any but his strongest to investigate, and he needed his strongest here.

"No. It could also be a trap," he said. "I know I'd have people in place to deal with a scout – even a powerful one like—"

"More reinforcements!" Lejihk warned.

Rielle turned to see shadows appearing behind the third group of Dahil's fighters, and for the next stretch of time her focus was on sending strikes to catch them at the moment they arrived. This time she managed to eliminate nine of them.

"Eliminate", she thought, tasting bile. *I'm already starting to think like a killer, reducing them to pieces in a game.*

"How are we doing?" Lejihk asked.

Baluka looked around. "Hard for me to tell . . ."

"We've lost five to lucky strikes from the enemy, and expended half of our strength," Hapre told him. The woman was clearly strong enough to read the minds of most of the Restorers' fighters. "The enemy are harder to read," the woman said. "They're not working in groups, as we are, and there is no leader. It's less efficient."

"But we can't read Dahli's overall strategy from their minds, only individual orders." Baluka shook his head.

Rielle could see him questioning the Restorers' strategy. The sorcerer shielding each group had to give the fighters within it gaps through which to strike, indicating where these were with subtle signs that could only be seen when close by. This meant that an attack from the enemy might coincidentally find a gap, penetrate the shield and kill someone within. Fighters inside the shield could also shield themselves to prevent this, but it doubled up on the use of magic. Each of Dahli's fighters shielded only themselves.

"We've killed more of the enemy," Lejihk observed.

"Yes, but only as they arrived."

Only those I killed, Rielle thought, and shivered.

"Deaths in sorcerous battles tend to come all at once at the end," Hapre told the Traveller. "Once one side is too depleted to shield." Her lips pressed together. "At least, that is true when the fighters are trained and organised. In a free-for-all, it can be bloody all the way to the end. Ah! There's another lot. They must have arrived elsewhere and walked here."

Rielle turned to look in the direction Hapre was squinting in. Sure enough, a group of about twenty sorcerers was marching towards the fight. Reading their minds, she saw that they had indeed arrived at a distance in order to avoid the weakness she had exploited.

"They believe they're the last group," she told Baluka. "From the furthest neighbouring world to Dahli's."

"So this is all of them?"

"They believe so."

"Now that they're all here, they'll start trying to work out how strong they are," he told her. "Watch and tell me what they conclude."

She did, and a little while later told him. "More than half of their fighters are depleted."

"And ours must be more than that by now." Baluka's frown deepened. "This is going to be close." *And we'll not have much left to tackle Dahli, let alone Tyen.* He was hoping Rielle and Tyen would cancel each other out in strength, though in reality it came down to how much magic either had been able to gather in preparation.

"More arriving!" Ankari warned.

"What?!" Hapre exclaimed. "Dahli must have kept this lot secret from the rest."

Rielle spun about to face the new threat, arriving behind one of Dahli's forces. She stretched out her mind to seek theirs. As she read their minds, she let out a gasp of surprise. "No!" she told them. "Not Dahli. These are ours!"

"But . . ." Baluka began, then he stopped as two more groups arrived behind the other enemy fighters. "What's going on?"

"They are some of the supporters who provided magic for our fighters," Hapre answered as she read the truth from the newcomers' minds. "Including most of the Travellers who came to us, led by Ulma. They decided to gather more magic after they left us, and these fighters volunteered to follow and join us."

Baluka looked stricken. "I told them to go home. Not all of us need die if we fail. There should be some of us left to continue the fight if the Raen returns."

"It is up to my people to decide how much they are willing to risk or sacrifice, and when," Lejihk told his son.

Baluka looked at his father, then grimaced and nodded.

Hapre nodded. "Their doing this without telling you – deciding at the last possible moment – means that Dahli's spies could not have learned of it soon enough to report it to him."

The reinforcements were indeed engaging Dahli's forces now. The barrage from the three enemy groups on the original Restorers' army abruptly weakened. Watching the minds of the enemy, Rielle saw doubts growing. Dahli had said they should retreat to his base world if they began to fail. A few had already concluded the battle was lost, and were waiting for others to give some sign they agreed. Nobody wanted to be the first to retreat, however, knowing how it would appear disloyal to their leader, a man known to value loyalty above all else.

Then one of Dahli's fighters crumpled as her strength failed before she could retreat behind the protection of the others. A moment later another collapsed, and a third shrieked as he was enveloped in flames. Shouts rang out among them and combined to form a mutual decision. Hands grasped arms. Men and women vanished, leaving a couple of fighters who hadn't linked in time. They were smashed to the ground before they realised their mistake.

The silence that followed was brief; then the reinforcements hurried to join the Restorers' army and the air filled with questions. Rielle lowered Baluka and the generals to the ground, then sought out Ulma. The ageless Traveller hugged her, then turned to watch Baluka as he moved through the fighters, seeking estimates of strength, replacing exhausted sorcerers with newcomers in each group. It was done quickly, and soon the crowd had been divided into two.

"Go," Baluka told the depleted sorcerers, and they disappeared, taken away by one sorcerer strong enough to get them beyond the dead worlds. He turned to the rest. "Stay in your groups, one shielding and the rest fighting. Hapre, Rielle, Lejihk, Ankari and I will travel a little in front again so that we may take the foremost position when we arrive." He walked into the centre and linked hands with Rielle and Hapre. "On to Dahli's base."

The pitted landscape of dead lakes faded into white.

TYEN

"INTO THE CENTRE OF THE ROOM!"
Dahli's shout made both Tyen and Qall jump. Looking around, Tyen saw that men and women were appearing in the hall, most within the square of lamps but a few within the danger zone. They walked over to surround the chairs. Many started as they saw Qall, bowing quickly before they followed Dahli's order to turn and to face outwards.

Qall ignored the reactions of Dahli's followers. He slowly rose to his feet, the box gripped tightly in his hands, and stretched his neck to look over the heads of the sorcerers. Tyen stood and looked around. A crowd of more than fifty now surrounded them. More were arriving.

The crowd parted briefly to allow Dahli and Zeke through. Without glancing at Qall or Tyen, Dahli strode to an empty chair and stepped up onto the seat, kicking the cushion out of the way. Zeke leapt up onto another.

"Shield and keep watch," Dahli called. "Call out when you see them." He looked down at Qall. "Do you remember what I said you should do?"

Qall nodded. At once the room darkened, and yet Tyen could still see clearly. His senses adjusted, telling him that it was the sudden lack of magic he'd noticed. Stretching out, he could not find a scrap of it anywhere in the world. He thought of the local people, and wondered if they'd guessed who Dahli was, and the price they'd pay for their world being the location of a magical battle.

Copying Dahli, Tyen pushed the pad of his chair to the floor and climbed onto the seat. He looked down at Qall, expecting the young man to do the same. Qall seemed frozen, his face pale, but as Tyen looked at him, he twitched, shook his head as if to wake himself and sat down.

He can watch the fight through everyone's mind, Tyen realised. *So could I.* He stayed put. It seemed too important and dangerous a moment to trust entirely to other people's perceptions.

The room quietened. Dahli's gaze constantly moved around the room, searching and alert. Reaching out to the minds around him, Tyen caught snatches of memory of the fight these men and women had left, retreating when reinforcements joined the Restorers. The enemy was more organised and had sustained fewer casualties, and when Dahli's fighters had begun to fall in greater numbers they'd retreated.

All had been afraid they were about to lose the battle, and their lives . . . until they'd seen Valhan. Now they were filled with hope and defiance – and some confusion. Why hadn't the Raen been fighting with them, instead of waiting here? Why was he now sitting, ignoring his surroundings?

A shout rang out, followed by a hiss of many indrawn breaths. Dahli's head snapped around towards the shouter, who was pointing out beyond the lamps. Tyen followed the direction of his gaze.

Five shadowy figures darkened the white room. As they grew more distinct, many fainter shapes formed a greater shadow around them.

"Wait," Dahli ordered, though none were considering wasting their magic on targets that hadn't yet arrived. Tyen sought Dahli's mind and saw a memory rushing to the fore as it was freed. Something about a trap. Something Dahli wasn't entirely sure would work, but was worth trying . . .

Then Tyen was distracted as the first five figures moved as one, skimming out from the middle of the Restorers towards Dahli's followers. As they passed the square of lamps, they stopped and formed a line, hands linked. The fainter shadows grew more distinct, taking the shape of people. These moved to form an arc, shifting either forward or back to avoid arriving with the lamps within their bodies.

Tyen could make out the faces of the first five now. His stomach sank as he recognised Baluka in the centre. Though it had been obvious who would lead the attack, it did not make being within the opposing army any easier. Two older Travellers stood to Baluka's right. On Baluka's left stood two women. Observing the one to the far left, Tyen's heart sank. Hapre had seen him, and her brows had lowered into a disapproving scowl.

He turned his attention to the other woman, and his heart stopped.

Rielle.

She too had seen him. She also regarded him with a frown, but her stare was more searching than angry. His heart lightened a little at that, but only a little. *Perhaps there is a chance to—*

"Ah," Dahli said. "So that's—"

A deafening sound knocked Tyen's mind into shocked stillness. Gasps and yelps of surprise surrounded him. Qall uttered a low cry, leapt up and climbed onto his chair.

Then the screaming began.

Baluka and his companions spun around to stare behind them. Where the hall had been empty but for the Restorers' arriving army, rows upon rows of poles now filled the space between floor and ceiling. Hanging from and embedded within the poles were limbs and torsos and heads – or pieces of them . . . some of which were coming loose and slipping to the floor.

Time seemed to slow as Tyen's mind struggled to comprehend and understand what had happened. Two-thirds of the Restorers' army had materialised outside of the lamps, within the trap. The poles had fallen a heartbeat before they'd arrived. The fighters

523

had no chance to move to a safer place. They'd materialised *within* them.

The lucky ones had died instantly. The rest remained alive, not just pierced but fused with metal, flesh slowly separating where the two met so that part of the victims continued to fall to the floor with a sickening slap, followed by a spatter of blood.

It was a brutal trap. An effective trap. Looking up, Tyen saw row upon row of dark circles in the roof. A few of the poles had not descended fully and hung over the carnage like sinister stalactites. So not a completely foolproof trap, but enough to weaken the army dramatically. Enough to turn the battle in Dahli's favour.

Then Tyen sensed something else. Magic was blooming within the room, released by the dead and dying sorcerers. As it did, it was drawn swiftly away towards Dahli's army. To Dahli.

It came with a gust of air displaced by the trap and its victims, laced with the smell of blood and vomit and faeces. A few of Dahli's followers began to choke or throw up. Tyen could see shock in their faces, or relief, and even admiration. He looked in their minds. Though many were sickened, all were glad to be fighting on Dahli's side.

Except for one.

Zeke was staring at Dahli. His mind was full of horror and disbelief. Dahli gazed back at him, his expression hardening.

"This is war, Zeke."

Zeke shook his head. "I can't love anyone who would do this," he said so quietly that Tyen only heard it because he could read Zeke's mind. "I can't let myself."

Dahli flinched.

Stepping down from the chair, Zeke turned to Qall. "I'm sorry, Qall. I can't do anything to help you. Know that I would if I could. I wish you all the best."

"Zeke—" Dahli began. But the young inventor straightened and faded out of sight.

Dahli reached out towards the shadow of the young inventor,

his triumph at the trap's success dissolved by guilt, regret and frustration. *I have to do this*, Dahli told himself. *I must be ruthless.* Yet he understood Zeke's rejection. The trap *was* terrible. It made him a mass murderer. Again. That thought made his heart burn with a familiar ache, and a desperate determination to succeed in his task. When Valhan returned, he would approve of what Dahli had done. He would say Dahli had made a difficult but correct decision. That he would have ordered Dahli to do it.

Tyen's stomach turned. He swallowed hard, tasting bile. For the first time, hate for Valhan pressed into him. *He used Dahli's conscience as well as his love to bind him. With Valhan to take the blame, Dahli could do anything.* What would happen if all possibility of the Raen's return was destroyed? Tyen had always assumed Dahli would be gone — having fought to the death. *But if he survived . . . he couldn't shift blame to Valhan any more. Would he self-destruct?*

Tyen looked at Qall. The young man held a hand over his mouth, his face pale and eyes wide. But as he saw Tyen looking his way, he lowered his hand and his expression hardened. He looked down at the box containing Valhan's hand.

"Qall . . .?" Tyen began.

The young man glanced up at Tyen, his eyes wide and frightened. He had never looked less like Valhan.

"I'm fine," he said. Then he bowed his head and his shoulders hunched. "Watch the battle."

So he can watch it through my eyes, Tyen understood. Straightening, he looked over the heads of the fighters to find that a more traditional sorcerous battle had begun.

The air hummed and glowed as the surviving Restorers attacked and Dahli's followers responded. The Restorers fought in organised groups, one member shielding as others attacked, with exhausted fighters retreating to the back. Dahli's followers shielded themselves as they fought.

Tyen sought the minds of each side. Baluka was worried. The

Restorers had been winning when Dahli's forces had retreated to this world, but with only a third left – and Dahli having taken the magic released by the two-thirds that had perished – their prospects weren't good.

Baluka looked at Rielle. Her face was hard with determination, her teeth pressing against her lower lip.

"Are you strong enough to transport us out?" Baluka asked her.

She did not answer.

"Rielle!"

"I'm not leaving without Qall."

"You'll die if we lose and are trapped here. We'll all die."

"Qall won't let them kill us. He'll insist that Dahli abandon us here instead. I'll make magic. We'll escape eventually."

"Can you see what Qall's doing?" Baluka asked.

"He's just sitting there, staring at a box," she replied.

"He must have heard Lejihk and Ankari calling his name."

She grimaced and shook her head. "He's not watching. He may not even be listening. Dahli must have done something to him."

"If we are to retreat, we should go now. They're bound to follow. We'll need extra magic to evade them."

She shook her head. "Qall will have to pay attention to us, if we stay to the end."

She's right, Tyen thought. *But it is a terrible risk to take.* And a terrible choice to force on the young man. Let the foster parents he loved die, or change sides and know Dahli's followers will kill all the Travellers in revenge.

And I . . .? A chill ran down Tyen's back. *He's not the only one who must decide between two terrible choices.*

Could he watch Rielle perish? His eyes found Rielle again and refused to move away. If he switched sides, it might save her, and the Restorers, but it would mean abandoning Qall. Dahli was sure to flee with the young man if he lost, and continue his quest to resurrect the Raen. Like the Restorers, he'd kept some of his supporters out of the battle, with instructions to follow if he lost – including attacking the Travellers. Qall would still be in his power.

Tyen forced his gaze away from Rielle to the young man sitting below. Qall's attention was still fixed on the box. *He needs advice and guidance. I should stay and be a voice of caution and reason to counter Dahli's manipulations.*

But if Tyen let the people Qall loved die, would he ever convincingly be a good influence again? Would Qall see him as another sorcerer as callous as Dahli? Would he model himself on them both?

Tyen looked up at the Restorers. They had formed one closely huddled group, protected by a single shield held by Rielle. Most had depleted their store of magic. Many were watching Rielle, their fears growing. They knew they had lost. They knew she was supposed to be transporting them away.

Dahli's forces were moving closer, slowly surrounding the Restorers. Dahli remained on the chair, though he was now positioned at the back of his army. He looked down at Qall, and a small smile of satisfaction curled his lips. He glanced at Tyen briefly – a cautious, calculating look – before turning back to the battle.

A creeping sensation ran across Tyen's skin. *What is he up to now?* Stepping off his chair, Tyen sat down and leaned towards Qall. The young man's gaze was fixed on the box, unblinking and glazed.

"Qall," Tyen said, keeping his voice low. "I'm going to switch sides. It's the only way to save Rielle and your parents. Come with me."

Qall's expression did not change.

"You are in a stronger position than you think, Qall. I won't pretend that Dahli isn't a threat to the Travellers, but if you destroy the hand and join the Restorers, they will help you protect them."

The young man's head moved slightly to the left, then back to the right. His mouth formed a single word. *Go.*

Tyen nodded and sighed. "I understand. It is your choice. Know that I wish you well. You are stronger and smarter than you think, Qall. Keep fighting."

Standing up, Tyen turned towards Dahli's forces. A row of backs blocked his path. Shaping magic into a wedge of stilled air, he forced them apart, pushing through the unshielded sorcerers who had depleted their strength. Yelps of surprise followed him, changing to words of encouragement as he emerged from the other side, and then cries of anger as he kept walking.

All attention shifted to him. Fighters stopped attacking. Silence spread.

Tyen looked at Baluka. The man's face was shifting from suspicion to dread to hope and back again. Tyen looked at Rielle. Her stance was protective and wary, but her eyes were wide.

Tyen encountered her barrier, then, pushing hard, forced it back until he was a mere step from the pair. Then he turned to face Dahli's forces, and stilled the air around the Restorers' army, protecting it as the enemy's onslaught resumed.

"STOP!" came Dahli's command.

The battering ceased. Tyen looked up, expecting to see Dahli's head rising above his forces, eyes glaring and accusing, but he had disappeared. Tyen sought the man's mind, but before he found it a voice rang out, shouting orders. The enemy fighters parted, revealing Dahli and Qall walking forward. Tyen's stomach turned to ice. The young man's expression was cold and haughty. As he surveyed what remained of the Restorers' army, a look of satisfaction twisted his face.

This is Valhan. Tyen stared in disbelief. *What happened? Qall was himself a moment ago.*

Tyen thought back, picturing Qall's glazed stare fixed on the box. *He doesn't have to touch the hand to access its memories. He only has to reach out to them with his mind . . .* Then he realised what

Qall had done, right under his nose. Desperate for another alternative, the young man had absorbed Valhan's memories. Had become Valhan, in order to save his family.

Except how could that save them? Valhan is as likely to kill them as Dahli. Unless he hoped to have some influence on the man . . .

"You're too late," Dahli said, smiling at the Restorers and Tyen. "All of you." He stopped and bowed to Qall. "Welcome back, ruler of worlds."

"No," Rielle whispered.

Slowly, but with grace, Qall approached the Restorers. The box remained in one hand, held lightly now rather than in a tight grip.

"The Raen," someone said. Tyen could not tell if it had come from the Restorers or Dahli's forces, but it was soon repeated on both sides in voices hushed with reverence and terror.

"No," Rielle said again, her voice stronger. She stepped forward, forcing Tyen to extend his shield. "Qall!" she said, glancing around. "It is Qall."

But Dahli's smile was full of smug confidence. He turned back to Qall. Or Valhan. "What is your first wish, Raen?"

Qall/Valhan looked at him and frowned, then seemed to recollect something. He smiled approvingly. The pause gave Tyen a moment of hope. The smile weakened it, and as Qall/Valhan spoke it shattered.

"Unblock your memories, my most loyal friend."

Qall's voice was gone, replaced by the deeper timbre of Valhan's.

Dahli nodded. As he removed the blocks, memories blossomed like poisonous flowers. He recalled how he'd accessed Valhan's memories himself, finding that the Raen had considered ordering Dahli to absorb them if the resurrection failed. As a combined Dahli/Valhan, he'd have been able to continue Valhan's experiments and in time find a way to complete a true resurrection.

Dahli had realised that a Qall/Valhan combination would do just as well — maybe was even better. The new Qall would willingly help him resurrect Valhan with no conditions on the process, unlike Tyen. Though he'd kept Tyen around in case he was wrong.

All he'd had to do was trick Qall into absorbing them. But Qall was too clever to be easily fooled into it. To ensure Qall had no time to consider the consequences, he'd lured the Restorers into attacking, forcing the young man into a desperate situation in which the risk of hosting Valhan's memories seemed worth taking.

Qall/Valhan's gaze fixed on Rielle. He broke from stillness into rapid motion, striding towards her. A single thought reverberated through Tyen.

He means to kill her.

"No!" Tyen gasped. Another voice echoed his cry – Baluka. Tyen hardened his shield, determined to protect her.

Qall . . . Valhan . . . suddenly blurred. Too late, Tyen realised the man had slipped out of the world to skim past his shield. Rielle raised an arm instinctively to fend off her attacker. Valhan took hold of it.

And they vanished.

PART ELEVEN

RIELLE

orlds flashed by. Rielle barely registered them. All her attention was captured by Qall's face, or Valhan's. Every shift in his expression lightened her heart or sent it diving. One moment it was cold and flat, the next softened with doubt and relief. The latter would have given her hope that some echo of Qall still remained, if it hadn't occurred to her that they were to be expected of someone who had been remade and was growing used to a new body.

Another sensation than fear demanded her attention, growing from the intensity of a whisper towards a scream. She looked away, trying to detect the source, and when she realised it was not coming from outside her but from within, a new kind of terror chased away both hope and dread.

She was suffocating. Instinctively, she opened her mouth in an attempt to breathe, but it made no difference in the place between. Her brief existence in each world was not enough to fill her lungs, though she tried to suck in air. Her awareness began to blur, to fragment . . .

A wall of dizziness and pain slammed into her. She was aware of gravity but had lost all sense of balance. The ground – or something large and flat – pressed into her back. Her lungs were on fire, her head pounded. Air was available, but she could not get enough of it into her.

As abruptly as the onslaught had begun, it faded. A familiar sensation spread throughout her body, though it had never been as powerful as this before.

She was healing herself.

But that's not possible. Unless . . . unless I was wrong when I told Ulma I was no longer ageless. Then that meant . . . what? That the worlds will end?

She could not rouse the energy to care. Only the retreat of pain and dizziness mattered. She grew aware of a warm pressure on her arm and the truth dawned on her. Someone else was healing her. Someone who knew pattern shifting. *Not me after all.* Her sight cleared, and she found Qall kneeling over her, his expression concerned, then relieved as he met her eyes.

Qall. But Qall couldn't pattern-shift. This must be Valhan.

But her foolish heart refused to give up hope. It told her Valhan would never have shown such emotion. Valhan wanted her dead. Valhan would have punished her for preventing his resurrection, not saved her from suffocation.

Unless he changed his mind. Unless he had forgiven me. But . . . why would he?

"Rielle," he said. "Rielle, are you all right?"

His voice was Qall's. High, not deep. With the accent of Lejihk's family. And yet, this could all be faked. She stared up at him, reluctant to speak until she knew who she was speaking to.

"It's all right," he said with a familiar impatient twitch of his mouth. "It's me. Qall."

She frowned, wondering if she wanted it to be Qall so badly that she was too willing to trust him.

"Prove it."

He smiled. "You're proud of Timane and what she's accomplished in Deeme, and guilty about not going back to check on the servant you had befriended at that suspended crystalline palace."

She frowned. Both had occurred after Valhan's death. She hadn't thought about them since she'd arrived in Dahli's base. How could he know about them?

Because he has Qall's memories.

"You can't be Qall. He isn't ageless."

He sighed and picked up a box. Opening it, he tilted it so she could see the contents. A hand, shrivelled and dried.

"I learned how to pattern-shift from this."

Valhan's hand. Qall had accessed the memories in Valhan's hand. Or was this Valhan, accessing Qall's memories in order to pretend to be him?

"But that takes many, many days and a great deal of magic."

"Usually, yes. I didn't have to imprint anything into magic, since the pattern was already in here. I just copied it into my mind." He tilted his head slightly. "If I was Valhan, wouldn't I have destroyed this as soon as I'd been resurrected? Wouldn't I have killed you and be ordering everyone about back at the battleground?" He closed the box and set it aside.

All her instincts told her this was Qall. The more he spoke and moved, the more she was sure it was not Valhan who knelt beside her. *If I'm wrong, there's nothing I can do about it. I have no choice but to play along with whatever game Valhan is playing. So I may as well act as if he is Qall for now, and see if something happens to convince me either way.* Pushing to a sitting position, she waited for a short spell of giddiness to pass.

"Take it slowly," he warned.

"I know," she replied, unintentionally curt.

He chuckled. The sound sent a shiver down her spine. It was the sound of an older man. A more mature, confident man than Qall. And yet Valhan would never have expressed such rueful affection. *Qall could have grown up a bit since he abandoned me. If it is him.* She slowly climbed to her feet.

"I owe you an apology," he said.

She shrugged. "You couldn't have known I wasn't ageless any more."

"No . . . Well, yes, but I mean for leaving you in that world."

"Ah." She frowned. "Why did you?"

"Hiding wasn't working. We'd been running away for less than a cycle and Dahli's searchers had already tracked us down. When it came to fighting, you were a terrible teacher. I know you did the best you could, but you've never been in battle. I read everything I could about Dahli and Tyen from you, then decided I'd rather try to deal with Dahli than wait and hope my family stayed safe. After all, I was stronger than him and could read his mind, and he couldn't kill me or he'd lose Valhan's vessel. The only advantage he had over me was that I would never be able to stop his people killing the Travellers in time if he gave the order. I can't be in more than one place at once. I knew he'd use you against me if he could. Trapping you in a dead world was the only way I could think of to keep him from using you against me." He paused. "How did you escape?"

"By becoming a Maker again." There was no point hiding the truth when he could simply read it from her mind. "Which is why I'm not ageless any more. It uses the same part of the mind."

"You have become more than an ordinary Maker," he said, now reading her mind. "Vella told me there's a prophecy that says if a Maker becomes ageless, the worlds will be torn apart."

At the mention of Vella, a tingle had run across her skin, but she was not ready to ask about Tyen. "Ulma said the same, but she said it was a very old prophecy and probably not very reliable."

He nodded. "Valhan didn't believe in Millennium's Rule, though he encouraged others to so that the rebels would come to fight him and instead rid him of the allies. I don't yet know if he knew of this prophecy about Makers. Dahli and Tyen don't believe prophecies are true predictors of the future either."

He doesn't yet know? Rielle wasn't sure what to make of that. "So Tyen let you read his book?" she asked, remembering that Vella could read the minds of everyone she touched. If he touched Vella now, she'd know if he was Qall or Valhan . . .

"No, I asked him to ask her some questions."

"About what?"

"I'll tell you later. We must keep moving. Dahli's bound to follow us." He bent and picked up the box, then held out his hand.

"Where are we going?"

"You'll see when we get there."

Again she noticed the new confidence in him. Ignoring the questions crowding her mind, she took his hand.

Qall – she could not help thinking of him as Qall – travelled quickly, but stopped regularly enough for her to catch her breath. They passed through dead worlds and rich, battle-scarred landscapes and scenes of prosperity. Some were familiar; most were not.

Then Qall began forging a new path through the place between. They arrived in the midst of cruel-looking peaks in a dead world. After she had caught her breath, he did not leave again, but skimmed over the mountains and across a desert, descending to a large, low dune in a desert painted gold by a rising sun. In the distance, the white walls of a city nestled into the crook of a silvery river. Rielle stared at it as they arrived, wondering why it reminded her so much of . . .

"Fyre!"

"Yes," Qall replied. "I saw it in his memories."

He'd brought her home. The realisation filled her with alarm. Did he think she wanted to be here? She stretched her senses out, seeking magic, and found none.

"This is still a dead world."

"Not completely. Some magic has been generated since Valhan stripped the world to leave."

"But so little it is barely detectable. Why did you bring me back?"

"So somebody knows where I am living."

"You?" She turned to stare at him. "Here?"

"Yes. I am known here. Not as who I am, or as Valhan, but

537

as someone most people will not harm." He frowned, but in concentration rather than anxiety or anger. His hair darkened and gained a sheen. The light that reflected off its glossy surface was tinted a dark, familiar blue. His skin was lightening to white. The Angel, returned to her world.

"Why?" she asked. "Why do you want to live here?"

"Because I need time to sort out which memories are mine and which are his without people who knew him influencing me." Qall lifted the box. "Because I want to be sure, if Valhan's personality does overcome mine, that he'll be stuck here, and will grow old and die. Before I absorb any more of his memories, I'll use up the magic I have – I'll probably need it to establish myself here, though I'll save a little in case of trouble but not enough to leave the worlds again."

She shook her head. "I don't understand."

"Valhan found that a vessel whose memories weren't erased contains both identities, each of which struggle to dominate. He thought that if he imprinted his mind on another's he would win eventually, since he'd lived longer and had more memories. As you know, he went on to develop a way to empty the mind of a vessel first, and his tests showed it was more reliable." Qall shrugged. "I learned this by accessing his memories. I also saw that doing so would take too long. The battle would be over before I discovered everything I needed to know. So I sought and absorbed only the memories I thought would be useful – enough to mimic Valhan so I could order Dahli to stop the fight, and to learn pattern shifting in case I needed to heal someone or completely change my appearance."

A chill went through Rielle. "You took a great risk."

"Yes. But I reduced it as much as I could. Even so, those memories . . . changed me." He looked down at the box, his face shifting into an expression of longing. "I want to access his memories again to find out who I was, but I dare not look until I am sure I am in control. What if he is lurking there, waiting for me to try, ready to overcome my identity? I must make sure that, if he does, he stays trapped in this world."

Rielle nodded slowly. Her heart was lightening. Valhan would not strand himself here willingly. Valhan would want to regain control of the worlds. "It really is you."

"Mostly," he replied, looking up at her.

His eyes were bright with pain. He lifted the box and lifted the hand out. "It is extraordinary, this thing. He made it before the rebels confronted him, so he was walking around with a dead hand for a day or so. The information in it is copied hundreds, maybe thousands of times, so just this finger – " He took hold of the smallest digit and bent it until it broke away from the hand with a dry tearing sound. "– holds many copies of the same information imprinted in the rest."

Rielle could not suppress a shudder at the sight of him casually breaking off the finger. He stowed it within his clothes.

"Dahli decided not to turn me into Valhan," Qall continued. "Partly that was Tyen and Zeke's influence. They both thought that if there was another way to resurrect Valhan, Dahli ought to try it. So he unlocked his memory of the hand's location and consulted Valhan's memories and came up with the idea of persuading me to absorb Valhan's memories. He thought that if I understood Valhan better, if part of me became him, I'd want to help him resurrect himself. Dahli's great weakness is his belief that, if we all knew Valhan as he did, we'd all love him as much." Qall looked up at Rielle. "Which is why your betrayal angered Dahli so much. You had the chance to understand Valhan, both in person and through his memories during a resurrection, in a way few ever did, and yet you refused to bring him back."

"He wanted to kill me."

"It wasn't just that," he reminded her. "You couldn't let him kill an innocent boy. For that, I owe you a great deal."

"You owe me nothing. Just don't . . ." She hesitated, realising the burden she could easily put on his shoulders.

539

"Don't become the monster Valhan was," Qall finished. "You didn't place that burden on me. I did. All I can promise is that I will do my best not to. And that is why I am here. If I am to gain even a fraction of his knowledge, I must risk that I become more like him."

She frowned. "You don't need to absorb his memories to find out who you were."

He nodded. "That's true. What is also true is that I will not survive long in the worlds without the knowledge he had. I am, after all, his Successor."

"Prophecies aren't—"

"It doesn't matter if they're real or not, if people believe in them, and act on them. When I return – if I return – I want to help the worlds."

"That's not as easy as you think."

"I don't think it's easy," he assured her. "I expect to fail. I also expect to succeed. What I can't do is not try. And my chances of doing good will be greater if I know what Valhan knew."

"Or you'll become Valhan. Don't take that risk. Take the slower path. Gain that knowledge yourself."

"That would take a thousand cycles." His smile was crooked, and faded quickly. He drew a deep breath, then let it out again slowly. "Will you come back here once every cycle to check on me? When I'm ready, if I am still myself, you can take me out of this world again. Will you do that?"

"Yes, but I can do better than that. I can stay here and look after you."

"No."

"You need someone with you who knows you. Someone who can tell you who you really are."

"Which cannot be you," Qall said firmly. "You knew Valhan. Your expectations of him will shape me as much as those of Qall."

Rielle opened her mouth to protest, but she couldn't deny it. Every time she saw him, she saw Valhan, even if for the tiniest fraction of a moment. Enough to send a frission of fear and fascination through her. Qall was watching her. *There must be another way*, she thought.

"What if you never read my mind?" she suggested. "I—"

Qall's gaze shifted away. "And here they come," he said in a low voice, his lips pressing into a thin line.

Turning, she saw two shadows resolving rapidly into human shape, then gaining detail. A man and a woman.

"Tyen," Rielle said as she recognised the man. "I suppose he expects me to forgive him after he saved us."

"He was always on your side. Give him the chance to explain himself."

She looked at Qall. He appeared to want to say more, but his attention shifted back to the arrivals. The woman was Ankari. Rielle wondered where Baluka and Lejihk were. As Tyen and Ankari arrived, she read the answer from the latter: they were back in Dahli's base world. Ankari, seeing Tyen push out of the world to chase Rielle, had followed and grabbed his arm.

Tyen started forward slowly.

"Let her go," he said.

Qall smiled. "She is not my prisoner."

"He's Qall," Rielle told him.

Tyen's eyes narrowed. "Are you sure he's not—?"

"As sure as I—"

"Dahli," Qall interrupted, his tone dark.

The three of them looked to Qall, then spun to face the direction he was looking in. A new shadow was resolving nearby. The Raen's most loyal was expressionless, but an unmistakable gleam of triumph and eagerness lit his eyes as he arrived. He glanced at Tyen and Ankari, then stepped forward.

"Raen," he said, bowing.

"Dahli," Qall replied. "I have done as you wanted. I have absorbed Valhan's memories." He lifted the hand, his grip hiding the missing finger. "It is done."

A flare of orange burst from the hand, spreading rapidly as it consumed the desiccated flesh, reducing it to ashes that fell to the sand.

Dahli froze, eyes moving from the fire to Qall and back again, over and over. When all of the hand had turned to ash, Qall opened his fingers and let the last of it fall, and Dahli's gaze settled on his face.

"I am not Valhan," Qall said.

Dahli's face hardened. "No," he acknowledged. "Not wholly. Yet you have him within you now."

"Some of his memories, yes," Qall agreed. "No more than that. The mind can only store so much. Certainly not every moment of a thousand cycles. Valhan chose what he retained or cast off for centuries before he created the hand, and in order to store what he considered vital, he sacrificed much."

"Like the ability to love," Ankari added.

All turned towards the woman.

"Ulma told me," she explained. "They were lovers many hundreds of cycles ago. She said even love can lose value when you have experienced it many times. Survival becomes more important. So Valhan told her. He thought power was more essential to survival than all else, so he sacrificed the better human traits in order to hold it."

"He sacrificed more than that," Qall continued, turning back to Dahli. "But he did retain the ability to value order and loyalty. He regarded you, Dahli, with a respect that was as close to love as he was able to feel. He did not deserve it in return, because he used your love against you. To make you choose to do things your conscience would never have allowed you to do otherwise."

Dahli straightened, his expression becoming flinty. "Don't you dare assume to understand—"

"I dare," Qall said, raising his voice to cut Dahli off, "because you too have used love as an excuse to do harm. You used my love to blackmail me. Tyen, Rielle and I know you had no choice but to serve Valhan. We know your grief at his death was terrible. But though you were free from him, you continued to be ruthless and murderous in his name. You threatened to kill not just the family that raised me, but an entire race. You brought about a battle in which hundreds died, many in a cruel and agonising trap." Qall's voice wavered, and he paused to swallow before staring down at Dahli again. "Tell me why I shouldn't kill you now."

"No!" Rielle gasped. "Once you kill—"

"Qall, you don't have to—" Tyen said at the same time, but they both stopped as Qall raised a hand to silence them. Oddly, the imperious gesture did not remind Rielle of Valhan. *This is Qall. Only he can resolve this grievance with Dahli, because to leave it to others to settle on his behalf is to be like Valhan.*

"Tell me, Dahli."

The sorcerer glanced at Rielle and Tyen. Realising how vulnerable he was, he immediately thought of the people he had in place, ready to kill the Travellers if he died or disappeared for more than a quarter cycle. Then he realised that if Qall killed him nobody would know, and the Restorers could possibly prevent most of the attacks on Travellers in a quarter cycle.

And it was exactly this kind of threat that angered Qall.

And nothing would be gained from it now. There was no chance of resurrecting Valhan. Only fragments of him existed within Qall. Not enough to remake even a shadow of the man.

His mouth opened and closed, but made no sound. His gaze lowered to the ground at Qall's feet. Looking closer, Rielle saw the fear and pain within him. Even as he acknowledged that Qall and the worlds had every right to want him dead, he could not help trying to justify his actions. *I had no choice but to serve the Raen, even after his death!* But that was a lie. Zeke had pointed that out. *I should have listened . . .*

"Zeke saw the remnants of conscience and morality in you," Tyen told him. "He gave you a chance to be the person you would have been if not for Valhan. I doubt many people would."

And I drove him away, Dahli thought. The guilt and regret lay heavy. *He'll never forgive me. Nor do I expect it.* He straightened his back. *I have lost. I have failed Valhan, and missed every chance to be free from him. I will face the consequences with dignity.* "Will you tell him what happened to me, Tyen?" he asked in a strained voice.

"Of course," Tyen replied. "Once the Travellers are safe. If he can forgive my part in this, he and I still have the insectoid problem to solve."

"He was close to a solution," Dahli said, then managed a smile. "He has a remarkable mind."

"You do not deserve him," Qall said. "But perhaps he could come to forgive you." He drew a deep breath. "Do you understand that Valhan cannot be resurrected now?"

Dahli looked down at the ash and nodded. All the plots and hopes that he had kept himself occupied with unravelled. The great hole of emptiness he had dreaded opened up within him, but to his surprise it did not grow to consume him. It was not infinitely deep. He felt . . . hope.

Is this what Zeke has given me? he asked himself. *Surely someone so young and unworldly could not have managed to get past my guard.* And there was something else. Something he'd never considered before. *Freedom.* He could be anything he wanted. He could be anything *Zeke* wanted. The kind of person he had never thought he could be again.

Though he would never get the chance. For what he had done, he expected nothing less than execution.

And yet why would Qall ask if he'd accepted that Valhan was gone if he didn't mean to give Dahli another chance? Qall wasn't the type to force an enemy to acknowledge his defeat, and the hope of redemption, just so he could kill him at his lowest.

Unless he has become Valhan . . .

"No," Qall said. "I haven't. But I won't let you go without extracting a promise."

Dahli nodded. "What is my punishment?"

"Oh, I think your conscience will provide enough punishment in the centuries to come. No, what I want from you is the promise that you will roam the worlds, redressing some of the wrongs you have done."

"But people might recognise . . . oh. I will have to change my appearance."

"Yes, and be very careful of stronger sorcerers, who can read your true identity from your mind. It will improve your chances if they can see that you truly mean to hold to your promise."

Dahli considered Qall, then slowly straightened. "I vow to dedicate my remaining life undoing as much of the damage I have done in the service of the Raen as I can."

Rielle shivered. She could see that Dahli did intend to honour his vow. She could also see something stir within him. His capacity for unflagging loyalty and attributing blame and responsibility to a master could easily shift to Qall. Who at least looked like Valhan . . .

"I do not want you as my follower," Qall snapped. "And know that if you use this vow to shift blame for your actions to me I will use everything I've learned from Valhan to find you and ensure you pay for it." His voice softened. "Be responsible for your own choices, Dahli."

Dahli nodded quickly, the desire for a new master shrivelling away. In its place came belated amazement and relief. Qall was letting him go.

"I understand. Thank you, Qall. And . . . I apologise for everything I did to you."

Qall acknowledged this with a nod. "Go," he said. "And give Zeke my best wishes when you find him. He can't have got far. Not with so many worlds around the base depleted of magic."

"I will." Dahli frowned. "I think . . . it might be better if I don't return to the base. Will you make sure the fighters there aren't trapped? They were near the end of their strength."

Qall inclined his head. "If anyone is still alive, I'll make sure they are freed."

Dahli paused, then bowed to Qall again. "Goodbye," he murmured. "And thank you." His gaze became wistful as he began to fade. Qall, Rielle, Tyen and Ankari watched until he had disappeared completely.

"Tyen," Qall said.

Tyen jumped and turned to face the young man. "Qall," he replied. His eyes narrowed. "You are still Qall, aren't you?"

Qall smiled. "Yes. Mostly."

"You absorbed Valhan's memories," Tyen guessed.

"Not all." Qall shrugged. "There wasn't time. Just enough to learn pattern shifting and a few other things. Vella was right: it has changed me. That is why I am here. I need time alone to be sure I am in charge. But I am glad you came here. I want to thank you for all your help."

"I don't know that I was of much use," Tyen admitted.

"Of course you were," Qall disagreed. He walked to Tyen and placed a hand on his right shoulder. "Your advice, the visit you made to the Travellers, all the information I read from your mind, questioning Vella for me," he listed. He smiled and shook his head. "You always believe the worst of yourself, Tyen. You are immensely powerful, but you let others manipulate you into doing things you wouldn't choose to. Keep going that way and you'll end up like Dahli.

"You've had good reasons for some of your actions, but you keep them secret from those who are most likely to understand and forgive." Qall glanced at Rielle pointedly. "You blame yourself for the war machines while not taking credit for all the good that mechanical magic has brought to the worlds. You can't have it both ways. Not when people will always try to turn new ideas to their advantage, especially in war." He placed his other hand on Tyen's left shoulder and shook him gently. "*It's not your fault.*"

Tyen's expression was a mix of surprise and humility. His mouth opened but no words emerged. Rielle could not resist a wry smile. He was no doubt marvelling at this remarkably outspoken and insightful Qall. She certainly was, especially compared to the old sulky and reticent one.

How much of this is due to him absorbing Valhan's memories? How much of it comes from the ordeal he suffered at Dahli's hands?

The young man released Tyen and turned to her, his expression suddenly sober.

"It is both," he told her. "It is you and Tyen and even Zeke and Dahli." He hesitated, then walked over and placed a hand on her shoulder, as he had done to Tyen.

"Thank you for protecting and teaching me," he said. "But now you must accept that I am no longer the child you rescued. The worlds need you more than I do. You are a Maker of extraordinary power. You can restore the worlds that have been stripped of magic since the Raen died."

The factory she had been stranded in sprang to mind. "I don't know. Maybe some worlds are better off without magic."

"You can't decide what people do with magic any more than Tyen can control what they do with insectoids and machines," Qall told her. "It seems to me that, when as much benefit as harm can come of something, you have to give people the chance to do good with it."

"And what of this world?" she asked. "Would you have me save others but not give mine that chance?"

He shook his head. "No, but this one has been weak for a long time. There are no civilisations built on plentiful magic, doomed to collapse when it is gone. Likewise, this world will not benefit from a sudden restoration. It needs a gradual healing. That is why I want you to return from time to time and seek me out. If all goes well, perhaps I can leave it in a better state. Unlike the last angel to visit it."

She frowned. "Is it right to lie to my people as Valhan did?"

"No. It is not entirely fair, and I will not pretend it is anything otherwise. But they will not believe the truth about magic and the worlds and angels from anything less than an angel."

"If the priests discover you're lying to them, they'll kill you!" she exclaimed.

"I still hold some magic," he told her. "And they have none. I will be fine. You, on the other hand, are an exile. You cannot return." He let go of her shoulder and glanced at Tyen. "We three are exiles and immigrants. Wherever we settle, there is an expectation we offer something beneficial in exchange for sanctuary. As I said before, I want to try to help the worlds. If there's a chance I can begin by nudging this one towards prosperity and truth again, it is worth the attempt."

She grabbed his arm. "Let me come with you."

"No, Rielle."

The voice was not Qall's, but Ankari's. A hand touched Rielle's back.

"Let him go, Rielle," Ankari said quietly. "All mothers must set their children free."

"He's not my son," Rielle told her, irritated by the woman's interference. Then she realised what she had said and grimaced in apology. "But he *is* my responsibility."

"Your responsibility is over," Ankari told her. "He no longer needs protection from Dahli."

"But he is still in danger of becoming Valhan."

"No, he isn't," Ankari told her. "He is only at risk of becoming *like* Valhan. You've done your duty, Rielle. You can't do the rest of his growing up for him. You have to leave it to him."

"Others need you more," Qall said. "Baluka and the Restorers' army need you to free them from Dahli's world. Timane needs you. All of the worlds depleted since Valhan's death need you. All I need is that you return after a cycle. Then we can argue about this again. Now go."

"Do as he asks," Ankari urged, squeezing Rielle's arm.

Rielle looked at the Traveller, then back at Qall, and nodded reluctantly. At his mention of Baluka, her heart had jumped in alarm. Were he and Lejihk still alive? Was Ulma? She could feel Ankari's need to return.

Qall stepped back. "We'll see each other again."

"Be careful," she told him.

He nodded. "Always."

Ankari's grip tightened. The desert, now bathed in early morning light, brightened further, then faded out of sight. Soon, all Rielle could see was the Traveller, who smiled as Rielle met her eyes.

"*He'll be fine,*" Ankari said, her mental voice ringing in Rielle's mind.

"*How can you be sure?*"

"*Because we raised him. You, me, the Travellers and even that young sorcerer back there. Between all of us, how can he not grow into a good, smart and resilient man?*"

Rielle could not help smiling. "*Well, since you and Lejihk did the bulk of the raising, if this all goes wrong, can I blame it on you?*"

Ankari's mouth widened and a moment later, as the next world surrounded them, the air rang with the sound of her laughter.

PART TWELVE

EPILOGUE

TYEN

"You're back sooner than I expected," Tarran observed.

Tyen sighed, shrugged out of his coat and tossed it over the back of a chair. A buzz of protest came from Beetle as it bumped against the wood.

"They want nothing to do with me." He dropped into another chair.

Tarran's eyebrows rose. "That's . . . that's not what my contacts at Liftre led me to believe."

"Oh, they made a good show of looking as if they welcomed me, but it was clear that half of them still regard me as a traitor, and the other half don't see any gain in hiring me as a teacher now."

"But you invented mechanical magic!"

"Not exactly," Tyen corrected. "I developed it to make insectoids. I brought what I knew out of my world and exchanged it for a place in the school." He shrugged. "I'm not sure I would be happy teaching there anyway. Liftre has changed. Too many of those who use mechanical magic have no scruples about its applications."

"Which is why I hoped you'd join them again." Tarran rose. "You would be a good influence on them. They should respect you as someone with more experience in the consequences of using it."

"They respect only my strength," Tyen said. "And that is not of much use in a place like Liftre. It wasn't before, and isn't now."

Tarran rested a hand on the back of the chair Tyen had left his coat on, his fingers drumming lightly on the wood. "Why don't you start your own school?"

Tyen laughed drily. "Even if people forgave that I worked for the Raen and sided with Dahli, it sounds like a whole lot of work I'm not qualified for."

"Oh, it's not that hard. When we started Liftre, people came to us offering help." He paused. "I'll help. You have some powerful friends who'd endorse it too."

"Who? Baluka? I don't know if he's even forgiven me."

"The Restorers say that you saved them."

"That doesn't mean that Baluka has forgiven me."

"Then you need to talk to him."

Tyen shook his head. When he'd returned to the scene of the battle, he'd found that Rielle had already taken the surviving Restorers and Dahli's fighters away. All that was left were the bodies of those killed. She'd reappeared to start the grim task of taking those bodies to the Restorers' base so they could be sent to the victims' families. He'd wanted badly to explain everything – why he'd joined Dahli and had spied for the Raen – but it was clearly a bad time. So he'd offered to help, and she had grudgingly accepted.

And he'd been present when she'd discovered the remains of a Traveller she had known. The Travellers' only ageless sorcerer. Older than the Raen. He didn't think he'd ever forget the expression of surprise on the dead woman's face.

He'd said he was sorry. Rielle had grown angry and told him she didn't need his help, and he should go. So he'd left. He'd returned to the workshop where he'd worked with Zeke, but the insectoids and humanoid were gone. So with nothing to do and nobody to meet, he'd returned to the only person he knew would still welcome him: Tarran.

Since the truth was out, he'd told the old man everything. Tarran accepted it all with a shrug. "You did what you did because you felt it was right, not because you would gain from it. Unfortunately, doing what we feel is right is no guarantee that everything will work out well." Then he'd patted Tyen's hand. "Stay here for a while. Help me teach if you need the distraction. Practise calligraphy – I find that calms most of my students."

So Tyen had, and as a quarter cycle passed, then another, the past grew less sharp and the future started to show a hint of promise. He enjoyed teaching – he realised he had missed it, and the sense of being among the exchange of knowledge. Missed the Academy, and Liftre. Tarran had encouraged him to consider returning to the famed school of magic to restart life as a teacher there.

So much for that.

Tarran had moved to the door. "I have a visitor who might be interested in helping too. Follow me."

The old man liked surprising people, so Tyen resisted reading his mind. Rising, he followed Tarran out of the room and through his sprawling mansion. As they left the building and started along the staircase that led to the circular cave, Tyen's chest tightened painfully as memories rose of his time here with Rielle. The glass panels that formed one side of the cave reflected dazzling sunlight, making it impossible to see through them. It was a relief to follow Tarran inside.

At once, the interior became visible, and its occupants. On the cushions strewn across the bench seat along the rear wall sat two women. The first was familiar, but he was not sure why. Pretty and poised, she gave him a frank and speculative look, but he forgot her immediately as he recognised the other.

"Rielle!"

A tangle of emotions rose. Delight to see her, worry that she still hated him, and guilt.

"Tyen." She stood and approached. Her simple dress whispered softly as she moved. It was similar to the one she had worn when he'd first visited her in Murai, he noted. The same silver lozenge pendant hung below her neck, resting on her brown skin. She was beautiful and graceful and it hurt to look at her, so he dropped his eyes to the floor. "How did your meeting at Liftre go?" she asked.

"Not well," he replied. "And you? Where . . .? What . . .?"

"I've just returned from rescuing Timane from the world I left her in when Qall slipped away to join Dahli." She glanced back at the pretty woman and smiled fondly. "Though 'rescue' is not the right word. She was doing quite well there. However, she now wants to see if she can establish a theatre in Murai, her home world. Do you remember her?"

He shook his head. "I apologise," he told Timane.

"No need," Timane replied. "I have changed quite a bit." She stood and walked over to Tyen. "I was Rielle's servant," she explained. "It is a pleasure to meet you again."

He took her offered hand. "I am honoured."

She squeezed his hand, then let it go and smiled at Rielle. "I will let you two catch up. I am tired after all that travelling between worlds. Tarran, will you lead me back to the palace?"

Tarran chuckled as she withdrew her hand from Tyen's, then hooked an arm around his. "I told you before," he said to her as they turned towards the door, "this is no palace. I am no emperor."

Rielle beckoned to Tyen and led the way back to the bench seat. "Wine?"

"Yes, please."

She leaned forward to fill a glass as he sat down. "Have you spoken to Baluka since the battle?"

"No. All I know is he's still leader of the Restorers. Have you spoken to any Travellers?"

"A few. I know Lejihk and Ankari have returned to their family, as have all the others who survived the battle." She paused. "Have you heard from Dahli?"

"No. I've not seen him or Zeke, but I have heard rumours of a pair of sorcerers travelling to worlds in conflict, releasing tiny insectoids that disassemble anything that uses mechanical magic. Their descriptions don't match Dahli's or Zeke's, but he would have changed their appearance to avoid being recognised."

She handed him the glass of wine. "I hope it's him."

"Will you seek them out?"

She took a sip of her wine, then leaned back against the cushions and regarded him speculatively. "Why? Do you think I might seek revenge?"

He shrugged. "Perhaps."

She shook her head. "I'm in no hurry to add a vengeful death to those already on my conscience. I can only hope Qall didn't make a mistake letting him go."

Tyen nodded. "So do I."

"And that Qall will still be Qall when I go back to check on him."

"I think he will."

She looked at him. "You sound so sure. I wish I was as confident."

He blinked in surprise. Confident was not how he'd describe himself right now.

"So what will you do now?" she asked.

He drew in a deep breath and let it out. "Tarran thinks I should start my own school of magic, but I don't see why anyone would want to work with me after what I've done."

"Does it appeal?"

He nodded. "Though it is a daunting task. He offered to help, but it would take more than Tarran to make it work. I think I'd like it to teach more than just magical subjects, too. As the Academy of my home world does."

"Would they accept you back?"

He shuddered. "I doubt it. They probably still think I'm a thief."

"A thief? Did you steal something?"

"In a manner of speaking. I prefer to think of it as saving something." *Or someone. Or at least part of someone, as Qall had pointed out that Vella was.*

He looked at Rielle and saw both wariness and curiosity in her face. Qall's words echoed in his mind. *"You've had good reasons for some of your actions, but you keep them secret from those who are most likely to understand and forgive."*

He had decided that, if he ever encountered Rielle again, he would tell her everything. There might never be a better moment to do so.

And so he did.

RIELLE

He filled the gaps, some of which she was aware of, and some she had no idea existed. He began with his discovery of Vella, saying he had avoided telling anybody more than necessary about the book, but now he felt he could do so. A tale of a corrupt teacher and a great castle's fall followed, as well as how he learned to travel between worlds. Then he skipped past his life at Liftre, which he had described before, to his meeting and deal with the Raen. There he slowed, explaining every part of his time with the rebels, giving both altruistic and selfish reasons for his spying and manipulation. He clearly felt guilt and sorrow for Yira, the leader he had replaced, and admiration for Baluka, who he had passed the position on to.

He described the Raen's death, and how in seeking Rielle he'd found Dahli and assured her that he'd chasing her down after the failed resurrection to ensure that Qall would escape. Afterwards he had become a spy for both Dahli and Baluka, mainly so that he could keep an eye on Dahli.

And then he explained that, once she had left Qall, he had made an agreement with Dahli. He would resurrect the Raen only if it did not involve destroying someone in exchange for learning how to restore Vella's body. This ought to have given Dahli less reason to hunt for Qall. He told her he had hoped that, if he succeeded in resurrecting the Raen, the former ruler would not find it easy to regain control. The Restorers had a

559

good chance of defeating him again. And in the meantime, he and Zeke had been working on a solution to the war machines, which had been much easier with Dahli's help. Of course, once Qall had joined Dahli his plans were spoiled, but he'd stayed to help the young man.

When he was done, she sat in silence for a moment, her expression thoughtful. Then she turned to him.

"And Vella? Have you found a solution for her? And what was the purpose of the machine body I smashed?"

A fleeting look of pain crossed his face. He shook his head, but though his mouth opened no words emerged. Her heart skipped.

"What happened? Did you lose her? Was she destroyed?"

"No. I . . . I've given up on restoring her body."

"Why?" She frowned. "Is it because you have to use someone else's living body?"

"No – but if that was the case, I wouldn't have done it. The experiments I did used recently deceased bodies of people who had no loved ones, and even that seemed wrong." He sighed. "The reason is I don't have her any more. I gave her away."

Rielle stared at him in disbelief. "But she was . . . unique. Valuable. She knew all your secrets. If I'm not mistaken, she was like a friend and mentor to you."

"Yes, she was," he agreed. "All of that. I miss her terribly. But . . . Qall once saw me talking to her, and what he told me made me realise something about her."

"What did he say?"

"He said watching me communicate with her was like watching me talk to myself. While her essential personality and morals were set and unchanging – which in itself is not how real people are anyway – her using my mind to interact with me meant that a large part of her reactions were really mine." He shook his head. "Not that I would have given her away because of that. I saw no harm in talking to her. But Qall also said that if I took what was left of her and put it in a body, she would no longer be the Vella I knew. She confirmed that what Qall had said was true. I realised that when Valhan had said that the process of giving her a body would destroy the book, this is what he might have meant."

"So you didn't want to destroy the person you knew. But what did *she* want? Would she have preferred to escape, even if it meant changing into another person?"

Tyen shook his head and let out a bitter laugh. "That is the essential problem: she did not mind either way. Though she knows that what was done to her was wrong, she has no ability to feel emotions, so she can't be unhappy about it."

"Nor can she be happy."

He grimaced. "No. But the hardest thing . . . what Qall opened my eyes to . . . was that the book isn't her. Vella died more than a thousand cycles ago. The book is merely an echo of her. A ghost. A part of her very convincingly preserved for many life-times after her death. I am so grateful that I got to talk to her, access her knowledge and keep that last shred of her safe but . . ." He spread his hands.

"But?"

He met her gaze, then looked away. "Someone else needed her more."

She sat up a little straighter. "Who?" She blinked. "Baluka?"

"No."

Her shoulders sagged. "Tarran?" she asked doubtfully.

He shook his head.

"Not Dahli?"

"Of course not."

"Then who?"

His smile was crooked. "From where I was standing, I could see a finger was missing."

She searched his gaze, weighing up the possible meaning of his words. Then, as she realised what it was, she sucked in a quick breath.

"Qall!" she gasped. "You gave her to Qall!"

"Yes. After you—"

Before she could think twice, and worry about the consequences, she leapt forward and wrapped her arms around him, squeezing so hard she heard air escape from his mouth.

"Thank you!" She said it over and over. Then, as his hands touched her back tentatively, she released him and moved away. *I don't want to give him the wrong idea. It'll take more than that for me to feel I can trust him completely.*

She stood and began to pace the room. "It's perfect! If he can get Valhan's memories into her he can access them safely, and then he can destroy the finger and there is no longer any danger of someone resurrecting Valhan."

"She absorbs knowledge by touch," Tyen reminded her. "He only has to bring the finger into contact with the book and she will take all of the memories in."

"It's a beautiful solution." She grinned at him. "Thank you, Tyen."

He nodded again. His expression was wistful, but his posture was hesitant. When he said nothing more, she turned to the table, took the flagon and refilled their glasses. He accepted his, sipped and watched her.

"We've talked mostly about me. What will you do now?" he asked.

She swallowed a mouthful of wine, set the glass down and returned to the seat.

"Restore worlds," she replied. "I expect Baluka has a long list for me. I'd like to tackle the ones stripped by Dahli's followers first. Then there's the one Qall depleted to trap me." She looked at him. "Do you know of any that need help?" She held up a hand to stall him as he began to reply. "Wait. What of your world? You said it was so weak you could barely leave it."

He nodded. "And most likely even weaker with the machines using up so much magic."

"Would you like me to restore it?"

He opened his mouth, then closed it again. "No. They will only waste it. Until the Academy acknowledges that creativity generates magic there is no point."

"If they see me making it, they can't deny the truth."

He smiled. "Or claim that women can't be great sorcerers." Then he sobered. "I can't return. I am a thief."

"They'd overlook that if you brought them magic."

"The Directors won't . . ." His eyes narrowed. "But the Emperor might." Then he shook his head. "No. Releasing one piece of knowledge from my world – mechanical magic – has had disastrous consequences. I don't want to risk spreading anything else that the worlds could turn to warfare. My world is used to having little magic. There must be many more important and worthy ones to save first."

"And you want to start a school of magic," she added.

He nodded. "Perhaps I could do what Dahli has, and change my appearance and name."

"Why would you do that?" She frowned, then smiled as the answer came to her. "You don't know, do you? Baluka has announced you as a hero. He's told everyone that you were spying for him, and that it was only thanks to your help that Dahli was defeated. People think you're so clever now, they'd jump at the chance of working with you."

He gaped at her in astonishment.

She laughed. "You *really* need to talk to Baluka," she told him. "He'll probably try to make you take over the leadership of the Restorers, but I think he will settle for helping you start a school."

He closed his mouth and swallowed. "I . . . I'll need it," he said. "Even with Tarran's help. It could take centuries just to build a library the calibre of Liftre's."

Rielle winced. "Well, when you do, if you come across any reference to Maker's Curse or Maker's Ruin, make a note of it for me. Ulma and I were going to search the worlds for information about it. I'm still going to. If there is a reason why being both ageless and a Maker would destroy the worlds, I want to know. And if there isn't, I want to know how to be both."

Tyen nodded. "I will. It's the least I can do."

"If you need extra magic at your school, I'll generate it for you."

"If you need someone to heal you, and give you more years to live, I will help."

They paused, then smiled at each other. Something of a pact had just been made. Not the sort of deal the Raen had liked, but a simple, well-intentioned offer of help to each other. She raised her glass.

"Here's to a future of healing worlds and friendships."

He saluted her. "And of learning and teaching – and no more spying!"

They raised their glasses to their lips, and drank.

The story continues in book four of Millennium's Rule.

ACKNOWLEDGEMENTS

The writing of *Successor's Promise* was unavoidably slow and the publication delayed thanks to the development of a very painful back condition, so I first want to thank my agent, Fran Bryson, my publisher and all my readers for their patience. I hope you find the book worth the wait.

A huge extra thank you to Fran Bryson, Liz Kemp, Paul Ewins, Donna Hanson, Shireen Hanson-Pou and Kerri Valkova for beta reading and helpful suggestions. And once again, a big hug for all the readers around the world who bought, borrowed, read and recommended my books. Your support and enthusiasm have got me through more than a few moments of doubts or struggle.

ABOUT THE AUTHOR

Trudi Canavan published her first story in 1999 and it received an Aurealis Award for Best Fantasy Short Story. Her debut series, the Black Magician trilogy, made her an international success, and all three volumes of her Age of the Five trilogy were *Sunday Times* bestsellers. Trudi Canavan lives with her partner in Melbourne, Australia, and spends her time writing, painting and weaving.

Find out more about Trudi Canavan and other Orbit authors by registering for the free monthly newsletter at www.orbitbooks.net.